AGAINST FEARFUL LIES

by
VIVIAN MOIRA VALENTINE

Wildflower Press
an imprint of Blue Fortune Enterprises, LLC

AGAINST FEARFUL LIES
Copyright © 2024 by Vivian Wise

All rights reserved. Printed in the United States of America. No part of this book may be used or reproduced in any manner whatsoever without written permission except in the case of brief quotations embodied in critical articles or reviews.

This book is a work of fiction. Names, characters, businesses, organizations, places, events and incidents either are the product of the author's imagination or are used fictitiously. Any resemblance to actual persons, living or dead, events, or locales is entirely coincidental.

For information contact :
Blue Fortune Enterprises, LLC
Wildflower Press
P.O. Box 554
Yorktown, VA 23690
http://blue-fortune.com

Illustration by Frankie Valentine
Cover design by BFE LLC

ISBN: 978-1-961548-08-4
First Edition: March 2024

Dedication

To my very dear Kelsey and Ryan,
who have been waiting very patiently for this.

Praise for
Beneath Strange Lights
Book I in the Amelia Temple Series

I think this might be my new favorite scifi series. This first book was FASCINATING. I loved Amelia as a character, she's so interesting. Being a government-owned secret with eldritch powers she herself is struggling to understand, the story weaves first love, time shenanigans, and an enjoyable scifi mystery throughout its many pages. The prose is fun to follow and easy to digest, even for the more math-centric parts. At multiple points I couldn't put the book down because I was just so fascinated with what was happening.

Amelia Temple is a lovely character, and I can not wait to read more of her adventures. What an absolute delight of a book.

B. Moon, Amazon review

Excellent Breakout Novel

Vivian does a wonderful job weaving a story about science fiction, the awkward journey of making friends after being completely isolated, and a budding lesbian romance. The world building and pacing of the book are nicely balanced to provide the reader enough detail to understand the world of the characters in addition to keeping tension and a nice pacing to the narrative. Even if you cannot relate to all of the struggles that Amelia is navigating through, she is easy to love and root for after her less-than-ideal start in life. I look forward to reading future releases in this series!

Alexandria, VA, Amazon review

I was absolutely HOOKED throughout this entire book! Vivian creates a wonderful world with complex characters, an absolutely wonderful plot line and beautiful visuals that ignite the imagination. I cannot wait for the second book!!!

Megan Anuci, Goodreads

Acknowledgements

This book insisted on being written.

After I finished *Beneath Strange Lights*, I tried turning my attention to other projects. None of them went very far, unfortunately, which was a big hit to my confidence. If there's one thing I think every writer or artist fears, it's that we only have the one work in us. Then I realized that Amelia was demanding my attention. She's been up to a lot since the disastrous Dowling Experiment, and I'm only just getting started with sharing her adventures.

My wonderful wife and fantastic cover artist, Frankie Valentine, is my best friend, favorite person, and number one fan. I wouldn't be anywhere without her love, support, and encouragement. I'm so thankful to have her by my side as I struggle through drafts, work out plot points, and spend at least a third of my waking hours with made-up people.

My found family, Kelsey, Ryan, and Johanna have been both behind and beside me throughout the writing of this book and the next. They're endlessly supportive and encouraging, and I hope they enjoy this as much as I did writing it. I love you all!

This book wouldn't exist without Narielle Living of Blue Fortune. When Blue Fortune picked up *Beneath Strange Lights*, it gave me the push to finish *Against Fearful Lies* and move on to the next book in the series. Thank you, Narielle, for loving Amelia almost as much as I do!

As always, thank you, you beautiful disaster, for reading along with me.

Two books is enough to call it a series now, right?

I crept close to the door: the organ broke out overhead with a blare. The dazzling light filled the church, blotting out the altar from my eyes. The people faded away, the arches, the vaulted roof vanished. I raised my seared eyes to the fathomless glare, and I saw the black stars hanging in the heavens: and the wet winds from the lake of Hali chilled my face.

And now, far away, over leagues of tossing cloud-waves, I saw the moon dripping with spray; and beyond, the towers of Carcosa rose behind the moon.

Death and the awful abode of lost souls, whither my weakness long ago had sent him, had changed him for every other eye but mine. And now I heard *his voice*, rising, swelling, thundering through the flaring light, and as I fell, the radiance increasing, increasing, poured over me in waves of flame. Then I sank into the depths, and I heard the King in Yellow whispering to my soul: "It is a fearful thing to fall into the hands of the living God!"

- Robert Chambers, "The Court of the Dragon"

01

The day was cool, even this early in the afternoon. Not yet cool enough to consider wearing anything heavier than a light sweater over my dress, though. The year was now well into autumn, but the true cold wouldn't come for weeks yet. Not that my body felt the so-called extremes of cold any more than it did of heat. Certainly not those the mid-century Maryland clime could produce. It would be necessary for the look of it, though. Most months, people might not do more than glance at a young woman walking down the sidewalk in a simple dress. They'd probably get curious once there was snow on the ground. I'd have to talk to Lucille about going shopping for a winter coat soon.

I'd have to talk to Luci about more than that soon, if I was being honest with myself.

Chatham Hills lay before me, a sleepy town of a few thousand minds slowly spreading up and down the Patapsco River. It was prospering—hundreds of homes were being built in a new housing development on the south end of town, likely in response to the arrival of a grist mill. Despite the construction, the region was quiet. Ultimately, it was a small commercial district clinging to Route 40 for dear life, surrounded by a wide, ragged band of houses that slowly tapered off into acres of farmland.

It was almost, but not quite, nowhere; a jumped-up waystation between Regina, Maryland and Washington, D.C... or vice versa, I suppose. The biggest entertainments were the Arcadia Theater, which boasted two movie screens, and the public library. The most exciting thing to happen in years was a major electrical fire that had claimed a downtown business. At least, so far as anyone knew.

All of which made it the perfect place for the Bureau of Extranormal Investigations to stash those things it felt needed to be hidden from the populace. Such as myself.

I closed my eyes and settled in my seat, feeling the road pass underneath the wheels of the bus. I let my senses spread out, seeing how much of the area I could take in. I could feel 5,347 people milling around the wood and stone buildings of the town and the open fields surrounding it, though at this scale I could get no sense of what any of them were doing. They were too many, too far away. I could only view them as a teeming mass, a swarm of indistinct individuals circulating through the life cycle of the town. I tried to narrow the span of my attention, focusing on one group: the people active downtown. Then I narrowed my focus again to the people going in and out of the diner on Main Street... and then on one person in particular, a young woman with red-gold hair about a year and a half older than me. I wasn't deliberately looking for her, but the second my attention drifted her way, she inexorably pulled it to her. As always, she filled the room, her presence radiating outward. Even from miles away, I could almost smell her scent, sweet like summer roses.

Lucille Sweeney was talking with the young lady at the diner's counter, a beautiful, dark-skinned woman with laughing eyes and a wry smile. While Luci was a summer day in the middle of autumn, Gloria Lane was a hearth fire in winter—warm and welcoming in the face of extremes. Gloria put a comforting hand on Luci's arm, and Luci's head was bowed, trying to hide the concern on her face. I couldn't hear what they were talking about, but I could guess at the gist. The tragedy that lingered over us. The incident at the bookstore a month ago. The thing we couldn't talk about to anyone else.

As I watched my friends comfort each other, I *turned* in another direction, looking not across space but back in time, and saw my last conversation with Luci. We sat in a booth in the rear corner of the diner, an unusual occurrence. Normally we sat at the counter, with Gloria making three. This time, Luci had insisted we sit there. For privacy, she said. It was a concept I only understood academically, not one I'd experienced.

For me, a lonely girl who grew up alternately tormented and neglected in a small box of a room, the Lane Diner was the closest thing I'd experienced to home. Even looking back from two weeks ahead, I was enveloped by the wonderful smell. Sirloin and grilled ham, southern fried chicken and chicken fried steak, crispy golden fries dusted with salt, and thick, creamy milkshakes swimming with chocolate, and of course the endless herd of hamburgers hot off the grill. Gloria's brother Andre captained the kitchen, following their parents' recipes and improving on them when he could. Just thinking of it makes my mouth water, all these years later.

The delicious food and feeling of safety couldn't overcome our sorrow that day.

Luci sat across from me, her food untouched and slowly cooling on her plate. I stared at the blob of ketchup splattered over her fries. A thin film slowly formed atop its surface as it congealed. It was easier than looking up at her face, turned away from me in sorrow. Not that I could help but watch that anyway. For the first time, I envied the limits of human perception. I didn't want to see the hurt in her eyes, the tears pricking at the corners, her lip trembling. It was bad enough hearing the quiver in her voice.

It was Ralph. Ralph Connor, her friend since childhood. A soft, quiet boy who'd bumbled around the neighborhood, eager and innocent, an easy target for bigger boys who'd wanted someone to push around. A nice boy that she, the only child of a troubled home, had stood up for on her third day in the neighborhood, promising a boy a head taller than her and twice her weight that if he didn't return Ralph's toy rocket, she'd make him sorry.

That quiet boy had grown into a quiet young man lying on a hospital bed after a louder, more forceful young man had dragged him into a half-baked scientific experiment that had, quite literally, blown up in all our faces. That tragedy left him unconscious for the past month. "Smoke inhalation", they'd called it when they took him in, but you don't spend three weeks in a coma from breathing in too much smoke.

We knew what was really wrong with him. Well, mostly. It might be more accurate to say we had a vague idea.

The half-baked experiment had been to summon something from another dimension. You see why we couldn't talk about it? It sounds ludicrous. That's what they did, though. They summoned an intelligent and very powerful entity from a more complicated slice of reality, a creature their patrons called a "Watcher Above". It infected Ralph. Infected the other young man, too, we thought, although it was hard to say for certain. No one had seen Ralph's "partner", Lucas Dowling, since that night.

"I can't stop thinking we could have done more," Luci said. "That we could do ... I don't know. Anything."

I covered her hand with my own, gently rubbing my thumb against hers. I gave her what I hoped was a reassuring smile, though I felt no such reassurance myself. She was right, although I didn't want to admit it. Surely we could try. More specifically, *I* could. The answer was within me. In a cold, alien box in a corner of my mind I no longer dared to look at.

Luci's face shivered as she held back tears. I could no longer bear to watch it, so I *turned* away to what I considered to be the present but still anchored on the Lane Diner. Luci had gotten up from her seat, while Gloria removed her apron and walked around the counter to join her. We weren't meeting for lunch, after all. Not today.

The nearest bus stop to the Chatham Hills Public Library stood a block away for reasons I couldn't confirm. I suspected it had to do with the building's otherworldly air. Walking across the grounds was like walking a fence-line, beyond which lay a mysterious distant shore. A step in the right direction, and one could end up somewhere quite far from sleepy Chatham Hills.

Perhaps all libraries were such liminal spaces. Perhaps it was the weight of all that collected knowledge and story doing odd things to time and space. But I suspected most libraries didn't boast alien gargoyles standing guard over the building's interior.

I gave the Genius of Wisdom a wary nod as I passed. The statue, an ethereal woman carved of an unidentified blue-green stone, had been donated to the library by a charitable organization called the Chambers Foundation for Higher Learning. We suspected the foundation had succeeded the mysterious gentleman's club that was once headquartered in the city. And, we suspected, this same foundation was behind the disastrous experiment that had left Lucas missing and Ralph in a hospital.

The statue did not respond to my greeting, and I hadn't expected it to. It was nothing more than a lump of expertly carved stone, albeit a particularly weird one. It triggered a twinge of familiarity that was uncomfortable.

I banished the thought as I crossed the threshold. The library was mostly empty. Gloria was already waiting at our customary table. To my pleasant surprise, so was Luci.

"I'm the last to get here?" I said, setting my purse down on the table. "What is the world coming to?"

Luci stuck her tongue out at me, then stood up to pull me into a tight hug a touch closer and longer than polite company allowed for two women our age. She pressed her cheek against mine. I closed my eyes and breathed in her scent. Her heart beat against my chest, spreading her warmth through both our bodies.

Mine, she thought. *My love.*

After two minutes, Gloria coughed once, politely. We broke our embrace. Luci gave me a quick, sad smile before recovering her composure. Not here, I knew.

We took our seats at the table, picking the two chairs across from Gloria. It put us close enough to discreetly touch one another, at least. Gloria gave us a look that was equal parts compassion and concern. She found our relationship somewhat puzzling—romance and sexual intimacy were as foreign to her as masculinity was to me—but felt protective toward us. Which was good, as far too often I suspected Luci would happily throw caution to the wind and kiss me the way I wanted her to, no matter who was watching. Risks, as far as she was concerned, happened to other people.

Which might have been funny to someone else. It certainly wasn't to Gloria. I found myself fascinated by Luci's lack of caution. Still, I had to admit Gloria would know far better than me what most of society said about people like us. About the way we loved. It was "unnatural".

Unnatural according to a society that had never treated me as anything other than a monster. Some days, I didn't understand why I was in such a hurry to join it. Surely there had to be better options. But that wasn't a problem I could solve today. I forced a smile for Gloria and Luci. It soon felt genuine. I *was* happy to see my only friends.

Gloria's side of the table was clean; she'd brought only her green notebook, half full of carefully organized notes. Luci's side, meanwhile, was covered in sketches and clippings from her "case file"—a thick three-ring binder stuffed with papers and multicolored dividers arranged according to a system that only made sense to her. I was glad I hadn't brought any notes of my own, as I wasn't sure where I would have put them.

"So," I said, as if calling the meeting to order, "how is everyone?"

"Tolerably well," Gloria said. "The diner's doing good. Bringing in plenty of customers. And the law hasn't come by to scare them off yet."

She gave me a funny look, radiating gratitude and concern. I nodded. My handler, Agent Walsh, was keeping up his end of our deal. So far.

"Unfortunately, that hasn't left a lot of time to study," Gloria continued. She was trying to get accepted at the Hampton Institute in Virginia when she wasn't preventing collegiate mad scientists from blowing up small towns. "Getting it in when I can, but all these shifts are running me ragged. I'm lucky I managed to get a couple hours off today. I'm trying to get Pops to hire more staff, but he isn't sure. He'd have to pay 'em more."

"How does that make sense?" I asked.

"It's family," Gloria said. "We're all pitching in to keep the family business running. Most of the money's going to the *whole* family, not any one part of it. Somebody else, they'd be working for a wage. Which is fair, but Pops won't go for it yet."

I nodded as if I understood. Family was another thing I'd only experienced secondhand. It made sense to Gloria and Luci, though.

"How about you, Luci?" Gloria said. "Midterms are coming up soon."

Luci had the grace to look embarrassed. "They'll go however they go. I've been focused on the project."

"I seem to recall you giving someone hell over that recently," Gloria said.

She'd tried to make a joke of it, but everyone's face fell as soon as she said it. It really didn't feel funny, considering. She opened her mouth to apologize, but Luci waved it off.

"No, you're right," she said. "I am being a bit of a hypocrite. I hounded Ralph for weeks about blowing off his studies over a private obsession, and here I am doing the same thing."

"You have better reasons, though," I said.

She nodded, mostly believing me.

"I'm not seeing any new movement from the Apollonian Society," she said. "Or the Chambers Foundation or whatever they're calling themselves now. Professor Blake has thoroughly disappeared, along with Lucas."

"Presumably not to the same place?" Gloria said.

"Who knows? I guess it depends on how disposable they thought he was," Luci said.

Professor Henry Blake had been instrumental in recruiting Lucas Dowling to the Apollonian Society's work. He'd been a visiting professor of mathematics at Del Sombra University in Regina. Luci attended that school, along with Lucas and Ralph. According to Luci, after Lucas disappeared, Professor Blake made a couple of appearances on campus before dropping off the face of the Earth too.

"The weird thing is, the U is acting as if Lucas is still there," Luci said. "It's been a month now, but his dorm room's still assigned. He's not attending classes, obviously, but it doesn't look like they've dropped him yet."

"Maybe they're waiting for the end of the semester?" Gloria said. "Has anyone else been asking around?"

"No, not yet." Luci turned to me. "Which is also weird. Your people know it was him, right?"

"I reported everything I knew," I said, ignoring the "my people" comment for love's sake. "Well, everything they needed to know. With an emphasis on Lucas' responsibility."

"That's definitely strange, then," Gloria said.

"I'd be more concerned if agents were there asking about him. And you," I said. "If they haven't come yet, that's their problem. Hopefully it makes things easier on us."

"What about Ralph?" Gloria asked, as gently as she could.

Luci took a deep breath and looked down at her hands, folded on the table in front of her.

"No change," she said. "They've stopped calling it smoke inhalation, but he hasn't woken up, and the doctors don't know why."

"Has *he* had any visitors?" I asked.

She frowned. "No. Only his mother so far. Mrs. Connor practically lives at the hospital these days."

Gloria glanced at me. "I'd have thought you'd know."

I shook my head. "They're keeping me in the dark. Which isn't unusual. What *is* unusual is that at least as far as we can tell, they're ignoring the two people they *know* were involved in this fiasco."

"The longer they leave Ralph alone, the more opportunity we have to do our own thing," Luci said. "There's got to be *something* we can do. How's your research going, Gloria?"

"I'm afraid it's not only my admissions studies that have hit a snag," Gloria said. "With the primer lost somewhere between 1925 and now…"

I winced. We'd "acquired" a primer on the bizarre mathematical language the Apollonian Society used in their experiments. Prospero's Keys, the society had called them. In the very short time she'd had the book, Gloria made great strides in understanding how to use the Keys. Until we'd been forced to leave the primer behind.

Gloria reached across the table to take my hand. "Don't make faces, sugar. It's not your fault. I'm the one who disrupted the experiment."

The experiment had been the Apollonian Society's first attempt to pull the "Watcher Above" into our part of space-time in 1925. I'd taken us there, or rather then, but Gloria had figured out how to reverse the process. Instead of pulling otherworldly beings in, the seal pushed them away. That category had apparently included me. I didn't like thinking about that part.

I'd barely managed to take Gloria and Luci with me as the reversed seal forced me back to where we'd started, 1954. We'd ended up at our origin point plus a few hours but without the primer. Gloria had a fantastic memory for the Keys, but I wasn't sure how far she would be able to go without that book. Further than I'd thought, it seemed.

"Besides, I did make sort of a breakthrough since then," she said. "Between my notes and what little we recovered from Lucas' experiment. It has to do with another set of Keys."

She was holding something back. Something that had helped her progress. Gloria cut her eyes to me. She knew there was no lying to me. She was less certain whether she was able to hide things from me. Whatever it was, she was trying hard not to think about it.

I wasn't going to pry. Not yet, anyway. Whatever was inside her head was her business. I had to trust she'd tell us when she was ready. I gave her a moment to speak, then asked if her breakthrough had to do with helping Ralph.

"Or with getting that thing out of Amelia's head," Luci said.

I made a face. "It's not in my head, exactly."

"That's not reassuring at all."

"My passenger is the least of our concerns right now," I said. "At least it's contained."

My passenger. More like my prisoner. We'd prevented the Apollonian Society from summoning the Watcher Above in 1925; we'd failed to prevent Lucas Dowling from doing the same a month ago. He was prepared for

Gloria's interference—Lucas had engraved his seal into a steel plate, making it impossible for us to alter. As a desperate measure, we'd imprisoned the Watcher in a corner of my mind when it tried to take the whole thing over. I could feel it, cold and damp, sloshing around in there, equal parts angry and afraid.

"It's contained for now," Gloria said. "We don't know if it will stay that way."

"The seal you created is holding," I said, letting a touch of irritation creep into my voice. "I would prefer if we left it at that for now. I don't want to do anything rash."

Such as trying the experiment in reverse. I could see the rough plan forming in Gloria's mind now—use the modification she'd applied to the 1925 experiment's seal to vacuum the passenger out of my consciousness and presumably into the higher dimension it had previously inhabited. It wasn't a bad plan. As long as she could figure out how to direct the seal to differentiate the passenger from me. She couldn't yet, and she wasn't willing to suggest it until she could. I was grateful for that.

"No, nothing rash," Gloria said. "And to answer your other question, I think I might have an idea or two about helping Ralph. I'd need to get in to see him, though."

"Oh! That reminds me," Luci said. "They're finally letting Ralph have visitors. Other than immediate family, I mean, which pretty much means his mother. I was thinking we could go. Maybe this Saturday?"

"Of course," I said immediately. As if she needed to ask. I'd go to Hell without hesitation if Luci were going, if there was such a place.

She smiled at me, then turned to Gloria. Gloria wanted to go as well, but instead of agreeing, she made a face and looked down at her dark brown hand.

"I don't want to back out after what I said, honey, but I think there's going to be a problem with that."

Luci's face clouded. "Ugh! I didn't think... this place is so *backward!*"

Gloria shook her head. "It's like that all over the country. Worse, in some places. At least they'll let me into the library here."

"I think I can make it not be a problem," I said. "If you need to get in, I should be able to do it without causing a fuss."

I couldn't just see inside people's minds—I could touch their thoughts. I didn't think I'd be able to change white folks' minds about Gloria, but I was pretty sure I could keep them from noticing her. At least for a while. Failing that, I could always take a shortcut. Transporting the two of us across a hundred meters of space would be much easier than across twenty-nine years of time.

"Let's put a pin in that," Gloria said. "I'm still figuring this out. We'll try it once I've got something, but in the meantime, you two go alone."

"Are you sure?" Luci asked.

"No need to make this more complicated than it has to be," Gloria said.

"You're right," I said. "So, Luci, I'll see you Saturday? And you the next time I'm at the diner, Gloria."

"So probably tomorrow," Gloria said with a wry smile.

"The blue plate's meatloaf tomorrow, isn't it?" I said. "So, yeah."

We all stood up and headed for the door. Halfway there, Luci grabbed my hand and pulled me in between the nearest bookcases. With no one to pry, she wrapped her arm around my waist and laid a passionate kiss on me.

"*That's* how you tell me you'll see me on Saturday, darling," she whispered.

Gloria, ever practical, shook her head but hid a smile. Luci and I barely noticed, briefly caught up in a world where only the two of us existed. That could never last, sadly.

02

I did return to town the next day. Although not initially to have lunch at the Lane Diner, more's the pity. Stephanie Baines, one of the office girls on the second floor, gave me a message from Agent Walsh requesting that I meet him in town. I felt a bit of trepidation, seeing where he wanted to meet, but I acceded to the request. It was an understandable one, after all.

Of course, as far as the Bureau was concerned, he was my superior. It's not as if I had a choice.

The first time I set foot in Chatham Hills, I'd felt something uncanny. An irresistible pull drew me to a seldom visited bookstore just off-center from downtown. I had followed it without thinking, like a stone rolling down a steep slope, to Luci and the boys and the start of this whole giant mess. The bizarre gravity disappeared after that first afternoon, yet here I was again, staring up at the burnt-out wreck of Orr's Used Books.

The city had thoroughly condemned the building by this point; they would likely tear it down soon. All that remained was an empty shell. The windows gaped open, empty staring eyes and disjointed maws edged by a jagged outline of shards. The glass, blown out by the heat of the fire, had long since been swept up, along with the ash of the destroyed books. The surviving stock, what little of it remained, had been carted out—to be pulped, I'd assumed. The last trace of personality in this place—of Maxine Orr's presence, or of the incident that had destroyed it—had been erased. Just as Maxine wanted it, I supposed.

I stared up at the bookstore from the sidewalk. If I turned my attention just *so*, I could see it the way it used to be. See myself browsing the stacks and meeting Luci for the first time, see Lucas Dowling and Ralph Connor's work together, see the last terrible experiment that tore everything apart.

But I didn't want to. I didn't want to see the way things used to be. There was no point, after all. I couldn't go back to stop it or recover what was lost. I was here and now, and what I needed to see was where and when I was.

Above me, Agent Walsh picked through the remains of the second floor with another Bureau agent. Stanley Dawes had been part of my first indoctrination class, just before the current catastrophe started. Now he was a field agent, albeit a probationary one, waving around a device that looked like the offspring of a television aerial, a transistor radio, and a vacuum cleaner. A coiled cord connected the wand in his hand to the instrument panel slung over one shoulder. The needles on its many gauges jumped and shivered as he waved the wand around. I wasn't certain what exactly it was measuring. Frankly, neither was he.

"Are you sure this is entirely safe, Agent Walsh?" I called up to him. "Half of the second floor has caved in, and the rest doesn't look structurally sound."

As if proving my point, the floor creaked ominously beneath Walsh's feet. He carefully crept to the front of the building, poking his head through a shattered window. He smiled broadly, as if to dismiss the danger he was putting himself in.

"Amelia! It's about time you arrived. Climb on up and we'll get started."

I folded my arms across my chest and quirked an eyebrow at him.

"Climb up there. After what I just said."

"It's perfectly..." Agent Walsh glanced around the ruined structure and shrugged. "It's mostly safe. So long as you keep close to what's left of the walls."

There were a few more creaks, and Agent Dawes' head appeared in the window next to Walsh's.

"Hey, Miss Temple!" he said. "It's going great so far! And the incident took place up here, so it's where we'll get the best readings."

That last was said in the tone of someone repeating what he'd been told but didn't entirely believe.

"Readings of what?" I asked.

"You'll have to come up here and find out," Walsh said. "I'm not going to shout it down to the streets. Come on, you said you wanted to get involved."

"No, *you* said you wanted me to get involved," I said grouchily, but I acquiesced.

Inside, the stairs had collapsed, but the second-floor rubble created a rough slope. As a ramp, it wasn't too bad, although it wobbled entirely too much for my liking. I could have taken a different way up, but the Bureau didn't know the extent of my abilities. Especially how easily I could move between dimensions. I wanted to keep it that way for as long as possible. Plus, for as much as they tried to select for a certain "steely" disposition, Bureau agents could be very excitable. Walsh believed he was comfortable with my extra abilities, or at least the ones he knew about. Dawes was an entirely different matter. He'd tried to be friendly when we first met, but he'd already heard stories about me. They flocked around the Bureau like wildly inaccurate pigeons. And while his hands were full, he did carry his service pistol in a shoulder holster. There were so many ways things could go bad if I was indiscreet.

To his credit, he gave me a friendly nod when I reached the second floor. "Good to have you with us, Miss Temple."

"Hello, Agent Dawes," I said. "Readings of what?"

"Spatial distortions," Walsh said.

"We think," Dawes added.

"The meter is still experimental," Walsh said. "That's why I wanted you here. I'm hoping that your..." His voice trailed off and he looked carefully at Dawes. "Your *perspective* will help confirm that we're actually picking up something."

The image that popped into Dawes' head nearly made me laugh out loud. I had to cover my face to hide my smile. I didn't bother explaining what was so funny.

"All right," I said. "Wave your magic wand around and tell me what you think it says, Agent Dawes."

He held the wand out and started walking carefully around the edge of the room. We were standing in the remains of the second floor back room—Lucas Dowling's secret laboratory. The needles on the instrument panel jumped, and a speaker set into the middle of it emitted a fuzzy static, which rose to an eerie, high-pitched whine whenever Agent Dawes aimed the wand at the hole in the center of the room. Where the Watcher Above had fallen to the Earth below.

"The distortions, or whatever they are, seem to be strongest here," Dawes said. "Although I'm picking up slight readings all over this part of the building."

"That makes sense," I said. "It's kind of like dropping a weight on a sheet of rubber. It'll stretch the most where it lands, but you'll get creases all over the rest of the sheet."

I could feel them—ripples in space-time radiating out from the point of impact. They were slight, almost imperceptible to a "normal" human, but they were there. I thought I could point out some of the larger ones.

"Look at this brickwork," I said. "There's a patch here about a foot across that's wrinkled, for lack of a better word."

The two agents stood behind me, Walsh peering over my shoulder and Dawes aiming his wand at the bricks.

"I *think* I see something," Walsh said.

"The meter's definitely *picking up* something," Dawes said. "The gauge jumps a bit when I get close."

"As you said, Agent Dawes, it's slight," I said. "Here, watch."

I passed my hand over the brickwork. As it got close to the distortion, it rippled. Just waves of half an inch, as if looking through a cracked pane of glass, but it was enough to make Walsh say a foul word and jump back.

"I saw something! I don't know what I saw, but I *saw* it!"

"Here, I'll go more slowly."

I passed my hand the other way, this time letting it crawl across the brick. Walsh let out a slow whistle as my hand passed through the distortion. Part of my hand seemed to bend, as if it was half-submerged in water. It bent into shape after passing out the other side. Moving slowly, the effect wasn't as dramatic, but the agents were still impressed.

"You seeing this, Dawes?"

"Yeah."

I bent down close to the distortion and then stood up, counting slowly out loud as I did. "One, two, three, f-four-r-r-r, five, six, se-se-sevnn, eight, nine, ten."

My voice skipped like a record needle as the sound passed through the distortion. Dawes' jaw dropped. I winked at him and wiggled my fingers.

"Jeez, Miss Temple… I mean, does it hurt?"

"I can feel a slight tingle when my hand passes through the distortion," I said. "Something like, um, a very low electrical current passing through my hand."

"Or, uh, like your leg waking up after falling asleep?" Dawes said.

I glanced away, thoughtful. "Maybe? That's never happened to me before."

"You never had your leg fall asleep after sittin' in one place too long?"

"No. Does that really happen?"

I stepped away from the wall, ignoring Dawes' confounded expression. "I wouldn't recommend anyone else try that, Agent Walsh. I think it might hurt you more than me. Though it will be difficult to avoid. There are small distortions all around this building, in a flat torus centered around the hole in the floor."

I crept carefully to the hole. Lucas' seal had sat there, inscribed on a flat sheet of steel. It was gone now, probably in a Bureau storage room. Likewise, so were all but the faintest traces of the Watcher's corpse. I could see the scar its passage had torn in the world, a twisted seam of space-time hovering in front of me like a heat shimmer. It forked like a lightning bolt. At the bottom, it terminated where the floor had once been. Halfway up, a twisting branch struck out through the central window, the one Lucas had leapt through while we grappled with the Watcher in my mind. The rest of the scar stretched *up*, past the partially caved-in ceiling. Past the sky and the stars that hung above it.

A chill and a sudden irresistible *need* rose in the back of my mind. To my horror, I realized my passenger could see the seam in space as well. The Watcher's consciousness, compacted and sealed in a corner of my mind. It writhed like a tank of fetid water that began boiling without warning. It strained against the bounds of the seal locking it away, reaching for the crease in reality that led to its former home.

It felt like an icicle shot through my head. But the seals held.

No, I said to it.

My passenger seethed. I could feel its anger—it was using a piece of me to feel it, after all. That I expected. I was less prepared for what I felt next.

Escape/return you/us

My eyes flew open. A chill crept down my spine. The fingers of one hand began to twitch, the flesh rippling. I hadn't heard the Watcher's voice in over a month. I hadn't been certain whether it even could speak to me. It wasn't a pleasant discovery.

Escape/return you/us. Compact/agreement yes query

"No!" I said again, only this time out loud.

"Miss Temple?" Agent Dawes said. By his tone, I could tell it wasn't the first time he'd repeated my name.

"Amelia? Everything all right?" Agent Walsh said.

I was crouched over the hole in the floor, the fingers of one hand pressed against my forehead, the others digging into the splintered floorboards. Walsh's question was fair. My body had moved, not unconsciously but following a lower-level direction. The concern in his voice was genuine, although less than that in Dawes'. My handler was accustomed to seeing me do unexpected things. Agent Dawes was not. He stepped forward, intending to help me up. He overestimated the structural integrity of the floor.

A loud crack split the air, and the floor tilted wildly beneath his feet. The badly burned joist supporting that part of the floor gave out under his weight. It was going to take a good chunk of the remaining floor and Agent Dawes with it within the next five seconds if someone didn't do something. I flung out a limb to grab hold.

Not my skinny human arm, of course. One of the many limbs of the greater part of my body, the one that bent at an angle no human I'd ever met could perceive. The part of my body that provided most of my unusual abilities, although I'd carefully hidden that explanation from the Bureau for nearly eighteen years.

My limb moved closer to the three dimensions of space the agents could perceive and wrapped around the broken joist. The meter's speaker began screaming electronic noise. I squeezed the limb tightly, forcing the joist into position. The floor stopped shuddering. Agent Dawes' arms stopped pinwheeling as he recovered his balance. Rather than flee for more secure footing, however, he stared at his meter instrument panel, which was now going wild.

"What the hell's going on?" Dawes' reading could pick up my extradimensional limb's presence, but the agents couldn't see or hear it. I wasn't inclined to explain.

"What's going on is that the part of the floor you're standing on is about to cave in, Agent Dawes," I said, not trying to hide a single drop of my annoyance. "You really ought to *move now*."

"Stop playing around and get over here, Dawes!" Walsh shouted. "You too, Amelia."

Dawes finally realized the danger he was in. He spread his arms wide and carefully reversed, eyes glued to the shaky floorboards, until he backed into the brick wall. I locked eyes with Walsh, giving him a look that reminded him very distinctly that I told him so, then carefully stepped across the floor to join the two agents. Once I was within a human arm's reach of Walsh, I let go of the joist. The floor groaned, rising to a wooden shriek as the boards snapped under the weight of its fall. It took a good quarter of the remaining floor with it. Dawes put his hands against the wall, as if trying to dig his fingers into the brick, and then slowly slid to the floor, his face pale.

"If you two need further encouragement to head for solid ground," I said, "the greatest spatial distortion appears to extend through that broken window. I expect you'll find something interesting to wave at in the alley."

Agent Walsh looked thoughtful. As I'd hoped, his thoughts had turned to Lucas Dowling and how to track him down. Dawes, meanwhile, didn't see how any of what I said connected but did want to get on the ground as soon as possible. He pushed himself shakily to his feet.

"You're sure the way down is safe?" he asked.

"I promise you, Agent Dawes," I said. I thought I sounded reassuring. "Just follow me and step where I step."

The slope of rubble where the stairwell once stood seemed sturdy, but I wasn't entirely certain about the floor between us and it. To be safe, I reached out and steadied the parts that appeared questionable while we carefully made our way down to the ground floor. Dawes was right behind me, matching me step for step and frequently glancing at his meter as it squealed and squawked. Walsh took up the rear, somewhat chagrined to have been proven wrong about the floor's integrity and, to my quiet amusement, guilty at putting me in danger.

Once we reached the ground, I let go of the various supports I'd been steadying. This time there wasn't a dramatic collapse, although what was left of the second floor let out a loud groan. Dawes was still looking at the building with trepidation. I tried to distract him from his entirely legitimate concerns by getting him back on task.

"Congratulations, gentlemen," I said. "You've successfully developed an instrument to detect distortions in space-time."

"Yeah!" Dawes said, with a commitment he didn't really feel. "Well, the lab boys did. Now we need to figure out how to measure 'em."

"Honestly, at this point I'm more concerned with figuring out how to track down Dowling," Walsh said. "But if Amelia's right about the distortion coming out the rear window—"

"I am."

"—then he might have left us a trail. Let's head into the alley."

The alley was a nondescript stretch of gravel-strewn dirt bisecting the block. A wooden fence ran down one side, blocking the backyards of the houses. Which was good for us, as it hid most of what we were doing from prying eyes. At Agent Walsh's direction, Dawes walked up and down the alley, wand held high. To my surprise, his speaker was silent and his gauges barely trembled.

"I'm not getting anything, Walsh," he said.

Agent Walsh frowned. He didn't like hearing me be contradicted. "Are you sure you're doing it right?"

"There's not a whole lot I have to *do*. The wand picks up weird stuff, the gauges move, the speaker squawks."

"Amelia, could whatever you detected terminate at the window?"

"No. I feel *something*," I said. "It's right here."

I pointed to a patch of dirt just outside the bookstore's back door, directly underneath the broken window. I could *feel* a wrinkle just by my feet, a narrow divot something had carved in reality. I leaned over and peered within. Then I gasped and stood up, hand over my mouth.

Something was growing in the seam, in a pocket at right angles to the rest of the world. It was a clump of fleshy polyps, pale blue-green only not. They squirmed and writhed, looking like a cross between mushrooms and thick, gooey worms. Until they realized I was watching them. They turned in eerie synchronicity, pointing their bulbous tips at me. I half expected them to split open and reveal unblinking eyes. Or to suddenly dart through the crack in space and attack.

Agent Walsh rushed over to me, putting a hand on my shoulder.

"Is everything all right?" he asked.

"Fine. I'm fine," I said.

I looked at the hand on my shoulder, then at him. He coughed awkwardly and let go, taking a step to the side.

"Agent Dawes?" I said. "Could you please come here and point that wand in front of where I'm standing?"

I stepped away as Dawes complied, suddenly wanting space from the two men. He knelt down, poking at the ground with his wand. I didn't expect the needles to jump wildly or the speaker to let out a huge burst of static, but I expected it to do *something*. To my annoyance, the gauges remained frustratingly inert.

"I may have to take back my judgment of that gadget's success," I said sourly.

Dawes pulled himself upright, somehow personally affronted at my criticism of a tool he'd had no hand in designing.

"Miss Temple, this 'gadget' is a precision instrument representing the cutting edge of aetheric research—"

"You don't even know what half of that means."

"*Amelia,*" Walsh said.

"Oh, fine," I said, cross. "But there *is* something there. It's not a big something, but I can still sense it."

"Okay, Amelia, okay," Walsh said, holding up his hands. "I believe you. The meter might just need some fine-tuning. What is it you've found?"

I hesitated. I wasn't certain what the polyps were, nor how they had gotten there. They appeared to be made of the same sort of matter as the body the Watcher had constructed when Dowling summoned it, but I could detect no more mind within the clump of worms than in a rosebush. What did that mean?

I had one avenue of investigation that was closed to the two agents. Another perspective, although the perspective here was already slightly warped. I *turned* my perception just slightly to one side along the axis of time. The alley was momentarily lit by a flash of not-green light, and then it was midnight dark. The bookstore was whole, except for the shards of glass falling from the window above me.

Lucas Dowling flew through the air. Or more accurately, plummeted. He crashed against the gravel-strewn dirt with a wet, bone-snapping thump. I winced at the sight. As much as I had reason to loathe him, I had no desire to see him hurt.

And hurt he was, though somehow not too hurt to slowly pull himself to his feet. I didn't think it was Lucas driving, however. His head and torso were covered in dark green ichor—the phlegm the Watcher Above had spewed at him shortly after it manifested. Pale fleshy growths, not unlike those hidden beneath the alley, poked through the skin on the left side of his body, from his face all the way down his arms and ribs. His right arm, which he'd landed on, hung limply by his side. The flesh of that arm was split where the bone poked out, leaking more of the weird fluid mixed with his blood.

A wide splash of ichor spread from the ground at his feet, where he'd landed. It roiled slightly, as if it was boiling. Or as if it was reacting with the ground or the space it occupied.

He staggered a few steps forward before collapsing against the wooden fence, leaving another splash of ichor across the boards, dripping down to soak into the dirt. Was it carrying some kind of spore? Had the element growing out of Lucas' flesh taken root in the alley?

I stepped toward him, meaning to get a closer look. The gravel crunched beneath my foot. Lucas' head jerked around. His left eye, now swollen with greenish-blue fluid, stared at me.

"*You,*" he said, his voice thick and glutinous.

I gasped and flung myself *forward.*

And nearly tripped over Agent Dawes, who was still trying to measure the spot where Lucas had fallen.

"Miss Temple?"

"Amelia!"

I stumbled back and propped myself against the brick wall. My head was reeling. It wasn't the first time I'd moved myself around in time. It wasn't the first time something had noticed me. It *was* the first time that something had once been human.

The Watcher Above had felt my presence in 1925. We fought. I only barely won. But this was different. Wasn't it?

"I'm fine," I said. "I'm sorry, I just…"

"Hey, Walsh, maybe we ought to wrap this up," Dawes said. "Miss Temple doesn't look so hot all of a sudden."

"I said I'm fine," I snapped, but Agent Walsh ignored me.

"I think you're right, Dawes. Amelia does look pale. I think she's overextended herself."

"Excuse me?"

"We'll call it a day. You've been a big help, Amelia, but I think it's time to take a break. Don't you?"

I bristled at his presumption. Yes, I was a bit disturbed by my unexpected encounter with Lucas, or whatever was driving him. And by my passenger's sudden vigor. They had both thrown me off balance for a moment, but I was still in control. I didn't need coddling. What I needed was to take a closer look at whatever was growing in the alley. To my annoyance, it was clear Agent Walsh wasn't going to budge. I took a deep breath to steady myself. Picking this fight would cost me more than I would gain. I could always investigate another day, and next time with partners I fully trusted.

I wasn't entirely ready to leave town, however. So I made a counter proposal. "Very well, Agent Walsh. I'll ride to the campus with you. Provided we stop for a bite to eat first."

03

I had been hesitant about taking Agent Walsh to the Lane Diner. *Obviously* it had the best food in town, although admittedly I'd only patronized one of the other three restaurants. Despite that, I didn't want to bring the Lanes to the Bureau's attention. Befriending Gloria had subjected them to enough scrutiny already. It was bad enough that Agent Walsh met her during the denouement of Dowling's experiment. She didn't need agents poking through her private studies.

It was plausible that I'd want to see my friend, though, and the Bureau had already decided the Lanes were safe enough for now. Walsh might be concerned about what I might tell Gloria, but he would have to trust my discretion. I wasn't foolish enough to tell her what we'd found at the bookstore in front of him. I had a trick in mind.

The diner wasn't terribly busy when we arrived. There were more tissue paper pumpkins on display than people, although that would have been true even if the place had been packed. Pumpkins hung from the ceiling on fishing twine, witches and skeletons with accordion limbs clung to the walls, and each table boasted a spooky paper centerpiece. Someone in the Lane family had gone all-in on Hallowe'en decorations. I suspected Gloria; her serious demeanor hid a developed sense of whimsy.

I was grateful for the decor, and not just because I'd never experienced a real Hallowe'en before. I hoped it would make the diner feel more familiar to the Bureau agents. I trusted Walsh up to a point, but I barely knew Dawes. I wasn't sure how he'd react when he realized this wasn't a white-owned establishment.

Gloria gave me a smile and a brief wave when I entered the diner, but it disappeared when she saw who was with me. Her entire demeanor shifted, as if she'd put on a mask. The two agents didn't notice. Walsh took the place in stride, but Dawes goggled to see Gloria behind the counter, and her brother Andre working hard at the grill.

"Miss Temple," he said, "you didn't say this place was a… a…"

I could see the ugly words forming in his mind. I turned to face him, locking eyes. I let my expression slowly melt from stern to quizzical, cocking my head to one side. He squirmed beneath my gaze like an insect on a pin.

"A *what*, Agent Dawes?" I asked, my tone mild.

With some effort, Dawes pulled his eyes away from mine. He looked to Walsh for support. To my handler's credit, he found none. Walsh shrugged and turned to Gloria, giving her a friendly smile.

"A… such a… nice place," Dawes said, giving Gloria a much less sincere smile. "When, uh, when Miss Temple said we were going to a diner, I figured it'd be a greasy spoon."

"We wash all our spoons reg'lar, sir," Gloria said. "Forks an' knives, too."

I hadn't heard her speak that way before, but I recognized it as a "talking to authority" voice, to make them underestimate her. Gloria's smile didn't touch her eyes, not that either man would notice. She picked up three menus and led us to a booth, picking one with a green cardboard octopus centerpiece. I narrowed my eyes and gave her a look. She responded with a sly wink.

If the agents noticed, they said nothing. Walsh and Dawes took their seats on opposite sides of the table. I slid in beside Agent Walsh, that being the less objectionable choice.

"The blue plate special is meatloaf, but I promise ever'thin's good," Gloria said. "Can I get y'all started with a coupla Cokes or sweet teas while y'all decide?"

"Coke's fine," Walsh said.

"Same."

"You know what I like," I said.

For a moment, when she was looking at me, Gloria's smile turned genuine. Then the mask returned.

"I'll have those right out. Meanwhile, y'all take your time."

Agent Dawes watched her, then shook his head.

"Interesting place you brought us," he said, low enough that only we could hear.

"It's the best food in Chatham Hills, *Mister* Dawes," I said. "And Gloria is a good friend, so I'll thank you to be polite to her."

Dawes' eyes widened. He glanced at Walsh, who nodded once in answer to both of his unasked questions. Yes, Gloria was my friend, and yes, I was allowed to speak to him that way.

Well, I'd said it politely.

In truth, Dawes' observation was correct, even if his tone was not. The Lane Diner was an interesting place. It was, to my knowledge, the only integrated business in the county. The sandwich shop on Main Street and the cafeteria at Woolworth's wouldn't serve Gloria, hence why Luci and I avoided them. There was another restaurant in Harwood, Chatham Hills' small Black neighborhood, but Luci and I had gotten awkward looks the two times Gloria had taken us there. We didn't face any hostility—not toward an attractive young white woman and her Plain Jane companion—but there was an understandable lack of trust. That left the Lane Diner, two blocks off Main Street, owned and operated by a Black family but patronized by everyone.

No, that wasn't the term people used back then. We're not in 1954 anymore.

I'd asked Gloria about it once, after I'd come to understand the town's segregation. She explained that the good people of Chatham Hills *liked* their little integrated diner so long as it wasn't *too* successful. That way they could tell themselves they were enlightened without actually having to change. That they didn't have a racial problem in Chatham Hills. Not like in other places.

It wasn't a good answer, but it was one that sadly made sense.

Gloria brought our drinks and took our orders. I wanted the blue plate, the two agents a burger and fries each. While we waited, the agents made small talk. Nothing important; they weren't oblivious enough to discuss even trivial work matters out in the open, even in code. Instead, they talked about some sporting event. I tuned them out—I'd never been allowed the opportunity to develop an interest in sports, so the topic bored me—and focused my thoughts inward. I didn't let my mind wander, exactly. I couldn't afford that, especially not with my passenger seemingly waking up. Instead, I simply pondered the current situation.

With what we'd discovered in the alley, it was more important than ever that I see Ralph. My passenger had clearly left more traces of their passage than we'd hoped. Pieces of it, or at least pieces of the vessel it had constructed, were burrowing into the space outside the ruined bookstore. Were they doing the same to Lucas, to Ralph?

The Bureau was likely looking into Ralph's medical condition, but I had little confidence in their ability to help him, or frankly, their willingness to do so. Most of the Bureau's agents, like Agent Walsh, believed it existed to identify ultraterrestrial anomalies and protect the American people from them, if necessary. Others saw the weird and the unknown as an asset. Or a resource, like iron, coal, or oil. Their nation had enemies, after all. To them, a human host with a fragment of "Subject 13" growing inside him would be valuable as a scientific experiment.

Unbidden, my hand went to my right arm. To the small scars that dotted the skin just below the shoulder. Where the electrodes had been attached. Agent Pickman loomed over me, looking down his thin nose.

"Note that the subject continues to be uncooperative."

The shock burned up my arm. My left hand clenched around it. My right hand pressed against the laminate tabletop. Then my fingertips pushed *through* it.

In a cold, damp spot in the back of my mind, my passenger writhed. The cold seeped down from my head, down my spine, into my limbs. The world darkened at the edges of my perception. For a moment, I didn't see Agent Walsh, a man who for three years had tried to do what he believed was right by me. I didn't see Agent Dawes, a naïve but well-meaning stranger. I saw two pale, hairy, soft-skinned animals. They were hideous. Weak. Replaceable.

Punish/protect/destroy.

I let out a thick, fetid breath. The air curdled around me.

No!

I slammed the full force of my attention onto my subconscious, brutally squashing the intrusive thoughts. I shook in my seat, jerking forward as if I'd caught myself in the act of falling asleep. The agents stared at me, Dawes with alarm, Walsh with concern. My handler reached out to catch my right arm.

"Amelia?" he said. "Are you okay?"

"What?"

"You, uh…"

"Looks like you had a fit or something," Dawes said.

"I wasn't going to go *that* far."

"I'm fine. It's nothing. I'm—excuse me," I said, standing up. "I need to go to the restroom. Female troubles."

As expected, that deflected their interest. It was ridiculous that they were so squeamish about simple biological functions because they didn't experience them but useful on occasion. I'd feel bad about encouraging it later. Right now, I needed to get away from everyone.

"Does, uh, *she* even?" Dawes whispered.

Agent Walsh shrugged.

I at least had the presence of mind to use the bathroom door instead of skipping around it. I let it close behind me, grabbing the sink and leaning all my weight against it; at least, as much of it as extended into these three dimensions. My shoulders hunched, holding so much tension they were practically cast in iron. I clenched my jaw so tight I could have snapped a metal rod in two, had it been between my teeth. I feared the sink might crack beneath my grip.

This would not do. I was in control of my body. Not my passenger and certainly nothing so mundane as fear. I forced my shoulders to relax and my jaw to unclench. I took a deep breath, and then another, until I could lay my palms flat against the sink instead of holding it like my life depended on it.

The Watcher Within was active. More, it seemed to have some sort of influence. Or at least it believed it had. Twice in one day it had reached for control of my body. I didn't know if it could actually take control, but it could communicate. Insidiously so. What else was it doing in there?

I stared at my reflection. My reflection stared back. I tilted my head, rubbing my fingers across my jaw, my cheeks, beneath my eyes. Trying to wrinkle out any changes that I hadn't deliberately made. Eyes, shape of my face, texture of my skin. Anything that suggested my passenger was affecting me the way it had Lucas Dowling.

I could see nothing different. Still the same face I'd always worn, accounting for the changes of late adolescence. I let out a shaky sigh of relief.

The seal was holding, I was certain of that. Gloria had done her work well, especially considering how much she'd had to improvise. Even so, now that the Watcher Within had made itself known, I could *feel* it there, somewhere. Like a cold spot of mold just out of view.

I needed to talk to my expert.

It was a good thing I'd gone to the restroom. I was going to want privacy for what I had in mind. I leaned away from the sink and settled my focus on the diner. Gloria was behind the counter waiting on another customer, while Andre was flipping a squad of burgers on the grill. Their middle brother Lucas was tackling the dishes at the sink behind them. That wasn't ideal. I had an idea for how to talk to Gloria underneath the agents' noses, but I didn't want her drawing attention to herself. I needed to get her out of the dining area, but not into the kitchen.

There was a small storage room next to the refrigerator, full of neat shelves holding everything a restaurant would need that didn't require cooling. Reaching between spatial dimensions, I grabbed a box full of tableware and dropped it. Forks and spoons clattered loudly against the linoleum floor, raising a racket that Gloria could hear from where she stood. Andre, nursing meals for seven different people between the grill, fryer, and oven, glanced in the direction of the crash and said a rude word.

"Gloria! Something fell in the closet. Go pick it up!" he called.

Gloria bit back the next three things she was about to say. She gave the woman whose order she had taken a dazzling customer service smile, then turned to the window.

"I'm with the customers! Send Lucas to do it!" she said, waving at their brother.

"I'm up to my elbows in dishes!" Lucas said over his shoulder.

"He's up to his elbows in dishes," Andre said.

It was a fair point. Lucas was doing a good job staying ahead of the diner's endless parade of dirty dishes, but there was always quite a queue behind him. Gloria rolled her eyes but conceded, heading through the employees-only door to pick up the mess I'd made.

Only to find me waiting in the storage closet. Kind of.

To her credit, she only blinked twice.

"Hi again," I said.

"You know this area is off-limits to customers," she said dryly.

"Oh, I'm not really here! I'm in the ladies' room. I'm sort of projecting an image of myself into the part of your brain that processes audio/visual information."

"I suppose that's better than pulling me into your mind again."

"I *have* apologized for that."

As we spoke, the bin for the utensils lifted off the shelf. The fallen tableware flowed up into it. I started to float the bin to the shelf, but Gloria held her hand out for it.

"They'll need to be washed."

"Are you sure? The floor in here looks scrupulously clean."

She smiled. "Momma taught us right. I'm not giving my customers forks that've been on the floor. Plus, it'll serve Lucas right."

I shrugged and floated the bin over to her. She tucked it under her arm.

"What's so important that you don't want your Feds to hear?"

I gave her the Reader's Digest version of their investigation of Orr's Used Books. I focused on how my passenger had reacted to it all. Gloria looked intrigued by the Bureau's newest toy but grew concerned when I described the way the Watcher Within had tried reaching for the hole in space.

"It was too much to expect it'd be over that easy," she said.

"It never really was over," I said, tapping the back of my head.

"True. We need to talk more about that too, although this isn't the time or place."

"Order up!" Andre called from the kitchen, as if to emphasize the point. Gloria looked at the door, annoyed.

"Can you still hear me if I think at you?" she asked.

I thought about how to explain that I could see what everyone around me was thinking at the forefront of their minds as casually as she could hear what everyone in the diner was saying from behind the counter. "Yes?"

"Good. Follow me."

Gloria led me out through the kitchen, where Andre waited impatiently with two plates in hand. The third, mine, was sitting on the window counter.

"What took you so long?" he asked.

"I had to make sure nothing else was going to fall, didn't I? Don't want Lucas to have to rewash all the dishes, too. Here you go, hon!"

Gloria dumped the tableware into the sink with a smile. Lucas rolled his eyes at his sister but set to washing the utensils without a complaint. Meanwhile, Gloria took the plates from their brother and backed through the door to the dining room. I watched all of this with a strange ache inside. I hadn't known anything like family until I'd met her and Luci last month.

I'm going to check the alley behind the bookstore after my shift, see what I can see, Gloria thought at me. *We already stopped that creature from eating the town. I don't want its kids running around.*

"I'm not sure if it is spreading," I said, "but that's still something to consider."

And it might lead to a more permanent solution for that nasty thing inside you.

Gloria slid the two plates she was carrying onto a tray. She picked it up and grabbed my tray off the window counter in one smooth motion.

If I have something by Friday evening, I'll give Luci a call. You can meet me at the library before you go on Saturday. Either way, meet me there Monday afternoon.

"That's assuming I can go," I said. I looked doubtfully at Agent Walsh.

Better get on that, then. And maybe go poof before you come out of the restroom? I like you, honey, but I don't know if I can take two of you.

"I bet Luci would think differently."

Gloria *thought* herself shaking her head at me. What she actually did was serve up the plates to the two agents with another beaming customer service smile. Dawes looked at his plate a bit nervously, but Walsh picked up his burger with gusto.

"Smells delicious, Miss Lane," he said.

"I'll be sure to tell my brother you said that," Gloria said.

I popped out of Gloria's view, then stepped out of the restroom, smoothing the front of my skirt with my hands. I gave the two men a slight smile as I retook my seat.

"You, uh, feeling better, Miss Temple?" Dawes said. To my surprise, his concern was genuine.

"Right as rain, I believe the saying is," I said.

Dawes took that with quiet relief. Walsh was more concerned with his hamburger. I couldn't blame him. I was certainly pleased with my meatloaf. We ate in silence for a few minutes. It wasn't as nice as eating with my friends, but I allowed that the agents' company wasn't entirely unpleasant. Particularly if they weren't talking. I was the one to break the silence, however. I put my fork down and folded my hands in front of me.

"I received some good news. Do you remember my friend Ralph?"

"The Connor boy?" Walsh said around a French fry.

My expression was carefully neutral, as if I were simply making small talk. Walsh's tone was also deliberately level, although I felt his tension increase. It was Dawes I kept my eye on, though, trying to gauge his reaction. I didn't sense any recognition when I said Ralph's name. That was good. Gossip about the investigation wasn't flowing around the Bureau campus yet. At least, not about that part.

"The hospital is allowing him to have visitors now," I said. "That's a good sign for his condition improving, isn't it?"

Walsh nodded slowly. He was already anticipating my question. "It certainly is. That's very good news."

He could hide his surprise from Dawes, but not from me. He didn't know anything about Ralph's condition or about visitations. That was interesting, and maybe a bit concerning. If he was leading the investigation into Lucas Dowling's disaster, he ought to already know about Ralph's condition. What did it mean that he didn't?

Agent Dawes, for his part, looked confused.

"You have a friend in the hospital?" he asked.

"Yes. The poor boy was in an accident." I glanced at Walsh, then turned up the "poor innocent waif" a bit. "They still aren't entirely certain how bad it is."

"Jeez. I hope he gets better, Miss Temple."

"Thank you, Agent Dawes," I said. "I'll pass on your well-wishes to his family this Saturday, when my friend Lucille and I visit. If I'm allowed."

"If you're allowed? What's the problem?"

"He's actually in a hospital in Regina because it's so serious," I said. "That's technically out of bounds for me."

"It's not 'technically' out of bounds, Amelia, it is out of bounds," Agent Walsh said.

"What, you got a friend in the hospital and you can't go see him?" Dawes said. "That's ridiculous!"

"I'm afraid so. Not unless Agent Walsh can pull some strings for me." I gave my handler what I hoped was a winsome smile.

Walsh shifted uncomfortably. "Amelia, that's kind of a big request."

"Cripes, Pat, have a heart," Dawes said. "She wants to visit a guy in a hospital, not hit up a gin joint downtown."

Agent Walsh bristled a bit at the other man's interference, but that was unwarranted territoriality. In truth, he wasn't opposed to the idea of my visiting Ralph. In fact, he seemed to like it, which surprised me. It was a question of what it would cost him.

"I'm not making any promises, Amelia," he said. "But Dawes is right. I suppose it's not too big of a request. I'll see what I can do."

"That's all I ask," I said, trying to look demure. "Well, maybe that and a slice of pie."

04

The beige waiting room at St. Audaeus Hospital is what sticks most in my memory. Four smooth walls in dingy off-brown paint with a ceiling to match and yellowish floors. Dark brown chairs, worn and saggy with use, pressed up against three of the walls in rows of five, leaving the center of the room empty. A duty nurse watched over the waiting room from a desk next to the door to the patients' wing. Well, in theory. The desk's current occupant was flipping listlessly through a fashion magazine. Someone had made a game attempt at decorating the room for Hallowe'en. The result was a scattered spread of wrinkled pumpkins crookedly taped up at random spots, and the hastily torn down remains of a poorly thought-out paper skeleton.

The large signs reading "WHITES ONLY" in big block letters were crisp and clear, though.

"This was really the best place your people could put Ralph?" Luci whispered.

"Not exactly," I said.

Agent Walsh had come through for me, much to my surprise. He'd gotten approval for a day trip to Regina. As we both expected, it came with a price, but I would be the one to pay it.

He had called me into his office Friday afternoon. Nothing like leaving important decisions to the last minute. To my dismay, he wasn't alone. Agent Randall Thomas was with him, leaning against the lone filing cabinet and scowling around his cigarette. Walsh looked like he had news for me, but despite Thomas' presence it wasn't bad, for once.

"Amelia, sit down." He gestured at the office's only other chair.

I did as he asked, warily eyeing Agent Thomas. He and I had a contentious history. Neither of us trusted the other; he because he believed I was a monster, and I because I knew that he was. He was almost certainly a member of the Bureau's Special Investigations branch, an inventive and devious band of hatchetmen I wasn't supposed to know existed. Thomas and his goons were deployed on those assignments that called for a particular sort of moral laxness. Worse, he was one of a handful of people whose thoughts I couldn't see. All I got from him was the mental equivalent of static and a headache. I tried to ignore his presence as much as I could, but it wasn't safe to keep an eye off him. It would be like ignoring a rattlesnake that was also a throbbing toothache.

Agent Walsh had the grace to look apologetic for Thomas' presence. He was sensitive to my discomfort around Thomas, even if he couldn't understand my reasons. He had no more desire to have Thomas interfering in my business, or in his handling of it, than I did. He was simply powerless to prevent it, or so he believed. The Specials had too much influence in the Bureau. They demanded oversight on, well, special investigations, and until the disastrous Dowling Experiment, I was the most special case around.

And, oh good, I was part of both investigations now.

Agent Walsh cleared his throat. "Shall we get on with it?"

"Please," I said, still looking at Thomas. "You've managed to get me permission to visit Ralph, but there are strings attached."

Agent Walsh blinked rapidly as he tried to reroute his train of thought. "I—yes. Hit the nail right on the head, there."

"Wasn't difficult," I said.

Thomas sneered. "For the record, I'm against all of this."

"Noted," I said, rolling my eyes but otherwise staying focused on Walsh. "So what *is* the catch?"

Agent Walsh shuffled the short stack of folders in front of him, keeping his hands occupied as he tried to catch his end of the conversation up to mine. My eyes widened as the thought formed in his head. I made an indignant noise.

"You want me to spy on Ralph for you?"

"No, not exactly," Agent Walsh said, stumbling over the words. Irritation bled into his stammer. "Look, if you'll give me a chance to explain—"

"You don't need to explain *anything* to hi—to 'her'," Thomas said. "Temple doesn't need to know the details, just the tasking."

"I don't think *you* get to decide what I *need*, Agent Thomas," I said, rising from my seat.

"*Both* of you, stop it!" Walsh said. "Randall, I *will not* remind you again who handles Amelia's assignments. You're a senior agent, for our sins. And you, Amelia, are practically an adult, as you keep reminding me. I should be able to expect better behavior from both of you. Especially in my own office!"

I didn't need to read Thomas' mind to see that he was ready to escalate. Faces were hard for me to read, but I knew what that red flush meant. I didn't care about his stung pride, but I didn't want to give him an excuse to go over my handler's head and get my permission revoked. So I swallowed my pride.

"I apologize, Agent Walsh," I said, returning to my seat. "You are correct, I shouldn't interrupt. And I ought to know better than to lose my temper."

I gave Agent Thomas an arch look. "It isn't lady-like."

Agent Thomas' face was still beet red, but he bit back whatever he was about to say next. I thought I could see a touch of hesitation in his eyes. If I was right, he was considering what I could do, should I *really* lose my temper. I was playing to his prejudices, but they'd be there regardless of what I did. A man of violence only understood violence.

"Let's get this over with," he growled.

"More than fine by me," Walsh said. He sounded tired. "As you surmised, Amelia, the Bureau is willing to approve a visit to your friend at the hospital. I've even gotten the AD to agree to let you go without an escort, for reasons I'll explain in a moment. But you're correct, this will be a working trip."

He shuffled through the folders again. They were personal files—those of my friends, as well as Ralph and Lucas Dowling. They were all a bit thicker than the last time I saw them. He moved Ralph's to the top. "It won't surprise you—"

"That Ralph is part of your current investigation."

Agent Walsh closed his eyes and breathed out, silently counting to five. "Your habit of finishing my sentences when you're irritated is only going to drag this out, you know."

"Sorry."

"It *might* surprise you that…"

Agent Walsh paused. I simply looked at him expectantly. Innocently. He narrowed his eyes. "Since Connor changed hospitals, we haven't been able to access him."

That *was* surprising. "You mean the Bureau wasn't responsible for his transfer?" I asked.

"Temple doesn't need to know that," Agent Thomas snapped.

"For pity's sake, Randall, she's bright enough to figure this out on her own. Sorry, Amelia," Walsh added, as what he'd *actually* said had been much coarser. "No, we weren't responsible for that. I think officially his mother was, but we're not one hundred percent certain. The Bureau can't be everywhere."

"Maybe if you were willing to flex a little muscle, Pat—"

"I don't need to, Randall, because we have a much more subtle method available." Walsh waved Ralph's folder in my direction. "You and Miss Sweeney should have no difficulty getting in as friends of the family, and you're already assisting me with this investigation. Whatever you can relay about Connor's condition will be helpful."

I arched an eyebrow. "So, I'm to be a field agent, then."

"No!" both agents said, one more angrily than the other.

"I'm thinking of you more as a trusted source," Walsh said, "and that's how you've been appearing in my paperwork. I don't need you to do anything fancy. Visit your friend in the hospital. Then write me a report."

The not-quite-promise that Walsh could get other privileges approved if I wrote a particularly useful report went unspoken. I didn't like that idea. What right did the Bureau have to dictate my coming and going? But that was how it had always worked, and I was already assisting him. Investigating Ralph's condition would let me influence the Bureau's attention in the direction I wanted. There was some potential here.

Also unspoken, but with far more emphasis, was that I was to keep that part a secret from Luci and Gloria.

"I'm not happy that they have you spying on Ralph," Luci said.

What Agent Walsh didn't know wouldn't hurt any of us.

"Neither am I, but at least this way we can have some control over what they're up to."

"For now."

I missed what she said next. I rubbed my upper arm with the hand that wasn't holding hers. It was twitching again. The half-dozen small scars burned, though thankfully not as badly as when I'd first gotten them.

Luci squeezed my hand, snapping me out of my reverie. "Amelia? Sweetheart?"

"I'm sorry, Luci. Did you say something?"

Her perfect brow furrowed with concern. "I said, 'It's strange that your keepers don't have anyone on the inside here. Didn't one of their doctors take him away?' And then *you* went away for a sec."

"Sorry. Yes, someone from the medical department arrived about half an hour after the two of you left."

Doctor Henry Vale. My personal doctor for the past six years, in fact. Not that I'd had many healthcare providers to choose from. He'd elected not to take Ralph to the Bureau campus, fearing it would raise too many questions with Ralph still having surviving family. Dr. Vale had placed Ralph at Hanners County General, the small hospital that served Chatham Hills and its surrounding area. Ralph had been transferred to St. Audaeus in Regina two weeks later. We'd simply assumed it had been the Bureau's doing until yesterday.

The door to the patients' wing opened. A stout, plump woman with messy blonde hair stepped out. She'd applied her makeup precisely, but it couldn't hide how tired her eyes were. Or how sad. She was all cried out, and there was nothing left but to keep hanging on. Despite that, she gave Luci the warmest smile she could muster and clasped her hand.

"Lucille," Beverly Connor said. "Thank you so much for coming. I know it means the world to Ralph."

"Of course." Luci rose to give Mrs. Connor a hug. "I'm only sorry that I couldn't come sooner."

"You know how doctors are. They always have to have it their way. I kept saying, 'If you'll just let him hear his Lucille, she'll call him back from wherever he's gone.'"

Luci held back a grimace. Something unspooled between them, a history of the near future that Mrs. Connor had sketched out without asking, born of a complete misunderstanding of Luci's feelings toward her son. Despite that, there was warmth between them. Luci smiled kindly and placed her other hand over Mrs. Connor's, trying to be reassuring.

"I don't know what we can really do, Mrs. C, but we're at least going to be here for him."

"And pray. Pray our boy home."

"Of course," said Luci, who to my knowledge hadn't set foot in a church in years. She waved a hand my way. "Oh, this is another friend of Ralph's, Amelia Temple."

I rose and offered my hand. "It's a pleasure to meet you, Mrs. Connor."

"Oh." Mrs. Connor took my hand, looking somewhat confused. "Another friend of Ralph's. Are you…?"

I could see the question forming in her mind. Another *female* friend of Ralph's. Could my interest in him be romantic? Was I Luci's rival? Such an assumption! Did everyone else assume that men and women's interactions could only be sexual in nature? Frankly, even describing me as Ralph's friend was a stretch.

"A student? No, ma'am," I said, hoping I could derail that train of thought at the station. "I'm not attending Del Sombra. Ralph and I, and Lucille as well, met at the bookstore. The one in Chatham Hills?"

A cloud crossed her face. The tears might not have all been cried out after all. "The one where all the trouble started?"

If only it *had* started there. I looked down at the floor, properly contrite. "I'm afraid so, ma'am. I'm so sorry. We would have stopped it if we could."

The cloud passed. Mrs. Connor let out a sigh and squeezed my hand. "Don't fret, dear. You couldn't have known."

Luci swallowed the confession that threatened to bubble out of her throat. It was killing her to keep the truth from Mrs. Connor. She couldn't believe the other woman didn't see the guilt in her eyes. But her smile stayed strong.

"Is it okay if we go in to see him?" she asked.

"Of course it is, dear. Go straight through. He's on this floor, third door on the right."

Luci thanked Mrs. Connor and hugged her again. I gave her a polite nod before we went through the double doors. The hallway beyond was quiet. And no less beige. I could sense the nurses and doctors throughout the ward, but no one was in this hallway. There were ten rooms in total on this floor. One was empty. Eight held two patients apiece. Ralph alone rated a single room.

Luci's brave face immediately collapsed when we walked through the door to his room. When she saw what was lying in the hospital bed, she let out a strangled sob and clutched me, burying her face in my shoulder. Nothing Mrs. Connor said had prepared her for the severity of his condition.

Ralph Connor lay beneath a gray sheet. Only his head and arms were above it, but they were far from exposed. They had been wrapped in thick gauze bandages, the splotches of blue-green fluid seeping through suggesting they were overdue for a change. The only exposed skin was a patch of his neck to facilitate a tracheostomy tube. The tube ran down to a piston respirator tucked beneath the bed. It hissed its steady mechanical heartbeat entirely out of time with the pulsing of Ralph's stomach.

"Oh God, Amelia," Luci whispered. "It's *horrible*."

I wrapped my arm around her waist and pressed my cheek against the top of her head. Ralph's condition had worsened considerably in just a month. The last time we'd seen him, his face and arms had been covered in weeping blue-green blemishes. Now, I was grateful Luci didn't have my senses. Inside, he was even worse.

Weird matter writhed beneath his skin. Fleshy polyps similar to the growths in the alley spread through his body like tumors. Blue-green tendrils dug into his muscles, spread down his veins, wrapped around and *through* his organs. It was no wonder he was on a ventilator. I couldn't imagine he could breathe on his own anymore. I didn't think he could even digest food. It was a small miracle his heart was still beating.

There was simply no way those growths hadn't shown up in x-rays. These were unlike the fungus in the alley in one respect. They existed entirely within the same set of dimensions as Ralph's living tissue. Palpating his body would surely reveal something wrong. Or just looking at the way his stomach pulsed.

Yet the doctors were still calling it severe burns and smoke inhalation. I was starting to suspect why the Bureau couldn't get a man inside.

"Luci," I said softly, "are you okay?"

She shook for a moment then straightened, taking a deep, shaky breath. Accepting the handkerchief I offered, she dabbed at her eyes.

"I'm sorry," she said. "I thought I would be able to handle it."

No one was near the door, no one coming. I cupped the back of her head and gave her a quick kiss.

"Don't. It's okay to be upset. You've got something to be upset about."

Not for the first time or the last, I silently cursed Lucas Dowling and his foolish experiment, and the sick, greedy old men who'd put him up to it. Somehow, I knew that none of them were paying the price Ralph was. Not even Lucas.

Yet.

Luci dabbed the last of her tears away. "You seem to be doing better than me."

"I've seen worse," I said.

I moved around to the side of Ralph's bed, more to look normal than out of any need of a closer vantage point. Beneath the bandages, his face twitched rapidly. Spasms from pain or from the growths plucking his nerves? I couldn't say yet.

I took Luci by the hand and placed my other hand on Ralph's shoulder, hoping the contact wouldn't hurt him. I bowed my head.

"We should pray," I said to her.

She cut her eyes at me, confused, but followed my lead.

I didn't know for certain whether we would be observed, my brass in kissing her notwithstanding. A pair of nurses were now making their rounds in the nearby rooms, but they didn't concern me. No one looked suspicious nearby, but that proved nothing. I certainly knew there were methods of observation that weren't so easily detected. If my suspicions were right, someone connected to this hospital might have access to them. I didn't know how much we didn't know, and that was frustrating and a little frightening.

But I guessed that at least one method of communication was secure.

Can you hear me? I said in Luci's head. *Squeeze my hand if you can.*

Luci blinked twice in surprise, but otherwise hid it well. She gave my hand a light squeeze.

Good. Don't speak. Just think what you want to say and I'll "hear" it.

I paused, chewing my lip. Then I added, *I'm sorry if this feels intrusive.*

It's not, she sent. *I like it. It's intimate. Not so much as last time, but close.*

A warm flush spread through her and toward me. Luci had to duck her already-bowed head further to hide her face. Despite our circumstances, despite the surroundings, she was having a hard time not smiling. She enjoyed having my mind touch hers. Especially now, it was a comfort. Feeling less alone, she relaxed ever so slightly.

So, what's the game? she sent.

I'm not one hundred percent certain yet. How much do you trust Ralph's mother? Does she have any reason to deceive you?

Bev? Luci stifled a laugh. *She loves me. I'm the daughter she desperately wants.*

Then anything she tells you about Ralph's condition is what the doctors are telling her?

Absolutely.

I apologize. I don't mean to impugn a family friend.

Luci radiated warmth toward me. *It's okay. You're putting pieces together. I think I could tell if you had any malicious intent right now. Not that you have a malicious bone in your body.*

An image of Agent Pickman flashed across my mind. His face slackened from fear to dull surprise. I banished him as quickly as I called him up. Thankfully, Luci didn't see that fragment of memory, but she felt my reaction to it. Her warmth changed, not lessened but flavored with deep concern.

Amelia? Darling? What was that?

Nothing. No one.

My pulse quickened. So did my breath. The room seemed to darken. The scars on my arm burned angrily. The muscles twitched beneath them, my skin rippling. I hadn't expected Luci would feel that. What else was she feeling? What could she see?

Her hand squeezed tighter. She pressed her arm against mine. Her scent filled my nose.

You're pulling away from me. Don't.

I...

Her grip loosened, though she kept her body close against me.

No. Sorry. Pull back if you need to. We can whisper if that's more comfortable. But I will want to revisit this as soon as you feel able.

I stood silent for a moment, letting her warmth surround and comfort me. I forced my heartbeat to slow. My breathing to deepen. My arm to still. I was safe, here with her.

Her warmth changed again, enveloping me like an embrace. *Better?*

Yes. I'm sorry.

Don't apologize. You experienced something.

Yes. Something I'm not ready to talk about yet.

That's up to you. Always. Another time. When you choose. Right now, we can focus on Ralph's condition. You were implying the doctors weren't giving Bev the whole truth?

Yes. I can see inside him. The things the Watcher spat at them are growing.

Her face paled. *Growing.*

The doctors should be able to see it. Even if they don't know what it is, they should be talking cancer, *not severe burns and smoke inhalation.*

Luci's eyes widened. She quickly came to the same conclusion I had. *We need to find out who really had Ralph moved to this hospital. Dollars to donuts it's the same sick old men who put him and Lucas up to this.*

That's your area of expertise, sweetheart. Meanwhile, Gloria and I need to figure out how to get this gunk out of Ralph.

Can you do that?

I have no idea, love. But we have to try.

I might not have been particularly close to Ralph Connor, but I couldn't let him be the victim of Lucas Dowling's machinations. Nor of his patrons. He didn't deserve this. He was primarily guilty of trusting the wrong person, not of malice. First, though, I needed to determine whether there was anything of him left to save. I certainly wasn't going to put it that way to Luci, of course.

I centered myself, trying to banish the thoughts crowding me. I needed to be clear-headed for what I was going to do next.

Luci, I'm going to pull away again. This time it's for your safety, not mine. I'm going to try to look inside Ralph's mind, and I'm not sure if it's safe for you to come with me.

I'd rather not, regardless. That feels too intrusive.

I paused. *Do you want me to not, then?*

I'm honestly uncomfortable with this. But it seems normal to you, huh?

More or less. This won't be like when you and Gloria helped me fight the Watcher. It's more thorough than talking. I understand why it feels wrong to you, but it's part of the way I perceive the world. I should be able to see what's happening on the surface of his mind as easily as you can see what's on the walls of his room, and I can't. It's like I'm looking through fog.

Or through mucky water. Blue-green water.

Have you ever seen someone in a coma before? Luci sent.

No. Catatonic, yes.

She squeezed my hand again. *That thing you're not ready to talk about.*

Yes.

Okay. I trust you know what you're doing, darling. And I'm right here if you need me.

Thank you, love. I'll only be a moment.

I dropped my connection to Luci with a great deal of reluctance. It was mutual; to my surprise, she almost didn't let go. I felt a pull as my mind slipped away from hers, a gentle pressure to stay. Easily overcome, as if I were slipping my fingers out of her hand, but it was so tempting to yield. Nonetheless, I dropped away. Not far. Just enough to create a conceptual gap, a psychic moat between Luci's mind and whatever might be waiting inside of Ralph's.

I pushed into the haze encapsulating Ralph's mind. It was like walking into a dark fogbank. I could sense vague shapes within arm's reach, but no details. Beams of ruddy light shone through the gloom, cutting momentarily through the fog before shutting off without warning. I cast my awareness out through the fog, looking for some sign of Ralph's consciousness. I could hear something in the background. A strange noise. For a moment, I thought it was my heartbeat, or perhaps Ralph's. But it was too irregular.

It sounded like something chewing.

It was an anchor, at least. I pushed forward, focusing on the sound. The fog was as gloomy as before, and the sound grew no louder, but I heard something beneath it. A quiet voice.

lucille? lucas? anyone? help me …

Ralph! I sent through the gloom, a psychic foghorn that should have been audible in every corner of his mind. *Ralph, it's Amelia Temple. Can you hear me?*

Then a beam of red light played over me. I felt a harsh pressure, a psychic heat against my conceptual form. It interrogated me, trying to identify me and my purpose here. I raised my own defenses, shielding myself with an aura of amnesia. The light refracted around me, then changed, becoming hostile. Now it burned. My conceptual form began to disintegrate as the light pushed me back.

Instead, I dove deeper. The light cut out as gravity tipped over. I sank into a sea of green-blue water, the surface falling rapidly away from me. Cold leached at my form.

I flailed as panic took hold, thrashing about as I tried to flee. But there was no way up. There was no surface, no sea floor. Just an endless volume of cold, fetid liquid, dark and silent as a grave.

Silent. Utterly, utterly silent.

When the Watcher attacked my mind, I experienced a riot of signal. Threats, entreaties, promises, deceptions, all bubbling out of a miasma of psychic gibberish. There had been so much noise I could barely comprehend individual thoughts. This was nothing like that. There was no noise, there was no signal. Just blank presence.

I cast my awareness out, hoping to catch some sign of intelligence. Nothing. Only formless quiet. I pulled my awareness away, focusing my attention as narrowly as I could, peering as closely as I dared at the volume of whatever I was in. Then I found something. Impulses. Commands. Reports. Back and forth, back and forth. Reflexive action. Autonomous function. A nervous system, instructing organs to function. But no consciousness, no awareness. Just a blank substrate, waiting to be imprinted.

And deep within me, my passenger lunged for it. I felt it strain against its seal, trying to break free of its bonds. To rejoin the piece of itself that had infested Ralph.

Mine/ours grow/change free/evolve/possess now!

"No!"

Luci grabbed me again, but this time I was the one who needed steadying. Her arms wrapped around my waist, her face pressed against my neck. I could feel her whispering her name against my skin. Her warmth, her rose-gold scent, enveloped my sensorium, banishing the cold that had permeated Ralph's mind. I let myself sink into it, recovering my balance in her.

Once I was steady, I patted her arm with one hand. "I'm fine, love. I'm here."

"You're cold as ice."

"So is Ralph." I pressed my fingers against the bare patch of skin on his neck. He was feverish. "At least, inside his mind."

"Is he still in there?"

"Yes, I'm sure of it. But the thing infecting him has buried him, for lack of a better word. So deeply that I don't think he can find his way out on his own."

Luci shuddered. She stared at his stomach, the growths bulging against his skin, visible even through the blankets. "That might be a mercy."

"It might. Or it might make things harder. There's no way to be certain."

"I suppose you're right. We should talk with Gloria as soon as possible."

"Yes. In the meantime, we should probably cut this visit short. I don't think we can accomplish anything more today, and I don't think we should be here when his doctors come to check on him."

"When you're right, you're right. Let's say our goodbyes to Mama Bev and get you to Chatham Hills."

We left the room and hurried down the hallway as quickly as we dared. Behind us, a man I was certain was Ralph's doctor had come around the corner. As I guessed, he was on his way to check on Ralph. He was a short, balding man, running toward stout as he approached middle age. He carried Ralph's chart in one hand, a leather bag full of unusual implements in the other. Pince-nez hung from a chain connected to his buttonhole. He stopped briefly to exchange pleasantries with a nurse, which fortunately delayed him long enough for us to slip through the door to the waiting room. He was a fatherly-looking man with a broad smile, and I had no desire for him to see our faces for the same reason I knew he was Ralph's doctor.

I couldn't see his thoughts at all. My awareness slid off the surface of his mind like water on a mirror.

05

The drive from Regina to Chatham Hills was scarcely longer than the one from town to the Bureau campus. Provided one was traveling by car. Such as, for instance, the one Luci had again borrowed from her unnamed friend. And had offered to drive me home in, with the implication that the trip could take longer, if I so desired.

She hadn't specified whose home she meant, either.

It was a *very* tempting offer, one that made my heart go faster and my palms sweat, but I turned it down. Day pass or no, I was still due at the Bureau campus within three hours. An electric trolley ran from Regina to Chatham Hills. I boarded with a half-dozen other passengers, few enough that I could claim a seat near the rear. Directly before the disgusting sign designating the last three rows for Black passengers. The trolley was slow, especially considering the way Luci drove, but it would still get me back before curfew. I didn't want to jeopardize my chances at future day trips by coming in late now. And I had something to occupy my time.

Gloria had trapped within my living brain an entity we did not entirely understand, using methods that were almost as mysterious. It had worked, as far as we could tell. The Watcher Within appeared to be confined, unable to access the rest of my nervous system. It had been quiescent for weeks. Then, within the span of six days, it had attempted to breach its confinement three times. Once was in response to my emotional state, the others due to external stimuli.

That meant three things. First, that the bodiless consciousness was able to detect things outside the ward, presumably using my own sensorium. Second, that the containment wasn't absolute; it could still communicate with me through the seal. Third, it at least believed it could still affect the world outside my mind, presumably using my own body.

The Watcher had failed so far, but it was a frightening thought. I didn't know everything I was capable of, but what I did know chilled me. My passenger had already proven it had malicious intentions for the world. I had to ensure it was contained. And learn what it was doing to Ralph. As the trolley trundled down the track, I settled in my seat, closed my eyes, and focused my attention *inward*.

The city, the railway, the trolley, all fell away. I opened my eyes. My seat now sat at the end of a familiar hallway. Wooden floorboards stretched out beneath a starry sky lit by auroras of strange light in no spectrum human eyes could see. Four doors were spaced along the right-hand wall. Empty space lay beyond the first three; I saw no need to extend the metaphor enough to build additional rooms. My dorm room lay beyond the fourth.

I took hold of my doorknob, but before turning it, I leaned in to listen at the door. I heard a quiet sloshing noise, as if a thick liquid was slowly moving in a small space. I rapped my knuckles against the door once. The noise stopped. The resulting silence was expectant. Waiting.

I opened the door and entered the room. It was a near-exact copy of my living room and kitchen. The door to my bedroom stood on the far wall, although unlike the real thing it was locked. A rumpled Chuck Berry poster hung on the wall to the door's left, and a small stack of paperbacks sat in the corner. My sofa was missing. In its place, a small aquarium full of sludgy green-blue fluid squatted on the floor, its edges glittering with weird light.

"Hello again," I said.

A folding chair leaned against the wall where I left it. I'd acquired it from a conference room two years ago; it was the only other seat in the room. I unfolded it and placed it in front of the aquarium. I sat, one leg folded over the other, one elbow on my knee, chin propped on my fist, and stared at the aquarium. My lips quirked into a slight smile. Possibly smugly, although I would never admit to it.

For a conceptual metaphor, it was quite fascinating. Peering closer at the glittering edges, I could make out the elements of Gloria's seal, the complex circular symbols the Apollonian Society had called "Prospero's Keys". The light was the power moving through them. My thoughts? Or metabolic energy? Or some other source?

Whatever it was, it contained my passenger successfully. The seal traced the edges of a rectangular cuboid, but within it, the blue-green fluid representing the Watcher's consciousness flowed along multiple dimensional axes. Compressed. Constrained. Cantankerous. The fluid churned, sending waves crashing helplessly against the faces of their prison. Within the convulsing mass, I glimpsed hints of my passenger's aetheric form. It was something like a squid, and something like a mushroom, and something like a jellyfish, and nothing like any of them as its form spanned five dimensions.

All locked within a small, dirty aquarium in the dorm room of my mind.

"This is interesting," I said. "Did you come up with this? I don't recall ever visualizing you this way."

To demonstrate the point, I altered the mindscape around us. My dorm melted away, replaced with the upstairs room in Orr's Used Books. The place where my passenger had successfully forced its way into the world and into my mind.

My chair remained, although I couldn't resist the urge to make it larger and more ornate. I sat on a dark wooden throne with armrests to accommodate my many limbs. It towered over the small aquarium, which sat on a wide steel plate. Lucas Dowling had used such a plate as the foundation of his summoning seal, but this one was blank, burnished metal. I had deliberately chosen not to replicate the seal. I didn't want to chance the memory of the seal having some effect. The last thing I needed was a *second* Watcher squatting in my central nervous system.

The Watcher Within swirled furiously. Its tendrils thrashed within the thick fluid of themselves. The aquarium wobbled on its stand, but it did not topple.

You affront/challenge I/We.

I *felt* rather than heard the words. I shrugged and leaned back in my chair, trying to emulate Luci's nonchalance. Resting my elbow on the closest armrest, I examined my nails as if I knew what I was looking at.

"You tried to take over my mind. You'll forgive me if I took that personally."

The Watcher writhed.

I/We agreement compact void You. You agreement/compact animal/natives. Discord/confusion. History/precedent/projection align/predict no. I/We comprehend no.

I sighed heavily. "Do I have to do this again? I already went over this with a representative of your swarm. I didn't break any agreement with you because I never *made* any agreement with you. I assure you, I have never forgotten a thing in my life. If I'd encountered you before last month, I'd remember it. For pity's sake, I wasn't even *born* the first time the Apollonian Society tried to summon you."

The Watcher stilled for a moment, processing this. Then it threw itself into an agitated swirl. The fluid boiled, thick bubbles bursting helplessly against the bounds of the seal. Its thoughts came with a panicked insistence.

I/We comprehend no. I/We agreement/compact yes.

A sudden fury rose inside me. "No, *you don't!*" I shouted.

The walls and the floor rattled, the floorboards visibly shuddering beneath my wrath. The lone window fractured, a crack racing across the glass like a lightning bolt. The imaginary arms of my chair splintered beneath my human hands. The Watcher cowered inside its prison, its fluids pulling further into itself, leaving only oily vapor coiling against the glass panes.

Around me, in the physical world, the trolley shuddered as if struck by a heavy gale, but the air was still. The other passengers let out cries of alarm, and the driver said a sudden foul word as the control stick jerked under his hand. The wheels on the left side lifted an inch off the rail for a second before the trolley fell heavily back down. Thankfully, the trolley didn't derail.

"Sorry about that, folks," the driver said, red-faced. "Guess we got hit with some wind."

My anger cooled, replaced by a cold lump of guilt. It had been a long time since I'd lost my temper like that. This was a stark reminder as to why. I forced myself to still. I was gripping the arms of my actual seat as tightly as I had in my mind. Thankfully, these arms didn't have the same strength. With some difficulty, I unclenched my hands and let out a long breath. A loose strand of hair had flopped down in front of my face. I fastidiously tucked it behind my ear.

I counted to ten, then returned my focus inward.

"I did not come here," I said, picking my words with care, "to have this argument. I came for what is certain to be an entirely different yet equally frustrating argument."

The Watcher Within slowly unclenched itself, letting fluid refill the aquarium. It was still wary of my anger, but I could feel curiosity radiating from the murky liquid. Five bubbles rose to the surface and popped. I thought that might be the equivalent of a raised eyebrow.

"I want to ask you two things. To be honest, at this juncture I really only want the answer to the second, but considering you're thinking with my brain, I suspect you'll have an even more difficult time hiding the truth from me than most would."

The surface of the fluid quivered. Was it trepidation or humor? Despite my bluster, its thoughts and emotions were difficult to read. Years of teaching myself to interpret human body language and facial expression were useless here. I could translate only its broadest, most overt signals. It was, after all, an utterly alien entity.

"The first. After we trapped you, you were quiet for weeks. Now all of a sudden you're talking. Or at least thinking out loud. Testing the bounds of your prison. I get that, I really do. But why now?"

The fluid swirled into itself, raising waves that crashed into a small whirlpool. Something like a shrug? Or a sulk?

I rolled my eyes at it. "Well, I suppose that's understandable. Being humbled by inferior beings and all."

You inferior no.

I frowned. "What?"

You inferior no. Animal/native inferior yes. Animal/native prey/asset/material. You ally/patron/tutor I/We. You open/lead gate.

All/One.

I shivered. Its attitude had changed. The resentment was still there, but now a sense of reverence overlaid it. It felt as if the Watcher was trying to pull me in. Or maybe to pull closer to me. As if I was a…

"This is ridiculous. I'm Amelia Temple. I'm a…" The words stuck in my conceptual throat. "I'm not an entity like you."

And yet the Daimon Seal had affected both of us. Drawn the Watcher into our world, blocked me from entering spaces warded with it. Whatever I was, it was something closer to the Watcher than to Luci and Gloria.

I dismissed the thought with an angry shake of my head. "I said I wasn't having this discussion. We're talking about the second thing now."

I called up an image of Ralph in his hospital bed, emphasizing it as strongly as I could.

"What are you doing to Ralph Connor?"

The Watcher sank into itself. The fluid burbled. The dueling emanations of reverence and resentment lessened, replaced by a growing sense of confusion or frustration. The physical being within the aquarium writhed, agitating the thick fluid. It reached out again and again, an empty mental signal. It brought to mind someone opening their mouth, then closing it without speaking. As if it was trying to find the words.

The room shivered, and suddenly we weren't alone. Ralph Connor lay on the floor in front of me. Lucas Dowling was slumped against the wall on the other side of the aquarium, near the lone window. Green-blue blemishes were spreading across their exposed skin. The tableau was moments after the Watcher Above had begun its ichorous song.

I came very close to saying a rude word.

Like the edges of the aquarium, the images of Lucas and Ralph were chased with strange light. Looking closely, I could see the way the Watcher Within had reshaped within its prison. It had pushed parts of itself into different shapes—human shapes, and apparently separate from a three-dimensional perspective—but still all one being.

"Aren't you a clever entity," I said, my tone flat.

Lucas, still contorted as he tried to evade the Watcher's ichor, turned his head to face me. Thick blue-green fluid swam within his eyes. "It's about time you noticed."

I frowned and folded my arms across my chest. "What exactly am I addressing?"

"This colony," the apparition said. "And our memory of the Lucas Dowling creature. Mixed slightly with your own."

"I *really* want to say a rude word right now."

"Go ahead. We won't stop you," the Watcher-As-Lucas said. "We recognized that we were experiencing a communications gap. So we extruded these forms to bridge it."

"I see. And why these, specifically?"

"B-because they're f-f-familiar to you," the Watcher-As-Ralph said. "And b-because y-you ch-chose to present yourself as one of them. W-we don't un-understand it, but we w-will honor it."

"We hope you get tired of it quickly," the Watcher-As-Lucas added.

"You want to honor me?" I shook my head. "Fine. Then will you answer my question already?"

The form of Lucas smiled ghoulishly. "You're worried that perhaps we are in communication with the pieces of ourselves inside these creatures?"

"Are you?"

The Watcher-As-Lucas sneered. It—no, they—turned their hand over, examining the way the light glittered along the lines of the seal. "No. We had thought perhaps we could reach the pieces of ourselves we had left behind, but it seems our imprisonment is obscenely thorough. Well done, Amanda."

"*Amelia*, thank you. And it's Gloria's work. You ought to respect it."

Guilt flashed across the Ralph form's sweaty face. "Y-you'll have to f-f-forgive us. W-we c-connected to these c-creatures too briefly to incorporate much. W-we're l-limited to y-your m-memories of them."

I narrowed my eyes. "You're able to plunder my memories?"

"After a fashion," the Watcher-As-Lucas said. "As *you* pointed out, we are stuck using your disgusting meat brain."

"If y-you re-relocate us to a d-different p-part of your f-f-form, it w-would be much easier for us to think c-c-coherently."

A different part of my form. Well, of course they knew about that. They'd seen another part of me. My human self was the part that normally intersected with the local four-dimensional space-time. The greater part of me existed at right angles to that, in a space not dissimilar to where the Watcher and their swarm inhabited. That part of my body was very different. I'd long avoided thinking about *how* different.

Did the rest of my body have its own form of nerve tissue somewhere? Other organs? What sustained all of it? Certainly I didn't *eat* as if I were supporting an exponentially larger amount of body mass.

I was drifting. Letting them get me off-track.

"Call me provincial, but I find this version of you a little easier to interact with. And being human-like might help with your rehabilitation. So I think we'll stick with this set-up for the foreseeable future."

The Watcher-As-Lucas snorted dismissively and turned to the window. They ran a finger along the crack in the glass.

"You don't want to interfere with the energy matrix imprisoning us, as you barely understand how it works."

"There's a fair amount I *barely understand*," I said, dropping acidic emphasis on their words. "For instance, what you're doing to Ralph. And to Lucas Dowling, I suppose."

The Watcher's avatars shared a look, then turned to the wall on my left. It melted away, revealing a scene out of a nightmare. It was an alien landscape, a city in ruins dotted with tall, fleshy fungoid plants. Their trunks were pale blue, streaked with pulsing veins of green, and they looked like a cross between a tree and coral. A yellow-green fog hung over the city. A cyclopean Watcher in the weird flesh towered over it all, a skyscraper-scale pillar of biological matter. A flat cap like a deflated jellyfish topped the tower, and tendrils as thick around as tree trunks hung from it, lazily brushing against the rubble-strewn ground. Long vents ran vertically down their trunk, rhythmically spewing clouds of green-blue ichor.

"What is this?" I asked. "A memory or your disgusting fantasy for Earth?"

"Memory," the Watcher-As-Lucas said. "A world from three spawnings ago. We called it," and then I smelled a complicated chemical scent, overlaid with a modulated burst of radio static. "We don't know how long ago that would have been as they measure time on this plane, so don't bother asking."

"Time passes differently on your home plane," I said.

The Watcher-As-Ralph looked mournful. "Th-that isn't our h-home."

"What? Then what is it?"

The Watcher-As-Lucas hesitated. "A way station, perhaps? It was meant to be a place to expand, a sanctuary for the next step in our development. We… miscalculated."

The Watcher-As-Ralph glanced at me, confused and wary. "Y-you're *sure* y-you don't rem-muh-member this?"

"I keep telling you," I said, struggling to contain my frustration, "until a couple of weeks ago, all I knew about your people was that something like you existed. I didn't even think you were sapient, let alone a colonizing force."

The Watcher-As-Lucas made a dismissive noise and turned back to the vision. I followed their gaze. Something was moving across the rubble. A stream of four-limbed figures picked their way through the ruined buildings around the massive Watcher. Myriad growths sprouted from their bodies, tendrils and boils of weird matter. They were undoubtedly the mature versions of the growths that infected Lucas in the moments he fled his disastrous experiment, the same that currently infected Ralph.

"What is this?" I whispered.

"Instrumentality," the Watcher-As-Lucas said.

The beings moved in alarming sync, silently clearing rubble from a circular space a hundred meters from the cluster of coral trees. Once the ground was bare, they surrounded the grove, seemingly tending to the plants. Some of them stroked the fronds, others massaged the roots. After a time, a third of the beings pulled yellow orb-like growths out of the coral trees' fleshy trunks. The group returned to the clearing. The orb-bearers took up positions within the clearing, while the rest spread out at the edges. Those at the edges began to dance, gyrating in sync, limbs contorting into a variety of shapes that traveled in repeating sequence around the clearing. Those within the clearing knelt on the bare ground, pressing the orbs against their torsos. The orbs split, releasing clouds of ichor, thin tendrils bursting from the rents in their skin. The tendrils flailed wildly until they found the creatures holding them. Then they wrapped around the creatures' bodies, burrowing into infected flesh. The creatures curled around the sprouting orbs, cradling them as they took root in the bare ground. Their limbs spasmed, but they made no sound. Or perhaps the Watcher's memory simply didn't include it.

When the last of the beings stopped twitching, those at the edges ceased their dance. They formed back into a line and marched a winding path through the ruins, on to whoever knew what next.

"Th-there are th-things w-we need d-done that w-we c-can't at our sc-c-cale," the Watcher-As-Ralph said. "W-we need t-tools that can operate at a m-more delicate s-scale."

"Those are *people*," I said.

"They were animals," the Watcher-As-Lucas said, sneering.

"Y-you have to understand, th-they were p-p-primitives," the Watcher-As-Ralph said. "B-barely rated as a civilization, l-like the animals on this p-planet. W-we *uplift* them. G-give them u-unity and p-purpose. W-we make them p-part of us."

"Literally, eventually," the Watcher-As-Lucas said. "It takes a great deal of mass to sustain our corporeal growth."

"That's *obscene*," I said.

"I believe these animals have a concept known as 'the food chain'?"

I glared at them. I knew that part already. I'd witnessed what the Watcher had done to the Apollonian Society members that had summoned them in 1925. They'd started with poor Eleanor Townsend, a mild psychic talent the Apollonian Society had convinced to serve as the Watcher's host. The Watcher had warped her body into a more suitable vehicle, the tower we saw in this memory but at a smaller scale. Then they absorbed the ritual's other participants. They would have kept going if Gloria hadn't succeeded in banishing them.

They'd tried to do the same thing weeks ago, when Lucas and Ralph summoned them into the bookstore. But to hear them say it so casually, to dismiss all these people as nothing more than raw materials, was disgusting. And infuriating.

"And that's what you've done to Ralph." My voice was flat and cold.

"That's what we tried to do to these animals," the Watcher-As-Lucas said. "We obviously didn't succeed."

"Wh-when y-you sealed us in y-your b-brain, y-you cut us off from the p-pieces of us g-growing in these animals," the Watcher-As-Ralph said. "W-without our p-presence, it's aimlessly g-growing."

"So it *is* like a cancer," I said. "And if it keeps growing …"

"It will probably kill him," the Watcher-As-Lucas said casually.

"How do we stop it? Can we reverse the process? Cleanse the infection?"

The two avatars looked at one another, then turned to me, faces blank.

"We have no idea."

"W-we've n-never t-t-tried."

I glared at them, fists balling. So dismissive. So arrogant. So unconcerned with those they deemed beneath them. So utterly similar to the society that grew around me. Humans had their disposable classes too.

"Of course you haven't," I said, my voice quiet and still.

I shattered the mindscape around us. The images of Lucas and Ralph dissolved, erased like sand in a strong wind. I floated in a blank void with the

Watcher's aquarium form. I leaned close to them, my jaw tight in quiet fury. The thick fluid quivered beneath my glare.

"I don't know how to explain to you why what you're doing to other sapients is wrong," I said. "So instead, I recommend you try to figure out how to undo it."

My eyes flew open. The trolley was still a few miles from the stop in Chatham Hills. I let out a shaky breath and wrung my hands together, trying to channel my anger into pointless motion. Part of me wanted to destroy the Watcher Within, arrogant and rapacious thing that it was. Surely that would be easier than trying to teach it empathy for "lesser beings". But almost as soon as I had the thought, the image of Agent Thomas appeared in my mind. His sneer. The way he looked at me as if I were a clever but dangerous thing. The mocking emphasis he put on the words "she" and "her" the few times he was forced to use them.

I didn't believe that destroying my passenger would make me morally his equivalent. I knew that killing a prisoner because it was convenient was the sort of thing Randall Thomas would do. So instead, I chose the hard way. No matter how much it hurt.

And it would hurt.

06

"You're going to need a coat."

"I assure you, Mister Newton, that I will not," I said. After a moment, I gave him a pleasant smile.

Terrance Newton, the technician in charge of Evidence Chamber Three, looked to Agent Walsh for support. My handler shrugged, accepting that I would do as I saw fit. Mister Newton shook his head and sighed, then handed Agent Walsh a clipboard.

"Print name and sign. Time in is 1015," he said. "Observation access only without Assistant Director's written approval, you understand? Object 13-153 is classified as Highly Dangerous Material."

"As it should be," I murmured, signing my name on the form. Sort of.

Eight outbuildings were spaced around the north side of the Bureau campus. They had a variety of purposes—laboratories, armories, evidence storage—and in most cases, the bulk of the space lay underground. I hadn't made a habit of exploring them, although if I really wanted, I could see what was in most of them. They were, by and large, boring. Most of the "evidence" the Bureau had collected over the years was mundane, the debris and detritus left in the wake of an ultraterrestrial object's passing. There was enough dangerous material, however, to warrant one evidence chamber with extra security. Material such as the leftovers from Lucas Dowling's disastrous experiment. The Bureau had the wreck of his summoning seal down here under lock and key, although that was harmless in its current condition. It was no more functional than the seals Luci, Gloria, and I had destroyed in the Apollonian Society's old headquarters. The other major piece of debris was far more troubling. It, too, was currently inactive, but it would serve for our purposes.

"These badges are for Basement Level Three." Mister Newton exchanged the clipboard for a pair of small orange placards on thin chains. "Make sure they're visible at all times."

"You know, I *am* a field agent," Walsh said sourly. All the same, he looped the chain around his neck and placed the badge so it was visible over his tie.

"Then you should appreciate how dangerous this trash heap is," Mister Newton said. He looked down at the clipboard, confirming we'd filled out every field on the access form. Then he did a double take.

"This says 'Object 19-001'," he said with a scowl, pointing at my signature with a dirty-nailed finger.

"That's correct." I smiled winsomely.

Walsh let out a heavy sigh and rubbed his hand down his face. Newton stared at him. Then his eyes went wide as understanding set in. He stepped away from the counter, holding the clipboard in front of him like a shield.

"Is… is this…?"

"Yes, Mister Newton. This is Miss Temple," Walsh said, not bothering to hide his exasperation. "Who else would it be? How many seventeen-year-old girls do you see agents escorting down here?"

"Please tell me the answer is, 'just this one'," I said.

"Don't pay to ask questions around here," Newton muttered, his face flushing. "Figured she was a secretary or somethin'. She don't *look* seventeen."

That was accurate, albeit uncomfortable, to hear from a man I didn't know. I'd never looked my age, not since I was a couple of weeks old. It's apparently quite disconcerting to see a six-month-old walking around with... not a dancer's grace exactly, but hardly toddling.

Hoping to let the matter drop, Newton left his office and unlocked the door to the elevator. Before letting us pass, he offered both of us a stick of gum. For the pressure, he said.

"Make sure you show your badge to the guard before you step off the elevator," he said. "Some of 'em are twitchy. Does stuff to your mind, being down here."

His eyes bugged beneath bushy eyebrows as he twirled a finger around his temple.

"You *sure* the, uh, the young lady don't want a coat? It's colder'n a... uh... it's mighty cold down there."

"I'm quite sure, Mister Newton," I said. "You can return to your girlie magazine now."

Newton spluttered but couldn't come up with a response before the elevator doors closed. Walsh gave me a sharp look. I looked back, innocence personified. "It's in the drawer underneath the counter."

Walsh sighed and pressed the button marked "B3". The elevator shuddered, then began making its creaky way down the shaft.

"I'm starting to think my superiors are right about these friends of yours," Walsh said. "That Miss Sweeney is a bad influence."

I simply folded my hands in front of me and smiled.

The elevator had dropped twenty-five meters before the floor indicator clicked over to B1. The temperature plummeted, and the pressure changed in our ears. Not for the first time, I was struck by how obnoxiously the human body had constructed itself. There was only so much I was able to change on my own—tell my body to produce *these* hormones instead of *those*—and something as simple as rearranging my inner ear? No recourse but chewing gum. Absurd.

At least I wasn't shivering.

"You should have taken the coat," I said.

"I didn't think it would be this cold."

Foolish man. The coats hung on a rack in Newton's office. I considered grabbing one, but I was pretty sure Walsh didn't know I could do that. Also, a closed-circuit camera hung from the ceiling corner behind us. Newton wasn't watching the screens—he had, in fact, returned his attention to his magazine—but I didn't want to chance it. Walsh would simply have to learn a lesson about sensible clothing choices.

"You're absolutely certain you need to see this?" Walsh's teeth started to chatter.

"You said you wanted to involve me in the investigation," I said. "That means I need to be involved in *every* part of the investigation. Including the alleged clean-up."

Including the parts Walsh didn't need to know about.

As planned, Gloria and I met at the library the day before. I shared what Luci and I had experienced at the hospital. Gloria shared her solution for the Watcher's infection. Or at least, what she hoped was a solution.

"I have a proof of concept," she said. "Two, in fact. They're modifications of the seal Maxine Orr used to summon the Watcher here and the ones the Apollonian Society used to ward their headquarters."

I failed to suppress a wince. Those wards had been designed to keep "otherworldly" things out of the building those mad scientists had called home. Or, possibly, to keep them contained inside. The seals hadn't kept me from physically crossing into the space they warded, just scrambled my perception and inflicted the most excruciating pain I'd ever experienced. And I had experienced a lot in my life. Agent Pickman had been quite enthusiastic about compliance via pain.

On top of the trauma they'd inflicted, the wards had incidentally outed me as something not strictly human to my girlfriend and our dearest friend. That part, at least, had worked out. Gloria recognized the source of my distress and covered my hand with her own.

"I know. We haven't had the best of luck with that design," she said. "But I think we can get this one running without all that trauma."

"I trust you." I squeezed her hand. "How does this work?"

"By carefully modifying the Structures." She held up a diagram of a complicated seal—myriad circular symbols arranged in an ellipse, linked by a complex web of curling lines. "This one, I'm calling the Transit Seal. It only moves objects within our set of spatial dimensions, and only a short distance."

"Objects." I examined one of the seal's many Refinements, the Key that determined the scope of its effect. It was the Daimon Key. The Key that targeted entities like the Watcher. And me.

"Look at the Keys surrounding it." Gloria tapped each one with her finger. "More Structures. These modify the Daimon Key, narrowing the seal's scope. This one only affects critters like the Watcher. Or its body, I suppose."

"That's clever," I said, impressed. "How'd you figure that out?"

"Oh… I had some notes left over from when we still had the primer," she said. "That and what I remembered of the seal from 1925. Before everything went haywire."

That wasn't the whole truth. She was holding something back again, but Gloria wasn't thinking about whatever the whole truth was. Was she deliberately hiding it from me? Why would she do that?

If I delved deeper into her mind, I could probably find out, but Gloria was my friend. Invading her thoughts like a Bureau agent rummaging through my dorm room didn't sit right with me. She hadn't done wrong by me yet. If she wanted to keep something private, it seemed to me that it must have been for a good reason. Right?

So I let it go. We'd come to regret that later.

"*If* it works the way it's supposed to, this seal will get that gunk out of Luci's little friend," Gloria said. She held up another diagram. "This one will keep it contained."

Where the first seal resembled an open flower, this one chased the edges of the paper like the bars of a cage. I recognized a few of the Structures. In addition to the complex set of Keys that apparently described the Watcher, I recognized the Guardian Key, the Shroud Key, and Lethe.

"This one actually isn't as complicated as the first," Gloria said, with what seemed to be uncharacteristic inaccuracy. "It's a typical ward but inverted. Kind of similar to the one I did inside your head, but hopefully a bit more refined. That one was kind of sloppy."

As you might imagine, hearing her describe the multidimensional equation written directly into my own consciousness as "sloppy" was far from comforting. "It's holding so far," I said, weirdly affronted.

"'So far' is right. You know that was a desperate move, sugar. We don't know that it'll hold forever. We need to do something more permanent before the thing inside of you…"

I squirmed awkwardly in my seat, wanting to get off this line of conversation as quickly as possible. Before Gloria gave my passenger ideas. I leaned forward, trying to think of a way to explain it surreptitiously.

"They, ah, they can hear you," I whispered.

"What!?" Gloria said, much more loudly.

Obviously, I didn't succeed. "My passenger. They're trapped inside my brain. Which is linked to my senses. So they can access them, apparently, as well as some of my memory."

Gloria's face went through a wide range of expressions as she rallied admirably in the face of this new information. "Okay," she said at last. "That's all the more reason to figure out how to clear the Watcher's infection." She sighed heavily. "Unfortunately, I don't have any means of testing these seals. It's all theoretical."

"What about the polyps in the alley?"

Gloria shook her head. "I believe you when you say you found something there, Amelia, but I don't know how. I've returned three times, and I can't find anything out of the ordinary."

"I choose to take that as a good sign."

"Maybe. In the meantime, that leaves me without a sample to test my work. The only source we can for sure access is inside of Ralph Connor, and I am *not* Lucas Dowling. I'm not testing this on a living person first."

"I wouldn't expect you to. What if we went to the alley together? I could try to pry the stuff out of whatever pocket space it's hiding in."

Gloria made a face. "I'm not sure that's a good idea. I'm confident in my work, but at this stage? If I've made a mistake? I'm a little concerned about releasing live samples."

"No, that's understandable," I said. Then a thought occurred. "What about a dead one?"

The floor indicator clicked over to B3, and the elevator stopped with a jaw-rattling clunk. The door shuddered open, letting in a rush of biting air. Agent Walsh groaned and wrapped his arms around his torso.

An armed guard stepped out of an alcove past the elevator, rifle slung across his chest. His trigger finger twitched nervously until he recognized our access badges. Then he relaxed a bit, though his rifle remained pointed at our feet.

"Should have worn coats," he said.

"Th-thanks for th-that," Walsh said through his teeth. "W-where is Object Th-thirt-teen One F-five Th-three?"

The guard made a face beneath his balaclava. A chill unrelated to the near-freezing temperature crept up his spine. He turned away slightly, gesturing down the long hallway behind him, unwilling to look at the things within the chambers.

"Chamber 3-09," he said. "Fifth on the left. No touching the glass. No flash photography. Door's locked and entry's only allowed with two authorized observers. Anything funny happens and I'm under direct orders to initiate anti-contamination procedures."

"Which are?" I asked.

"I pull that switch there," he said, pointing to a row of switches within his alcove, "and three nozzles in the chamber start spraying flaming napalm."

"That's dramatic."

"The stuff down here's nothing to fool around with, miss. I get nightmares.

You ask me, they ought to flip the switches right now instead of playing with that stuff."

"That w-would certainly be *a* c-course of action," Walsh said. "Assuming it even w-works."

"Let's not find out, then." The guard checked his watch. "Unscheduled visit. You get ten minutes."

"I'm sure that will be sufficient," I said.

The guard moved to one side, and we exited the elevator. Like the two floors above and below it, this storage space was a single long hallway stretching about three hundred meters, lit by red lights. Ten large chambers adjoined the hallway on either side, rectangular concrete shells fitted with heavy metal doors and large plate glass viewing windows. Most of them were empty. Chamber 3-09 was the closest occupied room. The Bureau rarely acquired samples that survived exposure to local conditions long enough to require this kind of storage. Either whoever designed this space was wildly optimistic, or it was the result of a huge budget with little oversight. Probably a measure of both.

Object 13-153, better known to me as the corpse of the Watcher Within, loomed in the dim red light. Its half-formed tendrils hung limply from the wide cap atop its slumping stalk. The vents that had spewed its ichorous spores were now crusted with dried filth. Small incisions scored nearly every part of the corpse, from the wilted cap to the thick root-like tendrils at its base. The Bureau's researchers had been busy harvesting samples. That was hardly a reassuring thought.

I expected the Watcher Within to react the way they had when I was examining Ralph. Cautiously, I turned my attention inward, expecting to give a warning. To my surprise, they sat quiescent within their confinement.

You're being awfully quiet. Not interested?

The Watcher Within stirred. I could feel them searching through my memories and tensed, waiting for an attack. Then a picture of a diving suit flashed across my mind, a page taken from a book I'd read. The original image was whole. Then it altered, the suit torn and the helmet cracked.

I see. I think. This isn't you at all. Just a suit you wore.

But for our plan to work, the suit was all we needed.

I looked down at my hands, turned them over, and examined my arms. I felt my heartbeat and the air going in and out of my lungs, the blood through my veins. Glands released various chemicals. Electrical impulses raced along my nerves. No, I wasn't like the Watcher. This body, for all its flaws, was me, or at least a part of me.

I couldn't decide whether I found that comforting.

This ultraterrestrial corpse was in the best condition the Bureau had acquired in over a decade. I could see signs of decay—it had started rotting as soon as the Watcher's consciousness had been sucked out of it—but some mechanism had arrested the process. The cold, I thought, had little to do with it. I peered around the space, looking for signs of Prospero's Keys, or some other method of achieving the same goal. I knew the Bureau had used the Keys once; I remembered them from the old Bureau campus in Massachusetts, destroyed ten years ago. At one point after that, the Bureau had seemingly abandoned their use. I couldn't recall encountering them between then and the trouble with Lucas Dowling, and I remembered everything.

I had reason to believe alternate methods were possible. The decimal numeral system was only one method to describe numbers, after all; they existed independent of the way humans wrote them. Maxine Orr had created a pocked space within her bookstore for her own studies and experiments, and I hadn't found any seals within the one time I was inside it. Nor were any seals to be found around this chamber. That was concerning. It meant I had no idea what measures might be in place, nor how they might also affect me.

I let my focus wander from Chamber 3-09, taking in the rest of the space. Only one guard had been stationed, but each chamber was fitted with the same brutal anti-decontamination system. A surveillance camera hung from the ceiling on either end of the long hallway. Both connected to the monitor thirty-three meters above us in the main guard office, being diligently ignored by Mister Newton. There were no monitors in the guard alcove on this floor, but he did have a phone that connected to the one up top.

Crucially, there were no cameras inside the actual chambers. Why would there be? Everything stored here was supposed to be inert. Surely anyone intending to access the chambers would have to come down the guarded, monitored hallway.

I turned my attention to the Watcher's corpse. With some trepidation, I extended a hidden limb into the chamber. I felt no pain, no resistance. I wrapped my tendril around a corpse and gave it a slight flick. It swung silently, as if caught in a momentary drift. No alarms sounded.

"I've seen what I needed to, Agent Walsh," I said. "We can go now."

"Th-that was quick," Walsh said, but he was eager to hurry after me as I walked toward the elevator.

"I wanted to be certain it was secure," I said. "Heaven knows what you meddlers get up to down here. We wouldn't want anyone getting up to mischief, would we?"

The elevator door closed behind us and up we went.

I returned to Evidence Chamber Three later that night. I left Agent Walsh to his own devices and brought two useful tools. One was a simple kitchen knife. The other was a blue Pyrex container Gloria had loaned me. The knife was utterly ordinary. From the outside, so was the Pyrex—a blue glass box big enough for two servings of dinner. Inside was a different matter. Gloria had etched a delicate ribbon of curling symbols along the interior and beneath the glass lid. To the right eyes, it glittered with faint light.

Three floors below me in the main building, Special Agent Oscar Hess stood duty. His primary responsibility was to monitor the phones and the alarms for various anomalies stored on campus. Technically, that included me, but a little over a month ago, a particular disturbance had culminated in four grown men barging into my room in the middle of the night. After that, the duty agents had become reluctant to actually check on me. It was nice, finally experiencing something like privacy. Not least because it meant I had a wider latitude in after-hours activity.

Still, better to be safe than sorry. On my way downstairs, I paused on the second-floor landing. Hess sat in the duty office with a thermos of coffee and a paperback book, occasionally glancing at the rows of alarm lights on the wall. He was already tired—he'd worked a full day and still had drawn the all-night watch—and it took very little to push him into a deep sleep. His head tipped gently forward, his eyelids drooped and then closed. He slumped in his chair, lightly snoring. I silently promised to wake him on my way back up, assuming it went well. Hess had never been specifically hostile toward me. No reason to set him up for trouble.

The night air outside the main building was pleasantly cold. This late, the Bureau campus was utterly quiet. It hardly bustled during the day, but now it was deserted. Other than myself and Hess, there were barely more than a dozen personnel present across the entire complex, and all of those were armed guards at sensitive posts. None of them would see me from the direction I was traveling.

I focused on Evidence Chamber Three, peering deep under the earth to the third sub-basement. I narrowed my focus to a pinpoint centered on the chamber holding Object 13-153. Looking at the space directly behind the Watcher's corpse, from the perspective of anyone looking in from the hallway. Keeping that point in space fixed in my mind, I stepped *forward*.

Reality rippled
    and
        I stood behind the Watcher's corpse.

I tensed, waiting for the klaxons, waiting for the flaming fuel to come shooting out of the nozzles in the ceiling corners. But nothing happened. The corpse sat still. The guard in the alcove sat quietly. There was no noise except my breath, coming out in small clouds. My passage had gone completely undetected.

I let myself relax but made sure that I was still positioned so that the corpse's thick trunk obscured me in case the guard made rounds. I didn't want to have to explain how I'd gotten down here. I'd kept my abilities hidden as closely as I could, and for as much as the Bureau had kept me under observation, it was sometimes hard to believe how little they understood me.

I wanted to stop and search, see if I could identify whatever force was arresting the corpse's decay. I didn't dare, however. No sense spending too much time down here. Gloria might be interested in whatever methods the Bureau was using, but she would be far more interested in a sample of Watcher matter. I set the Pyrex beside one of the stabilizing root-tendrils and withdrew the knife. I steadied the corpse, not with my human hand but one of my *other* limbs. No leaving traces of myself that the Bureau's specialists might identify.

Choosing a spot above the tendril, I sawed off a sliver of rubbery flesh and flipped it into the container. The seals activated once I replaced the lid, flaring with a strange light that I hoped only I could see. There were two, the containment seal Gloria had shown me and a preservation seal she had improvised after I explained my plan. She assured me they'd work so long as the lid stayed on and the seals intact. I would bind the whole thing in twine once I had it in my room, just to be safe.

I hoped this would be what Gloria needed to make her own plan work. We didn't know how much time we had left to help Ralph.

As it turned out, it was much less than we'd guessed.

07

While Gloria experimented with the Watcher's corpse and I tried to come to terms with their presence in my mind, Luci investigated the hospital. By which I mean, Luci was engaged in something between trespassing and breaking and entering.

Luci returned to the hospital three days after our visit to Ralph Connor. Dressed in a blue cardigan, white skirt, and oversized sunglasses, she told the receptionist she was here to visit a sick friend named Daniel Hardy. None of us knew Mr. Hardy and never would. He was simply another young man conveniently lying comatose and on a different floor from Ralph. In other words, a means to get Luci through the doors to the patient wing.

(I wasn't present for any of this, mind you. Much to my annoyance. I learned it all that Friday afternoon, on a date to the Arcadia. Luci shared the memory with me while we watched a movie about the truly improbable effect of radiation on insects.)

Luci signed in under a made-up name, then followed the nurse's directions to Hardy's room. Like Ralph, Hardy was the only patient in his room. Unlike Ralph, a small table stood next to his bed laden with get-well-wishes—flowers, cards, even a small box of chocolates sitting improbably on a clipboard. Whoever this gentleman was, he'd clearly made more of an impact on his community than poor Ralph Connor, alone in the hospital with only his mother and a trio of misfits to care for him.

The thought made tears well in Luci's eyes. She considered interrupting her mission, but practicality overruled sentiment. There was nothing she could do for Ralph by watching him breathe. He wouldn't even know she was there. Someone else surely would, if only a nurse. She couldn't afford to draw a connection between Lucille Sweeney and the woman who was about to be stalking the halls. So she wiped away the tears and set to work.

Apparently, most boxes of chocolate have a card in the lid identifying the filling of the various pieces within. Behind that, this box held a hastily sketched map of the hospital's first floor and basement with a room circled on each. It also held a note with a heart drawn in red ink. The note, along with the box of chocolates, clipboard, and the burgundy blazer hanging on the coat rack in the corner, had been left by one Dorothy Weathersby. Dorothy was a fellow Del Sombra co-ed who volunteered at St. Audaeus as a candy-striper. Not incidentally, up until five months prior, she had also been in a "something, it's hard to say, don't worry about it" with Luci, to use my darling's own words. Dorothy had broken it off but wasn't entirely over Luci. My darling clearly wasn't above taking advantage of her former flame's complicated feelings to further an investigation.

Luci replaced her cardigan with the blazer. She tied up her hair in a severe bun, sticking a ballpoint pen through it. She swapped her sunglasses with a pair of square, non-prescription eyeglasses in her purse. In the blazer's pocket, she found a small name tag that read "INSPECTOR". She pinned it to her lapel, stole a peanut butter chocolate from the box, and took the map from the lid but pointedly left the note behind.

"Sorry, Dottie," she said. "Guess you should have been a little less square."

Luci closed the box and slid the clipboard from underneath it, clipping the map to the board. Her disguise set, she blew Hardy a kiss and walked confidently out of the room.

There's a funny thing about beehives. A variety of creatures, such as wasps, are drawn to their honey. Bees defend their hive ferociously, repelling invaders with numbers and stings, so long as the attackers mount a frontal assault. If, on the other hand, a clever wasp can slip through a hole or crack in the hive, once she's inside, the bees will assume she must belong there.

Humans aren't any different. As Luci told me, walk as if you know where you're going, with your back straight and your head high, and most people will assume you must be allowed to be there. *Especially* if you're carrying a clipboard. Luci swore by it. *No one* wants to interfere with a determined person carrying a clipboard.

So no one bothered Luci as she left the patients' wing through the doors marked "Staff Only". She didn't avoid eye contact with the people she passed, heels clacking across the beige tile floor. Rather, they avoided eye contact with *her*. The combination of the clipboard and the vague title on her nameplate apparently warded her as effectively as Prospero's Keys and with much less fuss. No one wanted to chance being inspected.

Pity poor Theresa Grady, then. She had the misfortune of being the clerk on shift at the patient records room when Lucille Sweeney, Freelance Investigator, strode up to the window and placed a well-manicured hand against the counter. Miss Grady, who was only two years older than Luci and had worked at the hospital for less than a year, looked up from her crossword puzzle in surprise. The insincere smile that greeted her did nothing to settle Grady's nerves.

Or so I assume. I don't know exactly how Grady felt seeing Luci. I assume her heart beat a bit faster, and probably not for the reason mine would have. She smiled back at her surprise visitor, her mouth wide. Her eyes darted furtively to Luci's nameplate and then over her shoulder, perhaps hoping someone else was coming to take care of this. If so, she was out of luck. No one appeared to save her. Luci began drumming her fingers testily against the counter.

"May I help you?" Grady, who really did not deserve this, asked as brightly as she could manage.

"I am conducting a compliance inspection," Luci said. "I require access to this hospital's medical records."

"Oh! No one told me there would be an inspection today," Grady said, laughing nervously into her hand.

"Of course not," Luci snapped. "Why would we give any malefactors the opportunity to cover up their malfeasance?"

The unfortunate Miss Grady's eyes widened. "Oh! Oh, we don't have any of that here, there's nothing to hide—"

"Then you shouldn't have any problem unlocking this door and giving me access to the record files, should you?" Luci said. She pulled the ballpoint pen out of her hair and clicked it menacingly. "Unless you think I should note this in my report?"

"No! No, that's—"

Grady stood abruptly and fumbled for the small keyring sitting on a corner of her desk. She unlocked the door and pulled it open, jumping as Luci pushed into the room. Luci shut the door behind her. Grady was so flustered she didn't notice Luci slip the keys out of the lock and into the pocket of her blazer.

"This shouldn't take long," Luci said. "*If* everything is in order, that is. You can wait in the break room."

Grady nearly balked at that. This couldn't be standard procedure. She tried to stammer out an objection but froze under Luci's expectant glare. Luci held her pen above the clipboard, poised to take notes.

"Yes?" Luci said icily.

"Nothing!" Grady said. "I'll just... just..."

Grady slid around Luci, keeping her back to the wall until she reached the door, and fled the records room with as much dignity as she could muster. Which, in the moment, wasn't much. Luci waited until Grady was safely gone, then pulled the key ring from her pocket. Following Dorothy's instructions, she quickly sorted through them until she found the one engraved with "B5" and slipped it off the ring. She pocketed that key and dropped the rest of the keys on the desk roughly where Grady had found them. Then she turned her attention to the filing cabinet. She didn't know how much time she'd have before Theresa Grady, or whoever she'd run off to report to, became suspicious, but she only needed the one file.

For a moment before she pulled out the drawer, Luci worried that she wouldn't find Ralph's file at all. There it was, though, properly filed under "C". She slipped it out of the drawer and propped it open on top of the cabinet, poring through it as quickly as she could and jotting down notes on whatever seemed important.

In memory, the scene shivered. I appeared behind her in Grady's abandoned chair, holding a bag of Arcadia popcorn and looking a little cross.

"You understand how risky this was?"

Luci glanced over her shoulder, holding a page mid-flip. "As risky as going back in time to stop a mad scientist?"

"I suppose not," I admitted grudgingly.

I stood and came up behind her, wrapping my arms around her memory-self's waist and resting my chin on her shoulder. Luci hummed happily and pressed her cheek against mine. It was terrible that we could only be this casually intimate when our minds touched, but we were determined to make the most of it.

"Besides, it all turned out okay," Luci said. "Now stop grousing and help me search."

I read Ralph's file over her shoulder. Unfortunately, it was far less complete than she'd hoped. I gathered her general impression of what it said, but few specific details. Medical science simply wasn't Luci's forte. Most of the jargon appeared on the page as inky blurs.

"Anything jump out at you?" Luci asked.

"Just what you remember," I said. "You can tell it's a fraud because it's only talking about burns and smoke damage, but you don't remember much of the specifics."

"But I thought you were able to see everything?"

"I could if *I* had been the one to read it." I gave her a quick peck on the cheek. "I'm sorry, love, but your memory is terrible."

"I knew I should have stolen this, too," she grumbled.

"That would have been too obvious," I said. "They'd probably have realized it was missing by now, moved Ralph again, and likely put two and two together and made the pretty strawberry-blonde who'd terrorized the last clerk who'd seen it. They might have even gotten to six with the *other* pretty strawberry-blonde who keeps visiting Ralph."

Luci lowered her fake glasses. "I am *wearing a disguise.*"

"And you look terrific with your hair up like that. Nevertheless, you don't look *that* different. You got away with this on gall and gumption and the fact that you signed in as Samantha Bennett visiting Daniel Hardy."

"I don't think you're giving me enough credit." Luci sniffed. "At least this wasn't a complete bust. We already knew this record would be a fraud, but at least we have the name of the doctor who ordered Ralph moved from Hanners County General. Doctor Graydon Sutherland."

"Is that his attending physician here?"

"He's the one who filled most of this out."

"That means there must be another medical record here somewhere. A real one. You tried to steal it, didn't you?"

"Not today! It's in Dr. Sutherland's office if it's anywhere, but I didn't have his name so I couldn't ask Dottie where to find it. Found something else, though. If you'll come with me?"

Luci's memory-self, keenly aware of how much time had passed, snapped Ralph's record closed and re-filed it. Moving quickly, but hopefully not so quickly that she drew attention, she left the room and ducked down a side hallway. Just in time to avoid Grady and her supervisor coming around the corner. Their voices—the supervisor's annoyed, Grady's apologetic—quickly disappeared after Luci went down the stairwell to the hospital basement.

"So Miss Grady didn't entirely fall for it," I said. "Good for her."

Luci stared at me. "She was an obstacle keeping me from Ralph's medical record and you're rooting for her. You're doing that right now."

"You were very harsh with her. She was just doing her job."

"Well, nothing is missing so she shouldn't get into trouble."

"Except for the key to the hospital's other records room."

"Except for that, yeah."

The hospital basement was as beige and brightly lit as the rest of the building. Nonetheless, I could feel Luci's unease leaking through her memory-scape. There was nothing down here but storerooms, or at least that was how the doors were labeled. Nothing to cause the feeling of creeping dread that surrounded us like a low fog. Feelings that had nothing to do with the fear of getting caught. My fearless girl was absolutely confident in her ability to get in and out of the hospital without being found out. It was something else. Something hidden. Something *wrong*. And, inexplicably, something *red*.

Unfortunately, within the memory, I could only perceive what Luci had perceived.

The records room sat halfway down the gently curving hallway, along the outer curve. Like most of the doors in the building, a glass pane had been set in the upper half, with a shade drawn on the inside. Luci put her ear to the door, listening for movement inside. Once she was satisfied that she was alone, she unlocked the door and quietly ducked inside. Pulling a Rayovac flashlight out of her purse, she started perusing the filing cabinets. I hopped up on a cardboard box and watched, munching on popcorn.

"What exactly is it you were looking for?" I asked.

"Financial records. Personnel files. Some proof of who owns this hospital," Luci said. "Anything that connects it to the Chambers Foundation."

Of course, the hospital didn't stand still while Luci was digging around. Elsewhere, or more specifically two floors above us, Doctor Graydon Sutherland was making his rounds in the patients' ward. He, it will not surprise you, was the man I'd seen before, when Luci and I were leaving Ralph's hospital room. He smiled genially at a passing nurse as he entered his next patient's room, a comatose young man well-loved by his community. He performed a routine check of the patient's vitals, made a note in his chart, and turned toward the door. Before opening it, he stopped and sniffed the air. He must have smelled Luci's perfume, which evidently was an unusual scent, at least in this room.

This is another thing I didn't personally witness, at least, not as it was happening. I went back to observe much later, when we were trying to piece together how everything had gone so wrong. This, by itself, wasn't an important piece of the puzzle, but it was a piece.

Dr. Sutherland looked around the room for anything out of place. He saw the simple blue cardigan hanging on the coat rack. He picked up the sleeve and sniffed it, finding the source of the perfume. He dropped the sleeve and considered it, a curious expression on his face. It was such a minor detail. Most people would have overlooked it. But minor details were important in Dr. Sutherland's line of work, and this one thing apparently aroused his suspicion.

I couldn't say what drew Dr. Sutherland's eye to the gift-laden table and the candy box sitting slightly askew, thanks to whatever force blocked his thoughts from me. Whatever the reason, he casually lifted the lid of the chocolate box and peeked inside. He immediately found Dorothy's note. He held it to the light, turning it over curiously, then casually pocketed it. He stole a coconut crème from the box and resumed his rounds, humming to himself.

His loop soon took him past the patient records room, where a tearful Theresa Grady was arguing with her supervisor. Ordinarily, Dr. Sutherland probably would have walked on without even noticing the clerical staff and their problems. This time, something stopped him. I don't know for sure, but I suspect it was the hint of Luci's perfume still lingering in the air.

"What's going on, Gladys?" he said, addressing the older of the two women.

Gladys Harriman, the terror of St. Audaeus' administrative staff, was momentarily taken aback by his intrusion. She didn't answer to the medical team, not exactly. Nonetheless, this doctor was a powerful, and male, member of the hospital staff, and there was no sense getting on his bad side if it could be avoided. She plastered an insincere smile on her face and tried to explain.

"*Miss Grady* here apparently believes it is hospital policy to allow visitors unmonitored access to patient records," Mrs. Harriman said, "and then to lose track of them!"

"She said it was a surprise inspection!" Miss Grady said, clearly not for the first time.

Dr. Sutherland looked between the two women. He scratched his chin and hummed to himself, thinking it over.

"Describe this woman, Miss Grady," he said. "We'll want to know if anyone else has seen her."

"Eureka!" Luci whispered.

It had taken nearly an hour; even a hospital as small as St. Audaeus generated a lot of paperwork over the course of a year, and seemingly all of it eventually migrated to this room. Luci had constructed a small stack of files atop the room's lone desk. It leaned precipitously as she dropped the last file on top but didn't fall over yet.

"Listen to this," she said. "This hospital was founded ten years ago by a four-person board of governors."

"Let me guess," I said. "Maxwell Thorpe and his cronies."

Luci frowned. "No, I was expecting that too. His name's not on here. I don't recognize any of the names, actually, but I'm going to work on them."

True to form, Luci tore the sheet of paper out of the file and tucked it into her purse. I sighed heavily. There was no sense chiding her. It had already happened, and at least this file was unlikely to be read any time soon.

"No, here's the interesting bit," she continued. "They started with funding from three different groups: the Nova Anima Institute, North Central Dynamics, and the Chambers Foundation."

"So it *is* connected. Thorpe's crew is behind this place and keeping the Bureau out."

"And certainly up to no good! We have to get Ralph out of here."

"One step at a time, darling. First, we need to figure out how to get the

Watcher's gunk out of him. Gloria thinks she's got a method, and I've already requested permission for another visit next Saturday."

"Clever girl!" Luci said, kissing me happily. "After all, if he's cured, they have no reason to keep him here."

I thought about the Bureau and my impending eighteenth birthday. For a sufficiently amoral organization, having no justification to hold someone was less of a deterrent than Luci thought. I held my peace, though. I saw no reason to borrow trouble on either front.

"All right, we have a plan!" Luci said. "Now, I just need to get to Mr. Hardy's room and change on my way out. You can pop out, if you like. I promise it was much less exciting than it sounds."

"I suppose I could go back to watching the movie," I said. "These giant ants aren't very convincing, though. Have the filmmakers never heard of the square-cube law?"

"The gal sees four flicks and all of a sudden she's a critic," Luci said with a grin. "Come on. Let's enjoy the rest of our afternoon."

The memory-scape melted around us as we returned to regular consciousness. So I never actually saw Luci reach Mr. Hardy's room, exchange Dorothy's blaze for her cardigan, and let her hair back down. Not that it would have helped. Luci was oblivious to the nurse watching from the far end of the hall, taking careful note of who entered the room.

08

"You're certain this is going to work?"

"For the *fifth* time, Amelia, *yes!*" Gloria said, a trifle testily.

It had only been the fourth time I'd asked, actually, but from her tone I surmised Gloria wouldn't appreciate me pointing that out. Her attention was focused on the seals she was setting up in the alley behind the burned-out bookstore, and despite her body language, she was nervous. We'd never tried anything like this before, and if it all went well, we'd have to do it again tomorrow. That was cutting it close.

"You don't have to get it right this time," I said, in what I hoped was a helpful tone. "We don't have to see Ralph tomorrow."

Gloria straightened up and looked over her shoulder at me, her mouth tight. Not a helpful tone, then. Not at all.

"How did he look when you saw him?"

"Not good," I admitted.

"That gunk was spreading all through him, you said."

"I did."

"And it had only been a month. Now it's two weeks later. He might not have a whole lot of time left."

"You're probably right."

"So yes, it does have to be tomorrow."

Gloria turned back to her work. She had drawn five seals in ink and paper. The largest was the summoning seal, which she placed directly over the patch of dirt that hid a pocket full of Watcher polyps. The other four were positioned at the corners of a square five feet to a side, centered on the summoning seal. Ink-soaked twine connected these four to the primary seal, threaded through holes carefully punched into direction-defining Structures. Or so Gloria had said. As she explained it, a seal required three elements to work. It needed a focus, or the thing being acted upon. It needed power to fuel the effect, and a will to channel that power into the focus. In this case, power would come from twelve candles placed on the four subsidiary seals. They would catch the heat of the flame and direct it into the summoning seal. It was Gloria's innovation on Maxine Orr's set-up for the experiment in 1925.

"Why not incorporate the power source directly into the summoning seal, like she did?" I asked after Gloria was done explaining how it worked.

"Because when we do this for real, the summoning seal's going right on top of Ralph Connor's chest," she had said. "I don't want to risk giving him actual burns."

The seal itself was a sort of blueprint; when Gloria activated it, she would direct the flame's heat through the keys and into the focus. Or foci, in this instance, as there were two. One was the fist-sized knot of weird matter writhing within a divot of space-time beneath our feet. The other was the specially treated blue Pyrex that had held the sample of the Watcher's corpse. As if that wasn't complicated enough, the seal was built around a second innovation. The other seals we'd encountered had a set of Structures that acted as a sort of "lock", for lack of a better word. They drew more power than the seal needed and kept the power circulating through the framework to maintain the effect. That was why the wards in the Apollonian Society's former headquarters still worked decades later. Lacking those Structures, this seal would cease to function shortly after someone cut the power. Gloria said it was a safety measure, and one I was glad of. We didn't want the Watcher matter getting loose.

Although she insisted there was little to worry about. Absent an animating consciousness, she didn't think the Watcher matter could survive in open space. The sample I'd provided had rotted away to goo already, but the stasis seal had preserved it long enough for her experiments. She didn't see any reason to preserve this. Once it was out of its hidey-hole, hopefully it would also decompose. If not—that's why she'd waited until I was available to conduct this particular experiment. I appreciated her caution, although I wasn't sure what I'd really be able to do if this somehow went wrong. It was Gloria, after all, who'd prevented the Watcher from colonizing Chatham Hills the last time.

And it was Gloria whose will would drive this seal. When she was ready, we lit the candles, moving clockwise around the meta-seal. Then Gloria knelt in front of the summoning seal, placing her open palm on the Anchor Key. She closed her eyes and concentrated. I saw her run the equation that the meta-seal defined over and over again, a whirling sequence of arcane symbols rotating like a prayer wheel. The candles flared bright. Weird light, visible only to me, pooled within the curling lines of the power seals as they drank deeply of the heat. When it built to a critical mass, the light shot down the cords and into the summoning seal. The air above the seal shimmered as light ran around it, whirling faster and faster until an energetic vortex whipped up in the middle of the small alley, sending gravel and refuse flying away from us.

The world tilted around the seal as a new source of gravity coalesced in the center of the vortex. I heard a sound like rubber stretching. Then, at the very edge of hearing, a *pop*.

And a knot of iridescent matter wriggled wetly inside the Pyrex container.

I snapped out my limbs, snuffing the candles all at once. The air died down and the light vanished. Gloria fell forward, panting, sweat beading on her brow, and I ran up to support her.

"Are you okay?" I asked.

She nodded slowly, trying to catch her breath. Her eyes darted to the Pyrex. The lid wobbled. I placed a hand on top of it, holding it shut.

"It worked," I said. "It's in there."

Gloria grinned and punched the air. I picked up the Pyrex carefully with one arm and helped her to her feet with the other. She was unsteady at first, but quickly regained her balance.

"Told you it'd work," she said.

"So you did. Well done! What now?"

She looked past me at the stained bit of fence a couple of feet behind me. "You said there was more of it over there?"

"I did and there is, but I'm not sure you're in any condition to pull it out."

Gloria made a face but didn't argue. "No, you're right. I wasn't expecting that to take so much out of me."

"You've never done that before."

"Well, now I know. I'll rest tonight. We can clear the other patch out another day."

She took the Pyrex from me, handling it gingerly so as not to disturb the lid. "Now we have to decide what to do with this stuff."

"I thought we were going to let it rot."

"That's what I thought. But it's alive, right?"

The knot of weird matter writhed inside the glass container, like a school of eels knotting together. The polyps bumped against the lid and the sides of the Pyrex, their movements random, directionless.

"It might be," I said. "I don't sense any kind of mind animating it. Just a kind of hunger, for a lack of a better word. A desire to grow."

"That sounds like life to me, at least in the most basic terms."

"But why is this still alive when the Watcher's vessel died without them animating it?"

"That's a good question for another day," Gloria said. "I think I'm going to put this in the back of the diner's freezer for now. Hopefully Andre doesn't decide to serve it to someone."

Luci drove down to Chatham Hills in her borrowed car to pick us up the next day. She shared the results of her hospital break-in with Gloria on the way. I was still a little worried about what she'd gotten up to, but Gloria took it in stride.

"This isn't even the riskiest thing she's done this year," Gloria said. "And I'm not counting the thing with Dowling."

Luci stuck her tongue out at Gloria through the rearview mirror. That struck me as a mildly dangerous thing to do while driving. Gloria laughed.

"It confirms what we thought, and that's useful," Gloria said. "These same people are still behind all of it, and they're bigger than we first believed. What are they doing, though?"

"Experimenting," I said, rubbing my hand across the scars on my right arm. "To see what happens next."

Luci recognized my distress, although not the cause. She put a comforting hand on my thigh. I covered her hand with mine and gave her a small smile, but my scars still burned.

"Once we get that gunk out of Ralph, they'll have no reason not to discharge him," she said again.

The worst part was, she really believed that. I still didn't know how to tell her otherwise. We were going to have to cross that bridge when we came to it. Behind us, Gloria silently agreed. She looked out the window and shook her head.

"Men like that can always find a reason," she said to herself, too low for Luci to hear, "but at least we can save his life for a bit."

Luci parked the car at the far end of the hospital's parking lot. Gloria and I sat in the back seat while she went inside. Gloria had retrieved her summoning kit from the car's trunk—a small stack of seals, sixteen fresh candles, a book of matches, and a roll of ink-soaked twine. She had inscribed the interior of the crate with the same complex binding seal as the blue Pyrex. We were going to need a much bigger box this time, after all.

Gloria tapped her fingers nervously against the crate while I watched Luci sign in at the desk, this time under her own name. Ralph's mother was waiting with her. I didn't like that, but we would have to work around her presence. Maybe use her to run interference with the not-so-good doctor, should he be making his rounds.

"You're certain this is going to work?" I asked.

Gloria gave me a sharp look.

"Sorry. Oh, they're letting her in now."

Dr. Sutherland had emerged from the patient's ward. He shook hands with Mrs. Connor, who introduced him to Luci. I almost said a rude word at that. I didn't want him knowing any of our faces, let alone our names. I didn't realize it was too late. Dr. Sutherland was in fact drawing a connection between Luci and last week's mystery inspector, but he hid his recognition well. He only gave her a very intense look as he took her hand. In the moment, I chalked it up to typical male attraction. His thoughts were still closed to me, but Luci was a beautiful young woman and men typically reacted to her in a certain way. The doctor placed a hand on the small of her back and guided her to Ralph's room. I could feel her skin crawl, but she smiled pleasantly. I must have lost control over my facial expression, because Gloria looked at me with alarm.

"What's wrong?" she asked.

I looked down and realized I was gripping the seat cushion with both hands, hard enough to put some serious stress on the upholstery. I let out a slow, angry breath and forced my fingers and jaw to unclench. I tucked a stray hair behind my ear, trying to mimic my girlfriend's nonchalance.

"He's *touching* her," I said, utterly failing.

Gloria's alarm melted into disgust as she realized what I meant.

"So, he's one of *those*," she said. "Well, Luci can handle herself for the moment."

"Why does he think he can be so familiar with a woman he just met?"

"Some men, the thought that they might not be welcome never occurs to 'em," Gloria said. "All they see when they look at a gal is a nice little bit of something. I expect the nurses keep out of arm's reach around him."

"Disgusting."

Why did I want to be a part of this world, again?

Dr. Sutherland took his hand off my girlfriend's near-bottom when they reached Ralph's room, much to Luci's relief. And mine. And Gloria's, actually, who hadn't enjoyed sitting next to a suddenly furious monster girl. He picked up Ralph's chart, using it as a prop while he told a number of pretty lies about Ralph's condition. Which, to my eyes, was only getting worse.

The polyps in the alley hadn't grown much in two and a half weeks, but perhaps that's because they had nothing to feed on. The gunk within Ralph had grown by about a third. His abdomen looked bloated even from the outside, and ropes of viscous matter bulged beneath the skin of his limbs. Surely Mrs. Connor had to see that something was wrong, even with the heavy bandages, that what the doctor was saying and what she was seeing did not add up.

But no. Dr. Sutherland was an authority figure, and Beverly Connor had been brought up to listen to authority. Perhaps that was why her son fell so eagerly under the sway of Lucas Dowling—a petty, domineering little bully. Or perhaps I was being unfair. The doctor was meant to be an expert in a complex field, after all. Mrs. Connor was supposed to be able to trust that he was telling the truth.

Regardless, I had to get Mrs. Connor and Dr. Sutherland out of the room. I focused on Mrs. Connor's mind, reaching in to lightly entangle her thoughts with mine. I didn't need to just make her *say* what I wanted, I needed her to *believe* it. To keep doing as I wanted without my continual influence. I found a memory she was keeping very close to the surface. A brave young girl and a timid young man sitting on the steps of her front porch amid a pile of comic books, laughing and eating sandwiches. I pulled it to the forefront of her mind. It wasn't hard; I followed a well-worn mental path. Letting the memory play out, I urged Mrs. Connor to step outside.

Tears pricked at her eyes. She placed a trembling hand on the doctor's arm.

"Lucille and Ralph were so close," we said. "Why don't we give them some space while you tell me what can be done?"

Luci, picking up on the cue, started sniffling. She quickly escalated to a loud wail. Dr. Sutherland took a step back, uncomfortable with her sudden display of emotion. He allowed us to lead him out of the room. I let go of Mrs. Connor once they were in the hallway. She would take him to the hospital cafeteria on her own.

Luci counted to thirty, then stopped crying. She closed the door and turned in the direction she thought the car lay (she was wrong). She flashed me a thumbs-up.

"We're ready," I said.

Gloria double-checked the supplies in her crate. When she nodded, I took her hand. I focused on the open space to the left of Ralph's bed.

"I should warn you," I said. "I've never actually done this with someone else."

Before Gloria could respond, I pulled us *forward*.

A tiny gust of air ruffled Ralph's bedsheet as Gloria and I appeared in his room. Gloria gasped and Luci let out a surprised squeak. I let go of Gloria's hand and she fell backward, sitting on her bottom. She absently set her crate down and began slapping gently at her limbs, her stomach, her face.

"All there?" she asked, dazed. "Am I all there?"

"You're fine," I said, kneeling beside her and patting her shoulder in what I hoped was a reassuring manner. "That wasn't so bad."

"Sure," Gloria said. She looked down at her crate. "You know, I need all this junk to do that. You just *do* it."

"I know," I said, shifting uncomfortably. "I don't really know *how* I do it."

"You do it amazingly," Luci said. She reached out to help Gloria up.

"That's not exactly a scientific description," Gloria said with a shaky smile, "but it's pretty accurate."

She took a deep breath to center herself, then picked up the crate.

"Okay. We probably don't have a lot of time. Let's get this set up."

The three of us placed the seals in accordance with Gloria's instructions—the summoning seal on Ralph's chest, the four power seals on the floor around his bed—while she threaded the inked twine through the holes to connect them all. Luci set up the candles and pre-positioned the matches. When Gloria pronounced it ready, I floated the crate just so over the summoning seal's center. Luci and Gloria lit the candles. Then Gloria took up her position at Ralph's side, opposite mine. Holding the headboard to steady herself, she placed her other hand on the summoning seal's Anchor Key. As she had yesterday, she ran the equation through her mind again and again. Weird light flared above the power seals, pooling within their curving lines until it was drawn up into the summoning seal, like our trial run.

For a moment, the room was quiet.

Then everything went wrong.

The candles flared. The air whipped into a vortex centered on Ralph's bed. The seal's energy reached into his body, grabbing hold of the ultradimensional matter threading through him. I could see the energy matrix tracing the edges of the Watcher matter, isolating it from Ralph's flesh. Then sparks of baleful red light flashed amid the seal's energy. A wave of heat filled the room.

For one second, space went black.

I saw a red sun in the void.

Or maybe it was an eye.

Ralph's body contorted, his spine curling back as his swollen abdomen thrust upward. His eyes flew open, and he let out a blood-curdling scream. Until it was choked out by a gout of blue-green ichor. It splattered against the ceiling tiles and fell on us in a grotesque rain.

"Stop it!" Luci screamed, clapping her hands over her ears. "Make it stop!"

With a rip like wet cloth tearing, Ralph's skin split along his limbs and torso. Thick tendrils of Watcher flesh sprouted from the wounds, flailing, reaching for the crate. A seizure ripped through Ralph's muscles, while ichor mixed with blood poured from his wounds and onto the floor.

Gloria leapt away from the seal. She grabbed the two cords of twine on her side and yanked them hard, ripping the twine out of the summoning seal. The energy swirling within immediately dimmed. I dropped the crate and followed suit, tearing the remaining twine out of the seal while Luci dashed out the candles. Starved of energy, the seal sputtered out, but Ralph kept shaking. I grabbed Luci's arm.

"Go for help!"

Luci nodded and fled through the door, screaming for Dr. Sutherland. It wasn't an act. Gloria and I threw the remains of the seal into the crate as quickly as we could. Then I grabbed her arm and pulled us *out*, barely looking at where we were going.

We tumbled forward into an open field behind the parking lot, about a hundred meters from the parked car. Fortunately, no one was around to see us. While Gloria caught her breath, I stood and peered back at the hospital, into Ralph's room. He was still convulsing, the tendrils lashing angrily at nothing. At least he had stopped screaming.

"What do we do now?" Gloria asked.

I didn't answer.

09

We were silent on the drive to Chatham Hills. Luci stared out at the road, one hand on the wheel, the other next to mine. She barely registered anything but the road slipping away beneath us. Gloria stared at the ruins of her work, trying to understand what went wrong, praying to a god she barely believed in that she hadn't made Ralph's condition worse. And I? I stared at the thing inside of me, the hostile alien intelligence trapped in a corner of my psyche. They stared back, waiting for me to say something, anything. Just like my companions.

I said nothing. What was there to say? We were all in over our heads, the same as Lucas Dowling and the old men who'd inspired him. We were lucky that we hadn't killed Ralph or spread the Watcher infection through the hospital. Maybe we had. It was too soon to say otherwise.

Maybe the Bureau had been right all along. Maybe things like the Watcher—things like me—were monsters to be contained. If we couldn't be destroyed.

Maybe I should tell Agent Walsh everything come Monday morning. Wait for the Bureau to sweep through and clean up my mess. Let them bury me at the bottom of a mine shaft with the rest of the monsters.

What had I ever done besides hurt people?

I'd put Luci and Gloria, two people I claimed to love, at risk without ever telling them how. First by concealing the truth about myself. Then by pulling them thirty years into the past and into my own mind without warning. I used the threat of my powers to bully Bureau agents into giving me my way and to alter their minds when they wouldn't. I'd torn Agent Pickman's mind apart. I'd always told the Bureau, told myself, that it was in self-defense. But I had been angry and hurting and it had felt so good to hurt him back. Even my first victim, Agent Carlisle. Once when I was five years old, he had frightened me. I lashed out, barely aware of my own strength, and shattered his spine. He never walked again.

What harm could I inflict on my friends?

Or for them. When Dr. Sutherland had put his hand on Luci's back, I'd wanted to hurt him. I still did. It would be so easy.

Within me, the Watcher stirred. *Punish/protect/destroy?*

I stared at them, not knowing how to respond.

Luci turned onto Cook Street, driving into Harwood. We arrived at Gloria's house a few minutes later. Gloria said nothing as she double-checked the contents of her crate. Then she opened the car door and left the vehicle, walking wordlessly up the steps to her house. We watched her go just as silently, just as awkwardly, until she took hold of the doorknob. Before she could turn it, Luci flew out of the car and up the steps, catching Gloria in a tight hug.

"This wasn't your fault," she said. "What happened today wasn't your fault. You did the best you could."

Gloria didn't respond at first. She held the tension in her chest, her spine taut like a violin string. For a moment, I thought she would pull away. Then her armor cracked, and she slumped against Luci, burying her face in Luci's shoulder. Her chest shook as she sobbed, casting out her guilt and frustration until nothing was left but exhaustion and quiet sorrow. Then she pulled away, rubbing away the tears with her sleeve.

"Good?" Luci asked.

"No," Gloria said. "But better."

"That's a start." Luci kissed Gloria on the forehead. "We'll take tonight and tomorrow to rest. Come Monday, we're figuring this out. Usual place, usual time. Got it?"

"Yes ma'am," Gloria said, managing the ghost of a smile.

Luci squeezed Gloria's hand by way of goodbye. She waited for Gloria to close the front door behind her. Then she returned to the car. She put her hand on the steering wheel and looked at me with a stern expression.

"And that goes for you too, miss."

Before I could respond, she cupped my head with her hand and kissed me well. Her warmth flooded my mind, pushing away the Watcher Within's dank cold and the chill of my own self-loathing. I could see that she only half-believed what she said, that she was as full of recrimination as Gloria and I. That she thought she wasn't as useful, that she hadn't watched out for Ralph as she'd promised. I could see a fresh scar across her mind, something she kept turning away from to lessen the pain. She had reached out to me for comfort as much as she was reaching out to comfort me, as she had Gloria. I gave what I could, drawing her in as much as I dared, trying to envelop her summer warmth with my presence.

Too soon, she broke the kiss. She turned to the steering wheel and composed herself, fixing her hair in the rearview mirror. She had surely already drawn the neighbors' attention by hugging Gloria. Two girls making out in a parked car would only draw more. I could taste her desire in the air, the promise of excitement to come if only I asked. If only we had the time.

"Time to take you to your horrible home, I guess," she said.

I bit my lip. The hint of an idea came to me. But I wasn't sure.

"You'd better stop for gas first," I said, stalling for time.

Luci sighed and started the car. There was a Texaco station on Main Street. She pulled away from Gloria's house and headed for it, driving well under the speed limit to stretch the time out. She pulled up to the pump and hopped out of the car. I followed suit.

"Need to use the ladies' room," I said. "Do you want a beverage?"

"We usually say 'soda'," Luci said with a faint smile. "A Coke'd be nice."

The small station was empty of people except for a single clerk, bent over a car magazine. He didn't look up when the bell rang above the door, nor when I walked past him to the cooler. I grabbed two bottles and set them gently on the counter. I asked the clerk, who still hadn't looked up, if I could get the restroom key.

"Restroom's for customers," he grunted.

I coughed pointedly and pushed the bottles further across the counter. Then I fished two nickels out of my wallet and dropped them beside the bottles, letting them clatter loudly. He finally looked up. He swiped the coins off the counter, rang up the sale, then almost as an afterthought dropped a key attached to a long wooden bar next to the bottles.

"Thank you," I said.

I grabbed the bottles in one hand and the key in the other, then went around the back to the bathroom. It was awful. I had seen worse, but only because a month ago I'd watched a half-dozen people have their bodies warped into a flesh tower by a manifesting ultraterrestrial entity. By a regular person's standards, the restroom was vile. Fortunately, I didn't really need to use the toilet. I still didn't set the bottles down on any available surfaces.

I faced the sink, careful not to touch it, and stared into the grimy mirror. The girl who stared back was tired, sad, and about at the point where I would start picking out every flaw in her appearance. Everything that made me look less than feminine… less than human. The shape of my nose, the line of my brow or jaw. The set of my shoulders and the size of my hands. The subtly wrong shade of my eyes. The things that would lead a canny observer to conclude that something was amiss and start looking closer.

Enough. I didn't have time for this. I knew who I was and so did Luci. I pushed through those feelings and the reflection in the mirror, casting my attention out farther. Out past the city limits of Chatham Hills. It was difficult; though my sensory capabilities seemed vast to my friends, they still had limits. Even if those limits were described by other parameters. My attention fell away from my body, away from Main Street's 300 block, away from the small town entirely. I was caught up in a sense of motion, as if my focus was moving along the fifth-dimensional axis that defined the greater portion of my physical form. Which, perhaps, it was.

The Bureau campus swam into view. I narrowed my focus on the second floor, to the duty office where an agent sat monitoring alarms that thankfully never sounded. To my relief, the agent tonight was Stanley Dawes. For all his faults, Dawes had at least tried to treat me with respect. Like a person, rather than sensitive materials or a piece of unexploded ordnance. He knew I was expected back from the hospital soon. He also knew about Agent Thomas' embarrassing invasion of my dorm room during our investigation into Lucas Dowling. Knew of it and disapproved. Standing orders or no, he had no intention of disturbing me this evening. He trusted I was inclined to be responsible. Which, I felt, was a good assumption, even if our definitions of "responsible" differed. In gratitude, I left his mind and memory intact. If he could trust me, I could trust him.

In hindsight, it might have been kinder if I had tinkered with his memory. At least then Agent Thomas would have found something when he went digging for answers.

My mind made up, I went to the car and hopped in. Luci took the bottle I offered with a tired smile.

"So," she said. "Ready to go home?"

I took a deep breath, then put a gentle hand on her thigh.

"Do you consider your dorm room home? Because that's where I'm going."

Luci's mouth dropped open. She shook her head, trying to catch up to what I'd said.

"Are you sure? I mean, of course I'd *love* for you to come with me. What about the Bureau? What will they do if—"

I leaned in close and gave her a quick peck on the cheek. I whispered in her ear, "Why don't you let me worry about that, and I let you worry about sneaking me in?"

Luci bit her lip and shivered. She put a hand on my cheek. Desire swam in her eyes, along with sorrow. She needed this as much as I did. It wasn't the way she'd imagined it, but right now? She wasn't ready to let me go.

"I don't know what's gotten into you all of a sudden, Amelia Temple," she whispered, "but I certainly like it."

Some of the tension left her as she started the engine and pulled away from the service station. Her speed was sure to alarm any nearby police cars. Thankfully there weren't any. I settled in my seat and popped the cap off my Coke, entwining my fingers with her free hand. Consequences were for tomorrow. Today I needed her.

10

It probably comes as no surprise that it was significantly easier for Luci to sneak her belle into the dorms than it was for her neighbors and their beaus. I followed her inside to the ground floor lounge. It was a public area chaperoned by a severe-looking woman Luci identified as Professor Madison, a history professor and resident of the hall. The lounge was open to all students until 10 p.m., and the doors to the residence hall were locked at curfew, which was 1 a.m. on Saturdays. Guests weren't permitted up the stairs to the actual dorm rooms at all.

"Not even other women?" I asked.

"Nope. It's not that they're worried about gay couples. I don't think the U even considers the possibility. Well, Professor Madison might." Luci looked thoughtful for a moment. "It's a blanket rule across campus to avoid 'disruptions'. If it ain't your dorm, stay out."

There were ways around the rules, mostly involving an oak tree by the building's northwest corner and hoping the young ladies in Room 219 were feeling cooperative. The staff was hip to that ingress, however, so would-be paramours couldn't use it too often. Other students had tried more creative attempts to comingle and canoodle, but to hear Luci tell it, most lovelorn coeds simply resorted to the reliable automobile back seat.

That sounded extremely uncomfortable to me. Easier to duck into the downstairs restroom, wait for Luci to walk up two flights to her room, and pop across the intervening space to sit on her bed.

Even knowing that I was coming, Luci let out an adorable little squeak when I appeared next to her. Then she giggled and kissed me.

"That was so much easier than paying off Debbie and Evelyn in 219," she said. "I should've started dating teleporting gals a long time ago."

I pulled back, mock-offended. "Say, how many other gals have you brought up here, anyway?"

"Enough to know what I'm doing," she said, and pounced on me.

Luci pushed me against her pillow, hands on my shoulders and lips pressed against mine. I wrapped my arms around her neck, running my fingers through her soft red-gold hair. We held each other for a long, passionate moment. In fact, it was 197 seconds, but I've since learned that sometimes that degree of precision isn't sexy. Then Luci pulled back, biting her lip in concern.

"I'm sorry, I should have asked," she said. "Are you…?"

I shifted my right leg so that it was between both of hers. I raised my thigh just enough. Then I grabbed her shoulders and pulled her down.

Luci's tongue darted gently into my mouth. I ran my hands down her sides until they reached her hips, then pulled her closer. An electric tingle worked its way up from my abdomen as our bodies rubbed against one another. Somehow, through the suddenly too thick cotton of our dresses, our hands found each other's breasts. I moaned into her mouth as her experienced fingers attended me, while she somehow gasped with pleasure at my clumsy fumbling.

At some point she had to come up for air again, although my hands didn't leave her body. Luci propped herself up on one elbow, caressing my cheek with her other hand. I turned my head into her touch, gently kissing the heel of her hand.

"How far do you want to take things tonight?" she whispered.

I didn't know how to answer that. I looked into her soft blue eyes and tried to find the words. I wanted her, and I wanted her to want me. I was also afraid of that want, and of what she would think once she got my clothes off. There was a lot that was unusual about my body. She said she didn't care. I wanted to believe her. But it was one thing to say that in the front seat of somebody else's car with a stick-shift between us, and another when we were in her bed with only two layers of clothing separating us.

"I don't want to go 'all the way'," I finally said, pulling the phrase from her mind. "Not tonight, I mean. I *do* want to do those things with you. But—"

"But not right now," Luci said, giving me an understanding smile, followed by a gentle kiss. "It's *okay*. It was a while before I was ready for *my* first time. I told you before, we'll go as fast or slow as you like."

I snuggled close to her, feeling safe and loved. "Thank you. To be honest, I don't even know *how* we would—"

"Oh, you." Luci gently tapped my nose. "I have *so* much to teach you."

She rolled onto her back and slid the arm that had been propping her up beneath me. I rested my head on her shoulder, and she pressed her cheek against my forehead. She enveloped me in her warmth, tickling the edges of my mind with her own thoughts.

And you and I don't even need to use words, do we? she sent.

She followed up with a collage of sensual images showcasing the many, many things we might do together. A couple I had postulated on my own, but there were so many I had never considered. Each image was tinged with a hint of the specific pleasure it might bring. I very nearly reconsidered how ready for sex I was.

All that?

Well, not usually all at once. Luci gave me a peck on the forehead. *Or even every time.*

It's intimidating!

We can go one at a time, once you're ready. For tonight…

She rolled onto her side, wrapping her other arm around me. I burrowed into her arms, baring my neck so she could press her face against it. The cloak of sensual confidence she'd wrapped around herself slipped, letting out a ray of fear and sorrow. She shivered and nuzzled the hollow of my neck, seeking comfort as much as affection.

For tonight, just hold me, darling. Hold me and make me believe everything will be okay.

I held her close, enveloping Luci in my presence. Our lips found each other again, this time less passionately but no less tenderly. We took solace together, in her narrow bed, each guarding the other from her fears.

I awoke to someone gently tapping me on the face.

I opened one eye to see Luci's mischievous smile. She leaned in and kissed the tip of my nose before pushing herself up on one elbow. She rested the other hand on my stomach, gently tracing circles with her fingertips.

"Not that I mind you staying over, but are you sure you're not getting yourself in trouble?"

Two and a half hours had passed. It was now 8:50 pm and well after my curfew. I would be in tremendous trouble if anyone happened by my dorm.

"I'm not," I said. "Promise."

The Bureau headquarters was twenty-one miles from the Del Sombra campus. That should have been far outside the usual limits of my perception, at least without losing the sense of myself as an individual, physical being. I could see it easily, though, simply by casting my attention southwest. My perception warped around it, bringing it into focus as if through a lens. The buildings were mostly empty, save for a few unlucky stragglers. There was Agent Dawes at the duty desk, and Agent Walsh working late in his office, and the handful of guards spread through the evidence chambers. It was effortless. Perhaps I had spent so much time on these grounds that they warped space for me, like a massive object distorting gravity around it. That was a sobering thought.

So far away and yet so close. I wondered if I could step across space from Regina to the Bureau campus? Agent Dawes still had no intention of bothering me, but it would make things easier if I were seen after curfew. I'd never tried to cross spatial distance at that scale before. Was it really that much harder than moving myself and two people across twenty-five years?

Luci's honey-sweet voice interrupted my speculation.

"In that case, would you be a dear and move the other bed over here? Not that I mind being so close to you, but I think one of us is setting herself up for a backache tonight."

We were still entangled in her twin bed, and she was right—it wasn't made for two. The other bed was on the opposite wall. Luci's side of the room was decorated in what I assumed was standard college style: a Del Sombra pennant, a poster of a dark-haired actress I should probably recognize, a corkboard covered in notecards, photos and newspaper clippings connected by variously colored strings. Her roommate's side was even more bare of ornamentation than my own dorm room.

"Are we not expecting company?" I asked, realizing that probably should have come up sooner.

Luci laughed and rested her head against my shoulder.

"No, Roberta had to drop out earlier this semester. 'Family emergency', she said. It's way too late in the semester for new admissions, so I doubt I'll see a new roomie until after the holidays. If even then. Lucky for us." She kissed me. "Now shift, darling, and I'll steal you fresh sheets from the linen closet."

I disentangled my legs from hers with a token grumble and rolled out of bed. She slipped behind me, giving my bottom a quick squeeze before leaving the room, humming happily. She didn't bother to fix her messy hair on the way out, but there was no one in the hall to see her. Not that she cared in the slightest, wrapped in the euphoria of intimacy.

And burdened by a storm cloud of despair. Our failure today still weighed on her. She tried to hide it beneath the thrill of being with me and very nearly succeeded, but that shadow covered her. In her mind, the disaster today was of a piece with her failure to protect Ralph from Lucas Dowling in the first place. She didn't blame Gloria for trying her best and failing; she blamed herself for letting Ralph get hurt in the first place, and only slightly less blamed Lucas Dowling for doing the hurting.

There was something else. Something in a corner of her mind, a void nibbling at the edges of her thoughts. I saw it when I first asked to spend the night, but once we arrived, I was too preoccupied to dig deeper.

I'd also been too preoccupied to examine her cork board. What I'd taken for a collage was a roadmap of her investigation into Lucas Dowling and the strangeness we'd encountered, but his photo was in the center of the board. Everything, all her anger, revolved around him.

A notecard in the upper right corner was labeled "Apollonian Society". Yellow string connected to several cards bearing names we'd identified, some with photos pinned to them. I recognized about half of the names. Professor Henry Blake. Maxine Orr. "RF". Maxwell Thorpe, the seeming ringleader. Yellow string ran from Thorpe to Orr to Blake, ending at Dowling. Dowling connected to a photo of Ralph via green string. Ralph connected to a photo of St. Audaeus, which connected to a card in the bottom right labeled "Chambers Foundation". That card connected to a fan of others—the Chatham Hills Public Library, Whitehead Academy, Maxwell Thorpe, other names I didn't recognize.

The section on the Bureau dominated the board's upper left. Blue strings connected to cards labeled with the names of agents Luci knew, as well as "Site One", "Site Two" and photos of each. One string also connected to a photo of me. Luci had taken it outside the Arcadia last week. She'd connected it in red to a card in the upper middle labeled only "Cold Man", which was the only name I had for the man who had attended my mysterious birth. He connected to the Apollonian Society in yellow, as did Site One and Site Two. It all tied together, possibly even more than we knew.

"I've been busy," Luci said behind me.

She closed the door, a gently folded bundle of crisp sheets resting on one arm. Her emotional state was a mixture of guilt, defiance, and pride. Of anyone on Earth, I knew her face well enough to see it all in her expression, even if I hadn't been able to see her thoughts.

"So I'm not the only thing you're glad to keep private," I said, trying to make a joke out of it.

Luci didn't find it funny. "I'd rather be public. I'd walk out in the sunlight with you, your hand in mine, and kiss you whenever I wanted. No matter who was watching."

She dropped the sheets on her roommate's bare mattress. Then, as if to prove her point, she took my hand and kissed me hard.

"There are places we can do that, you know," she whispered into my ear. "We can go. Together. Tonight."

I leaned into her embrace, resting my cheek against her forehead. I almost held back a tear. Instead, it dropped into her red-gold hair. I let out a long, slow breath, my shoulders shaking. Then turned and placed one finger against my photo. I traced the blue string up to the card marked "Agent Walsh" and from him to the Bureau.

"They'd find me," I said.

Luci sighed and put her head against mine. "I know."

We held each other for a long minute. Then she straightened, the cloak of decisiveness falling across her shoulders.

"So that's Step Two. After we figure out how to save Ralph, we get you free of the Bureau."

"Just like that?"

"Just like that." She winked and tapped my nose. "Now c'mon, you gonna move that bed or what?"

"Oh. Right."

I blushed, which apparently my girlfriend found ridiculously endearing. Then I lifted the empty bed and carefully floated it across the room, setting it down snugly against the other one. Luci went to unfold the fitted sheet but let out a surprised squeak when it suddenly unfolded on its own. It settled on top of the mattress, elastic snapping quietly underneath the four corners.

She turned to me, hand on her hip. "Show off."

I smiled prettily (I hoped) and gestured to the other sheet. Luci smirked and grabbed two corners of the top sheet, then squeaked again when invisible arms took up the other two corners and pulled it flat.

"You're having too much fun with this," she said, giggling.

"I've never had too much fun in my life."

We floated the top sheet over the mattress and spread out the comforter. All smiles and laughs, we both sat heavily on the bed. Luci leaned over to rest her head on my shoulder. I put my arm around her waist and my own head over hers. We sat there for a long minute, trying to hang on to the laughter, to hold the tension at bay. It couldn't last. The smile slowly fell from Luci's face. She dropped her eyes and let out a deep sigh.

"So," I said, as gently as I could, "do you want to talk about what else is eating you? It's not only what happened to Ralph, is it?"

Luci didn't say anything at first. Her eyes stared at the blank wall across the room, while her mind churned with the things she wanted to say. I tried to look away, instead following the connections she'd made on the cork board. She deserved the space to work out what she needed to say on her own and in her own time, without me trying to skip to the end. Even if that would have been more efficient. It was normal. Human.

Nevertheless, I couldn't help but see the void inside her mind. Her thoughts whirled around it. It was like an open wound in the middle of her memories, and it hurt to perceive. How much more must it hurt to experience? Yet outwardly she refused to show her distress. She kept her face turned from me—pointlessly, although I didn't think she knew that—and held the hem of her dress in her hands. The only sign of upset was the way she worried the fabric between her delicate fingers.

"I'm sorry," I said, the words rushing out of my mouth. "I overstepped. You don't have to say if you're not ready."

Luci tried to choke back a sob and couldn't. Her face screwed up as she burst into tears. She turned in my arms and buried her face against my shoulder.

"Oh God, Amelia," she said through sobs, "I *can't remember*."

I pulled her into my lap, letting her sob against my neck. The dam broke. I could now see the nature of the wound via absence. Luci had no memory of anything that happened in the hour between our arrival at St. Audaeus and our departure. When her mind tried to turn to it, all she found was a scar lined in weird flickering light, floating in an abscess in her thoughts.

11

Luci was right, as ever. I should have been more concerned with whether the Bureau would notice my absence. More specifically, certain elements of the Bureau.

Between grief and desire competing for my attention, I'd been entirely too careless when I checked in on the campus. It was a Saturday, after all. Other than the guards and the duty agent, I'd expected the buildings to be empty. I hadn't considered that a newly opened investigation so close to the Bureau's headquarters would have kicked up a veritable hornet's nest. Eleven agents worked over the weekend and well into the night, all focused on the Dowling Incident and its fallout. Yes, Agent Walsh's presence should have been a clue. I'll remind you I was in bed with my wonderful girlfriend at the time.

Walsh had spent most of the week reviewing witness interviews. One hundred thirty-five citizens of Chatham Hills—a little under a tenth of the population—had reported unusually vivid nightmares on the night of Dowling's experiment. Each person would have been a component of the Watcher's growing terrestrial body had we not pulled their intelligence out of it and into mine. One hundred thirty-five dreams of eerie music, of barefoot walks along twisting paths, up a steep hill beneath an alien sky, the air thick with a sickly sweet stench. Can humans smell in dreams? They did that night.

Over the past month, Agent Walsh's team had surreptitiously interviewed forty-seven dreamers. Walsh spent that Saturday evening trying to combine those forty-seven interviews into a coherent report. At the time, I wasn't quite certain how they'd managed it. The America of 1954 was not a place and time in which the average person was inclined to seek psychological counseling. I would later suspect the involvement of the mysterious "Dreamland" facility, but I was too late to prevent the Bureau from turning it to terrible purpose.

Agent Thomas, I would later learn, was hot on the trail of Lucas Dowling. Only he wasn't. He was room temperature at best, trending downward to moderately clammy. Dowling had disappeared entirely, far easier to do in 1954 than it would be now, even with a raging alien spore infection. A month of leveraging all the resources at Thomas' disposal had turned up nothing more than a former roommate quite grateful to be former and a university administration unconcerned with his absence from class. Most curiously, he had made no new waves in the occult underground. Either he was keeping an uncharacteristically low profile or someone or some*thing* was keeping him hidden.

It was a disturbing thought, and one I assume must have occurred to Thomas. It couldn't have helped his usually sour mood, which explained why his subsequent conversation with Walsh went as poorly as it did. It didn't have to. Perhaps Thomas had genuinely come to Walsh for assistance but had been too proud to ask directly. Perhaps, when he saw the light on in his fellow agent's office, he'd only wanted to commiserate on their shared difficulties. It might only have gone badly because both men were frustrated with their tasks as much as with one another, and in their frustration spoke a little too hastily.

I really have no way of knowing.

But I suspect the truth is that Agent Thomas was simply spoiling for a fight.

Walsh didn't bother looking up when Thomas burst into his office without knocking. He calmly set one interview transcript aside and picked up the next.

"Randall," he said, his tone as flat as his desk. "Forget which office was yours again?"

"Can it, Pat. You're not clever," Thomas said. "We need to talk about this Dowling business."

Walsh looked over the top of his reading glasses, not bothering to hide his skepticism. "Is your division finally willing to cooperate?"

"That's not how this works and you know it," Thomas said, his lips twisting into an ugly sneer.

He grabbed the office's only other chair and pulled it in front of Walsh's desk. He sat heavily, leaning forward with his left elbow propped on his knee. His right index finger stabbed out like the barrel of a gun, nearly poking the papers Walsh was holding.

"*You* people provide us with information, and *we* handle the situation. Only you're not providing me with squat, and now Dowling's in the wind!"

Walsh took off his reading glasses and gestured to the stack of as-yet unread transcripts to his right.

"I don't know if you've noticed, Randall, but at the moment we have a small hill of data to sort through. I'm personally expecting it to grow into a mountain by the time we finish learning what we don't know. Do you want it done quickly or do you want it done correctly?"

"What even is this?" Thomas snatched the papers out of Walsh's hand. "An interview? Some yokel having a bad dream? This is what you're wasting my time with?"

"I hardly consider forty-seven people psychically attacked by an ultraterrestrial entity to be a waste of time," Agent Walsh said. "I consider them to be victims, but if it helps you justify it, you can think of them as potential time bombs. We should know if they're about to go off. You should be aware that my team has been covering multiple potential issues stemming from Lucas Dowling and his failed experiment. Assuming you've been reading the reports I've sent you. Have you?"

Thomas snorted. "Oh, I've read your reports, all right. That's why I've got half a mind to take this entire case away from you."

"Don't do me any favors, Randall."

Walsh held out his hand for the transcript. Thomas rolled his eyes and dropped the papers on the desk in front of him. They scattered messily across the surface.

"I know everything you and your little team have been doing, Pat. Or at least, everything you've bothered telling us about."

Color rose in Walsh's cheeks. He set his reading glasses down carefully and put his hands on the desk, slowly pushing himself to his feet. He leaned forward, resting his knuckles on the wood, and let his carefully composed expression slip.

"You're not the type I'd like to dance with, Randall. If you have something to say, come out and say it."

Thomas practically leapt out of his seat. He stood nose to nose with Walsh.

"You wanna hear it? Fine. What are you up to with Temple?"

"What am I…? I'm *cultivating an asset*. As I've made clear to the AD multiple times, Amelia is a tremendous resource that the Bureau has mismanaged *spectacularly* over the past seventeen years. Thanks entirely to following the advice of short-sighted men like *you*, incidentally. Right now, she's *engaged* in this investigation, and I intend to run with that for as long as I can. The Bureau would have been caught entirely flat-footed by the Dowling Incident if it hadn't been for her cooperation, and frankly, we've given her no reason to offer it."

That was true. I wouldn't have reported it to the Bureau at all if we'd been successful at stopping Dowling from summoning the Watcher Above. If we hadn't arrived at the bookstore an hour too late. The only reason I'd been grateful for their involvement was that Ralph had been hurt in a way we couldn't fix and look how useful they'd been on that end.

"I'm utilizing both Amelia's incredible talents *and* her personal connections to our benefit, and she's given us access to information we'd never have," Walsh continued. "So you're welcome, Randall."

Thomas snorted like a bull about to charge. He pounded the top of the desk, sending papers flying, then jabbed a finger into Walsh's chest. "You really expect me to believe we got the alert from one of Temple's dreams?"

"I don't give a damn *what* you believe." Walsh slapped the finger away. "That's what she told me, and that's what I wrote in my report. Deal with it."

That was partially true. I had told him to write that I'd seen the experiment in a dream. We couldn't think of a better explanation for why I was at the scene of the crime after curfew. Most of the Bureau had accepted it.

"We've been monitoring her dreams for over a decade for this very reason, Randall. We have an entire filing cabinet full of her dream journals in Evidence Chamber Two. It finally paid off. And I don't know *why* I'm explaining any of this to you, because Amelia's care and application falls entirely under *my* responsibility, *not yours. We don't answer to you.*"

"So you think you can send your pet monster wherever you want? Out into town, down to the evidence chambers, into a hospital we don't control?"

"Is that what this is about? Are you really that pissed off that I managed to get an asset into St. Audaeus when you never could?"

"An *asset?* Are you out of your mind?"

"No, clearly I'm the one thinking rationally." Walsh yanked open a drawer in his filing cabinet and pulled out a cardboard envelope. It held the report of my first trip to the hospital. He threw it on his desk. "Amelia reports that Ralph Connor's condition is poor but stable and that the hospital is lying to his mother about his affliction. Which is no surprise, but it's better than anything *you've* come up with in the past month."

It felt uncomfortable, giving the Bureau the essential truth, but Luci and I had agreed it was easier than trying to come up with a plausible falsehood. We'd gambled it would encourage the Bureau to keep letting me visit Ralph. So far it had worked, but a gambit only works out so many times.

"This is ridiculous, Pat," Thomas said. "You know what this confirms? Why we can't get a *real* man inside? *They* control St. Audaeus Hospital."

"The Apollonian Society doesn't exist anymore," Walsh said, as if he was speaking to a child.

"Some of the ringleaders still do. This isn't good enough. We need control of this situation, and that means moving Connor into a facility *we* control."

"That's on your team, Randall." Walsh sat, trying to organize the scattered papers. "I have my own part of the investigation to oversee."

"Yeah. It *is* on my team. I don't want Temple going near that hospital again, clear? That's under *my* jurisdiction."

"And Amelia's well-being is under *mine*." Walsh's tone was far more patient than he felt. "That's her friend in there. I'm not going to let you deny her compassionate visits. I'm a human being."

"Temple's not. Get that through your head."

The memory of a young girl in a white nightdress flashed across Walsh's memory. Her hair was limp and damp with sweat. Her cheeks were pale. He jumped to his feet, hands balled into fists.

"I suggest you leave," he said through gritted teeth. "*Now.*"

Thomas stared at him for a moment. Then he let out a short, dismissive laugh. Shaking his head, he turned to go. He stopped with one hand on the open door, looking over his shoulder at Walsh.

"You're a sap, Pat. That thing's playing you."

Thomas slammed the office door behind him. Sadly, he couldn't see Walsh's refusal to respond. Thomas stood in the hallway, an awful, thoughtful look on his face. Then he turned on his heel and strode toward the nearest stairwell with terrible purpose.

Agent Walsh tried to resume his work. He still had a pile of interviews to review. He dug through the stack of papers until he found what he'd been reading, before Thomas' hostile interruption. He scanned through it, trying to find his place. It was no use. The words swam beneath his eyes. The transcript might as well have been written in a foreign language for as much sense as it made. The fight with Thomas had shaken him more than he was willing to admit.

Walsh set the transcript aside with a heavy sigh. He rested his forehead in his hands, grinding the heels into his eyes. *He wanted to trust me. For reasons I couldn't entirely explain but had everything to do with the girl in* the white dress, he *needed* to trust me. But he knew me too well. He knew I was hiding something from him. He didn't know how much.

It wasn't my fault. Walsh believed that very strongly. He was trying to convince himself that my actions were simply a young woman asserting herself as she stepped into adulthood. A sign that he'd done something right as my guardian. He tried to ignore the small part of him that agreed with Agent Thomas. The part that worried he'd overcorrected, giving me too much freedom. That maybe I really was dangerous.

With a disgruntled sigh, Walsh pushed himself to his feet. He told himself that he was being unfair to me, that he was tired. What he needed was a break. Coffee. Maybe a donut. The cafeteria was closed, but there was a break room on this floor. He could refresh himself and get his mind right.

Walsh made to leave but stopped with his hand on the doorknob. He looked at his desk, covered with papers, and grinned sheepishly to himself. I'd chided him weeks ago about his bad habit of leaving sensitive materials lying out in the open. Walsh told himself that it showed I was a good kid after all and went to clean up.

He sorted the transcripts into two piles—the ones he had read and the ones he hadn't. The latter he scooped into a folder and locked in his filing cabinet. The former went into a different folder, one that reminded him of another way to improve his mood. He tucked the folder under his arm and left his office, a strange half-smile on his face. He went down the hall to the break room and emerged ten minutes later with two cups of coffee and a plate of slightly stale pastries.

Annette Vance was one of four clerks who managed the Sensitive Materials records room. It was the Bureau's morgue for reports and artifacts that were actively being used, instead of archived in an evidence chamber. Vance was the only one working late that night, and for reasons I suspect had little to do with making sure her records were available.

I'm not saying she wasn't dedicated to her job, I'm just saying she had more than one motivation that night. If you'll stop interrupting?

I'd spoken to Miss Vance twice a day for two weeks when I was teaching the indoctrination class for new agents. She'd *never* smiled at me the way she did when Agent Walsh poked his head through the door. I hadn't thought of her as a person who could be friendly.

"Good evening, Miss Vance. Burning the midnight oil too?"

"Someone has to make sure you boys get what you need." Vance set her crossword puzzle aside and stood, leaning both hands against the counter. "Dropping off or picking up?"

"Dropping off, for now." Walsh set the coffees on the counter, then the folder. "This needs to go back where it belongs. As for these, well, I figured you might need a little pick-me-up."

"I certainly wouldn't say no," Vance said. She hopped up on her side of the counter, leaning against the window separating them. "Which one's mine?"

"This one." Walsh pushed the paler of the two coffees through the gap beneath the glass. "Creamer and two sugars, right?"

"Just how I like it, Agent Walsh."

"Please, Miss Vance. Call me Patrick."

Vance ducked her head and smiled. "Then you should call me Annette, Patrick."

I'm sure you can imagine how the rest of their conversation went. It was certainly more pleasant than what Agent Thomas was getting up to.

I have no way of knowing, obviously, but I genuinely believe Thomas expected to find me when he burst into my dorm room unannounced. I think his intention was to interrogate me on whatever it was he thought I'd been hiding from the Bureau (which, to be fair, was a lot) and incidentally discover how complicit Agent Walsh was in my illicit activities. Still, if he was surprised to find my bed empty when he banged open my bedroom door, he hid it well.

Thomas checked his stride when he entered my room, swallowing whatever horrible thing he was about to shout. His brows knitted together, but his lips turned up in a sneering smile. He had me now.

He made a slow circuit of the barely furnished room, stopping once to look under the bed and again to open the closet door. He ran his hand over the row of dresses hanging on the rack. Three new frocks, colorful but subdued, had recently joined the half-dozen identical gray dresses the Bureau had requisitioned. He rolled his eyes at my attempt at fashion and shut the door.

I'll credit him exactly this much—he knocked quietly on the bathroom door and waited ten seconds before slowly opening it. Apparently even Thomas had the decency not to barge in on me peeing. Seeing the toilet unoccupied, he went in and yanked the shower curtain aside. Satisfied that the dorm was empty of any other presence, Thomas let out a snort. Irritated? Triumphant? Perhaps a mixture of both?

He carefully closed each of the doors as he left, no doubt trying to hide the evidence of his intrusion. Then he went down to the second floor—not to Walsh's office, but to the duty agent's desk. Dawes sat watching the alarm lights out of the corner of his eye while reading an issue of *Amazing Stories*. Thomas opened the door slowly. The other man had no inkling he was about to have company until Thomas' hand fell heavily on his shoulder. Dawes hurriedly stuffed the magazine in a drawer and turned to face Thomas, who grinned down at him malevolently.

"Whatcha got there, Stan?" He reached over Dawes to fish the magazine out of the drawer. He held it up between two fingers and laughed rudely. "Aren't you a little old for rocket ships and ray guns, Stanley?"

"Actually, considering our line of work, I think it's pretty appropriate," Dawes said, trying not to rise to the senior agent's bait despite the flush running up his face. "I may not have seen any little green men yet, but I'm pretty sure our lab boys are cooking up ray guns."

"Keep that under your hat." Thomas shook the magazine and sniffed. "I guess this is more professional than the last magazine I caught you jokers reading on duty. Barely."

He tossed it aside, and it landed on the desk with a soft splat. Dawes rolled his eyes and picked the magazine up before the pages could get bent and put it in the drawer.

"Something I can help you with?" he asked sourly.

Thomas grinned, as if the junior agent's pushback amused him. "Yeah.

Checking up on something. Have you made your rounds upstairs yet? Made sure Temple's staying out of trouble?"

"Of course I have," Dawes said without a moment's hesitation. The lie slipped out of his mouth as smoothly as a pat of butter on a hot pan. "Amel—Miss Temple has turned in for the night."

I don't know whether he would have seen the lie if he hadn't already seen the truth for himself. Not that it mattered now. Agent Dawes had mostly told the lie for himself, covering the fact that he'd neglected one of his duties, but that neglect was out of compassion for me. Poor Stanley Dawes. I don't know if I'd call him a good man—I don't know if there was such a thing in those days. He was racist and sexist in ways that were disgustingly acceptable in his society. His occasional flashes of sympathy for me didn't erase that. But he didn't deserve what happened to him, and he sowed the seeds for it in this moment.

But that was yet to come. In the now, Agent Thomas said, "That's good. That's *real* good, Stanley. You make sure you keep an eye on Temple, you understand? That thing's trouble. A lot of men here don't want to see that. Don't you be one of them."

"Sure, Thomas. Whatever you say," Dawes said, biting back the words he really wanted to use.

Thomas nodded again and turned away, leaving Dawes to his magazine. The smile dropped from his face as he reached the stairwell. This time he went up to the third floor, winding through the building to a section of the southwest corner marked in black. This wasn't the headquarters of Special Investigations. It was their office on the main campus. Men like Thomas didn't like direct oversight. Nonetheless, this space had what he needed for his purposes tonight.

(What did the other agents think the Black Zone was? Good question. They didn't. They didn't even register that it was there. Even I barely noticed it, and looking back in time to this moment gives me a terrible headache. Prospero's Keys at work, or something much like them.)

The Specials' office suite was a simple space. A large triangular room dominated it, something between a lounge and a shared workspace. Five smaller rooms surrounded it on two sides. Two were offices, one held files and records, one stored equipment, and the last was blank to my senses. Three men sat in the main room, a stack of papers distributed between them. They looked up expectantly when Agent Thomas entered.

"We have three problems," he said. "I have solutions for two."

He turned to the first Special, a tall, slender blond man whose eyes were hidden behind the reflection of his spectacles. This, I would learn later, was Special Agent Philip Stark.

"I have reason to believe Stanley Dawes has been compromised," Thomas said. "Book him a session at Dreamland. I want his mind looked over with a fine-toothed comb and scrubbed out as needed."

Stark nodded and went to the red phone in the corner. He didn't bother dialing. Thomas turned to the second Special, a stocky man with close-cropped black hair starting to retreat from his forehead. His nose had been broken more than once, and his jowls gave him a face like a bulldog. This was Special Agent George Drummond.

"St. Audaeus Hospital. I'm tired of pussyfooting around with this. I want a canary in that coal mine."

"One of the new guys," Drummond said. "The Opposition shouldn't have them on file yet."

"And they're expendable." Thomas nodded in agreement.

Stark paused, covering the phone's mouthpiece. His voice was almost entirely without inflection. "Two birds, one stone?"

"No. No time. I want Dawes under a light tomorrow and a man in the hospital Monday morning. Even if Dreamland's done with him by then, he won't be in any shape to work."

"Pity," Stark said. "It would be more efficient."

"Sometimes we gotta spend chips," Drummond said. "Though I dunno how much we're gonna buy off this bet. This isn't a lotta time, boss."

"We don't need him to get high up, and we don't need him to last long. Just long enough to get the lay of the land and report back before he gets made."

"And the third problem?" the last man said.

His voice was sepulchral. He was tall, with close-cropped dark hair that had long ago given over to silver. He loomed over the others. A scar ran down his age-lined face, starting beneath his left eye, then down his cheek and hooking up at his chin.

"Subject 19," Agent Thomas said. "Temple's acting out of bounds, and our old pal Pat doesn't know how to put it back in."

"Could Agent Walsh have been compromised as well?"

"Don't know yet. I'm leaning toward Pat getting suckered. Never thought he was good for much. Still, I'll keep an eye on the situation. Might need to book a second suite at Dreamland. In the meantime, Crux, I want you to get real familiar with the sanction protocols for Subject 19. This experiment might have run its course."

The scarred man—Agent Crux—favored Agent Thomas with a cold smile. "No need to worry, Agent Thomas. I am very familiar with the subject."

12

Eventually Luci stopped crying. Her shuddering stilled and her head sank against my neck. At first, I thought she'd fallen asleep. Then she hiccupped. Her head jerked up off my shoulder. She stared at me with wide, tear-streaked eyes. Then she hiccupped again.

She would later insist that I was the first to start giggling, but I've looked back to watch this moment so many times. It was her, although I followed suit a second later. We sat on the second bed, our arms around each other, heads pressed together, giggling like fools, our laughter punctuated periodically by more hiccups. Her fear didn't dissipate entirely, but I felt the terror recede from the fore of her mind.

When the giggles finally subsided, I took her face in my hands. I kissed her once beneath each eye, then her forehead, and finally on her soft lips. I pressed my forehead against hers, keeping her face cupped between my hands. She slid her hands up my arms, holding onto my wrists as if they were lifelines.

"I can still see it," I said softly. "The hole in your memory. You can't remember anything from this afternoon, can you?"

Luci bit her lip and shook her head.

"I *was* trying not to think about it," she whispered. "I think I'm *supposed* to not think about it, but it's like a sore tooth I can't stop poking. I think about what's going on... about you, the Bureau, Gloria's studies, *Ralph*, poor little Ralph, and I try to remember what happened today and then I *shove* myself away—"

"It's only going to get worse because you can't let it go."

Luci nodded and whispered, "I used to think that was a strength."

"It is." I kissed her forehead again. "Because it means you won't stop until we've fixed this. Right?"

She let out a deep, shaky breath and sat up straight, looking me in the eye. That fierce light I loved so well flared in hers again.

"You're damn right."

"Good," I said, finally letting myself smile. "Because I have an idea on how to fix it, and you're probably going to like it."

"What's that?"

"I want to go into your mind and let you into mine."

Despite her fear and sorrow, a warm flush rose in Luci's cheeks. And elsewhere. She smiled hungrily.

"Oh, *absolutely*," she said, or rather, purred.

"I have no idea why this excites you so much."

"Because I want to *know* you. To feel what you feel. And I want you to know me the same way. I know you don't have any experience to compare—*yet*—but it's even more intimate than sex."

She gave me a wink and kissed me. "Just not as fun."

I blushed and ducked my head. "I'll have to take your word for it."

"We're not rushing. We'll take the time you need. In the meantime, come on in. You're welcome. *Always*."

"All right. Think of someplace comforting. Somewhere you feel at home and safe."

Luci slid into my lap and leaned against me. "I'm already there."

I wrapped my arms around her waist and pressed my cheek against hers.

Then I spread my consciousness, slipping my mind inside hers. Just as she said, her mind opened to me instantly, welcoming me into her. The room shivered and dissolved, at least partly. The walls and floor behind us melted into the main room of my dorm, while those in front remained Luci's bedroom. The pushed-together beds replaced my couch, and the rumpled Chuck Berry poster next to my bedroom door melted into Luci's corkboard. Meanwhile, in the space against the left-hand wall where the second bed once stood, my passenger's aquarium lurked sullenly. Luci's smile fell when she saw it.

"What the awful word is that?"

"My passenger," I said. "I'm afraid a side effect of their imprisonment is unwanted chaperonage."

"That's appalling. Now I *really* want that thing out of you."

The sludgy water in the tank burbled grumpily at her.

"I wouldn't worry about that now. It appears that they're going to be quiescent tonight."

Indeed, the Watcher Within simply sulked in their tank. I could feel them watching us as we went to the door (a hybrid of our two real doors), but they said nothing. Perhaps they were as shaken by what had happened this afternoon as we were. Or perhaps they simply anticipated my lack of tolerance for nonsense tonight.

The door opened not onto either of our dormitory hallways, but to the patients' wing at St. Audaeus. It was a composite of our respective recollections, made hazier by the imperfection of Luci's memory, and the damage it had suffered.

After a moment, she said, "This is certainly something."

Nurses drawn from our overlapping memories roamed the halls, repeating snatches of overheard conversations. They phased in and out as different memories rose to prominence. Most of their faces were indistinct; Luci had been here more often than I, so imperfect as they were, her memories dominated the mindscape. The lights flickered on and off, and shadows writhed in the corners. Flashes of strange light, like sickly lightning, ripped through the darkness. She slipped her hand into mind the third time we were plunged into momentary darkness.

"What's wrong?" she whispered. "I don't remember this."

"I think this is the scar of whatever erased your memory of this afternoon. It's not just affecting that memory. When you think about the hospital at all, the gap in your memory approaches the surface. That may be one reason why you can't stop picking at it."

"Because I keep thinking of Ralph and how to save him. So I keep thinking about the hospital. So I keep thinking about—"

Darkness crashed again.

"—about the thing I'm not supposed to think about."

Her hand tightened in mine. I drew on my memory, and the lights came on.

"I don't really know how to heal you," I said. "I can take you to see *my* memory of today. It might replace the one you lost. In a manner of speaking."

Luci clung to my arm and laughed hollowly. "You're making this up as you go along."

"I'm learning from you."

"Good. Let's see it."

Ralph's room shouldn't have been far away. Nonetheless, the hallway stretched and bent as we tried to reach it. The lights flickered more frequently, leaving us in darkness longer. I could see things in the snatches of darkness, inhuman figures momentarily lit in strange light. Reaching for us, screaming at us. Dissipating into nothingness before we could do more than startle when the lights returned.

Luci held my shoulder tightly with one hand, the other firmly clutching mine. Her normally pink face was almost bone white. Her breathing, technically unnecessary in this place, came in ragged bursts. Her fingers trembled against mine—both here and in the world outside our two heads.

"It's all right," I said. "Focus on me. None of this is real. We've created it for our convenience. We're in my mind, going to see my memory. My memory is undamaged. The way is clear."

"The way is clear," Luci repeated. "The way is clear."

The hallway stabilized to a point. Ralph's door stopped retreating, although the lighting remained inconsistent. A figure sat in a chair outside the room—my memory of Beverly Connor. Or so I thought. She rose as we approached, a sad smile clinging to her face.

"We're here to see him," I said.

The smile spread further across Beverly's face until the skin around her mouth split. Fissure cracked open in her face as if it were mud drying in the heat. Her eyes and mouth sank into her face, becoming empty black pits.

"Nothing here for you nothing here for you nothinghereforyou *nothinghereforyou*," the creature screamed.

The door to Ralph's room fell inward, spilling emptiness into the hallway. Luci screamed as the false Beverly lunged for her. I grabbed the specter, trying to push it away from her. Its limbs elongated, bony claws ripping through the paper-like skin of its fingers to tear at my dream flesh. I slammed it against the nearby wall, or I tried to. That wall, the one that held Ralph's door, sank into emptiness. The specter clung to me and dove backward. Gravity flipped, and I felt myself diving into the void, the wound within Luci's memory.

"NO!" Luci screamed.

She lunged for me, wrapping her arms around my waist. We tumbled together, falling with the laughing specter into the widening nothingness. Into the weird lights that flashed at the edge of the void. I could feel Luci reaching elsewhere, trying desperately to grab something firm. Something to anchor us. Something to fall onto.

"Ralph!" she cried, her voice coming from far away. "Amelia, think of Ralph!"

I tried. I pictured him lying in his hospital bed, wrapped in ichor-stained bandages. Gloria's seal sat on his chest, the engraved crate suspended inches above it. Luci, Gloria, and I stationed around the circle, ready to activate the seal. Just seconds before it all went wrong.

We slammed into the tile floor, the specter trapped beneath me, Luci clinging to my back. Ralph's hospital room flowed into vision. I could see the four of us frozen in a moment in time.

The specter screamed and beat at my limbs. I snarled and grabbed it by the neck, flinging it over my shoulder at the far wall. It shattered, the specter flying not into the hospital passageway but my dorm room. The monster slid across the floor, crashing hard into the filthy aquarium. It rocked on its stand, but nothing spilled.

The mindscape shivered, and the Watcher-As-Lucas stepped out from behind the aquarium. Luci sucked in a sharp breath and grabbed my hand, asking rather coarsely for clarification.

"My passenger again," I said. "I believe I mentioned I'd been conversing with them? They've learned to take on a more comprehensible form."

"A more limited one, you mean," the Watcher-As-Lucas said, looking with disgust at Lucas' infected human limbs.

"Not one I'm happy to see again." Luci scowled, glaring daggers at them.

The Watcher-As-Lucas' face twisted into a poor attempt at a smile.

"We could appear as Ralphie instead. Would that be more comfortable? Oh, but he's already right there. Although we suppose there *are* two of you here as well."

"*No*," I said. "I see you've learned nastiness."

"You provide such an effective example. Miss Sweeney, would you like to see how she treats the animals in her 'Bureau' swarm? It's quite horrible."

"Animals?" Luci looked at them with confusion.

"They mean the agents," I said. "I'm afraid they haven't quite picked up the knack of treating humans as *people*."

"Oh. Geez."

Ambivalence wafted off Luci like a cloud of perfume. On the one hand, she figured the Bureau's agents deserved any sort of rudeness they received, especially from me. On the other hand, the thought of agreeing with the Watcher on anything troubled her, particularly where the treatment of humans was concerned. Interacting with them at all was unsettling enough, especially in the guise of one of her least favorite people. Finding common ground? That was truly awful.

"With that sort of attitude, I figure it'll be quite a while before we agree it's safe to let you go free," she said at last.

"If accepting a horde of spatially locked protoplasmic clumps as our equals is the price of freedom, your animal is certainly correct," the Watcher-As-Lucas said to me. "How amusing."

The Watcher-As-Lucas looked at Luci as if she were no more than a mildly entertaining insect. Something they could use or abuse at their convenience. The way the specter had looked at her. The way Agent Pickman had looked at me. Rage rose inside me. The mindscape rumbled. My form melted and flowed, my skin becoming rugose. My mass doubled, then tripled. Multiple long, flexible limbs sprouted from my thickened trunk. I shifted the mindscape to a different part of my brain, one composed of forms of matter vastly different from that which made Luci's. For her safety, I pushed her away. The mindscape melted as her portion of it fell behind me, leaving only myself and the Watcher. The hospital walls tore away as if they were paper in a hurricane, revealing an endless field of stars shining coldly beneath weird aurorae.

Speak to her in that way again, I sent, my thoughts a frozen wind tearing through space, *and I will find a way to destroy you.*

The Watcher-As-Lucas trembled, their form rippling like dirty water in the wake of a stone. They tried to stand proud, glaring at me defiantly.

"You can't destroy us," they said. "If you could, you would have done that instead of imprisoning us."

I hissed, my head tendrils flailing in outrage. I spread my many limbs, and the void trembled. Strange light flashed in distant writhing nebulae. At the very edge of hearing, discordant chimes rang out.

I couldn't destroy you then. That doesn't mean I can't, if I decide I want to badly enough. In the meantime, do you really think this *is the worst place to be imprisoned?*

I reached into the depths of unknown memory and pulled up a vision of a small, irregular rock tumbling through the interplanetary medium. Its cold face was pockmarked by millions of years of impacts. The lonely planetoid's orbit was so far from my world's sun that it was no more than a pale yellow dot far, far below us.

Perhaps you'd rather be left clinging to the barren plains of Kor-Mitra? Sheltering from radiation within the abandoned temples of the Ixikan? Hurtling forever through the stagnant trans-Neptunian meteoroid fields?

I grasped for another vision and found an anti-sun, its ancient mass radiating darkness so bright it hurt even my myriad eyes.

Should I cast you into the gravity sewers of Izulz? Leave you orbiting helplessly as the antimatter winds tear your energy lattice to shreds?

A third vision, this one far less grand in scope, but more fearsome in aspect. A simple room with a black and white tile floor, the walls hung with velvet drapes that were almost green. A low black table of unknown material sat in the exact center of the room, surrounded by three metal chairs. An entity sat in each of them. It lifted its head when it realized it was being watched and turned to face us.

She waits on the threshold. Are you ready to face Her? To have even the comforting illusions I've permitted you to be stripped away?

Where should I leave you, Watcher Within, conqueror worm, alien infection, locust of the cosmos? I would be rid of your loathsome presence. Which blasted wasteland will you haunt, you insufferable pestilence?

The Watcher-As-Lucas fell to their knees, wrapping their thin arms around their chest and trying to bury their head in the crook of their elbows. Tears of brackish water ran down their cheeks. The sludgy fluid within the aquarium churned, and it rocked on its stand as the Watcher Within thrashed in fear.

"Forgive us, One From Beyond, The Opener Of The Way, You Who Are The Gate And The Guide. Abandon us not on the Fearful Shores. Deliver us to the bountiful hills that we may spread our souls and prosper. We, who are but pale shadows of Your perfection, offer You condign obeisance."

They cowered at my feet. Through their senses I saw myself towering over them, glorious and terrible, a writhing figure wrought of weird matter, lit by strange lights. A figure of awe. Of fear. Of worship.

Behind me, Luci screamed.

I collapsed into myself, reasserting my Amelia shape. My mindscape plummeted, rushing to join up with Luci. She cowered on a handful of tiles, the hospital room collapsing around her, falling into the hole in her memory. I grabbed her and held her close, murmuring reassurances into her ear.

"I'm sorry," she whispered. "The room fell apart after you left. I tried to keep it together, but…"

"No. *I'm* sorry. I lost my temper, I didn't think…"

I looked at the Watcher-As-Lucas, still cowering where I left them. I didn't know how to feel about them. They were a horrible thing that had tried to consume everything without caring about the consequences to any other life form. And I was a horrible thing that could somehow commit even more terrible acts if I put my mind to it. And worse, it would be *so easy*. I just had to accept it…

I pushed the thought away.

"If you're willing to be civil to my girlfriend," I said, "I'm willing to restart this conversation."

The Watcher-As-Lucas looked up carefully. Seeing that my rage had ebbed for the moment, they picked themselves up from the floor. They bent down and grabbed the specter, who remained cowering at the base of the aquarium. They held the creature up, inspecting it as if it were a particularly distasteful bit of refuse. It now appeared significantly less substantial than before. It was a wonder it had caused me any trouble at all.

"Wretched little thing. We hope it's not staying. This place is already crowded enough as it is, especially if you insist on bringing your companion here."

"What did I just say? She's far more welcome than you are."

"We're more than willing to take our leave of your mind."

"I'm sure you are. You seem to know what that thing is. Care to share?"

The Watcher-As-Lucas hesitated. They had just seen my temper and were terrified of the consequences. Yet my question was inconceivable.

"Is this a test?"

I let out a sigh. "Yes. Sure. It's a test of your willingness to cooperate. I will look favorably upon you if you pass. Get on with it. Please."

My passenger nodded slowly, trying to comprehend. "*Zedu heth baagu.* Vulgarly, a dream eater. Or rather, the traces of its predation, at any rate."

An odd expression crossed their face. "You know barren Kor-Mitra and the lost Ixikan but not this thing? We suppose it should be beneath your notice, but…"

I didn't. But I felt as if I should. Something about that name, in an unknown language, stirred a vestigial pattern in the base of my memory. It was familiar, but in a way I couldn't reach. A shape vaguely appraised in dim light. I scowled as I tried to resolve it and couldn't.

Name of an unspeakable name, is this what forgetting was like? How appalling!

Seeing my consternation, Luci stepped in front of me, fists on her hips.

"And why should she? Where would she have run into a saydoo hayth bahgoo, anyway?"

The Watcher-As-Lucas winced at her pronunciation but made no further comment. They were learning. "In dreams, perhaps? Your mind touches on the subtle spheres as readily as any other, and hers far more readily than either of ours."

"The subtle spheres?" I said, somewhat absently. It tickled something just as the dream-eater's name had.

"Do you mean the astral plane?" Luci asked. Off my expression, she continued, "Research, remember? Nineteenth century spiritualists, like the Theosophists, believed the soul could travel to other realms. Non-physical ones."

"They weren't entirely wrong," the Watcher-As-Lucas said, sounding both annoyed and vaguely impressed. "There are phases of reality that even animals such as yourself can reach psychically. An ethereal realm—"

"A dreamland," I said sharply.

The Watcher-As-Lucas looked pained. "That's putting it vulgarly, but we suppose not inaccurately. Some sapient beings can reach that sphere in dreams, some even without training. But this sphere has its own ecology. The *zedu heth baagu* is part of it. Predators, or so they imagine themselves."

"And that thing *ate* my memory?" Luci said, horrified.

"The actual *zedu heth baagu* did. This is an echo, if you will. A reflection of itself left behind after its attack."

"But that attack was from *today*," I said. "Luci didn't sleep until well after the incident at the hospital, and the injury was present before then." A horrifying thought occurred. "Could one of these entities be controlled?"

The Watcher-As-Lucas snorted with disgust. "The animals of this world have learned to summon such puissant entities as ourselves. Do you really think they couldn't control such a miserable creature as *this*?"

Luci said something truly impolite. "How do we fix it?"

"How do you fix an amputated limb?" the Watcher-As-Lucas said dismissively. "You *don't*. It's gone. Even if your corporeal form was capable of regrowing it, it would be all-new matter replacing what was lost."

"I see you've decided to stop being helpful," I said. "I do have a sort of idea, darling. I don't remember only my experiences. I also remember what everyone around me is thinking, or at least what I can perceive of it. I perceive quite a bit of what you think. I'm sorry… you're always in focus when you're near."

Luci ducked her head and smiled shyly. "That's maybe the most romantic thing anyone has ever said to me."

I smiled back. "If we can transplant my memory of your thoughts into your mind, it could sort of seal the gap."

"We don't see how that disproves what we said," my passenger said grumpily.

Luci looked from me to the Watcher, eyes wide. "Will that work?"

"We don't know why you're asking *us*," the Watcher-As-Lucas said. "We have no idea. This isn't the sort of thing we *do*."

"I've never done it before," I said, "but it sounds plausible, doesn't it?"

"I certainly trust you." Luci looked at my passenger. "Do you mind? I'd like some privacy."

The Watcher-As-Lucas rolled their eyes but stepped away, taking the remains of the dream-eater with them. The walls of the hospital room knit back together, leaving us alone with our memory selves.

"Okay," Luci said. "What do we do?"

"First, we need to know exactly what's missing. Can you tell me where your memory from today stops?"

Luci frowned and took my hands. She closed her eyes and looked within. The lights flickered as she cast her memory across the scar left by the dream-eater's predation. Her fingers trembled within mine, but her voice was strong when she spoke.

"I remember driving to Chatham Hills to pick you and Gloria up from the diner. We had lunch, then drove to Regina. Around Centerville my memory cuts out, and then I skip over to the three of us driving down the highway in the opposite direction, hours later. I remember that we failed to help Ralph, I remember being sad and angry about it, but I don't remember what happened."

"Okay. We can run all the way to the trip up to Regina if you want, although at some point the memory will start to get weird. I didn't follow you into the hospital right away."

"I'd remember about fifteen minutes of you watching me from a distance. Yeah, that feels like a step too far."

"I understand."

"And I'm fine losing the trip up. I space out a lot during long drives anyway."

"Yes, and it's very concerning."

"Let's just skip to the good part. That's what I really need."

"All right. I'll start at the point when Gloria and I enter the room."

The scene flickered. For a moment, Luci was alone with Ralph. Then a burst of air rippled Ralph's sheets as Gloria and I appeared. Luci—and Luci—let out a surprised squeak. I focused on my memory of Luci's thoughts, trying to pass them to the real Luci as we watched ourselves set up the apparatus for Gloria's seal.

Luci was silent until the experiment went wrong. When the tendrils of weird matter ripped through Ralph's skin, she burst into tears, burying her face against my neck. Not that it protected her this time. For one terrible moment she perceived reality as I did, unable to look away as the memory settled into the hole in her mind.

I stopped the memory when her past self fled, screaming for the doctor.

Luci let out a shaky breath. "Okay. I think I can put the rest of the pieces together myself. It's a deduction. I went to get the doctor. I took him to see Ralph—"

"And after he saw what happened to his patient—"

"He sicced the dream eater on me. Can't have a hysterical female letting the cat out of the bag," Luci said with a scowl. "Probably did the same thing to Bev and any nurses who saw what happened to Ralph."

"What else did he do? He can't have left Ralph like this."

"No. He must have done something to get the reaction under control. Or just moved him. How long was it before I rejoined you in the car?"

"Exactly twenty-eight minutes and forty-six seconds. I couldn't see you for nineteen of them. I was more than a little worried."

"Can't say you weren't right to be," she said. "He could have done anything in that time. Absolutely anything."

"We can go back to the hospital. I can take us to see exactly what happened."

"We're going back, all right. Because we can say one thing for sure. He's got the dream-eater locked up down there."

I stared at her. Then we said in unison, "The basement."

"I told you that place was creepy!"

"Yes, I felt it in your memory."

"Let's break in and find out what else is down there. Because whatever they're up to, I'm starting to think it's more foul word than we thought."

13

I believed my absence had gone unnoticed, so I thought nothing of it when Monday came and went with no consequences. Thomas was biding his time. Breaking curfew was a minor infraction, expected from someone my age. Walsh would likely be able to shield me from any significant punishment, although it would cost him. Thomas wanted us both dealt with permanently, which meant giving me enough rope to hang myself with.

I went by Walsh's office late Monday afternoon to write my report on the second hospital visit. Luci and I had spent a good part of Sunday morning trying to figure out how much to share with the Bureau. We had agreed that "basically the truth" wouldn't cut it this time. Learning that Ralph's condition had dramatically worsened, never mind why, would surely have spurred the Bureau into action. We'd debated whether that was a good idea. It might have put Ralph within our grasp, leaving us the devil we knew to work with. On the other hand, it might have put him under the Specials' jurisdiction, in which case I would never be allowed by his side ever again. Both of those were best-case scenarios, assuming the Bureau gained the upper hand in a direct confrontation with the Chambers Foundation. There was a very good chance the Foundation would bury Ralph somewhere we would never find him, or that he would be hurt in the crossfire. Reluctantly, we decided it was too great of a risk at this juncture. I would report that his condition looked to be declining and that the hospital was considering its next steps. That was probably still true.

Agent Walsh wasn't pleased to hear that, though he was grateful for the information I'd provided. One would think that would have made him more inclined to share his office for a couple of hours. It wasn't *my* fault that the Bureau had neglected to teach me typing skills.

"Are you almost done, Amelia? It's been an hour."

"I'm going as fast as I can, Agent Walsh."

"Look, just put your left fingers on ASDF and your right—"

"I'm doing perfectly well, thank you."

Walsh put his hands on his hips and looked up at the ceiling, grimacing. "I know you have a hard time accepting criticism…"

"I am very good at accepting criticism. You're bad at giving it."

He raised his eyebrows, giving me a wide-eyed stare. I ignored him, poking at the keys with my index fingers.

"Additionally, if you're so reluctant to share your typewriter, you should have granted my request for my own two weeks ago."

"As I explained, the Bureau's budget doesn't cover that sort of thing. You have a stipend for personal goods."

"Half of the offices on this floor are empty, Agent Walsh. With perfectly good typewriters going unutilized."

"Those typewriters have been requisitioned for the use of those offices—"

"Then I'll take an office!"

"And those offices are for duly appointed agents of the Bureau of Extranormal Investigations, so unless you're thinking about joining…"

"Oh, just let me take one! No one will notice."

"No one will notice what, Temple?" Agent Thomas said, swinging the door open.

I glared over the paper at him for five seconds. Then I dropped my eyes to the keys and carried on typing. Walsh looked at his colleague with a less openly hostile expression, but the temperature in the room dropped a few noticeable degrees. Metaphorically speaking.

If the cool reception bothered Thomas, he didn't show it. He favored me with his tiresome sneer. "What's going on, kiddo? You up to something? Youthful hijinks and what not?"

"Agent Walsh, do I answer to Agent Thomas?" I asked, keeping my tone light.

Walsh locked eyes with Thomas. "No, Amelia. No, you don't."

"Agent Thomas, my handler says I don't answer to you."

I continued pecking away, not bothering to spare Thomas another glance. He laughed, a nasty chuckle that I could tell was somehow at my expense. He shook his head and ran his hand across his chin. Nerves? Irritation? I had no way of knowing.

"Your little pet's getting feisty, huh? Must have had a good weekend."

Internally, I bristled at that, but I kept my expression carefully neutral. The arrhythmic sound of my keystrokes filled the silence. Walsh put a comforting hand on my shoulder. Under the circumstances, I allowed it.

"Considering that she went to see a friend in the hospital, Randall, I think we can assume Amelia's weekend was tough."

I let the mask drop just a bit. Enough to let some of my genuine grief show. Not enough to give Thomas satisfaction.

Thomas blatantly telegraphed his disbelief. "That's a shame. Connor not doing so hot, then?"

"You will learn all about Ralph's current condition whenever Agent Walsh forwards you my report, Agent Thomas."

"And I'll have to review her work before I feel comfortable passing it along," Walsh said. "It might require revision. Amelia is new at this. It's a process, Randall. I'm sure you're familiar with it."

"Could take hours." I offered an insincere attempt at a smile. "I like to be thorough."

"Is that so?" Thomas said. "You know, some of the higher ups might consider anything related to the Dowling Incident to be high priority. No pussyfooting around."

"You're quite right, Randall. And since that's the case, it would probably be best if you stop distracting Amelia so she can finish her work. Unless there's some actual reason you're darkening my office door this afternoon?"

Thomas let out a short, ugly laugh and shook his head. "Nope. I guess there's not." He stepped into the hall. "You carry on with your work, Temple. Can't wait to see how this shakes out."

He slammed the door and walked away, whistling jauntily. I watched as he went down the hall until he reached the closest stairwell, in case he did something unexpected. I set my mouth in a tight line.

"I really hate that man," I said.

Walsh agreed, but professionalism prevented him from admitting it. He idly considered reprimanding me but dismissed it as pointless and hypocritical. Instead, he turned to me, eyes pleading. "You aren't really going to take another hour, are you?"

We were due to meet at the library to plan our next incursion into the hospital. But I also had another meeting that week. This one was entirely my idea. I'd spent three days mulling over the things the Watcher had said when we were exploring Luci's scarred memory. We needed more information, and it seemed they were starting to feel cooperative. Wednesday night, I turned inward to visit with my passenger.

This time, the Watcher-As-Lucas was waiting for me when I entered my conceptual dorm room. The aquarium still stood where my couch would have gone, but the human presentation stretched out on something like a chaise lounge. It was carved of a dark wood I didn't recognize, and in place of upholstery, a thick pad of pungent yellow fungus dappled in shades of green grew over the seat and side. A translucent red sap dripped down the legs, pooling on the floorboards in sticky puddles. A smell I could only describe as "infected honey" wafted from the seat.

I pulled the folding chair over near the lounge and sat. The Watcher-As-Lucas was holding a blue hardcover novel—a Nancy Drew mystery I'd read three years ago. They didn't look up from their reading when I coughed.

"I see you've done some redecorating," I said.

The Watcher-As-Lucas turned a page. "We thought that as long as we were going to occupy this space, we ought to make ourselves comfortable."

Thick cables were strung across half the walls and ceiling. They were overgrown with tendrils of mossy fungus. Asymmetrical *objets d'art* hung from the cables, glowing faintly with internal luminesence. Admittedly, I knew little about art—my haphazard tutoring at Bureau expense had largely neglected the humanities—but they were so diverse I couldn't recognize a common theme or medium.

"What is all this?" I gestured to the décor.

The Watcher-As-Lucas cocked their head to the side thoughtfully. "Mementos, we suppose. Keepsakes. In the aether, we don't have what you would call space for souvenirs. Instead, we build our museums in the mind."

"I see. Yet you're still taking an interest in the local culture," I said, approvingly.

"We have experienced these multiple times before. We can see why you like this Nancy Drew animal. She reminds us of your companion."

"You understand that Nancy Drew isn't real? She's a made-up person."

The Watcher-As-Lucas looked at me sharply. "We are familiar with the concept of *fiction*, Amanda."

I folded my arms across my chest and quirked an eyebrow. "I didn't think that was funny when the real Lucas Dowling did it."

Shame and fear radiated off the human presentation. The book disappeared. The Watcher-As-Lucas folded their limbs around their torso, bowing their head contritely.

"We apologize, Amelia. As we said before, our communion with the Lucas creature was limited. We have only a few hundred seconds and your memories as a foundation to emulate. It is less than ideal."

You could say that again, I thought. "Then why do you keep presenting yourself as him? It cannot possibly be for my benefit."

"But it *is*." The Watcher-As-Lucas partially unfolded. "You experienced difficulty interfacing with our core persona. Thus, we have manifested a subsidiary. One that matches your presentation, out of respect. Unfortunately, we have limited options in that regard. Unless you would prefer to interact with the Ralph Connor... *person*?"

"*No*. Definitely not," I said. I tried to push away the wave of guilt that washed through me. "This will have to do, for now. I need to speak with you."

The Watcher-As-Lucas unfolded all the way. They looked at me with curiosity tinged with more than a little greed. "About what?"

"Saturday night. You named the dream eater in a language I—" I paused, trying to put the sensation into words. "I didn't entirely recognize. *Zedu heth baagu*. That isn't your native tongue, I'm certain of that. What is it from?"

The Watcher-As-Lucas rippled like stagnant water after a stone. "You really do not know?"

I pinched the bridge of my nose, letting out a deep sigh. "For the last time..."

The Watcher-As-Lucas held out their hands, their fingers waving in agitation. "We apologize again. This is difficult in ways we are not prepared to explain. We accept your words. You do not know. Very well."

They stood, walking across the room to a particular vine. A tower built out of hundreds of tiny, rectangular black stones hung from it, capped by a shining dodecahedron. The Watcher-As-Lucas plucked the tower from the vine, stroking its ridged length. It emitted a low jangling hum, as if it was filled with metallic bees. The resonance filled the mindscape and shivered, like bubbles passing through thin liquid. The dorm room crumbled away, though the myriad vines remained. We were standing on a small rock, tumbling through space. A black planetoid hung in the void below us, catching our vantage point in its gravitational embrace. Far above us, an elderly sun burned weakly, an inert clinker left behind after the last of its hydrogen blasted off. A multicolored shell of gas and dust spread out for light years around the clinker star, the whirling echoes of that great explosion. It should have obliterated the planetoid, as it had any others that once called this gravity well home. Some force had saved it. Or, perhaps, moved it into this orbit much later.

"Where are we?" I asked. "And when?"

The Watcher-As-Lucas cocked their head to one side, calculating. "'Where' is simple. We're orbiting a star several hundred light years from Earth. 'When' is more complicated. Dozens of spawnings ago. Approximately ten thousand years from now, as they reckon time on this planet."

I goggled at them, trying to process what the Watcher was telling me. They were showing me a memory from the *future?* "I'm sorry?"

"Time works differently in the aether. The swarm skips over epochs like stones across the water. And not in the straight line that time passes here.

"That isn't relevant to your question, though." The Watcher-As-Lucas pointed to the planetoid and a violet spark burning on its surface. "*That* is."

I followed their finger, my attention plunging down to the surface. A massive rocky hill burst up to meet me. A tower stood at its crown. It was a hundred meters high, a gently twisting spire topped with a shining metal dodecahedron. It was shot through with kilometers of curving tunnels and vaguely ovoid spaces. Luminescent crystals grew through the surfaces at odd angles. Thousands of beings roamed the tunnels and worked within the spaces, which were packed floor to ceiling with shelves of metal scrolls.

The model, or perhaps frozen memory, had vanished from the Watcher's hands. In its place, they held one of the scrolls. They unrolled it, revealing thousands of sigils written in metallic ink in a spidery hand. The writing spiraled around a diagram composed of hundreds of crisscrossing lines. After a minute of pondering, I guessed that it might be a map.

"What is this?"

"A bestiary. Specifically describing the fauna, if that's the correct term, of what your companion called 'the astral plane'. It is one of nineteen volumes in Izz-kelthan's *Treatise on the Mind Sphere*."

"I assume the original is in there?" I gestured to the tower.

"It was and will be."

The Watcher-As-Lucas turned to the tower. I followed suit. Deep within, in a chamber hidden a hundred meters below the surface, five of the denizens gathered in the gloom. Like their fellows on the upper floors, they were squat creatures with six limbs—three arms and three legs. Their thick, beaked heads had three eyes. Most of their soft ochre skin was protected beneath bulky shells. They wore heavy violet robes, belted with dark blue sashes covered in silver hashmarks. No two were the same; I wondered what the markings signified.

"Who are these beings?"

"Memory labels them 'the Archivists'. They were, or will be, an order of academics—a fairly heretical one, by the standards of their civilization. They amass the greatest library of research in this epoch, spanning nearly every known realm. The aether, the astral, what we would consider the material, infraspace, on and on. They catalogue the methods of transit across and between realms, the conditions within, the beings one might find there, from the most meager to—" the Watcher-As-Lucas gave me a careful glance, "those one might consider gods."

The five Archivists were writing something on the floor. Like the diagram on the scroll, it was composed of hundreds of diagonal lines crossing one another at various points and angles. It struck me as strangely familiar. At first, I thought it might be their version of Luci's conspiracy board. As it took shape, I realized how wrong I was. The design was all fractal angles instead of dizzying curves, but it was unmistakably a seal composed of a variation on Prospero's Keys. Perhaps even the antecedent.

"What's going on?"

The Watcher-As-Lucas gave me a sharp look. "The Lucas Dowling persona finds this mask of naiveté you have adopted charming, up to a point. Surely you recognize the protocol? They are making contact."

The seal was complete. One of the Archivists took up position just off from the seal's center. The other four squatted at significant points around the seal's edge. They began to chant, their words melting into a high-pitched nasal drone. Nine crystals jutting from the chamber's sloped walls began to glow with eerie light. Energy, invisible to nearly anyone without my senses, arced from the crystals and into the seal. The weird geometry pulled the energy into a vortex of ever-increasing speed. It caught the air within the chamber in its spiral, the sudden windstorm whipping debris around the edges of the room. The air grew hot and thick.

Then the Archivist anchoring the seal began twitching. Their shell shattered with a gut-churning *crack* as their ochre flesh erupted upward, forming a fleshy pillar. Thick root-like tendrils dug into the rocky floor, while their elongating arms struck out like whips, grabbing three of their fellows. The mutating Archivist dragged them into the seal, screaming and digging their sharp stubby fingers helplessly into the stone. It was no use. It wasn't an Archivist anymore. Rents opened along the manifesting Watcher's trunk, spewing out its ichorous song.

"The swarm was still mastering the art of manifestation," the Watcher-As-Lucas said, as casually as if they were discussing a painting in a gallery. "This is a very early form, but it served its purpose well."

The fifth Archivist screamed and fled the chamber, finally experiencing a sudden burst of self-preservation. It was too late. The Watcher's mass had quadrupled, but that wasn't nearly enough to accommodate the vast presence falling into this dimension from the aether. The fleeing Archivist only heralded a wave of chemical coercion as the Watcher spewed its spores into the atmosphere. More tendrils stabbed out from right angles to realspace, grabbing the nearest Archivists and slaving their minds to the Watcher's. Many resisted it, either via psychic training or the application of warding seals. Too few couldn't, and the Watcher had taken them all by surprise.

"It's impressive when you consider how primitive this vessel is," the Watcher-As-Lucas continued. "In the end, they successfully assimilated nearly sixty percent of the archives before their vessel was destroyed. Fortunately, the Archivists didn't know what they were dealing with. They didn't understand our relationship to these constructed forms. The colony abandoned its vessel and returned to the aether once it had suffered too much damage. They distributed the archive's contents to the swarm, and we were enriched."

They turned to me, their mouth curled upward. At first, I didn't recognize the expression. Then I realized it was a smile, a genuine smile. They radiated possessive and reverent emotions.

"And thus, we found a better method for reaching the material world."

I stared at the Watcher in horror. In their memory, a scene of carnage played out inside the alien monastery. I understood what they had intended for Chatham Hills and beyond, but it was one thing to know it. It was something else to witness it, even from multiple steps removed. To see the way the Watcher enslaved their victims, consumed their minds, warped their bodies to become fuel for their own form… and a temporary one, at that!

From seemingly miles away, my body tried to retch.

"You… you killed all these people… stole the work of lifetimes. Of multiple lifetimes."

"*We* didn't. We hadn't been spawned yet. And they aren't dead. Oh, sure, their bodies ceased to function. Dramatically, in most cases. Their minds live on within this colony, even now. Echoes have been passed on to every colony within the swarm. They're immortal. Frankly, they ought to have thanked us."

"*Thanked* you?"

"They were all going to die, Amelia. The swarm watched this period from every vantage point available. Without our intervention, they would have died within a millennium. As we told you, they were heretics. In sixty-two percent of potential timelines, their parent civilization experienced a particularly zealous period and purged the Archivists. In twenty-eight percent, a research project went spectacularly wrong. In the rest, they were the victims of some great cosmic accident. Look, do you know what a gamma-ray burst is?"

"No."

The clinker star and its nebula melted away, replaced by yellow sands and tall violet fungal growths. We stood atop a low hill, looking down at a coastal village. The buildings were squat huts woven from red reeds, arranged around a wide pool separated from the sea with a low rock wall. A menhir of gray-green stone grew up from the middle of the pool. The villagers were frog-like, with glowing yellow eyes, slick blue and violet skin, and six limbs: four legs and two arms. Many crewed long, flat-bottom boats woven from the same reeds as their houses. They cast nets into the water, pulling out hundreds of many-limbed mollusks. With each full net, a boat's crew let out a thick-throated chant of joy.

"Neither did this world's inhabitants," the Watcher-As-Lucas said. "It's a jet of immensely energetic radiation. We believe they are the result of massively dense stars collapsing into singularities."

"I don't understand. What does that mean?" I asked, although the answer tickled at the back of my mind.

The Watcher-As-Lucas' body rippled with momentary agitation. "You do understand, although maybe not in those words. It's the last phase in a truly massive star's lifecycle.

"And, in this instance, the last phase in these creatures' lifecycle, as well."

One villager sat in the pool, surrounded by what I assumed were their larval children. Their bodies were thick, flat oblongs with twin tails. They thrashed the pool excitedly as the elder spoke. The elder wore a cloak made of pale green feathers, and their body was covered in phosphorescent markings. Was it paint, or natural pigment? I would never know.

"This is the last generation that would be born to this… let's be charitable and call it a 'civilization'. Approximately two thousand years prior, a star that local observers named 'Izitorth' finished collapsing in on itself. As it did, it released a gamma-ray burst—a massive explosion that blasted across the void between stars.

"Today, it reaches this world."

The villagers looked up when a brilliant aurora filled the sky with ribbons of color. They cheered, waving their many-fingered hands at what they must have believed was a powerful omen. A deep-throated chant rose high above the village and the bright sea.

Then they began to twitch.

Thick, dark ichor leaked from their mouths, nostrils, and luminescent eyes. The chant fell to choking silence as one by one, the villagers collapsed. Their bodies spasmed as if subjected to an electrical current. Then they died in pools of stinking ichor. Thousands of them, dead in minutes.

"In some ways, these were the lucky ones," the Watcher-As-Lucas said, their voice as nonchalant as if describing the menu at Lane's Diner. "Yes, their bodies absorbed a lethal amount of radiation, but at least they died quickly. Their species—the Utsuoggtha, they called themselves—had spread across their planet. The civilizations on the far side of the globe lasted longer. By decades.

"The effects of the radiation in the atmosphere rapidly depleted the planet's ozone layer, exposing the surface to increased radiation from its own star. The atmosphere itself became toxic. Thick smog blocked the sunlight that photosynthesizers fed on, disrupting the food chain. Ironic, isn't it? That the atmosphere would deny the parts of the electromagnetic spectrum that fed life on this world but not the parts that ended it."

"I don't find that to be particularly amusing."

"No? We suppose these creatures would agree with you. Their climate rapidly cooled. Their skies rained down poison. Their food sources died out. The last Utsuoggtha died, cancer-riddled, frozen, and starving, approximately fifty-two of 'your' years later."

"How do you know all this?"

The Watcher-As-Lucas looked down on me, radiating puzzlement. "Isn't it obvious?"

We turned away from the stricken village. Our viewpoint rushed away, crossing three thousand miles in a single jump. A familiar fleshy tower grew atop a larger hill, its chemical song calling out to the minds around it. Thick tendrils hung from its flat cap, brushing the bare earth it had anchored itself to. Alien trees, like a cross of fungus and coral, grew in groves around the hill.

As we watched, a troop of Utsuoggtha hopped up the steep slope. Their bodies were riddled with growths, tendrils and boils of weird matter. They had been infected by this Watcher, slaved to a hive mind under its control. Eventually it would absorb them, fueling its own growth as it consumed all the biomass it could reach.

"Of course you colonized them," I said, disgusted.

"Of course we did. The swarm had been watching this planet for some time. We had long considered it as a potential spawning ground. When we detected the gamma-ray burst, the swarm determined it was an appropriate time to enter this world and consume what we could before the mass extinction event rendered it pointless."

"You could have *saved* them!"

"But we *did* save them, Amelia," the Watcher-As-Lucas said, furrowing their brow in genuine confusion. They thrust out a finger at the fungal tower. "That isn't just any part of the swarm. That is *this* colony. We were spawned here, on this world. We cultivated our first instar from its biomass. The Utsuoggtha, their history, their culture, their artworks—all of them worth preserving, at least—it's all saved within us. Us and five older colonies that took root here. This colony is in the truest sense a scion of this world, and we will carry its history into the eons."

I looked back to the stricken village. The bodies rotting in the thickening air. "Do you think that matters to the dead?"

The Watcher-As-Lucas looked affronted. "It should, damn it! We don't *have* to share our perfection with the animals. We can feed and grow on lesser beings. We could have let them all die, let their paltry civilization be scoured away by an uncaring universe. Instead, we incorporated them into our selves.

"We carry the echoes of our predecessors. We carry the minds of a million Utsuoggtha. Millions of minds from a half-dozen other species across the centuries. Not to mention the templates of at least twenty-five percent of this planet's animal kingdom.

"We've searched your memories, Amelia. We know the danger this world faces. Its primary civilizations stand on the brink of annihilation. They'll do it, you know. We've seen it before. We've lost worlds to their own self-destruction, poisoned by power the animals weren't wise enough to wield. Left unsuitable for our growth."

The Watcher-As-Lucas spread his hands, offering them for me to take. "We can save them. They can join us. Lucas Dowling, or at least the piece of him we took, is immortal now. Don't you think that's what he wants?"

I stared at the Watcher, reading their borrowed face, their mismatched body language. They needed so badly for me to understand. For me to approve of them.

"Not like this, he wouldn't," I said softly.

I withdrew, letting the mindscape melt away behind me. The Watcher Within lurked in the darkness, disquieted and disbelieving. They wrapped their presence into themselves and fell silent and cold.

I didn't know that I would ever reach them.

14

"I suppose it's a testament to our friendship how comfortable I've become with breaking and entering," Gloria said.

By night, the hospital squatted in the middle of an open field like a slumbering beast. Stretches of new housing lined the streets on three sides, fencing it in with common humanity. At the hour of midnight, the building seemed to pull away from them, huddled in the night like a miser hiding a bauble in his coat. Lights shone in random windows, bringing to mind the many eyes of a titanic spider, peering at the three of us as we crept across the dark parking lot.

"It's not *really* breaking and entering," Luci said, trying to sound more chipper than she felt. "Someone's letting us in. We have permission to be here."

"Does she have permission to let us in?" Gloria asked.

"Details, details."

We stopped near the staff door, outside the circle of light cast by the single bare bulb above the frame, and waited. Luci glanced at her watch. "Right on time," she said.

Time certainly wasn't something we'd given ourselves much of. Our plan was based entirely on the work schedule of the red-haired young woman in the candy-striped dress currently wheeling a gurney down the hallway and fighting second, third, and fourth thoughts about helping us. That, and how long it would take Luci to pressure her into helping us. That had turned out to be three days, and she still insisted she couldn't possibly do it until Sunday. The last day of October. The date gave both of my friends chills. They tried to dismiss it as childish superstition, but both of them stood outside the light, shivering for reasons that had nothing to do with the late autumn cold.

Dorothy Weathersby unlocked the staff door and poked her head out. "Luci!" she hissed. "Are you there?"

"Of course we are," Luci said, stepping into the light. "These are my friends. I'm sure you'll understand if I don't share their names."

"Of course," Dorothy said after a long pause. She glared briefly and Gloria and I, then turned to Luci. "Look, I really shouldn't be doing this."

"Where have I heard that before?" Luci's tone was sweet, but her smile turned nasty. "It's fine, *darling*. Just hand over your keys, and we'll be out of your pretty red hair in no time."

"I don't think so. I'm risking enough trouble as it is without handing these over. I know what you're like. I'm not letting you run off and make copies."

That was, in fact, what Luci had been planning, though she feigned offense. We all exchanged a look. Dorothy radiated so much nervousness that it was difficult to focus on her thoughts. It might have been for the best if she just stayed behind, but we had no such luck.

"What is the plan, then, Miss Weathersby?" Gloria asked.

"I'm coming with you." Dorothy tried to sound confident but stumbled over her words.

"I don't know about that," Gloria said quietly.

"I don't know that we have much choice," Luci said, resigned.

I spread my thoughts just wide enough to link Luci and Gloria to me. *I could knock her out for a bit*, I sent. *You could take the keys then.*

Luci gave me a sharp look. *Safely?*

I shrugged.

Jealousy doesn't suit you, dearest, Luci sent. She turned back to Dorothy.

"I guess you're coming with us. Lead the way, Miss Weathersby."

We knew we would only have one chance at this, assuming Ralph was still here, and a week was a big assumption. It was obvious from Dorothy's expression that Luci had used up the last of the goodwill that came from her lingering attraction and guilt at the way their relationship had ended. Hence the gurney, and the van currently parked with forged staff credentials. If possible, I was to teleport us all to the van to make our getaway once we found Ralph. If not, we were hoping Dorothy could give us some cover while we wheeled Ralph out to the parking lot. Gloria carried her inscription supplies in her messenger bag. She secretly hoped she was up to the task of improvising whatever seals she needed to overcome what Dorothy's extremely limited authority and Luci's charm couldn't.

I, meanwhile, would be what Luci called "our ace in the hole".

While Dorothy locked the door behind us, I cast my focus over the entire building. The hallways of this floor and the two above us were mostly empty of staff. Patients occupied roughly half the rooms. A handful of duty nurses waited at desks or made their rounds, but on the first floor, we had a clear path from the staff door to the elevators if we started walking now. Only the ER was busy—there had been a bad car accident in town and apparently a nasty fight at a downtown bar. Triage was holding most of the hospital's attention, which I supposed was a good turn for us. I felt a stab of guilt immediately after that thought. It was tragic for the victims.

The one we wanted was empty. I gave Luci an apologetic look as I said Ralph wasn't there.

"I told you that already," Dorothy said to Luci. She refused to look at me. "Your friend Mr. Connor has been moved. I don't know where to."

"We'll find out," I said. "How long until a nurse makes another round in that hall?"

"Let *me* handle that," Gloria said, interrupting Dorothy before she finished her first word.

"I don't know if—" Dorothy began, her eyes wide, darting between the three of us.

"You *said* you would help us." Luci leaned in close to her. "You *promised*."

Dorothy's mouth worked wordlessly as Luci's perfume filled her nose. Five months of indistinct togetherness passed between them. Her breath caught in her throat. I could practically feel her pulse raising. She swallowed once. Then her shoulders slumped as she gave in. One hand crept to her ear, tugging it nervously.

"Follow me," she mumbled, grabbing the gurney for dear life.

We followed her through the halls in silence. Gloria was tense, expecting another staff member to jump out of every hallway and door, demanding to know what we were doing here. Luci was on the opposite end of the spectrum, radiating supreme confidence and only worrying about what we would find once we finally did reach Ralph. Dorothy was simply a bundle of nerves and desire. Her fear was practically written on every atom of her body. Obviously, the fact that she was committing a firing offense was at the forefront of her mind. Getting caught now would certainly end her nursing career before it really began. Not that she particularly liked volunteering at St. Audaeus. She had a deep-seated revulsion of the place, wrapped around a fear I couldn't quite perceive. Her memory wasn't scarred like Luci's, but it seemed to me she had a similar injury. I didn't want to peer too closely, both out of respect for her autonomy and concern for how it might affect her. I assumed I was perceiving her mind's attempt to protect itself from something horrible she'd witnessed. Certainly, Ralph Connor couldn't be the only unusual patient.

Halfway to Ralph's old room, I broached the subject with my usual tact.

"Why do you keep working at this hospital if you hate it so much?" I asked.

"What!?" Dorothy goggled at my abrupt question.

"Regina is a large metropolitan area. There are many hospitals to volunteer at, if you must. Presumably most of them don't carry the same terrors. Why stay here?"

I didn't want to ask outright if she was being compelled or deceptive. I only hoped that if either was the case, broaching the subject would make her think about it, bringing the truth to the surface. Or proof of whatever had been done to her mind. I immediately saw flashes of Dr. Sutherland and other officials, but they were doing nothing obviously untoward. Dorothy was simply afraid of them, and not without reason.

"I don't really have a choice," she said, hesitantly. "The nursing program at Del Sombra has an agreement with St. Audaeus. We put in volunteer hours each month, and they *have* to be here. To quit, I'd have to transfer to another school, and I just don't know that I can afford to."

Sweetie, what's this about? Luci sent.

I think they've done something to her. Maybe to all the staff. They might be interfering with all their minds, everyone who isn't part of the conspiracy.

That makes sense, Gloria sent. *If they're up to shenanigans, they have to keep the help quiet somehow. And there's Del Sombra attached to the conspiracy again.*

Yeah. I can't wait to find out what hideous nonsense they're up to in the journalism program. Luci's thoughts came with a sour taste, like biting into a lemon.

We turned into the passageway, and Dorothy picked up the pace, the gurney's wheels squeaking loudly as she sped down the hall. She let us in the room, parking the gurney against the wall and gesturing at the empty bed.

"There, you see? I don't know what else you were expecting to find."

"Nothing. At least, not at this time," I said.

"It would take too long to explain," Luci said, vaguely attempting to sound soothing. "How much time do we have?"

"I told you, let me worry about that," Gloria said.

She withdrew two sheets of paper out of her bag, connected with a length of ink-stained twine. One was marked with her well-refined power seal. I caught a glimpse of the Lethe Key on the other as she taped it to the door's outer face. She threaded the twine around the door and under the gap, then closed it. Sliding the power seal against the wall to keep it out of the way, she set up four candles, lit them, and concentrated, silently running the equation. Energy pooled within the power seal, then shot through the twine and across the door's outer face.

"There we go." Gloria dusted her hands off as she stood. "Now no one who looks at that door will remember it exists, at least as long as the candles are burning."

Dorothy stared, eyes wide. Gloria ignored her. She nodded to me, ready for me to do whatever I intended to do. I returned the nod and walked to the center. Closing my eyes, I cast my perception *back* eight days. It was easy, and not just because it was a short temporal distance. Between Gloria's weird science and my own teleportation, this moment was churning with temporal-spatial turbulence. It was like looking at the surface of a lake to see where a large stone had crashed through it; you would have to try hard *not* to find it.

Ralph lay screaming in his bed, his body wracked with seizures as tendrils of weird matter sprouted from his flesh. They flailed like a jam of sea anemones. The space around him rippled from the wake of our teleportation. The tendrils grasped for the seam left by our passage.

Ralph's mind was too full of pain for me to see anything else. The torment of our failed operation hadn't pulled his consciousness out of the gray haze surrounding it. At least, not yet. I didn't know what I could do to relieve his body's agony without making things worse. It was very likely there was nothing that could be done. I whispered a useless apology and hoped the doctor returned swiftly with morphine.

I forced my attention away from him, following the path of Luci's flight. It wasn't difficult; even across time, the red-gold warmth of her presence shone like a beacon. She had run down the hallway, screaming for Dr. Sutherland. He came barging around the corner with Mrs. Connor in tow, drawn by Luci's entirely genuine panic. She grabbed him by the arms before he could ask her what was wrong.

"You have to come quickly!" Luci said, any attempt at subterfuge abandoned. "Ralph is having a seizure!"

Without waiting for a response, she ran to Ralph's room, pulling Dr. Sutherland by one arm, Beverly Connor stumbling two steps behind. Two nurses rushed after them, not knowing what was going on but determined to help. Luci ignored the doctor's loud questions and Beverly's stammered pleas for explanation. Dr. Sutherland's round face went pale when he saw Ralph's writhing form. Beverly began sobbing, begging to know what had happened to her baby boy. One of the nurses fainted at the sight. Another crossed herself and whispered, "Mother of God." She couldn't have been more wrong.

Ralph Connor's body hovered a foot above the bed. The sheet had fallen, leaving the pulsating bulges in his abdomen visible for all the world to see. The tendrils of Watcher matter had ripped entirely through the bandages now and were clawing furiously at the empty air, splattering the walls and ceiling with thick ropes of ichor. His eyes stared into nothingness, but his throat strained against the tracheostomy tube as he emitted ceaseless glossolalia.

Dr. Sutherland said a foul word. Then he withdrew a small pewter medallion from his pocket. He held it aloft, cutting his thumb on the sharp edge, and intoned five significant syllables. A wave of pressure spread through the room, filling it with aggressive silence. The women stood stock still, mouths slightly open, eyes unfocused. From across two hundred hours of time, my skin crawled.

The doctor returned the medallion to his pocket. He pulled a handkerchief from the other and mopped his brow.

"Badly," he said. "This has all gone so badly."

Sutherland took Luci by the chin and turned her face up to face him. Her unfocused eyes stared blankly through his head. In the present, I ground my teeth. The walls trembled, drawing a gasp from Dorothy.

"I knew you would be trouble, Miss Sweeney," Sutherland said. "I didn't realize how much."

He exited, leaving the transfixed women behind him. He hurried to the nearest nurse's station. I still couldn't read his thoughts, but the relief on his face when he recognized the nurse was palpable. Tandy Sullivan, a middle-aged woman with dark hair and a stern expression. I couldn't read her thoughts, either.

"Nurse Sullivan," the doctor said. "Patient Connor's condition has worsened severely. Please see to him while I handle a related matter."

Sullivan nodded and picked up the phone receiver. As she dialed a number, Dr. Sutherland returned. He fiddled nervously with the medallion in his pocket, mopping his brow all the way. His expression was difficult to read, but I thought I detected a sense of frustration and defeat from the slump of his shoulders and the set of his jaw. I'd seen similar body language in various Bureau agents over the years when faced with an intractable case. I might have been sympathetic had he not been keeping my girlfriend's adopted brother prisoner. I couldn't feel satisfaction either. Not with Ralph suffering from our failure. Instead, I let anger burn within.

Once in Ralph's room, the doctor let out a long-suffering sigh then snapped his fingers. As one, the women's faces went from blank to engaged. They focused their attention on him in perfect sync. He led Luci, Beverly Connor, and the nurses out and down the hallway. Nurse Sullivan was waiting beside the door. She closed it behind the second nurse without looking at her. Sutherland gave her a perfunctory nod, then led his train of hypnotized witnesses through the hospital to the elevators. They crowded into the first to open and rode it down to the basement. He led them down the gently curving hallway to the third door on the right and ushered the four women inside. A slender man with wispy hair lay on a bed in the mostly empty room. He wore only a stained white shirt and underpants. He did not react as the other entered, nor when Sutherland closed the door behind him. His eyes flew open when the doctor said his name. It wasn't whatever label his parents had given him.

"*Zedu heth baagu.*"

The man's eyes twitched. His irises were colorless. He slowly turned his head to stare at the doctor. A thin line of spittle dripped from the corner of his mouth. The doctor said something indistinct—

And everything went blank.

But I could fill in the rest.

I turned to meet Luci's eyes. "We were right. It's in the basement. Whatever he did to you, he did in there. Room B03."

Dorothy's face paled. "You don't want to go down there. There's bad things down there."

"You're right," Luci said, "but that's where we're going anyway. Is Ralph down there?"

"Let me see."

I *turned back* to the moment of our failure. This time I didn't follow Luci, but instead anchored my attention to Ralph. I dove for the point at which she and the others followed Sutherland out. He continued to writhe, his body contorting into joint-cracking positions while Sullivan stood guard at the door, shooing away anyone who approached. She left Ralph alone, writhing in pain as his body continued to warp, for two hours and fifteen minutes. Until two identical blond men arrived, pushing a gurney. They wore identical one-piece jumpsuits, mostly blinding white with black shoulders connecting to a V-shape running down the torso. Brass pins were affixed over the left breast, displaying a stylized image of the Vitruvian Man superimposed over a sunburst. A stylized "N" and "A" surmounted the image.

The twins, if that's what they were, nodded to Sullivan in unison. She glanced at their pins and stepped out of the way. The twin in the lead opened the door, and they wheeled the gurney inside. The man in the rear closed it behind them, leaving Sullivan outside.

They stared up at Ralph for a moment. Then they pulled the sheet off the gurney, revealing a complicated apparatus that looked like four horns connected to a transistor radio by long rubber tubes. They set the horns on the corners of Ralph's bed. One of the men fiddled with the control mechanism. A high-pitched electrical squeal filled the space, setting my teeth on edge. It sounded like a handsaw being deliberately bent back and forth, wobbling aggressively up and down the pitch meter. Ralph's seizures didn't stop, but he slowly floated down. When he settled onto the bed, the nearest man withdrew an oblong coin from his pocket and placed it on Ralph's forehead. He held it in place while the other man tuned the mechanism again. The tone changed, and Ralph's shaking finally stopped. He didn't go limp, nor did the Watcher matter bursting through his skin. His entire body locked up, freezing him in place. The men grabbed his limbs and none-too-gently moved him to the gurney. One man strapped him down while the other packed up the apparatus. They set it on the gurney between his splayed legs and covered the whole thing with the blanket. Then they rolled him through the hospital and out the same side door we would use a week later. None of the hospital staff looked at them, other than Sullivan. Once they were gone, she locked the door and returned to her station.

The men had a van waiting. Its décor identified it as belonging to the Langley Flower Company. They loaded the gurney into the van and drove away. I wasn't sure whether I could still follow them, so I returned to the present.

"Ralph's almost certainly not here," I said. "Two men came and took him from the hospital not long after we left. They may be part of another group."

Luci said a rude word. "He's not here at all? You're sure?"

I swallowed my impulse toward a sarcastic response. Luci didn't deserve that. She was just worried. "Yes. I watched them take him away. It's possible that they brought him back later, but…"

"Most likely he's somewhere else. That makes sense," Gloria said. "After what happened on Saturday, they'd want him somewhere less public."

"Sure. Okay," Luci said. She paced, one hand to her head. "That complicates things, but that doesn't change the plan. They've got something nasty in the basement. I want to know what it is and take it from them."

I wanted to ask if she was sure that was the best course of action, but I could feel her determination and her affront. What Sutherland had done to her and the others was inexcusable, and she could not bear for him to do it to anyone else. Nor should she.

"It's your plan, darling," I said. "I'm with you. What next?"

She turned to Dorothy. "Which way to the elevator?"

Dorothy blanched but made no protest. Her fear was obvious enough that even Luci and Gloria should have been able to taste it. Despite that, she led us out after Gloria took down the invisibility seal, leaving the gurney behind. We followed her through the hospital along a now familiar path to the central elevators. The way was still empty of people. There were no nurses or staff to watch our procession and see something out of the ordinary. That should have been suspicious, but I suppose there were other things on our minds. I was and am a lot of things, but even I am not omniscient.

When the elevator doors opened, the three of us entered. Dorothy hung back, looking uncertain.

"Come on," Luci said. "What are you waiting for?"

"Look, I can get into a lot of trouble," Dorothy said, her pleading edging into a whine. "Can't you find the way on your own now?"

"No, we can't," Luci said, looking cross. "You know this place best."

"Not the basement."

"It's where we're headed next," Luci said. "We can't leave you behind."

"We're burning up time," Gloria said, her voice low.

Dorothy Weathersby stared at the three of us, her eyes full of fear, her mind full of fog. Her eyes pleaded for us to just let her go. To end her involvement in whatever we were up to. Unfortunately for her, we couldn't. We couldn't trust her to stay behind.

"Dorothy." Luci's voice was quiet but merciless. "You *promised*."

It worked as well on her ex-girlfriend as it would have on me. Dorothy stared at her for another heartbeat. Then she slumped her shoulders and stepped into the elevator. Luci released the "door hold" button and pressed the one marked "B". The doors closed smoothly. The elevator shuddered to life, then slowly lowered itself down the shaft. It was only eight feet, but somehow it felt as if we were slowly dropping into the bowels of the Earth.

The elevator finally shuddered to a stop. An emaciated man in a dirty hospital gown was sitting in a wheelchair, waiting for us. Bandages wrapped around his head, covering everything but his ears and wide, scarred mouth. More bandages wrapped around his limbs. The visible flesh was pale and jaundiced, drawn tight across atrophied muscles. Leather straps held his arms and legs to the chair. His head was bent to his chest, but when the elevator went "ding!" it lifted. The doors slid smoothly open, and his scarred mouth twisted into a dingy-toothed smile.

And then the whole world was red.

15

The police car cruised slowly down the curving street. No siren blared. It wouldn't do to disturb the good folks slumbering behind the curtains of eighteen identical houses lining both sides of the street. This was a nice neighborhood, after all, populated by good people with good jobs. No need to intrude on their quiet, upright lives just to catch one curfew breaker.

The car rolled through the next intersection, coming to a stop beside one of the suburb's seven identical parks. A hand-carved wooden sign declared it to be Nathan Bedford Forrest Community Park. Carefully arranged bushes surrounded the sign, each one trimmed with mechanical precision. No uncontrolled growth would be permitted here, no shocking change or deviation from the standard. The covenant declared that these decorative bushes would be 30 inches tall and 80 inches around, always. An inch out of bonds in any direction and the neighborhood association would have someone's head.

The patrolman in the passenger's seat leaned out of his window, shining a sun-bright flashlight beam across the park. The lance of red light revealed nothing but a splash of paint across the sign, blotting out the park's heroic namesake. Someone had finger-painted a rude word above it, but the culprit was nowhere to be seen. Lucille Sweeney had already moved on.

The patrolman clicked off his flashlight and returned to his seat. The police car drove on, red light strobing as it searched for the miscreant. They'd find her. They'd find her and put her in her place.

Luci watched them go from up a tree two feet from the vandalized sign. She let out a shaky breath when they turned left at the next intersection, disappearing behind another row of assembly-line ranch homes. Easing her grip on the branch above her, she silently counted to ten. When the patrol car didn't reappear, she let go of the branch and dropped quietly to the ground. Then she ran, cutting a diagonal path across the street in the direction the patrol car had come. This was a tricky run; she was going up the short side of the block three houses and then another intersection. So much open space. She'd stick out in the streetlight easily. Still, she only had to go up three blocks before making a right turn. A hedgerow ran between the sidewalk and the street. She could duck behind it, hidden from street view by the hedge and mostly from the first-floor windows by the machine-cut picket fences on the other side. It was far from perfect cover, but hopefully it would be enough. No one should be looking through the windows this late at night anyway. All the good people were snug in their beds, blissfully asleep. Safe from the dangers of the world outside, the fear and perversion of the city.

The city. If Luci could get to the suburb's rec center, she could find her way to the city. There had to be a map of the suburb there. She could finally escape this mass-produced Hell, back to the safety of the city, of people like her.

Luci leapt over the hedgerow and threw herself down on the sidewalk, palms and belly flat against the cold concrete. Her gaze darted left and right, taking in the street and the windows of the nearest house. Her heart pounded in her ears. She didn't dare breathe. Her breath would steam in the cold air, rise in a cloud above the hedge, give away her hiding place to any man chasing her. Her fingers and chin were numb, her body heat sinking into the frigid concrete. The nerves in her limbs screamed at her to run. The tension in her chest demanded she stay put.

A light clicked on. Red light spilled out into the night air as a silhouetted man pulled open the curtain. Luci clapped her hand over her mouth, holding in her breath. She forced herself to lie still, to ignore the chill seeping into her limbs. Better to freeze than be caught. Better to die than go back. To be "fixed".

Despite herself, she was counting. One, two, three, four. Numbering the seconds from her last breath. Eight, nine, ten, eleven. She could definitely make it to sixty. Sixteen, seventeen, eighteen, nineteen. She could probably make it to ninety. Twenty-five, twenty-six, twenty-seven, twenty-eight. By a hundred twenty, her lungs would be screaming. Thirty-four, thirty-five, thirty-six, thirty-seven. Her body would surely force her to take a breath before a hundred fifty. Forty-four, forty-five, forty-six, forty-seven. If she somehow made it to a hundred eighty, her brain would start to die. Fifty-two, fifty-three, fifty-four, fifty-five.

Luci's eyes slid up to the rectangle of red halfway up the dark house. The silhouette stood in the middle, one hand on the curtain. He turned left, then right, then left again. Scanning the street for whatever had disturbed his slumber. Had deviated from the norm.

Eighty-two, eighty-three, eighty-four, eighty-five. A convulsion ripped through Luci's body—whether from the cold or the tension in her limbs or her lungs begging for air, she couldn't say. Ninety-six, ninety-seven, ninety-eight, ninety-nine. Her lungs were burning now, her diaphragm spasming as her body reached for precious air. One hundred four, one hundred five, one hundred six, one hundred seven. Tears stung the corners of her eyes. It was so cold she expected them to freeze against her face. One hundred ten, one hundred eleven, one hundred twelve, one hundred thirteen. She was going to take a breath. She was going to suck in a lungful of cold night air and exhale a blast of steam that would alert the man in the window that he had a trespasser. One hundred sixteen. He was going to call the police. One hundred seventeen. They were going to take her away. One hundred eighteen. She was never going to see… see *her* again. One hundred nineteen.

What was her name? One hundred twenty. What was her name, what was her name *what was her name?*

The man in the window let go of the curtain. Two seconds later, the light went out. At one hundred twenty-five seconds, Luci let go of her mouth and sucked in a huge, cold breath. She exhaled in a slow, hot shudder. She huddled on the sidewalk for thirty seconds longer, waiting for the light to come on, for a flashlight beam to slash across the freezing night, for the policeman's boot behind her. There was nothing but darkness and silence. Eventually, Luci lifted her head from the cold concrete. She stared down the long stretch of sidewalk, her quiet breath steaming in the dark.

Luci pushed herself to her feet and took off running. She sprinted up the three blocks, houses blurring away to her right. At every crosswalk, she expected white headlights and flashing red lights, harsh voices shouting for her to stop. Instead, she saw nothing but streetlights, heard nothing but her own footfalls.

She couldn't believe her luck. She crossed the last short block without seeing a police car or another lit window. She stopped at the street corner, pausing briefly at the edge of the streetlight. She looked down the street to her left, the far border of the park. The last patrol car had disappeared in that direction. She looked to the right. A row of lights marked the path to the rec center. Fourteen streetlights. Sixty houses. A mile and a half, if even that. All she had to do was make it that far. Then she could figure out the next step. It was easy now. Duck behind the hedge and crawl. Pause at the driveway. Listen for a patrol car. Count to ten. Skitter across the driveway. Pause at the hedge again. Creep down the length of the next lawn and repeat. She would crawl to freedom one lawn at a time. Keep her head down and continue moving forward until she could escape. There was a place where she could be free again,

(again?)

where she didn't have to swallow herself to make it through another day. Swallow herself and a bottle of wine and a handful of pills to tolerate being married off to some man who thought he was king of one out of a thousand identical castles. No. She was cold and her palms were scraped and her knees were dirty and her dress was torn, and she'd take all of that over one more night in this prison.

It didn't have to be this way. But it was.

Down the street. Dash across an intersection. Duck behind a hedge. Crawl across an alley. Back against a trash can, one hand clamped over her mouth as a patrol car cruised down the street throwing beams of red light across the neighborhood. Twice they almost caught her. The first time she wedged herself beneath a hedge and counted down until the patrol car drove on. The second time she threw a glass bottle down the other end of an alley and took off running in the opposite direction. After that, she spent what felt like an hour curled up beneath the bandstand of the closest part, hoping without hope that she'd escape. She couldn't believe that she'd gotten away again. Surely, they had to have heard her. She must have made as much noise running as the trash can she'd knocked over.

Something creaked above her. Luci caught her breath and slowly turned her head. Through the dim glow of the streetlights, she could just make out the dark outline of someone standing above her. The boards creaked over her head as the stranger slowly walked around the bandstand. They stopped at the far side, then turned and came back. Back and forth. Back and forth. Was it a policeman? Were they searching for her?

Luci's heart beat a tattoo in her chest. Her breath came short and fast as the panic took hold. Her shoulders tightened and her fingers shook. She forced herself to breathe steadily, to uncurl from a ball. She needed to be ready to move.

Slowly, carefully, Luci rolled over. She turned her head to look at the hole she'd crawled through. It was a gap in the trim, maybe two feet across. She could see a stand of decorative bushes three feet away. If she was careful and quick, she could slip out and hide in the bushes, then see who was stalking the bandstand. If she had to, she could dart across the park to a new hiding place. What hiding place? She didn't know yet. It didn't matter. She couldn't stay here. She had to move.

Luci crept forward, inching her way to the gap. The boards above her creaked again and again as the stranger continued pacing. Her breath, hot and fast, had to be louder than his footfalls... He was following her. He knew about the hole. He was toying with her, waiting to reach down and pull her out. Take her... not home.

(regina)

it wasn't

(moved when I was)

her home was

(not colorado any)

it was red.

A heavy footfall thudded above her head. Luci froze, inches from the gap. Her shoulders hunched and her fingers dug into the cold earth. She waited for the policeman's shout. The hand reaching down to grab her neck. The long drive to the hospital. The sting in her arm, the sickness in the pit of her stomach. Would it only be the chemicals, or would they use electricity? Her hands became claws. She swore he'd at least lose an eye.

The wood groaned as the stranger turned. Footsteps clomped across the boards again, going the other way. He hadn't noticed her at all. She almost laughed. Then she darted through the gap, rolling into the bushes. She held her breath and curled up into as small of a ball as she could. She craned her neck high as she dared, trying to see the stranger through the screen of leaves.

The stranger turned. They crossed the bandstand again, putting a hand on the railing and peering out across the park. They'd heard her but couldn't see her. The stranger leaned forward until the streetlight illuminated them. Luci nearly gasped. It wasn't a cop. It was a girl, no older than Luci, wearing a simple crimson dress. Her blonde hair fell on either side as pigtails. Her wire-frame glasses glinted red in the streetlight.

Luci remembered another girl. A serious young woman with dark hair and a sensible gray dress. She and Luci were

(what are you doing)

she and Luci

(dirty)
were close. Her name was
(do that with other girls)
her name was her name was her name was ...

"Hello?" the other girl called, her voice a loud whisper. "Is someone there?"

Luci slowly uncurled. She wasn't sure about this stranger. She could be a trick. Even if she wasn't, two people together would draw more attention. Two would slow each other down.

"Hello?" the dark-haired girl said again (dark-haired?). She jumped down from the bandstand, crossing the wet grass to the bushes. "Are you trying to escape too?"

Two could watch each other's backs.

Luci remembered another girl. The one who lived down the street. The one who had never returned. And she slowly stood up.

"Yeah. I'm trying to get out of here, too."

The dark-haired girl's face dissolved into tears. "Oh, thank goodness. I thought I would never escape!"

Luci grabbed the other girl's hand and pulled her into the bushes as gently as she could.

"Quiet! Hide! We can't be out in the open like this!"

"Oh! I kn-know..." the dark-haired girl said, sniffling. "I-I-I've been ruh-running from the p-p-police all n-night."

"Yeah, same." Luci glanced over her shoulder, expecting a patrol car to come rumbling down the nearby street at any moment. "I don't know how many cars they have out right now. I never see more than one at a time, but that doesn't mean anything. One's enough to be dangerous. Last one I saw was heading—whatever that direction is. South? Doesn't matter. It was less than an hour ago."

"They c-could be anywhere. Anywhere they n-need to be," the dark-haired girl said. Red light glinted off her glasses again. "I don't know if there's a way out of here."

"The rec center," Luci said firmly. "There'll be a map of the suburb there. We can use that to find the train station. That'll take us to the city."

"The train won't be running. Not at this hour."

"But the tracks will still be there. They'll lead us out of here."

"Are you sure?"

"I'm positive." Luci nodded with conviction. "That was our plan. Get to the city. And then we could—"

"Our plan?" Behind the red glare, the dark-haired girl's face showed confusion.

"Yeah, way back when." Luci's voice stumbled. "She and I were gonna run away together."

There had been another dark-haired girl. Not the one with the shiny glasses or the one in the sensible dress. This girl had long, straight hair that fell down her back. A gingham dress. Pink lips that quirked up into a clever smile. She was thirteen. So was Luci. They were thirteen and they were

(unnatural!)

close.

"Luci?" Concern filled the dark-haired girl's young voice. She pushed her glasses up with one hand. "Is something wrong?"

Luci felt dizzy. Everything seemed so much bigger now. She pushed herself up on her thirteen-year-old legs and set her jaw.

"Yeah. Everything's wrong. I'm cold and I'm tired and I'm scared and I'm a weirdo. And I'm getting the hell out of here."

She held out her hand to the other girl. "You comin'?"

The dark-haired girl stood, brushing dead leaves from her gingham dress. She took Luci's hand. "You're so brave."

"I have to be," Luci said, with a cocky grin she knew was a lie. "Let's go."

The two young girls ran across the park together, hoping without hope that they were heading in the right direction. If they were, the rec center was only a few blocks away. Luci was sure of it.

They came to the sidewalk at the far end and saw flashing lights down the block, coming around a corner. Luci dashed across the street, pulling the dark-haired girl with her. They ducked into the alley between two houses, crouching behind the trash cans. They huddled together, clutching each other for comfort as they waited for the patrol car to pass.

"They *won't*," Luci said. "They didn't see us. They're going to drive past."

The red light strobed down the street as the patrol car drew closer. Despite herself, Luci's chest tightened. The rumble of the engine shook her in the middle of her stomach, growling like a predator ready to flush its prey. She shrunk down against the trash can, silently willing the car to keep moving, ready to bolt if it didn't. If she heard the car stop, the door open, she'd be off like a flash. The heavy thump of the policeman's boot on the asphalt would be her starter's pistol. She would run in whichever direction was open. She'd leave the dark-haired girl behind if she had to. Just like she'd left the other dark-haired girl. The first girl she'd ever

    (a sin!)

        would save herself. If she had no

          (doctors will fix her)

            other girl clung to her. Her sharp fingers dug into Luci's arm and shoulder. They had to have drawn blood. Her breath came hot on Luci's neck. It stank like rotten meat. Luci wanted to tell her to move away, to shove her, but she didn't dare make a noise.

The patrol car slowed. It drew even with the mouth of the alley, red light flashing down the gravel-strewn stretch between houses. The driver's window rolled down. Luci gritted her teeth, waiting for the policeman's shout.

The window rolled up. The patrol car pulled away. The growl of its engine diminished as it continued down the street. Luci let out a shaky breath, letting the tension ebb again. She covered the dark-haired girl's hand with her own, then pulled it away from her arm.

"You can let go now," she said.

The dark-haired girl did, with some reluctance. Luci looked at her bare arm, half-expecting to see a row of bloody crescent moons gouged into her flesh.

"I thought you were leaving me," the dark-haired girl said, her voice accusing.

Luci stared at her. She didn't know what to say. She found that she couldn't meet the dark-haired girl's gaze. She looked down at her shoes, guiltily.

"Like you left that other girl."

A sick chill skittered up Luci's spine. "What did you say?" she whispered.

"The other girl," the stranger said, matter of fact. Red light glinted off her glasses. "The one you left. The one you let them drag away."

"I didn't ... that's not—"

The world swirled around her. Her stomach lurched. Red light filled her vision.

"It was

(i was thirteen)

so long ago."

"You left her." The dark-haired girl leaned closer, her stinking breath fouling the fresh, cold air. "How could you do that?"

"That's not—"

She and the other girl giggled beneath the pale blue blanket, alone in their shared world. Their slim fingers intertwined. The other girl leaned closer. Her breath smelled like bubblegum. Her lips were so soft.

"Did you tell her you loved her?"

A heavy hand fell on her shoulder. A rough voice shouted the other girl's name, stinking of whisky and tobacco. They screamed.

"I... we were children... it's not—"

"Does that sound like love?"

She watched them through the bushes. A white van pulled up to the house. Two men in white opened the rear doors and pulled out a bed on wheels. They carried it into the house. Minutes later, they came out with the other girl strapped to the bed. The other girl's mother cried from the open door. Her father stood on the curb, face blank behind a cloud of cigarette smoke. The other girl called Luci's name as the men in white loaded the bed into the van. Her cries cut off when they slammed the van doors shut. Luci said nothing. She watched silently as the van drove away, taking the other girl.

"Do you even remember her name?"

"*Cora!*" Luci screamed, forcing a name through the red haze. "Her name was *Cora* and I *never* forgot her!"

A heavy hand fell on her shoulder. A flashlight beam filled the alley with red. The policeman hauled her to her feet.

"Got her!" he shouted.

Luci screamed in fear and rage. She swung a wild fist at the policeman. It smashed into his gut, which was solid as oak. He wrapped his arms around her waist and picked her up off the ground, carrying her to the patrol car in a bear hug. She kicked, striking nothing but air. The other policeman opened the patrol car's rear door, then grabbed at her feet. She flung one foot out, catching him across the nose with a satisfying crunch. The policeman's head whipped back, then jerked forward, like a poorly operated puppet. He stared at her for a moment. Then he struck her across the face. Red stars exploded around her. She snapped her teeth at his hand, but too slow. The world spun.

The second policeman grabbed her ankles, and the two swung her into the back seat. The second policeman slammed the door shut as she was diving for the gap. She banged her fists against the glass, to no avail.

As the patrol car drove away, the dark-haired girl stood in the street, watching her. An eerie smile stretched too far across her face. The lenses of her glasses burned with red light.

16

Raucous laughter filled the dining room. Champagne flowed from fluted glasses into wide, grinning mouths like fizzing liquid gold, but these people needed little lubrication to celebrate. Vicious gossip and witty *bon mots* made their way around the long table, fusing with plates of canapes and other appetizers. This one is sleeping with that one's husband. That one is embezzling. He has a second family hidden upstate, hadn't you heard? And can you believe what she's wearing?

If they looked up, they would see the moon through the high window on the dining hall's northern wall, hanging full and red in the dark sky. Not that these people would look up. Not unless it was to admire the fine glass of the chandelier or the expensive paintings. The moon meant nothing to them, nor the nine stars in the east that marked the Sign of the Gate. These people feasted on food and wine, the cost of which would feed entire families for years, happy and comfortable in a house marked by the Sign of *Tahmu-Ammon*, known by the Wise as Hell's Banker. The high window was his sigil, worked in wrought iron and colored glass so it could catch the moon's rays as it rose. Beneath crimson moonlight, the Illuminated and their wives and mistresses celebrated their plenteousness.

Gloria stepped out of the kitchen hall with a tray of *salmon en papillote*. The smell wafting from the fish made her mouth water and stomach grumble. One might think the help would eat well after the feat, once the men had finished their cigars and brandy and retired to their rooms. Or someone's rooms, at least. The salmon was no doubt delicious—her brother was the head chef and the best cook in the county. But even as she held out the tray for a society lady to take her helping, Gloria knew she'd never taste it. The food that remained would be thrown out with the rest of the waste. The butler's evil eye would be on them as it was disposed of. Any leftovers would go to the dogs before they'd go to the help. Even the scraps on their plates, and there would be a full meal left on each. These folks couldn't stop themselves from taking more than they needed.

The Illuminated and their women didn't see Gloria as she passed. They saw the silver tray. The immaculate white gloves. The fake smile plastered across her face. But Gloria herself? Her, they looked right through. It was impressive, in a horrible sort of way. Taking food from a tray held aloft by nothing more than a pair of gloves. Reducing an entire person down to nothing but the service they performed for you.

Gloria knew them, though. Not every face had a full name, but they all had at least a title or a description. Something that summed up what they were to one another, or the terror they had inflicted on the help. Here was Mitch Haight, the banker, and his wife, who chaired the boards of various fashionable charities and was known to slap any maid who looked at her "with disrespect". There was Mr. Wolfe and his mistress; he was a Great White Explorer, she ought to be home on a school night. There was the one they called "Dicky"; he had come alone, but was sleeping with Judge Carlton Mann's wife, sitting across from him. There was the one at the far end of the table, who was difficult to look at and whose voice sounded like a saw blade on rusty metal. A half-dozen others, all rich as sin and too bored or greedy to be satisfied with the mundane world. And the worst of them all, the old man sitting at the head of the table. The man in ornate black robes with gold filigree. A thick white sash across his barrel chest, bearing a gold sunburst pin. He wore a black blindfold with the eye in the pyramid embroidered in red thread over his right eye but could see as clear as day. His name was

(his name)

    Maxwell

(his name was)

the old man. They only called him the Old Man. This was his house, under the Sign of Hell's Banker. His country. His world. And like every soul in it, Gloria was nothing more than another tool. A tool that only mattered when he needed to use it.

Which meant the Old Man knew nothing of the books she had secreted out of his library.

Gloria understood that everything about this was wrong. She wanted nothing more than to leave the hall, go to her room, where, if she was right, she had an escape. There had been yet no time for that, not with all the preparations for tonight's dinner party. If she missed her appointed tasks, she'd suddenly become very visible. No way to escape chastisement for such an unforgivable act. So she kept her head bowed and kept moving forward, on a path that led her down and around this long hardwood table, pausing at each place setting to offer her tray. Half of them ignored her. Half of them took a helping far too large to eat after so many courses. And one made her heart stop when he spoke.

The man's voice, if he was a man, was like a fistful of rusty nails being dragged over a tin roof. The intonation dug into her ears and hooked into her nervous system. She could feel them crawling down her spine, along her nerves, a swarm of radio ants biting and stinging. There were no words, but there was information.

She felt like an insect under a magnifying glass, with the noonday sun overhead.

"Salmon, sir?" she asked, her fake smile faltering.

The smile on the other face (was it a face?) widened. A hand rose to touch the tray. The barest pressure guided the tray down. A second hand lifted the spatula and claimed two filets.

The guest at the end turned away from her. Gloria felt her heart start beating again as she moved past. She bent to offer her tray to the next guest—Mr. Wolfe's mistress, who was turning up her nose at another guest's vulgar joke. Then the guest at the end spoke again. This time, Gloria swore she understood him.

///goodluck///

She dared not turn around. She kept her smile fixed and her tray level as, one guest at a time, she made her way up the table. Back straight, she left the dining hall through the double doors to the kitchen hallway. She locked eyes with the next server, carrying a tray of steaming roast. They said nothing, but the other woman gave her a slight nod before fixing her own fake smile to her lips. There was nothing to say. The banquet continued. The servants' dance continued. More dishes left the kitchen on silver trays, spinning widdershins around the long table. The trays came back half-full, their contents unceremoniously dumped in a trash bin. Like water in a prayer wheel, churning out a hymn to excess and waste.

But Gloria was ducking out of it. Dropping her tray in the soapy sink, she mumbled a whispered apology and hurried to the cold storage. The other servants watched her go with sympathy. They recognized the look in her eyes. They had all been there. It was more than the degradation of serving their haughty "betters". It was the song of the guest at the end of the table playing up and down her spine, tingling her finger and toe tips.

Gloria walked to the cold storage and rested her head against a wire rack. The cold metal leeched the heat from her forehead. She imagined the tension flowing up her limbs and out through her head. Let the contempt go with it, let the disgust and the disrespect heaped upon her skin dissipate in the cleansing cold. Most of all, let that horror man's song go along with it. Gloria's education might have been largely self-directed, but she had gathered what knowledge she could beneath the selfish gaze of the house's so-called master. She knew what the guest at the end of the table was.

"The Ageless Stranger, whose voice is a sickness, whose laughter is venom."

He, or it, had appeared in a dozen grimoires and esoteric histories scattered throughout the Old Man's library. Usually in the margins, always as a warning. And these fool white men had invited him as a dinner guest. Gloria had to get out of this hell before she was consumed in their folly.

She heard a cough from the door and looked over her shoulder. Her brother stood in the entrance, love and concern written across his dark face. It was a look she'd seen so many times. When she'd fallen and skinned her knee, when she'd come home from school crying, when she'd been stuck at home with the younger boys while he and his friends were out in town. Even here, even now, it touched her heart. Even when she knew better.

"Shouldn't you be seeing to dessert?" she asked with a sad smile. "That greedy old man will have your head if it doesn't come out just right."

Her brother said that he let one of the junior cooks handle the cake. She didn't quite make out the other man's name, to no surprise.

"He's got steady hands," her brother said. "Better for the frosting. Are you all right? Did those men—?"

"They didn't say nothing that matters," Gloria said. "Nothing for you to worry about."

She crossed the room and put an arm around her brother's big shoulder, letting herself feel safe against his broad chest for a moment. A moment was all she would allow herself.

Because I don't think you're real, she thought.

She tried to build a symbol in her mind, a silver circle crisscrossed with lines and loops. She imagined energy racing along it, writing a shimmering pattern in blue fire. She tried to hold the image in the front of her mind, just as she had a hundred times since she woke up here. In this house under the Sign of *Tahmu-Ammon*.

Her brother shimmered. A sick red light filled the cold storage closet. Gloria felt *change*, like a needle skipping over a scratched record.

The image fell apart, as it had a hundred times before. Her big brother stood in the entrance to the cold storage, as real and solid as an oak tree. His face was a picture of love and concern stolen from an eight-year-old girl's memory. She couldn't remember his name, not for love or money.

"I have to go," she said. "I'm not feeling well all of a sudden."

"What about dessert?"

"Have…" She reached for another serving girl's name and failed to grasp it. "Have that pretty girl you keep looking at serve it. She owes me."

She said it with such conviction that it might as well have been true. The pretty girl, she was sure, was taken from a memory of a neighbor four doors down. Her brother had, in fact, been sweet on her. He hesitated, but as she spoke, the connection formed inside his head. When she put a hand to his arm and squeezed, he nodded.

"Run upstairs and get some rest," he said. "We've got the rest of the dinner."

"I'll be back when it's time to eat," she said, hoping to mollify him. She felt silly saying it, but there was such a look of relief on his face. The exact look her real brother had when their middle brother turned up late but safe.

Gloria slid past him and ducked into the servant's hall, ignoring the dirty looks from her phantom coworkers. None of them mattered. They probably wouldn't even be there once the door closed behind her. Nothing mattered except getting to her room before her roommate returned.

In contrast to the rich décor in the front of the house, the servant's hall was bare boards and exposed wires. A narrow strip of wood hardly wide enough for a single person, it looked like the builders had laid down the floors and walls and then left for a break and never returned. There was electricity, at least, the bare red wires running along the inside of unfurnished, uninsulated walls. The wall on her left was studded with doors leading to work rooms, storage rooms, laundry rooms, all the chambers where the real housework was done. All except for the door in the middle, which opened onto a narrow stairwell. The servant's quarters waited atop the one flight, two dozen tiny, two-person rooms. The men lived on the north end of the hall, the women on the south. Two doors kept the men's and women's quarters locked off from one another after hours. The head maid kept the key to the women's quarters, the butler the key to the men's. To protect the virtue of the maids, which was at least three different tasteless jokes. It wouldn't protect a single woman from the men at the front of the house if one of them should happen to catch a rich white man's eye.

It made more sense to Gloria to keep a supply of preventatives on hand and let folks do what they were going to do safely. Not that it would benefit her directly; she'd figured out long ago that she wasn't interested in that sort of thing. It would save a lot of energy spent trying to prevent people from doing what most of them were going to do anyway. And without the Miss Grundies keeping their judging eyes peeled for horseplay, it would be easier for Gloria to get away with her own shenanigans.

The hall, fortunately, was empty. Everyone was still downstairs serving the party. Either none of the snitches had gone running for the head maid or her brother had successfully intervened.

You sure do have a low opinion of people, Miss Lane, she thought. *Or of the sort of shades that populate this trap.*

She opened her door carefully. Her roommate was nowhere to be seen. She let out a quiet sigh of relief and ducked inside, closing the door behind her. There was no lock. Nice girls didn't need to lock one another out, the head maid always said. She considered dragging the one chair in front of the door but dismissed the idea. It would only cause more commotion if someone did come looking after her. She would simply have to work quietly and quickly.

It only had to work once.

A small chest sat at the end of each bed, the meager storage for their personal effects. Gloria's chest held a few sets of clothing for her infrequent nights off, and beneath that, her journal and a small tin box. The journal was stuffed with loose pages—the fruits of Gloria's late-night searches in the house library—and her attempts to pour out her own compromised memories. The box held what supplies she'd scrounged—candles, matchbooks, a few sticks of charcoal, and other sundries. As magical tools, they were pretty tatty, but Gloria knew the truly important factors were her knowledge and her will. She could only hope she'd gathered enough of both.

She laid the book and the tin open on her bed and flipped through the pages of the journal. Each was covered with many interlocking circles,

connected by curving lines. The symbols
  (keys)
              were like gears; if she could arrange them correctly, they would form a machine that would open the door to this cage. Whatever this trap was, she'd escape.

She had labeled the circles after her previous attempts. Each symbol did *something*, she just wasn't certain exactly what. She *had* known, but her memories were frustratingly blank. Lost to the red. She had picked up some answers from the library of the Illuminated, but not enough. Their knowledge was too well-hidden. Or, more likely, was far less complete than they believed.

As was hers. She knew more, she was certain of it. Something was hiding it from her. She could feel the pressure at the back of her mind when she tried to recall the details. It was building now, as she flipped through the journal, finding the symbols she would need. This circle here, it was important; one of the most. The
  (seal)
              machine was built around it. It described people, somehow. This other was for protection, a third for fire. She selected the ones she was sure of and copied them onto a blank page, connecting them with lines that hopefully described the way the light would flow through the machine. Turning the gears. Generating the effect she needed.

She drew each line as precisely as she could—if the machine was flawed, it might sputter out, or it might explode in her face. But she also worked quickly, because she wouldn't be alone for long. She couldn't do what she needed to do from a makeshift lab in a room she shared with a busybody.

As soon as she completed the thought, the air in the room changed. Behind her, the second bed creaked ever so slightly as a body settled onto the mattress. She gritted her teeth and set the charcoal stick down, trying not to smear her formula in the process. She hadn't heard the door open, but that never seemed to matter.

"Good evening, Prudence," she said without turning around.

"Hullo, Glory," her roommate said. "You're not working with the others."

"I came over poorly all of a sudden," Gloria said.

"So you came upstairs to kneel in front of your bed and draw funny circles again," Prudence said. There was a giggle in her voice that Gloria's hand itched to slap out of her mouth.

Her hand twitched, but she resisted the urge. Instead, she turned around, careful to keep her workings hidden behind her. Prudence sat in the middle of her own bed, one stockinged leg crossed daintily over the other. Her black and white maid's uniform was perfectly pressed, as always. Her head was cocked to one side, as if she thought Gloria was doing something particularly curious. A smile that was nearly a sneer hung across her dainty face. The one face that Gloria was certain hadn't been pulled from her memories.

Prudence's glasses glinted with red light.

"I don't see how it's your business what I came upstairs to do, Prudence," Gloria said. She deliberately turned her back to the other maid, focusing on her journal. She carefully selected a candle from the tin and placed it in the middle of a circle labeled "Hearth".

"It's my business if it gets the rest of us in trouble," Prudence said, her voice hot with venom. "It's all well if the master gets up to heathenry. Don't you drag it up here."

"That's the difference between us, Pru," Gloria said. "I don't have a master."

She grabbed a matchbook just as Prudence jumped up from the bed. Before she could do anything, Prudence grabbed her wrist and pulled it back painfully.

"What's this? Lighting candles?" Prudence said, laughing cruelly as she twisted Gloria's wrist. Flares of pain ran up her arm. "Did you really think that was going to do anything?"

Gloria grinned through the pain. She leaned in close to Prudence.

"Of course not," she hissed. "The candle's not real."

She fixed the symbol she'd drawn in the forefront of her mind, running through the equation.

"I don't think anything here is real except for you and me. I just thought it would distract you."

The engine flared to life inside her head. Lines of blue fire ran through symbols that described the length and width of a circle full of light. Into the central circle, the one marked "Demon".

Prudence screamed as a pulse of power erupted from Gloria's machine. The bare walls and floor melted away, replaced with cold blue and white tile. Prudence's bed and storage chest disappeared, while Gloria's transformed into a hospital gurney. Prudence vanished like morning fog. In her place was a withered figure in a dirty hospital gown, collapsed into the seat of a wheelchair. A dirty cloth wrapped around its head, covering its eyes and ears. Leather straps bound its arms and legs to the chair. The stranger's head was cocked to one side, jaw falling slackly open. Rotting teeth jutted out from cracked and bleeding gums.

It made a rattling noise. Gloria wasn't sure if it was laughing or crying.

Gloria looked down at her clothes. She was wearing a tartan skirt and a turtleneck, the same clothes she wore the night she broke into St. Audaeus with Luci and I. She could remember that. She could remember everything now.

Her clothes weren't soiled. Her mouth was dry but not gross. It couldn't have been long, then. An hour or two at most.

"An hour or two," she whispered. "You did all that to me in an hour or two."

She looked around for the rest of us but saw nothing but murky air. She was kneeling in the center of a hemisphere that only extended for a few feet around her. Reality crackled at the edges of the spell. As she watched, the bubble rippled and pulled in two inches.

Because there was no seal in reality. She had drawn it in the dream-world. Which meant it only existed within her mind. She was powering it with her own metabolism. That might work for me, but Gloria knew it was something she couldn't do for long.

The creature in the chair rattled at her, and this time Gloria was positive it was laughing.

17

The chair's metal seat was cold against my bare thighs. I have always maintained that the cold doesn't affect me, but the men behind the glass had at last found an extreme of temperature that could trouble my human flesh. My muscles seized painfully as they tried to shiver some warmth into my body. At least, as best they could with the leather straps holding my limbs fast to the chair. I was bound at the chest, forearms, wrists, and calves. So tightly bound that my convulsions should have sent the chair toppling over with me in it, had someone not thoughtfully bolted it to the cement floor.

The clicking-clacking noise echoing across the chamber nearly drove me to my wits' end until I realized it was my teeth chattering.

I couldn't tell the temperature, but the observation room on the other side of the glass had a gauge. It read -50 degrees Celsius. I ought to be dead. Certainly, the three men observing me thought so.

The glass was meant to be one-way, but of course that was meaningless for someone with my perspective. Leather straps could contain my body, but they still hadn't figured out a way to restrict my senses. I could see the three men watching me, three men in black suits with pale, sour faces and sharp, poking fingers. They stroked their pointy chins with dry, bloodless fingers and muttered to one another in sneering voices. Behind them, a quiet woman in a shapeless dress sat at a small desk, hunched over a legal pad. She scribbled the agents' every utterance in shorthand. Filled legal pads littered the floor around her. We had been at this for a very long time.

Red light glared down from a recessed bulb in the ceiling, directly over my head. It was as bright and merciless as the noonday sun, yet somehow it provided no more warmth than the merciless eyes of the agents. Their thoughts were hidden from me, although I didn't need to read their minds to know their intentions. There was no mental static, not like the Bureau's Specials, nor the strange sensation of slick glass like the remnants of the Apollonian Society. Instead, their thoughts reflected between the three of them and back at me, a cacophonous echo of malice that drove a spike of hostility into my mind. It was a neat trick, and a nasty one. I couldn't help but feel the echo when my attention drifted toward them, and what else was there to focus on in this blank, red-lit frozen cube? In contrast, the quiet woman's mind was simply silent, blank. An empty room. I'd never seen that before. Perhaps it was how she'd learned to protect herself from the horrors of her job—by shutting down entirely.

"Another five degrees?" the agent on the right asked, his thin lips twisting into something that might be a smirk.

"Why not?" replied the agent on the left.

He lifted his skeletal hand and snapped his fingers. A sound like dry twigs breaking echoed through the observation room. The quiet woman stood and shuffled across the room with her head down, her indistinct face hidden behind lanky blonde hair. She put three trembling fingers to the dial beneath the temperature gauge and rotated it exactly five degrees. Then she shuffled to her seat and sat down heavily. Lifting the pen as if it was a great weight, she noted the time and the change.

Above me, the great machinery controlling the chamber's air flow roared a touch louder. Over the course of ten long minutes, I felt the chamber grow that much colder. I glared at the one-way glass through frost-rimmed eyelashes, directly into the flat eyes of the agent in the middle.

"Fascinating," he said, his voice wheezing like air out of a punctured bellows. "I'd almost believe it could see me."

"Entirely possible," the agent on the right said. He removed his wire-rimmed spectacles and drew a handkerchief from his breast pocket, polishing the lenses between his narrow finger and thumb. "Experiments 95 through 157 all indicated a degree of extrasensory perception."

"Exact degree still inconclusive," the agent on the left said. He stuck the pinkie of his right hand into his ear, twisting it, then bringing it to his nose for a sniff. He wrinkled up his face at the result and flicked it away. "Subject 19 was non-compliant with procedures."

"Hence the switch to measuring environmental adaptation," the agent in the middle said.

He bent forward, folding neatly at the waist. One hand clicked the switch of the microphone protruding from the base of the one-way window. He stopped with his dry mouth inches from the apparatus.

"If you are ready to cooperate," he said, enunciating each word as if it hurt his bloodless lips to move, "we can return to the schedule of sensory capability experiments. If not…"

He shrugged.

"Repetition is the bedrock of scientific inquiry."

I sat quietly in the chair, my breath steaming in the frozen, red-tinged air. My ten-year-old frame hung stiffly against the leather straps. I willed my swollen tongue to move, then my numb lips to part. As if I was pushing a heavy boulder up a hill, I worked up a small measure of saliva and spat it at the one-way glass.

It crystallized into ice immediately and dropped to the cement a foot away, cracking into three pieces as it skittered across the floor. As acts of defiance went, it was far from impressive. Still, it got my point across.

The agent in the middle looked at me as if he was sucking on a lemon. Although, in fairness, that was just the way his face was shaped. He bent forward again and clicked the microphone on.

"Experimentation team will break for lunch. Experimentation will resume with direct stimulus methods in one hour." His eyes glittered with malice. "Subject 19 will remain in place for... stationary observation."

He turned to the quiet woman. "Stay here and observe. Leave this room before we return, and you can join it in the testing chamber."

The quiet woman only bowed her head in response. The three agents filed out through the door in the rear of the observation room, snickering to one another. After a moment, the quiet woman recorded the time of their departure. Then she dropped the pen and sat with her hands in her lap, like a toy that had wound down.

I stared at her, reaching into her empty mind, for thirty breaths. Thirty clouds steamed into the frigid air before dissipating. We both sat still, my mind working furiously despite the chill, hers a bowl with no water. I looked for some sign that she was active, a twitch in her limbs or face, a groan or sigh, a shift in her seat. There was nothing. She was perfectly still, doll-like except for her breathing, which was so regular it could have been used as a metronome. She couldn't have been a person, but I couldn't guess what she really was.

I cast my perception out, trying to map the facility. It was eerily impossible. Whatever wards that had been put in place around the chamber were too good. I could sense the boundaries of the chamber, a cube ten feet on each side. An attached observation room extended the space, the same length and height but half the depth. Beyond that was the hallway the agents had exited into, but I had only detected that when they'd opened the door. I had no sense of its dimensions. It faded out of my perception three feet from the door. Another door stood behind me, but I could sense nothing about the space beyond it. Even though the agents had brought me into the chamber through it.

Hadn't they?

I thought back to my arrival at this place and found
    (elevator door)
        discontinuity. I

(we went to the basement)
couldn't
(pressed the button)
couldn't remember
(through the side door)
I couldn't remember
(strawberry blonde, screaming)
couldn't remember how I got here
(ding!)

I realized ten minutes later that I was screaming.

I flung my small body forward against the straps. The thick leather bit into my slender limbs and chest as I strained against the bonds. The chair began to give, cold metal screeching as it scraped against the bolts. I remembered that I had other arms tucked away at right angles to everything. They lashed out at the walls and floor, gripping fast. The cement cracked beneath me, sending cold chips flying every which way. My limbs strained, dragging me forward. The cement shattered as the bolts of the chair's rear legs ripped free of the slab. A sound like dry bones rattling in a metal cup filled my ears and *(doors open, someone sitting in a chair)*
discontinuity.
(the doors slid closed)

I sat shivering in the steel chair, my feet planted firmly on the smooth cement floor. The red glare of the recessed light beat down on me. My limbs ached deep inside, from the cold and the seizing. Droplets of sweat had crystallized into ice chips across my face, chest, and limbs, glittering crimson in the light.

The quiet woman's head jerked up, as if someone behind her had yanked on a string. Thoughts squeezed into her mind like dough from a tube, red and thick, filling the hollow space. She unfolded jerkily into a standing position. She turned away from the table and took two steps forward, toward the one-way glass, hands folded neatly behind her.

That wasn't as clever as you thought it was, she sent.

I winced at the words dropping into my mind, scattering across it like chips of hot, red glass. I tried to make words with my mouth, but my blue lips were too numb to form shapes. All that came out was a chattering moan.

The quiet woman cocked her head to one side.

You needn't bother with sound. Like an animal. So vulgar.

What are you? I sent.

An instrument. A means to an end. The Eye sees and the Cage imprisons.

What end? Torturing me?

The quiet woman cocked her head to the other side. Curiosity bounced across her mind.

Containment, she sent. *Your pain is irrelevant. It is simply what I found inside you. Inside most of you. It seems to be an inevitable consequence of this plane's physical laws. Like heat or gravity.*

Inside me. Inside
        (strawberry blonde, roses in summer)
    most of
                (messenger bag packed with power, a hearth in winter)
                    inside my friends.

The walls shivered. The light above me flickered, then flared so brightly the temperature raised a couple of degrees. Pain stabbed into my mind, but there was more of my mind than what was here, wasn't there? More than the pain could reach.

Luci and Gloria! My friends are Luci and Gloria and... and the other one. Luci's old girlfriend.

The quiet woman stepped away from the one-way glass. I could feel the fear flickering across her human-shaped mind.

Where are they? What have you done with them?

The air whipped into a tight torus. My friends were missing. I was in the agents' clutches. But I wasn't in this body. I wasn't ten years old anymore. I wasn't what they had tried to force me to be, the boy they had tried to cram me into. I never was, and I never would be again.

"You *dare* confine *me?*" I screamed.

I stood, my limbs and torso lengthening to their proper height as the chair shattered behind me. Dark hair spilled down my back as it rejected the short boy-cut. The hair whirled around my head, snapping like angry tendrils. Elsewhere, my other limbs thrashed at empty space. I flung one at the wall, smashing it against the one-way glass. It bowed inward, cracks spiraling across its surface. The quiet woman fell back, screaming. An alarm screamed in harmony with her. The door to the observation room burst open, the three agents spilling into the room. I braced myself, readying my limbs to attack. I lunged forward and

(luci pressed the button marked "b")

discontinuity.

(the doors slid open)

Space spun around me and

(ding!)

the first agent pulled the door open. The other two dragged me inside, fingers digging into my arms. I realized, too late to react, that the scene had changed. No longer in the observation room, now I was in a tiny prison cell. They threw me onto the concrete floor, then ran out of the room. A red lamp burned above the metal door. The first agent slammed it shut with a bang that echoed across the small space. The lamp winked out as he rammed the deadbolt through.

I pushed myself off the floor. I stood in the center of the room, rubbing life back into my limbs as I took stock of the space. It was even smaller than the laboratory chamber, only seven feet to a side, and somehow even more featureless. The single steel door and the lamp above it were the only fittings. The floor, walls and ceiling all appeared to be poured black concrete. My sense of the space beyond the door was already disappearing.

At least it was warmer here. My body, thankfully once again seventeen going on eighteen, tingled painfully as feeling returned to my frozen flesh. It wasn't a sensation I was eager to ever repeat.

"Where am I?" I asked no one in particular.

No answer. My voice echoed across the room, mockingly.

"Who are you?"

Again, no answer but my own reflected voice.

"Where are my friends?"

The echoes bounced around me and through one another, combining into a haunting susurrus. My reflected voice grew louder with every rebound until I feared my own echoes would deafen me. I clapped my hands to my ears, but it was no use. My plaintive questions mocked my imprisonment, my friends' disappearance. A deep rage rose inside of me. I clenched my teeth until I thought they would crack. My fingers dug into the sides of my scalp. The floor beneath me trembled.

"*Give them back or I'll tear this place apart!*" I screamed.

The lamp above the door snapped on, filling the nearly empty room with its red glare. I felt a sudden sick sensation in the pit of my stomach as the room tilted. I stumbled backwards, then fell head over heels, tumbling as the floor became a wall, the wall behind me became the floor, and the door opened on the ceiling. An agent appeared in the doorway, strong-arming another person forward *(down)* into the room. One hand on the base of their neck, the other on their arm, twisting it painfully behind their back. The agent shoved the prisoner into the room. They stumbled three feet forward before collapsing painfully on the floor *(wall)* in a splash of dirty water. The agent slammed the door shut. The light snapped off again. Gravity returned to its previous configuration, and I fell to the floor with a knee-scraping *smack*.

The prisoner groaned and pushed themselves up. They pushed their hair out of their face. To my immense disappointment, it wasn't Luci or Gloria, nor the third woman. Lucas Dowling's face glared at me through damp hair.

"What a fine mess you've gotten us into."

I shifted my legs around, coming off my scraped knees to sit on the black floor. I wrapped my arms around them and pulled my legs to my chest, regarding my companion over the horizon of my kneecaps. They were bleeding. Somehow that didn't seem fair.

"You're here," I said, my voice flat. "That explains most of this. We're not in the physical world."

The Watcher-As-Lucas smirked. "Enjoying your mind prison? Finding it pleasant?"

"You were going to eat an entire town. Don't try to play the victim," I said.

I looked around the small room. It was still the only place I could detect. Now I suspected it was the only place that existed, at least for the moment.

"I am not finding it pleasant," I admitted. "As a matter of fact."

"No entity can thrive confined to such a small space," the Watcher-As-Lucas said. Their tone was now reflective, rather than sneering.

I looked down at my knees, remembering the laboratory chamber. I'd accepted it so readily because it was familiar. It had clearly been drawn from my memory of another laboratory. A horrible one, under the control of a horrible man. This tiny space was familiar, too, and drawn from a worse memory.

Agent Carlisle screamed at me. He called me a monster. He swore he would tame me. Then he struck me across the face, not for the first time. But this time, I struck back.

Other agents surrounded me, corralling me with metal cards that only brought pain. They threw me into a tiny room. Into *this* room. And they left me here alone for one year. I turned six years old, alone in the dark.

"No," I said. "I certainly never did."

I lifted my head and met the Watcher's eyes. Dowling's had been dark, but the Watcher's irises were colorless, swimming with greasy fluid. They couldn't hide the entity's fear. Nor the barest touch of sympathy.

"We must find a more humane solution for dealing with you," I said. "If we can escape this."

"You're doubtful," the Watcher said. Their emotional state was a mixture of fear and confusion.

"I don't know what's happened to us. To any of us," I said. "I can't ... I can't *remember* things."

I jumped to my feet and paced around the room. One hand slid across the rough black wall, the other clenched and unclenched rapidly. The Watcher moved to the exact center of the room, crouched in their puddle of dirty water and watching me with trepidation.

"I don't know how I got here. I didn't know Luci and Gloria's names until moments ago. I still can't remember the name of Luci's ex-girlfriend, although at least I can remember that there was a fourth person now. I'd even forgotten you existed until they threw you in here."

"We are unsure—" the Watcher began.

"*I don't forget things!*" I shouted. "I remember *everything* that ever happened to me! Until now! Now I can't remember anything before—I don't even know how long ago it was. I've never not known the passage of time. I have no *references!* Not time, not space, *nothing!*"

The Watcher shrank away. I ignored them, continuing my angry stalk around the room. "What could have done this? The dream eater? Did it steal my entire life?"

I stopped pacing and rested my head against the wall. It was cold stone, rough against my skin. Hot tears burned at the corners of my eyes.

The Watcher waited for me to resume ranting. After ten breaths, they said quietly, "You remember the dream eater. That's interesting."

"Not until just now. I don't remember where I encountered it. I just remember that it exists."

"It was the hospital. But you didn't encounter it. Your... the Luci entity did."

I clenched my hands into fists. The Watcher was silent again, waiting for my outburst. When they were sure one wasn't coming, they resumed.

"We do not think this was *zedu heth baagu.*"

I lifted my head, turning to face them. It wasn't strictly necessary—I could perceive them equally well from any angle—but it seemed like something a human would do. Hot tears spilled down my cheeks. I didn't bother wiping them away.

"Why not?"

"This is rather beyond a dream eater, Ama-... Amelia," the Watcher-As-Lucas said. "To ravage a mind so thoroughly? Particularly yours? It would take a horde of them, and even then, they would need far more time than has passed."

"How much time has passed?"

"By the measurements your animals use? We think forty-seven minutes."

I stared at them. Then I sank to the floor, laughing humorlessly. "We've been in here for less than an hour?" I said, bordering on hysteria.

"We think so, yes."

"How can you tell? Why can't I?"

The Watcher held up one thin hand. The light of Gloria's seal glittered prettily in the darkness. "A helpful side-effect of our prison, we think. The enemy has locked you in a portion of your mind. It has likely done the same to your servants. This is another point of evidence against the *zedu heth baagu*, by the way. They might damage a lesser mind but could never create such an illusion in their wake.

"Regardless, the enemy cannot reach our presence. At least, not directly. We're trapped with you, but our memories remain inviolate."

There was an unmistakable sense of relief in the Watcher's voice. I felt a pang of sympathy and of jealousy. There was no time for that, though.

"So it hasn't been torturing you?"

"It's tried." They shrugged. "We've been wandering this space, trying to find its limits. We think the enemy finally got tired of us."

"I'm amazed you could find anything. I can't sense anything beyond this room. Just void."

"Yes. We are accustomed to traveling in such environs, albeit not in physical form. Or an approximation thereof."

"Did you find anything?"

"No. Other than echoes of your trauma. Localities form in the void as necessary. Either as a stage for you or for the enemy to mine your memories."

"You keep calling it 'the enemy'."

"It seems like an accurate descriptor, yes."

"Don't get smart. Do you have any idea what it could be?"

The Watcher thought for a moment. "There are several entities that could exert such mental control. From such potent presences as yourself to the astral equivalent of vermin. That number shrinks considerably when we consider what could confine you. As opposed to your animals."

"*Friends.*"

The Watcher-As-Lucas blinked twice. "Yes. Your friends. So. An entity capable of shackling you, but weak enough to be bound by the ani— the creatures... the entities you have been fighting." They shrugged helplessly. "We cannot imagine. Not under these criteria. This scenario is completely impossible."

"And yet," I said. I thumped my head against the wall behind me. "I spoke to it. Through one of its puppets, but I'm sure I was speaking to the enemy directly. It said 'the Eye sees and the Cage imprisons'."

"The Eye..." the Watcher said. Then their eyes widened. "*Shomo-Elnak.* The Gaze That Chains."

A shiver of recognition ran through me. "Stronger than a dream eater?"

"We should say so. Stronger than us. Possibly stronger than the entire swarm. For these entities to have acquired it—"

"Could it be working with them willingly?"

"We suppose it is possible," the Watcher-As-Lucas said, sounding doubtful. "Neither the Eye nor these 'Illuminated' are the sort of entities who seek partnership."

"No. That's a mistake," I said. I sat quietly for a moment. "Perhaps that's something we should reconsider ourselves."

The Watcher tilted their head to the side. "A partnership?"

"Yes. *All* of us."

The Watcher sat silent for a moment, then nodded slowly. "We... will consider this."

They looked down, pondering my intent. An alliance with me, they could easily comprehend. With Luci and Gloria... to them that would be like entering a partnership with a pair of dogs. They couldn't conceive of humans as having significance, let alone of being their equals. Or mine. They traced their finger idly through the dirty water at their feet, flicking droplets here and there. They screwed up their face in confusion and lifted their head again, meeting my eyes.

"Why did you permit it?"

I almost took offense until I realized what they meant. They'd seen the worst of my memories as the Eye looked for weapons against me. They were even sitting in one of them. I let out a long sigh, dropping my head.

"I couldn't prevent it. I was a child."

That answer didn't satisfy them. They put their hands together, twisting their fingers in distress. They couldn't conceive of mere humans—of animals—being capable of hurting me, of constraining me. Any more than they could think of the dream eaters as being a threat to me. Or the Eye. For the first time, I saw a sense of their true feelings toward me, not buried beneath my memory of Lucas' posturing. There was fear there, but also reverence.

"No more sideways talk," I said. "Just what is it do you think I am?"

"The Opener of the Way," they said without hesitation. "The Gate That Is The Guide. What the Archivists named *Teshu Ung Maya*. Something as far above us as we are above these animals you love."

I laughed bitterly, still not understanding. "I'm just a teenage girl with a messed-up body."

"Yes," the Watcher said, frowning. "We do not understand. Perhaps whatever has been done to your mind has also been done to your physical form."

A spark of fear flared up in my breast. My stomach clenched.

"What do you mean?" I asked, though somehow deep inside I knew. I had always known.

"There is more to you than this animal flesh. Far more than you can perceive. You were… compacted. Or pruned. Forced into that rotting frame of meat and seawater. But unlike us, you could not be contained."

My arms. My body. My senses, unbound by mere organs of sensation. My eternal self, stretching out in and around the pitiful four dimensions of time and space until I had met myself, however far into the future.

"Something limits you. Perhaps you limit yourself."

I heard my voice echoing from the other end of time.

"It's a choice."

I could do more. I could feel myself waking up, the pins and needles stretching far beyond my slim frame. I stretched. I grew.

"There is more of you. Too much for *Shomo-Elnak* to chain. It caught you by surprise, caught the you in this flesh, but it can't contain you. Not if you accept what you are."

A leviathan stirred, sending waves of gravity through space at oblique angles to everything.

"I... I can't," I whispered.

"You can. You must."

"I'm *afraid!*" I screamed. "I'm afraid of what I am. What I'm supposed to be!"

The Watcher fell silent again. Then, "We were afraid, too."

"What?"

"It was so many spawnings ago. Before any of them. Our star was dying. Our scholars said they had a way. To abandon the flesh, send our minds and anima into the space between the stars. We were afraid. Would we die? Be torn apart by the weird radiation of the aether? Disperse under the weight of ego death?

"Our predecessors almost didn't join the ritual. They were going to abandon themselves to fate. To die with so many others."

I thought of what the Watcher had said before. To my first and last conversation with the greater swarm. Only it hadn't been the first, had it?

"And then I came."

"No. Not yet. The cataclysms struck our world, and our predecessors realized that they would rather risk dying in the void if it meant a chance at life."

"And that's your point."

The Watcher paused. "That is half of our point."

"Go on."

"We realized that we were right to fear the void. That the aether could not sustain us. To survive, we would have to change further. Into something that could still feed and grow. To do that, we needed worlds. Warm, wet worlds bursting with life. We tried methods to reach them. They were successful, up to a point, but the summoning was inefficient. Good for a handful to feed, not the species as a whole.

"And so we consumed the Archivists. And from them we learned of you. We called to you to take us to the first spawning world in exchange for our service."

"Why? Why did I…?"

"We don't know. We cannot understand your motives. As we said, you are an entity far above us. Your needs, your desires, they are not ours. They are not those of your servants. You *must* accept that if you are to escape this prison. If you are to survive."

"I don't want that! I'm just a girl. That's all I want to be."

The Watcher-As-Lucas stared at me. Sympathy mixed with contempt on their damp face. Then their form rippled. The image of Ralph Connor stood behind them.

"I-if you d-don't, you c-c-can't save Luh-Luh-Luci," the Watcher-As-Ralph said.

I covered my head, although I could still see their face. "That's a cheap trick."

"Sh-she's caught tuh-tuh-too. Whuh-whatever *Shu-Shomo-Elnak* d-did to yuh-you, it's d-doing to her. And p-probably wuh-worse."

"Stop it! You have no right!"

"D-do you think she can g-get out on her own?" the Watcher-As-Ralph asked.

"She's just a human. She doesn't have your power," the Watcher-As-Lucas said.

"No!"

"Th-they're g-gonna h-hurt her."

"They're hurting her right now."

I screamed. The force of my rage cracked the concrete shell around us. The air in the chamber whipped into a vortex, sending chips of black stone skittering around the room at flesh-shredding speeds. The Watcher's forms fell to the floor, covering their heads and faces with their arms.

The light above the door flared to life, bathing the room in its baleful red glow. The Eye was watching again. The temperature in the room plummeted. The room tilted, the walls twisting and shrinking until there was only room for me to kneel, limbs pressed against the walls, staring up at the crimson Eye blazing above me. My skin burned with cold. I screamed in rage and pain.

Elsewhere, I shuddered, sending a wave rippling through space-time.

Dimly, I recognize a sense of constriction in a past-point of my consciousness. Memory flashes. Earth/1954. The Lucille-Sweeney/Gloria-Lane/Dorothy-Weathersby social configuration. Referencing the *Amn-Zahad* matter. Local cross-section caught in the *Shomo-Elnak* mind trap.

Yes. It was time to handle this again.

I *turn*, my vast form rotating through dimensions. *Shomo-Elnak* does not detect my presence until the wards put in place react to my passing. Dimly, I register feedback—heat and light, an ostentatious display of energy. It would disturb my local cross-section, so I temporarily relocate her to a safer space.

There is screaming. I dismiss it as irrelevant.

18

Gloria stared at the thing in the wheelchair. It stared back, its bandaged eyes somehow still finding hers. She took three steps to the right, her back braced against the gurney. Its head followed her. She took three steps to the left, and then three more. Its head continued to follow her, silently swiveling. The thing in the chair made another rattling noise deep within its sunken gray chest. It didn't make her think of laughter this time. More like the warning rattle of a desert snake.

Keeping her eye on the bandaged thing, Gloria took two more steps to the left, then two more. The warning rattle grew more intense. A section of wall peeked through the edge of her reality bubble. She looked at it, then smirked at the thing.

"So," she said. "Door's that way, I'll bet."

The bandaged thing hissed. Its obscured eyes were fixed on her. Its slack jaw drooped, the corner of its dry, cracked mouth turning down in a crooked scowl. She felt as if she was staring down the barrel of a bent, rusty gun. It could go off at any moment, and God knew what would happen if it did. It was as likely to explode as it was to shoot.

Before she could think of her next move, a spike of pain stabbed through her stomach, forcing her to double over. At first, she thought the thing was attacking. Then the reality bubble shivered and pulled another two inches inward. A wave of nausea rolled over her as she realized what was happening. The seal in her head consumed a tremendous amount of energy, and she only had so much in her. Either she had to find a way out of the thing's trap, or she'd end up shriveled and dried out like a gourd left in the desert.

Her messenger bag. It was full of supplies. If she could find that, she could do something with her seal. Transfer it to paper, set up a circle of candles to power it. Maybe even push it back further to find us. At least she could remember our names now. Luci and Amelia and Dorothy Weathersby, who wasn't really her friend at all but had gotten dragged into their foolishness just the same. She felt a stab of guilt at that. We should have let Dorothy go as soon as she'd gotten us into the hospital. She was a bystander, far more so than the Connor boy we were working so hard to save.

I'll get you out of here, Gloria thought. *Can't promise you more, but we owe you at least that much.*

She hurried back to the gurney, trying to reason things out. The room couldn't be that large. The wall to the left was about ten feet from where she'd been laid. Assuming she was at about the center of the room, that would make it twenty to thirty feet across, widthwise. Lengthwise, who knew? There wasn't enough data yet. She would have to explore some. But how would the thing in the wheelchair react? It had grown hostile when she'd approached what she thought was the exit. She wasn't ready to pit her makeshift seal against it if it got its dander up. Not while it was running off her own metabolism.

As if on cue, the bubble shivered again, contracting another two inches. That was half a foot in less than fifteen minutes. At this rate, she wouldn't have to worry about starvation. Another couple of hours and she'd be stuck in the creature's mind trap again.

So I have to get my bag, she thought. *Where would they have put it?*

That was assuming it was in the room at all, but she couldn't let herself think about the possibility that it wasn't. If it wasn't in this room, it could be anywhere in the hospital, and that might as well be the dark side of the moon for all the good it would do her. She had to grasp at the straws in front of her now.

If it's in here, she thought, *I'd put it near the monster. Because it's the only thing in here besides us. Because if it wasn't, I'd already be caught.*

Gloria stepped toward the thing in the wheelchair. Its attention darted back to her. She walked forward slowly, pausing between each step to gauge its reaction. On the third step, the monster rattled a warning at her. Her bubble of reality rippled, but the edges held for now. The monster sat still. Its fingers and toes twitched, and its toast-rack chest filled and emptied like a torn squeezebox, but otherwise it was still. Even without the bonds at its arms and legs, Gloria didn't think it could move much on its own.

"Well, why would they need you to?" she asked aloud.

Despite what it had done, Gloria felt a measure of disgust for the men who had bound whatever it was. It was emaciated and filthy, its body clearly scarred by neglect. She'd felt its malice, true enough, but she suspected it was the meanness of a junkyard dog that had been kicked too much. She wouldn't trust it, and she didn't dare take it off the leash, but she could pity it. Nothing deserved to be treated like this.

She took two more steps forward, coming within arm's length of the creature. Now it reared back in its chair as best as it was able. Its neck creaked as it tried to push its face away while keeping its bandaged eyes fixed on her. The rattle was louder now, but it did not strike at her. She peered closely at it… at him. A skeletally thin figure with ruined muscles and dry, cracked skin. Familiar markings had been working into its pale, unwashed limbs and chest. The tattoos were old enough that they were blurry and faded, but the seal they described was holding. Whatever the creature was, it had been bound to this wretched man the same way she had bound the Watcher to me. Only rather than being imprisoned in a corner of his mind, they must have given the thing the poor man's entire body. She hoped silently that he was dead. It was a horrible thought, but it was the more merciful alternative.

Behind the creature, the room's rear wall swam into reality. Gloria saw a row of glass-faced cabinets lining the wall. And praise be whatever power was watching over us—her messenger bag was inside one of them. It must have been easier for our captors to leave it in here when they had rolled us into this room. Now she had to hope her supplies were still inside.

Gloria took two steps back. The wall fell away, lost in the rippling darkness. The creature stilled but kept its eyes locked on her. She looked to her left, in the direction of the presumed exit. She then looked past the creature, considering whether she felt safe walking right past it. She decided she did not. It *probably* couldn't move on its own. "Probably" wasn't the same as "definitely".

Instead, she slid to the right, tracing a slow arc anchored on the creature in the chair. It stayed silent. Their eyes remained locked, but it made no noise, no twitch. Just steady, ragged breaths. So long as she didn't approach it or the exit, it seemed content to watch her.

As Gloria approached the rear wall, a low table swam into view. She moved around it, keeping it between her and the creature until she reached the cabinets. She couldn't say why, only that the flimsy barrier made her feel somewhat safer. The creature's neck tilted at a spine-breaking angle trying to keep its eyes on her. When she finally passed out of its field of vision, the creature slumped forward. Its head fell back to its chest. Gloria paused for a moment, watching it. Then she pressed her back to the cabinet, sliding along it with her behind pressed to the wood, her eyes never leaving the creature.

She stopped right before she reached the cabinet holding her bag. Eyes fixed on the creature, she bent at the knees, sliding down to open the cabinet door and retrieve the bag. She let out a sigh of relief as she felt its familiar weight in her hand. All her supplies were still there.

Gloria hitched the bag over her shoulder and crept back around the other way, a little faster this time. Her stomach clenching harder now, grabbing her entire midsection in a viselike grip. Desperate for food to meet the sudden demand for calories. Her vision swam, but she willed herself to stay upright.

If I'd known I was going to be working this hard, I'd have had a bigger meal.

She made a mental note to add candy bars to her list of supplies.

The moment she entered the creature's field of vision, its head snapped back around. She tried to ignore its dusty gaze, even as gooseflesh broke out across her neck and shoulders. Its eyes burned against her back until she reached the gurney. As soon as she set her bag down on it, its head dropped to its chest. Gloria nodded, understanding. As long as they were where they were supposed to be, it was dormant.

Not so hot stuff, are you? she thought. *You're the big man on campus when we're stuck in our heads, but out here? Barely even a watchdog.*

That thought gave her some pause. Were they really alone in there? Surely their captors couldn't have thought this one creature would be enough to contain them. Not when it was helpless in the physical world. But no, of course they did. They'd left Ralph out in the open for an entire month. Because they were lazy and overconfident. They wouldn't think to add a proper watch because it would never occur to them that four young women could escape the mind trap.

Not that we've escaped yet, she thought, as the reality bubble shuddered and contracted again. *Three inches this time. You need to get to work, girl.*

Gloria spread out her supplies on top of the gurney. Her hand trembled as she picked up her pen. She could swear that she saw bones beneath her skin. She tightened her grip, willing her hand to stay steady, and closed her eyes. Gloria tried to summon the feeling of being back in the mind trap, of *being back inside my mind.* A hazily remembered image of her room in the illusory servants' quarters coalesced around her. The seal in her mind burned on her bed. It was crude—she hadn't been able to do her best work at the time—but the framework was solid. She felt a burst of pride at that. Even with an incomplete memory, she understood the Keys well enough to free herself. She could see where her work needed improvement, but it wouldn't take much. Outside of her mind, she put pen to paper and started to draw.

Once she had the seal's basic framework down. Gloria opened her eyes and glanced over her shoulder. The creature was still dormant, its shoulders slumped, its chin resting against its thin chest. Clearly it couldn't recognize what she was doing. It might once she activated the seal. That was fine. By then it should be too late.

Working as quickly as she could, Gloria added new Structures to the warding seal. Some were to expand the area it covered; others she hadn't yet had the opportunity to test. These were an innovation on the Structures that locked the initial charge of power inside the system. They would double the energy back on itself again and again. That would increase the power drain considerably, but she was prepared for that. She had two dozen candles in her bag, most of them fresh. If she had to, she could consume her spare paper for extra heat. If it came to it, there might be medical supplies in the cabinets as well. Alcohol burned well enough.

As she fished in her bag for her pre-prepared power seals, a wave of dizziness almost knocked her off her feet. She gripped the side of the gurney with both hands, eyes screwed shut, hoping it would pass. Another pang of hunger ripped her abdomen like a sawblade. Her breath was coming in sharp bursts now. Even through the darkness behind her eyelids, the room spun sickeningly. The dizziness wouldn't pass. She opened her eyes, trying to focus on something stationary, something to anchor herself. It was no good. The room tilted and blackness crept in at the edge of her vision.

I'm going to starve to death, she thought. Panic gripped her chest.

The creature sat stock-still, or at least, so she thought. Her reality bubble had shrunk again. She could only see about half of it—arms, legs, the front of its bandaged face and torso. The rest of it was lost in the rippling nothingness at the edge of her ward. She didn't know what would happen when the creature no longer fell within the area of effect. Probably nothing—probably she was safe until it collapsed completely—but why take that chance? The thought of it being out of sight made her shudder or would have if she wasn't so weak from hunger.

Another pang ripped through her abdomen. Her head swam. Carefully, carefully, she slid down to the floor. Better to work on the floor than to risk falling onto it. She felt as if she hadn't eaten in days. There wasn't any food nearby, nor did she know where she might find it even if she could go searching. Would she starve to death in the next few minutes? No, but she certainly would pass out, and then she might as well be dead. Someone would be by to collect everyone before long. She had to get out.

Which meant Gloria had to eat. Or at least, the next best thing. She curled up like a shrimp, trying to ease the pain in her abdomen while she grappled with this problem. Energy. The problem was energy. The power seals drew energy from the heat of the candle flame. Or any other source. Dowling's seal had used electricity. This warding seal was burning out Gloria's metabolism. Energy was energy. A seal could run off the energy of a candle or the energy of a wall outlet or the energy of a body. The energy was the same. Yes.

Why couldn't it work in reverse?

There was no reason. None. Energy was energy was energy. Yes. She was rambling. She had to focus. She had to set up a power seal. She had ready-made power seals in her bag. Yes. Draw a new seal for it to power—simple. The Adamite Key to anchor it. Structure Keys to draw power and direct it into the anchor. Into her body. On her body. She had to draw the seal onto her bare skin. Yes. To ensure the energy went where it was needed. A risk. An acceptable risk. Carefully draw each Key. If they weren't enough, if it went wrong...

She had to get it right the first time.

She pulled the bag down after her and swore when it spilled its contents across the floor. The papers and twine stayed close by, but the candles rolled every which way. She grabbed at what she could without crawling across the floor. Nine candles lay close at hand. She didn't think she had the strength to go after the others. The nine would be enough to start with. They would have to be.

She fished a pen out of the mess and forced herself to lay flat, ignoring the way her stomach clenched and screamed. She hiked up her sweater and began to draw. She had to stop three times to steady her hand. It felt like it took hours to draw the seal across her abdomen. The end result was far from perfect. The lines looked wobbly, but they would have to do. There were spots in her eyes, and her head hung like a block of cement from her neck. The pen fell from her trembling hand, no longer strong enough to hold it. No matter. She was done with it for now.

Gloria grabbed a power seal from the pile on the floor and smoothed it out. She placed the recovered candles on the relevant Keys, forming a ring around the seal. She taped the ink-stained twine threaded through the paper to her stomach, right on top of the first Directional Key. When all was ready, she propped herself up on one elbow and grabbed her matchbook. Her thumb fumbled at the paper cover. She glared at her shaking hand and willed it to steady. Clumsily, she thumbed the cover open. Moving the matchbook to the hand propping her up, she tore off a match and dragged it across the striking strip. The match didn't light. She struck it again. And again. On the third attempt, the paper match tore in half. The sulfur tip flew coldly into a corner.

Gloria screamed out a foul word, tears pricking at the corners of her eyes. The creature's bandaged head jerked up at the noise. It stared balefully at her. The edges of the reality bubble rippled and shrank again, everything but the creature's hands, calves and feet disappearing into inky nothingness. Hot red light flashed in the void. Gloria thought she could hear echoes of the party, the mocking laughter of the idle rich, waiting to pull her back. To put her in her place.

Her breath was coming in quick, ragged hitches. She bared her teeth in a defiant snarl, but her head shook. She was on the verge of passing out. Was it from hunger or the creature's renewed assault? She couldn't say.

"We don't die here," she whispered, her voice hoarse and fierce. "This isn't how it ends."

She tore another match from the book. She dragged it across the striking strip. Too slow, too slow. She scraped the sulfur off the match to no effect. She tore out a third match and tried again. And again. And again. Until there were only three left.

The creature made its mocking dusty rattle.

Gloria stared at the matchbook, weaving unsteadily. Only three left. Only three. She didn't have time to scavenge for more.

"Should… should have brought more," she mumbled, on the edge of delirium. "Gonna bring more… next time. Gonna… be a next time."

She hooked a finger behind the remaining three matches and folded them over until their heads touched the strip. She folded the cover over them and rolled onto her back. She put her hands together, holding the matchbook between her palms. Gritting her teeth, she dragged her palms across one another as hard as she could. The matches flared, catching the paper book on fire. It burned like hell, but in that moment she didn't care. She let out a cry of triumph and thrust the flaming matchbook at the nearest candle. The wick caught immediately. She threw the matchbook away and grabbed the lit candle, lighting those that remained. Their nine tiny flames burned brightly in the void, like her hopes.

"Now we'll see," she said.

She placed her unburnt palm against her stomach, touching the Adamite Key drawn there. Closing her eyes, she ran the equation in her head. The seal blazed with energy. Gloria couldn't see the flaming vortex that erupted in the middle of the power seal, nor how the energy arced up the string connecting it to her abdomen. She could feel the fire as it traced the lines drawn on her skin. She grabbed onto the gurney's frame, trying not to scream as the seal burned itself into her body.

Her skin was on fire, but the seal was working. Power flowed into her. Her stomach twisted itself into a knot, but her strength was returning. Her vision cleared. Her hands stopped trembling. If not for the pain from the seal, she thought she could stand again.

When she could take the pain no longer, she ripped the twine from her stomach. She let herself lie still for a moment, feeling the life return to her shrunken flesh, waiting for the pain to fade. The warding seal still spun in the back of her mind, burning up the metabolic energy she had restored, but hopefully not for much longer. Now—set up the next ward. After another minute, she pulled herself into a sitting position. Gloria blew out all but one of the candles. Then she got to work again.

When the new warding seal was finished, she sat cross-legged in front of it. Relighting the candles, she ran the new equation. She felt much more confident of this seal. She hadn't considered what would happen when the two seals overlapped.

The energy wound through the amplifying Structures, building and building, creating a vortex of power that swept back the creature's influence. The gloom disappeared, revealing the entire room. The creature seized, shaking the wheelchair and rattling angrily. Three people lay strapped to gurneys behind Gloria; Luci, Dorothy and I. Not that she saw us. The energy of the new seal fountained up and entangled with the energy of the old. Feedback blasted into the seals, into her mind. She screamed and fell backward, clutching her head as a lance of agony seared through her consciousness.

The world was dark.

Then she was sprawled on the hospital room floor.

Then she was sprawled on the servant's room floor.

The visions overlapped. They separated, then intertwined. At one hand, a seal burned in a ring of candles. At the other, a seal blazed brightly on a simple bed. Strange light arced between them and through her, throwing sparks across the rooms. She burned like a mouse with a mouthful of live wire. She had to end one of the seals, or they were going to end her.

One of the seals was going to kill her anyway.

Which one?

Gloria rolled onto one side, muscles spasming against the cool hospital tile. She braced her hands against the rough wooden floorboards and pushed herself up. She reached out to the seal on the bed. On the floor. On the bed. She grabbed the paper and crumpled it, ripping the heart out of the seal. She prayed it was the correct one.

19

Tears streamed down Luci's face as she hammered her fists against the glass divider. The officers did not respond. They ignored the banging, took no notice of the screams and paid no heed to the stream of frankly improbable insults she spat at the backs of their heads. The driver only moved to turn the steering wheel. The cop in the passenger's seat didn't even move that much. They sat still as statues bathed in the patrol car's red lights as it raced down the suburban streets, mercilessly escorting Luci to her doom.

She refused to go easily. She hooked her fingers under the edge of the seat, bracing herself. She leaned against the seat, lifting her feet. Then she smashed them against the glass divider, heels first, screaming in fear and rage. The glass didn't budge. Neither did the officers. She pulled her feet in and kicked the glass again and again. Her heels made a horrid racket as they crashed against the glass but did no damage whatsoever. It wasn't even scuffed.

Luci kicked and kicked until she was worn out. She lay sprawled against the seat, panting and staring at the unmarked glass. Tears streamed down her cheeks. Then she threw herself at the door, slamming her fist against the window over and over. She scrabbled for her shoe, ripping it off her foot and hammering it against the glass. Nothing. Once again, the glass didn't so much as scratch, and the police didn't budge.

She let the shoe slip from her fingers and clatter against the floorboard. Leaning her head against the window, she finally allowed herself to cry. Her shoulders shook as huge wracking sobs rocked her skinny child's body. Fat tears fell from her eyes, splattering against the door like the rain that was now pelting the patrol car's roof. A bolt of red lightning tore across the black sky, and an ear-splitting thunderclap followed not even a second later. Luci jerked, flinching, and then she saw her destination.

The endless suburb had fallen behind them, replaced by an expanding forest of dark towers. The tallest was directly ahead of them. It stabbed at the rain-belching sky like a basalt spear. Near the summit, a massive red sphere bulged out of the building's skin, an architectural tumor, a swollen, rotten fruit covered in gooey webs. The bulge rocked back and forth, revealing a misshapen dark spot swimming across its crimson skin. A sickening chill churned Luci's stomach when she realized it was an eye. A swollen eye the size of a small house.

The eye-spot rolled in their direction. Luci's skin crawled as a wave of *something* passed over her. Then a spot on the patrol car's ceiling began to pucker. A thick black fluid leaked from the spot in long ropes that hissed when it spattered on the black seat. A bubble the size of her fist pushed its way through the metal. It split with a wet tearing sound, like a peach bursting through its skin. Dark ichor splattered the car's interior. Another red eye lolled amidst the ichor. A wet black film swept across it twice, then it swiveled to stare directly at Luci. Its baleful gaze burned into her, seizing her muscles. She tried to fight against it, but the eye's gaze paralyzed her as it burned through her mind, peeling back her memory to find her worst, most shameful secrets. The things she'd said to Dorothy in their last conversation. Nights out at sixteen, looking for adventure, not caring that her mother waited up at home. Walking through the five and dime at twelve, pocketing a handful of candy that she didn't even want.

Luci tried to curl her lip, but her face was frozen. She imagined herself spitting right at in the thing's eye and threw that image at it as hard as she could.

That's the best you've got? she sent. *Youthful rebellion? A little girl on Santa's naughty list? You're pathetic.*

The film swept over the eye again. Then it shivered. Luci thought for a moment it was laughing.

Then she saw herself at eight years old. Kneeling beside her bed, listening to the screams coming from her parents' room. Praying Daddy would die.

A hot tear ran down her cheek.

How... how dare you? she sent, but weakly. Her mental voice had choked up.

The eye narrowed its gaze. Its gaze burned hotter, brighter. Tearing into her little girl memories. The screaming. Whiskey on his breath. The bruises. Plates shattering against the wall. Neighbors not meeting her mother's eye as they passed. Luci helpless in the corner, clutching her stuffed bunny.

Please. Stop.

The eye pressed harder. Its gaze was like a scalpel. It

(creature seized)

eye rolled back

(a vortex of power)

screamed and lashed out with her foot. Her bare heel smashed against the eye, popping it. A gout of black ichor splashed against the glass divider. The *car* shrieked and slid to one side, screaming across the slick asphalt until it crashed against a nondescript storefront, rear first. The impact sent Luci flying across the seat, smashing her head against the left door's window. The glass was still undamaged. Not so much her skin. Blood splattered against the glass, mixing with the ichor. Luci slumped against the door, leaving a streak of

(discontinuity)

r e g a i n e d

consciousness. The patrol car was smashed against the building, and she was still trapped in there. The police officers were slumped in their seats, unconscious or dead. Dark violet ichor poured from a torn patch in the ceiling, covering the floorboard in stinking muck.

Luci's head was splitting. She absently put a hand to her right temple and winced. She was unsurprised to see it come away wet, stained with black blood.

"Have to get out," she mumbled.

She slid across the seat, trying to avoid the slime pouring out of the patrol car's wound. She tested the door handle. No luck. No surprise, either. She slammed a fist against the glass divider, shouting at the police. They didn't respond. Not so much as a twitch.

"All right," she muttered. "All right, then."

She put both of her heels against the passenger window and braced herself against the seat. The first kick shook the window without damaging it. The second left cracks spiraling across the window's center. The third kick shattered it entirely, sending chunks of glass scattering across the road. The glass tore a deep cut across her bare heel up to her calf, but she took no notice of the pain. She crawled through the open window, heedless of the scrapes on her arms, legs, and belly. She landed hard on the asphalt, bruising her shoulder. She pushed herself to her feet and fell against the patrol car, wincing as the impact drove shards of glass into her arm. She stumbled away from the vehicle, limping on one leg, holding one arm against her side, her head aching and fuzzy.

The patrol car's carcass slumped against the broken façade, hissing as various thick fluids leaked from its myriad injuries. It had barely missed the mouth of an alley. Luci let out a laugh without any humor. Three more feet and it might have slid into it easily.

She staggered around the car to the alley. She wasn't sure why. Nothing was there but trash and debris. Perhaps she was looking for an escape route or a place to hide. Perhaps she wanted shelter from the pouring rain. Or more likely, she wasn't aware of what she was doing. That head injury was serious.

I need. A weapon, she thought. *I need. Defend myself. Something.*

Another bolt of red lightning tore across the sky. Luci hid her eyes from the flash with her hands. Then something *changed*. The light glinted off a length of metal pipe poking out of a trash pile. Luci knew this was what she had been looking for. She grabbed it and held it high. It was about three feet long, jagged at one end. She stared at the length of it. She gave it a hesitant swing. Then she slowly turned to the patrol car lurking behind her and stared at the slick black and white surface of its hood, watching raindrops scatter off the surface. The pipe dropped to her side, swinging idly in one hand.

Then she screamed and charged the patrol car.

The hood dented when she hammered the pipe against it. Then it buckled. Then it rent with a metal shriek. Gouts of thick ichor spurted out where the metal split. Thick rivers of gunk poured out as pieces of the hood and front panels came loose. Eventually there was nothing but a mound of slime splattering wider with each impact. Luci swung wildly, screaming her pain and outrage at the dissolving hulk of the patrol car. She only stopped when she heard a firm but caring voice behind her calling her name.

She turned to respond and immediately covered her eyes. Strange light streamed through a rift in the air. A dark-skinned young woman stood in front of it, wearing a shimmering blue outfit. There was something weirdly familiar about her. She was older than Luci… no. That wasn't right. They were about the same age.

Luci lowered the pipe and took a stumbling step forward. The light from the rift played across her own dirty, bloody skin. She was suddenly overcome with exhaustion. Her shoulders slumped, her head hung low, though she did not let go of the ichor-stained pipe. She grew with every step, aging from thirteen to nineteen as she remembered who she was. Who the other woman was. Luci lifted her head and smiled weakly at her best friend.

"Gloria?" she whispered.

Despite her weariness, she ran into the light, throwing an arm around Gloria. She laughed softly, more in relief than anything, and kissed Gloria on the cheek. Gloria held her close. Luci rested her head on her friend's shoulder and cried, letting the fear and tension bleed out of her. The pair held each other up in the rain, until distant sirens pierced the air.

Gloria gently lifted Luci's chin, saying softly, "We have to go."

Luci looked hesitant but took Gloria's hand. "That's all I've wanted for… for I don't know how long."

"Would you believe less than an hour?"

Gloria led her through the rift. Luci felt a wave of distortion as she stepped into the light. She stumbled forward, letting go of Gloria's hand and catching herself on a wide counter of blue metal. It ran around a full third of a curving metal wall. They were in a hemispherical room covered in metal plates. The floor was shining chrome grillwork. Three large, oval-shaped viewscreens hung from the ceiling in front of the counter, which was covered in an entire electronic shop's worth of switches and dials. Gloria paused for a moment, putting an arm around Luci for support before taking a spot in the middle of the console. She turned a dial and the rift snapped shut, leaving the metal room lit by a half-dozen round blue lamps affixed to the walls.

Luci stared at the room for a moment, trying to process what she was seeing. Gloria continued to work at the console, matter-of-factly messing with the controls. Luci's face was serene, although inside her head she was screaming.

Still, when she finally spoke, she kept her voice level.

"Gloria," she said, as if they were discussing what movie to see next Saturday, "what the foul word is going on?"

"That is a rather big question." Gloria didn't look up from her controls. "Do you want to break it down some?"

"You're enjoying this. I'm in shock and you're enjoying this."

"Of course I'm enjoying this. I've pulled off something pretty impressive, if I do say so myself."

"Fantastically impressive. I'm flabbergasted. Possibly gobsmacked. Are you going to explain any time soon?"

"Well, since you asked so nicely." Gloria grinned despite her tension. "Whatever pack of evil wizards is running this joint has more haunts down here than we thought. One of them put a whammy on all of us. We were trapped in nightmares. You, me, your ex... even Amelia."

Gloria flicked a trio of switches. The viewscreens snapped on. One showed Luci lying on the bare floor, a small seal marked onto the tile under her head. A second showed Dorothy in a similar position. A thin ribbon of seal ran down the floor away from their heads, terminating somewhere off-screen. I was on the third viewscreen, still on a gurney. Frost covered my bare face and arms.

"*Amelia!*" Luci cried. Now free of the mind trap, she remembered my name. "She's so *cold*. Where is she?"

"Less than ten feet from you."

Gloria turned a dial. The view on the screen showing me zoomed out, displaying half the room. I lay on my gurney in the back of the room. Luci and Dorothy were on the floor, their gurneys tipped on the side. The lines of seal around their heads ran down the floor to the bottom of the screen, presumably connected to wherever Gloria was sitting.

"I... I forgot her name." Luci's cheeks burned with shame.

"I forgot yours," Gloria said. "Yours, hers, my own brother's. It was part of the nightmare. To keep us off-balance, I think."

"So why do I remember it now?"

"Because you're out of the nightmare. You're out of your own head, actually. I brute-forced my way free with whatever scraps of Prospero's Keys I could hold on to. Then I built a connection between the three of us. Sort of like what Amelia did the night Dowling almost destroyed Chatham Hills, except hopefully a little more controlled."

"So this...?"

"Is a conceptual space in my mind. It helps me focus."

"And I thought Amelia was a sci-fi nerd," Luci said. "Amelia... wait, you said 'the three of us'. Where is Dorothy? Where's *Amelia*?"

"I built a pathway into Dorothy's mind, same as I did for you. We're going to have to get her ourselves. As for Amelia..."

On the viewscreen, I began to thrash in my gurney. Luci went pale, and Gloria's mouth tightened as she turned to Luci with a stern expression.

"I did this on the fly and from memory," Gloria said, in a tone that brooked no argument. "Not to overly worry you, but I didn't have time to properly test this. And seeing what was going on with Amelia? I didn't want to risk us to whatever's happening inside her mind under these conditions. Sorry."

"That's cold, Gloria."

"Amelia has powers that none of us understand, probably including her. I have far more confidence that she can survive on her own than I do your ex. Unless Miss Weathersby also has some supernatural gift you've neglected to share with me?"

"No. Okay. I don't like it, but I guess you're right." Luci sighed heavily. "Let's go rescue Dorothy. Then we can figure out how to save Amelia."

"Hopefully she can rescue herself."

Gloria manipulated the controls. A rift opened on the opposite side of the room, crackling in imaginary air. Luci tightened her grip on the pipe and took the lead, crossing into Dorothy's nightmare.

The hospital lurked on the other side of the rift, but it was nothing like the one we had entered. A dark, worn hallway stretched in front of them, warped and lit by flickering red lights. More than one lamp had broken, scattering shards of glass across scarred tile the yellow of old nicotine. The paint on the walls was dirty and peeling, and disgusting mold grew in dark patches running down the walls. A distant scream rippled through the stale air, soon matched by more terrified voices.

"What is this?" Luci asked. For a moment she wanted to step back through the rift. This was too familiar.

"Dorothy's nightmare," Gloria said. "The hospital is her nightmare."

"Dorothy's. We're in Dorothy's nightmare," Luci repeated. She grabbed Gloria's shoulder to steady herself.

"That's right," Gloria said. She gave Luci a wary look. We hadn't shared all the details of our experience within Luci's memory, and she didn't understand why Luci was suddenly on the verge of paralysis.

"Come on, then." Luci set her shoulders and gave her pipe a reassuring swing. "We're getting her out of here."

The scream—Dorothy's scream—had come flying up from deep inside the rotting building. Luci propelled herself down the hallway, not stopping to see if Gloria was following. The passage seemed to breathe as they followed it, sucking them along with a gust of fetid air. Dark doorways yawned open. Strange noises, like strangled voices and gasps of pain, drifted out of the doors as they passed. Sometimes there was a scrabble of motion, as if something was crawling along the floors toward the tiny square of light at the room's mouth. Whatever it was dared not come into the light. Passing one room, Gloria thought she saw a pair of pinpoint eyes reflecting the flickering light, but when she got Luci's attention, she saw nothing but darkness through the door.

"She's not in there," was all Luci said. "Let's go."

Luci stalked off without another word. Gloria stared at her retreating figure. Her single-mindedness had brought them this far, more so than Gloria's inquisitiveness. Now it was dragging them down into this Hell, where people suffered and monsters lurked. This version of the hospital was a nightmare, but it was a reflection of Dorothy's very real fears. Of her knowledge, buried or otherwise, of what went on behind the scenes. How many people were imprisoned here? How many more lives had been ruined? Didn't Luci *care* about them?

What did Dorothy know and when did she know it?

Luci stopped in the middle of the hall. Then she turned around, her blue eyes blazing with pain and anger, tears running down her cheeks, and Gloria realized she had said it all out loud.

"It's *my* fault Dorothy's trapped in here," Luci said. "*I* dragged her into this, after she'd already said we were through. *I* put her in here. Because she was convenient and because I was still *hurt* and I was *mad* and I… I wanted to play with her feelings a bit."

"Luci…"

"She'd be home and *safe* right now if it wasn't for *me*. So *no*, I *don't* care about anything except getting Dorothy out of this nightmare before it hurts her more than it already has! You said Amelia can save herself, and so can…"

Her voice trailed off. Her chest hitched. Tears streamed down her cheeks. She looked down at the dirty floor and whispered, "... and so can everyone else."

Far away, Dorothy screamed again. Luci whipped around, but before she could take off running, the hallway lurched, twisting beneath their feet. Luci and Gloria fell forward, sliding down the slick floor toward a widening rectangle of dim red light. It was the elevator, doors open, eagerly gobbling them up as they smashed into the back wall. The doors snapped shut.

The elevator floor fell out from beneath them, sending Gloria and Luci plummeting down the long, dark shaft. In the gloom, the far-away basement floor rushed up at them.

"What happens if we hit bottom?" Luci asked, shouting to be heard over the roar of rushing air.

"I don't know!" Gloria said. "I don't want to find out!"

Gloria grabbed at a door as it flew past her, hoping to get some purchase on the ledge. By some miracle she did, slamming into the shaft wall with a rib-cracking *thud*. Then Luci crashed into her, knocking her from the ledge and sending them both tumbling again. She could see the shaft bottom now, a dirty square lit with red light. They were going to crash. They were going to

(give me back my friends)

        discontinuity

               (or i'll tear this place apart!)

                          lay in a tangle on the shaft floor. Luci lifted her head, staring up the dark shaft. She reached out to touch Gloria's side, closing her eyes in relief when she felt her friend's ribs move.

"We're alive," she said.

"Not even hurt," Gloria said.

Gloria covered Luci's hand with her own, giving it a reassuring squeeze. Then she pushed herself up. She too stared up the dark shaft, lit only by dirty illumination from a couple of open doors.

"What happened?" Gloria asked. "We were falling and then..."

"And then we weren't."

Luci rolled over onto her stomach and picked herself up off the ground, using her pipe for support. She scowled at the mold-slick walls around them.

"You know, I liked it much better in Amelia's head," she said.

"I'll bet."

Luci rolled her eyes. "It's not like that."

"So you say."

The rusty elevator doors at the shaft's bottom were firmly shut. Gloria worked her fingers into the narrow gap between the doors and gave them a test pull. To no surprise, they didn't budge. She looked over her shoulder at Luci.

"Help me pull this open."

Luci came around the other side and hooked her fingers into the gap. The pair braced themselves and pulled on the doors with all their might. They pulled until their knuckles paled and their fingertips bled. The doors wouldn't budge.

Growling a foul word between gritted teeth, Luci stopped. She leaned forward, panting, hands on her knees. It didn't seem fair, being this tired in a dream. "Can't you magic this open?"

"It doesn't work that way," Gloria said. "I need something to power a seal. We're in Dorothy's head right now. I'd have to power it with her metabolism."

"Like you did with Amelia."

Gloria nodded. "Right. Only we're regular folks, not whatever Amelia is."

"Amelia's amazing, that's what she is," Luci said defensively. "We've got to save her. Right after we save Dorothy."

"We have to get through this door first," Gloria said. She examined the empty elevator shaft again. "We could try going around? I see an open door two floors up. We could climb up, try to find the stairs."

Luci frowned, glaring at the door. She tapped the end of her pipe on the concrete floor.

"*This* door is going to open."

She picked up the pipe, holding it like a baseball bat.

"I'm not losing anyone else."

She pulled the pipe back and swung it at the elevator door. It crashed against the dingy metal with a terrible *clang!*

"I'm not running away again!"

She smashed the pipe against the door again.

"You won't take her from me!"

And again.

"Do you hear me!"

And again

"Give her back!"

And again.

"Give her back!"

The pipe swung through the fetid air, striking the door with such violence it threw off sparks. The metal doors bend outward, opening the gap between them. Luci pulled the pipe back and jabbed it into the gap, wedging it between the two doors. She tightened her grip on the pipe's end and threw herself backward. With an ear-splitting grind of metal on metal, she levered the doors apart until there was enough of a gap for Gloria to squeeze through. Luci followed, half-expecting the doors to snap shut on her, but they stayed open as she slipped into the nightmare hospital's basement.

They faced another hallway half-lit by flickering lights. Far down the hall, a light exploded, sending a shower of sparks onto the concrete floor. The walls ran black with mold, oily liquid dripping from the masses to form sludgy puddles. Down the hall, a woman sobbed. Luci took off, gripping her pipe between both hands. A pile of sludge reached for her as she passed. She swung the pipe, and the slime retreated, hissing.

Luci passed nearly a half-dozen open doorways, barely registering the macabre tableau within. A woman sat on a bare metal chair in the first, her arms caught in a straitjacket. Her head was shaved bald, dotted with dark stubble. Crudely stitched surgical scars ran across her scalp. She stared out the open door with wide, colorless eyes and called Luci's name. There was nothing in the woman's face she recognized, and Luci ignored her and pressed on.

A fire burned in a rusty barrel inside the second room. Hunched figures in fluid-stained white coats scuttled around the room like giant beetles. They were gathering papers in manila envelopes and throwing them into the fire. Leather gas masks covered their heads. When Luci passed the doorway, one of them scuttled to the threshold and hung out of it. The figure hissed at her in a voice like radio static. Again, Luci ignored it. Gloria, coming up behind, gave the creature a wide berth. The dirty figure stared after both of them, hanging in the doorframe and muttering in high, electric clicks.

Darkness filled the third door. Or rather, dark water somehow filled the room up to the open door without spilling out into the hallway. Small bioluminescent fish swam blindly through the murk. They scattered as Luci passed, but not from her presence. A large beast loomed out of the inky fluid. Tooth-lined jaws opened impossibly wide as it lunged through the doorway. Luci spun on her heel, swinging her pipe. The jagged end passed through the creature's head, dragging sparks behind it in a long arc. The creature exploded, splattering the walls, floor, and women with a thick luminescent fluid. Gloria shrieked in disgust and outrage, but Luci took no notice.

The fourth room was lined with bones of all shapes and sizes, many of them clearly non-human. All of them were inscribed with strange markings and glowed with an eerie inner light. A man hung by one ankle from the ceiling. His throat and stomach had been slashed open, dripping dark green fluid into a rusty bucket on the floor. His dark eyes blinked independently of one another.

Dorothy's sobbing came from the fifth room.

She was strapped to an operating table. Strange symbols were drawn along her face, limbs and torso, nightmare distortions of Prospero's Keys. A huge domed lamp shone red light down from the dirty ceiling. A hulking figure in a stained white coat loomed over her, holding a set of retractors in one gloved hand. Luci was utterly unsurprised to recognize the distorted image of Dr. Sutherland, tiny pince-nez perched atop his enlarged red face. A rail-thin nurse stood on the other side of the table, the skin of her face rippling with knotted tissue like a tangle of tree roots. She held a wriggling *thing* between her claw-like hands, all eel-slimy skin and jagged teeth.

Dorothy screamed when the nightmare doctor grabbed her shoulder. He clacked the implements menacingly.

"Time to open you up!" the nightmare doctor said in a movie-monster voice.

He stuck the retractors into Dorothy's mouth, prying her jaws apart. The nurse held out the wriggling monster. The doctor grabbed it by its squirming middle and held it up, ready to plunge it into Dorothy's mouth.

Luci let out a scream of fury and charged through the doorway, swinging the pipe wildly. She caught the nightmare doctor across the middle, sending him flying against the filthy cabinets on the near wall. Luci slammed the pipe down, smashing his neck with a loud *crack*. The brute tried to clamber to his feet, his head drooping at a sickening angle, but Luci wouldn't let up her assault. She cracked him across the head, dislodging his jaw and popping a bulging eye out of its socket. She smashed his head open on the backswing. It burst, releasing a gout of rotten red meat and thick purple fluid that splattered the ceiling.

Gloria froze, shocked by her friend's sudden violence. This was a part of Luci she'd never seen before, and she wasn't certain how to react. While indecision stopped Gloria, the nightmare nurse was under no such difficulty. The monster screamed, her voice muffled behind her ruined face. She rushed at Luci, claws ready to rend and tear, but Luci whirled on her and stuck the pipe out. The nurse ran into it, ramming the jagged end of the pipe through her thin torso. The nurse let out a choking squeal, her claws still thrashing in the fetid air. Luci tightened her grip on the pipe and braced one foot against the nightmare nurse's thigh. She kicked hard, tugging the pipe free in another gout of purple ichor, and sending the nightmare nurse flying across the room. Luci raised the pipe above her head and smashed it against the monster again and again until she was no longer moving. The floor was now slick with stinking ichor.

The wriggling creature squealed in a tiny voice. It slithered across the wet floor, trying to escape through the open doorway. Just as it crossed the threshold, Gloria stomped on it. She made a face and scraped her suddenly soaked shoe against the concrete floor, silently thankful that this was all in Dorothy's head.

Dorothy sobbed in terror. Luci quickly undid the straps binding her. Once she was free, she flung herself into Luci's arms. The two sank to the floor, Luci supporting Dorothy, Dorothy wrapping her arms around Luci's waist and sobbing into her neck. Then Dorothy turned her face up and kissed Luci. She ran her fingers through Luci's hair, pulling her face close. Luci held Dorothy tightly, returning her passion. Until she realized who was kissing her. She put her hand on Dorothy's shoulder and pushed her out of her lap and out of her arms. Dorothy stared at her, tears sparkling in the corners of her eyes. Luci's mouth hung open as she tried to work out what to say.

Gloria shook her head. They didn't have time for this.

"Catch her up quick," Gloria said. "We have to keep moving."

The mindscape shattered behind her as she reopened the portal to her own mind. Weird light streamed into the filthy hallway. Without waiting for Luci to respond, Gloria stepped through the rift.

Luci coughed awkwardly and stood. She put a careful hand under the other woman's arm and gently pulled Dorothy to her feet, ignoring her protests. Luci smoothed out her clothes with her free hand, then brushed her hands through her hair. She wouldn't meet Dorothy's eyes. It wasn't Dorothy that she wanted. She was just scared and desperate for reassurance, for relief. From the way Dorothy was looking at her, she could tell her ex was rather more invested.

"Come on," Luci said. "I don't have time to explain, but Gloria's right. We have to get out of here."

"Luci, what's going *on*?" Dorothy wailed.

"This place isn't real. Look, I'm sorry I dragged you into all of this. I'm getting you out, but you *have* to follow me. Okay?"

"Okay," Dorothy said, hesitant.

Luci turned away and hurried out of the operating room. Dorothy was half a step behind her. She reached out to take Luci's hand, but Luci pulled it away. She didn't see the hurt in Dorothy's eyes.

Luci stepped through the hole in Dorothy's dreamscape. Dorothy hesitated for a second, but screwed her eyes shut and jumped in after Luci. She let out a gasp when she saw Gloria's gleaming conceptual space-age control room. She stood stock still against the wall as the portal closed behind her. Luci left her there, joining Gloria at the console. Gloria's eyes were focused on the viewscreen. Each of them focused on me, still lying on the gurney. The frost was evaporating off me, but I continued to thrash.

"Oh God," Luci said. "What's the plan?"

Gloria was silent for a moment, focusing on the controls. Then she said, "I don't know. I didn't plan this far ahead. I was really hoping Amelia would have freed herself by now."

Luci stared at her. Then she let out a laugh, bordering on panic.

"We really fouled this one up, didn't we?"

"You ain't kidding," Gloria said with a tired smile.

"Don't say 'ain't', it ain't sophisticated," Luci said. She stared up at the viewscreen and bit her lip with worry.

"You and her go back to your bodies," Gloria said, nodding in Dorothy's vague direction. "After that…"

"I want to go in after her," Luci said, eyes on me.

"I don't think that would be safe."

"I don't *care*. She's hurting, and I have to save her!"

"Luci." Gloria put her hand on Luci's arm. "We will. But we can't do that if we all get hurt in the process. She wouldn't want that."

Luci's shoulders slumped. "Yeah. I know."

Gloria looked up at the screen, running possibilities through her head. "I can try another seal. One to put her under. Just long enough to get us all out of here."

"You can't be serious!"

"Look, why do the gurneys have straps? In a *real* hospital, I mean? It's to protect the patients for when they do *that*." She gestured at me. "She's my friend, too. You know I would never hurt her."

"I know. Okay. But what about the monster?"

Gloria turned a dial. One viewscreen swiveled as she turned her real head to look at the creature in the wheelchair. The chair rocked back and forth as its own shriveled body shook. In the conceptual space, Gloria nodded at the pipe, still dripping ichor all over her clean metal floor.

"Plenty of blunt objects around. Think you can do that in the real world?"

Luci curled her lip at the creature. "Just watch me."

"Okay. First, we get you two where you're supposed to be. Then—"

Before she could finish her thought, my eyes snapped open. The shout of joy died in Luci's throat when I flew off the gurney, leather straps snapping. When I landed, it wasn't on two feet. My body was *turning* in space, shifting this weak human flesh somewhere safer.

"Oh my God!" Dorothy cried. "What is *that?!*"

Reality shivered as I let out a mind-piercing shriek. Cracks spread across Gloria's mindscape, weird light streaming into the chamber. The control room shook as the force of my anger caught it, buffeting it with winds from beyond. Gloria's hands flew across the console, trying to maintain her mindscape's integrity, but to no avail. The mindscape shattered against the force of my eldritch power, sending the three plummeting into the void.

20

Reality rippled as my other self tore into this plane. My mass had quadrupled. Long spines and tendrils sprouted from the back of my wedge-shaped head. Many long, powerful limbs grew from my rugose torso, snapping at the air. Seven glowing eyes blinked individually, taking in the space. I didn't recognize the debris flying across the room in my wake. I noted the three human bodies lying in a tangle amid the wreckage of an energy matrix. Whorls of power connected them, now pale and fouled. One part of my existence shouted a warning, but I did not heed it. This matrix was no threat to me. Therefore, it was not relevant.

A fourth human form, withered and covered in dirty cloth wrappings, was confined to a wheeled metal chair. I remembered it now. It had been waiting in the hall when the elevator doors opened. My enemy lurked within it, an orb of violent red light squashed like a parasite into stolen flesh. Its furious gaze tried to burn my skin, still scarred from the Watcher's assault not long ago, but now I was prepared. My skin rotated, sliding damaged flesh through space to be replaced with unsullied matter.

The Gaze That Chains made a dry animal noise inside its stolen body. I could see the lines of energy chaining the Eye to that flesh. Red tendrils wound through the animal matter, bound by sutures of light. It was clearly torturous. I decided to help. I am the Opener of the Way. The Gate That Is The Guide. To me, bounds and boundaries were an affront. I would offer myself a prayer and release my enemy.

I pushed two of my limbs through space on either side of the Eye's flesh prison. They grabbed its own limbs and pulled it from the chair. The leather bonds snapped. As did most of the metal rods composing the chair. As did three of the flesh's bones.

I manifested a third limb in front of it, and that limb reared back like a scorpion's tail. The Eye's flesh face twitched, staring at the limb's sharp tip. Perhaps the expression it made beneath the stained cloth was fear. Then I stabbed forward, plunging the striking tip into the stolen flesh and piercing the Eye. I hooked the limb through *Shomo-Elnak*'s intangible form and tore it out of its prison.

The flesh ripped apart against my strength. It was irrelevant now. I made to toss it aside, but I heard a distant voice begging me to stop. To be careful. That voice was familiar. Synchronized. Was it mine? Tension rippled through my form until a second voice emerged. This voice was hesitant but soothing.

I-it's ok-k-kay. H-he was already duh-duh-dead.

I looked within the stolen flesh. My interlocutor was correct. There was no consciousness active within the body's brain, no memories, no sensation. The Eye's presence must have driven out or consumed the original occupant. Without the Eye driving it, the stolen flesh would already be dying, even absent the horrific damage to its thorax. My initial assessment was accurate. It was irrelevant. I tossed it aside.

Shomo-Elnak thrashed at the end of my striking limb. No longer confined, its presence expanded, just as my apocalyptic form had. It had taken on mass, becoming a scarlet orb shot through with veins of black matter. A half-dozen tentacles sprouted from the lower third, thick ropes of black and purple flesh dotted with bright red blisters. Four of the tentacles flailed in the empty air. The other two wrapped around my striking limb, digging their tips painfully into my flesh. Viscous violet fluid leaked from the orb where I speared it. It reacted aggressively to the local atmosphere, bubbling and stretching. The residue quickly congealed into a dark purple webbing that coated my limb and spilled onto the floor, holding the Eye fast to me. And me to it.

Florescent yellow spots swam across the orb's scarlet surface. They coalesced into a spiraling shape that looked uncannily like an iris. The shape focused on me, and the air between us grew thick. A looming presence rose within my mind. The space around us crackled with energy. Externally, my senses could detect no change in gravity or the floor's integrity. Nonetheless, I felt as if the floor fell out from beneath me, sending me plummeting into empty space. The Eye laughed in mind-splitting radio static, tentacles writhing.

The hospital room fell away. A star field replaced it. Clouds of colored dust and gas floated at the extremes of my senses, buoyed by cosmic wind. I stood on a desert plain, a wasteland of pulverized black glass. A blood-red star blazed in the void far above me. A flare lashed out from its burning surface, showering me with harsh radiation.

Beyond the star, I could just perceive my limb holding the writhing Eye fast.

This is not real, I sent. *This is another illusion.*

Reality is what I perceive it to be, the Eye replied in a voice made of solar radiation. *I see you, Subject 19.*

The blasted plain rumbled beneath the hateful star's glare. It showered the desert with charged particles, whipping up a devastating wind. Dunes of pulverized glass formed in the storm's wake. The wind speed picked up. It screamed across the glass plane, shattering the newly formed dunes. Glass sand flew at me at flesh-flaying speeds. It poured over my apocalyptic form, ripping the weird matter away until there was nothing left but Amelia. I crouched in the desert, covering my face with bloody arms, screaming at the pain.

Then it was over. I was curled into a ball on the floor in the middle of the lab. Blood froze against my torn limbs and chest. The trio of agents sneered on the other side of the one-way mirror. *Shomo-Elnak*'s red light pulsed behind their eyes.

The middle agent leaned forward, clicking the microphone on. "We will recommence environmental testing now."

He snapped his fingers, making a sound like dry twigs breaking. The temperature in the room plummeted. The shreds of my simple dress fluttered in the sudden draft. I stumbled to my feet, baring my teeth in a snarl.

"You vile little *object*," I said. "I've already *been* here!"

The room tilted. My apocalyptic form ripped through the lab's concrete floor and charged the observation room. I shattered the one-way mirror with one sweep of a limb, then dove through the gap. The agents fled to the sides of the room, fumbling in panic for the weapons in their jackets. I roared in rage as they fired on me, although it was a pointless gesture. Even if mere bullets could pierce my rugose skin, I had no definable organs in this form, no bones, no muscle. My apocalyptic form operated on its own physical laws.

I lashed out, breaking the nearest agent in two. I grabbed the next closest and flung him across the observation room, striking the concrete wall hard enough to send cracks spiderwebbing across its black surface. These were nothing more than figments, after all. Fragments of nightmare, puppets of the Eye's fancies. Sent to torment its victims. They weren't alive. They didn't matter.

But oh, it was so satisfying to break them.

The final agent determined discretion was the better part and ran through the rear door. My apocalyptic form gave chase, destroying door and wall in a wave of distortion. As Amelia, I followed. My small human body had waited in the freezing laboratory chamber. Now I walked it forward, crawling through the shattered window into the observation room. I stared down the warped hallway, watching the distortion of my furious passage. As before, I could sense nothing of the space around me, nothing but this chamber and the stub of a hallway stretching into nothingness. But no, that wasn't true, was it? I could *feel* the Eye far away, writhing like a bloated worm on the hook of my striking limb. And I could feel this space, hanging not in the void or in nothingness, but in a deep red miasma of potentiality and memory. This was *Shomo-Elnak*, more so than the swollen thing struggling in my grasp. A mutable substance out of which it could mold any scene. Scenes pulled from its victim's memories. But for a powerful psychic, that connection flowed both ways.

I raised my left hand and opened the way.

The broken wall rippled and the hallway twisted and transformed. No longer a terrified child's memory of a Bureau campus hall, now it was a nightmare corridor through a warped reflection of St. Audaeus. I would later realize I had found a reflection of Dorothy's mind-prison. At this point, I assumed it was simply a manifestation of the Eye's malice.

I stalked the hallway, ignoring the screams and moans coming from the rooms around me. They weren't real, or if they were, they were pieces of memory. A distraction, meant to confuse and unnerve me. I wouldn't be sidetracked from my goal. I didn't know for certain what it was, but I knew that I would find it here. Within the Eye's foul mind.

I grabbed hold of the mindscape and *twisted* it, pushing deeper. I was no longer following a passageway. I was standing in an operating theater. A dozen white men in dark suits stood in the shadows with me, watching the scene with detached interest. Men in white coats surrounded a man strapped to an operating table. He was thin from malnourishment, though his body had been recently washed, or at least disinfected. His body was covered in poorly healed wounds and sores. His face and head had been shaved, although judging by the dozens of small nicks and cuts, whoever did it hadn't been particularly careful. He wore a hospital gown, one that he had soiled several times. The doctors took no notice. One busied himself tightening the leather straps holding the man in place. Two more jabbed ink-tipped needles into the skin of his arms and legs, marking him permanently with a seal. The last stood at the man's head, double-checking a complex equation in a thick book. A matching equation had been painted onto the bed beneath the man—the victim—in the form of an intricately recursive circular seal.

When the binding had been fully tattooed onto the victim's skin, the three doctors stepped away from the table. A pair of nurses emerged from the shadows, carrying thick cables with alligator clips. They fastened them to copper caps at the head and foot of the table and hurriedly stepped away. The doctor who appeared to be the lead nodded to one of the juniors. That man threw a heavy switch on an electrical cabinet. Sparks flew on the cabinet and on both ends of the table. The smell of ozone filled the air. The lead doctor raised one hand and read the equation. Reality skipped, to those with the senses to detect it. A vortex of energy whirled into being around the victim, who screamed with a voice hoarse from abuse. The gravity in the room shifted, centered on the seal in the middle of the table. The vortex picked up speed, and reality unfolded before me.

As if looking through a tunnel made of lightning, I saw a distant space lit with red. A huge scarlet star burned in atomic merriment, flinging radiation through a space seven light years across. The space curved in on itself, forming a closed ovoid. A dozen worlds spun along wobbling orbits around the star, the largest of them still tiny next to their stellar parent. Each of these worlds teemed with life, from the nearly molten orb nearest to the star to the frozen worldlet at the system's farthest reach. I let my senses go wide, absorbing it all in a single glance. All manner of life, from single cells to civilizations of millions. They lived and died beneath the light of the red star. Under its Gaze.

A torus of energy formed deep within the red star. On the far side of the system, a span of space a kilometer across buckled and inverted. Another vortex opened, spilling something through—a building, six sides, three stories, with a hexagonal gabled roof. Fifty-three people were inside, beings with segmented bodies and six multi-jointed limbs. They screamed, immersed in acrid chemicals as the building—their home? A school? A temple?—tumbled across the red space. Matter coalesced around and beneath the structure. Within minutes, subjective ones, a stable worldlet 312 kilometers around had formed beneath the building. It drifted across space in a lazy orbit that would eventually lead to its capture by the sixth planet out, a striated violet gas giant with twenty-one other moons.

The Gaze That Chains. The Eye saw, the Cage imprisoned. This was *Shomo-*

Elnak's truest form, this space dominated by a malicious living star and its child worlds. Nothing had evolved naturally on these planets and moons. They hadn't coalesced out of cosmic dust in a millennia-long dance of gravity and matter. The Eye had built all of this. It was a garden. And a prison.

The newer vortex closed. The one I watched through dove closer to the star. I feared I would tip through it, perhaps joining the hexapods on their newly formed worldlet. Then I realized this portal's pull was reversed. Instead of forcing us out, it pulled the Eye *in*. A prominence erupted from the Eye's surface, a towering spire of scarlet flame. The ejecta flew toward the portal, forming a tight spiral as it was sucked into our plane. Into the poor man on the operating table. He screamed, his back arcing away from the table as the alien energy scoured his mind and body, erasing any hint of his consciousness. Once his mind was gone, he collapsed against the metal table. His nervous system burned with energy, but his brain lacked activity. Then his eyes flew open. Crimson light burned within them.

His eyes fixed on me. A wave of rage crossed my mind. Then the vortex reversed, pushing me out. It was so quick I was caught off-guard, flying out of the Eye's memory and into one of mine.

I landed in my dorm room in the Bureau's old headquarters. From the way the dingy white walls loomed over me, I knew it was many years ago. When I was very small and scared. A shadow of that old fear passed over me. My lips trembled. I wanted to hide in the corner, curl up into a ball. Make myself too small to be found when he came.

Heavy footsteps clomped in the hall outside. The floor trembled with the angry giant's coming. I screwed my eyes shut, but it was no use. I could see him through the walls, smell the aftershave that failed to cover the rank stink of his sweat. Heat radiated off him in thick waves. He was already angry.

The towering door slammed open. I flinched when it banged against the wall, knowing it would only make things worse. Agent Carlisle, my first handler, stormed into the room. His eyes blazed with crimson light. He glared down at me, teeth bared.

"WHAT ARE YOU DOING IN HERE?" he roared. "I TOLD YOU

TO BE IN THE TRAINING ROOM TWENTY MINUTES AGO!"

I wanted to shout, to hurl invectives at him. To stand with my back straight and head high, telling him exactly what he could do with himself. Instead, I curled into myself, tears streaming down my hot cheeks.

"I'm sorry, I'm sorry, I'm sorry," I blubbered over and over in a voice I couldn't believe was once mine.

"YOU'RE *SORRY*? DO YOU THINK THAT *MATTERS*?" The giant smashed his fist against the wall, denting the cheap plaster. "YOU ARE WASTING MY TIME!"

That only made young me cry harder. Agent Carlisle shook his head and spat.

"I'LL GIVE YOU SOMETHING TO CRY ABOUT, YOU LITTLE FREAK."

He raised a hand larger than my head, ready to strike. He'd probably break something this time. My nose, my lip. Maybe my jaw. I flung a tiny arm over my face, for all the good it would do.

Why did you permit it?

My eyes flew open. The Watcher-As-Lucas looked at me from a shadow in the corner of the room, radiating confusion. I was so much stronger than this.

I was. Even then.

As I learned.

I thrust my arm out… and my *arm* out. A limb I'd only barely become aware of lashed out at Agent Carlisle from right angles to reality, catching him across the abdomen. He flew through the room like a rag doll, slamming back-first against the wall, his spine shattered in three places.

In real life, Agent Carlisle had laid there, moaning, until others came upstairs to investigate the commotion. In this distorted memory, the Eye within the Carlisle puppet struggled up. It assailed me with a radiation scream, trying to force some new vision upon me. Agent Pickman loomed out of the shadows, electrodes sparking in his skeletal hands. The cold man and his scar-lipped companion appeared behind me, grabbing my shoulders. Agent Thomas shouted up at me from the stairs below, claiming we were surrounded. For just a moment, I felt a stab of panic. There were so many. And there would be so many more. Always.

The Watcher-As-Lucas stepped out of the shadows. They regarded the human figures with unmistakable disdain. They laughed in a voice that stank of ammonia and honey.

"They are so far beneath you."

My head hung. They had all hurt me so. Again and again. Treated me as if I was less than them. But maybe the Watcher was right.

"Maybe I'm more."

I struggled to my feet, shaking off the hands on my shoulders, growing to my proper size. I laughed at the Eye, despite the rage building inside me.

"I told you. I've been here before."

I lifted the Carlisle puppet and shook it. "Do you think this frightens me? I've already dealt with you." I flung Carlisle at Pickman. "*And* you." The two smashed into the far wall, dissipating in a cloud of red smoke.

I turned to look at the cold man and his henchman. They blanched against my implacable fury, stepping back. Raising their hands in surrender.

"I don't even know who you are," I said. "What do you think you can do?"

I made a cutting motion with my hand. They collapsed like marionettes whose strings had been snipped. I turned to the open door, where my biggest monster waited. Agent Thomas had a hand in his jacket, resting on his service pistol. The Eye's red glow pulsed in his pupils in time with his heartbeat.

"As for you, Randall Thomas," I said. "I'll deal with you when the time comes."

I waved my hand and the door slammed shut. Agent Thomas shouted imprecations behind it, but his voice shrank as if a volume dial had been turned all the way down. I looked over my shoulder up at the ceiling, where the single naked bulb glowed bright and red.

"Anything more? A memory of a skinned knee? What about a flashback to wetting the bed?"

The memory-scape shivered, falling into pieces. The swollen Eye writhed at the end of my striking arm. The yellow iris whirled wildly, desperately. I curled my lip in disgust.

"I didn't think so. I see what you are. I've seen where you're from. I'm *almost* sorry for you. You were stolen
(like me)
from the place where you belong. You were shackled to someone else's body. Lashing out in pain because pain is all you know. You didn't even realize freedom was at hand. That you could have asked for help."

I folded my arms across my chest.

"I *could* send you back, you know. If I wanted to."

The Watcher-As-Lucas stepped behind me. They looked up over my shoulder at the Eye, watching it bleed purple ichor. They sneered. Then they whispered into my ear, "It doesn't deserve your help."

The fabric of the mindscape rippled. The last of the Eye's phantoms burned away, dissolving into the nothingness of its soul. Images of Luci, Gloria, and Dorothy flickered into place around me. They glared up at the Eye in cold judgement.

I took a deep breath, centering myself. Outside of our linked minds, I tightened my grip on the Eye's fleshy core.

"You hurt my friends."

I cast the Eye out of my mindscape. On the physical plane, I grabbed it between two limbs. Ignoring its radiation screams, I pulled its tentacles and *tore*. Its form dissolved into a pile of scarlet slop, leaving only its immaterial self writhing in my grip. Scarlet lightning danced harmlessly over my limbs. The Watcher's glee was palpable.

We hear Izulz is lovely this time of year.

I thrust out a questing limb, tearing open a hole in space and time. The portal yawned onto a burning vacuum dominated by a hideous orb of matter-scouring anti-radiation. The vacuum sucked at the atmosphere, pulling debris with it. I pulled the Eye through the portal, slamming it shut after me.

The titanic anti-sun churned beneath us, a vast engine of nuclear fusion that dwarfed even me. We couldn't stay long here without its anti-solar wind unmaking us. Fortunately, I wouldn't be.

The orb of crimson lightning that was the Eye's consciousness sparked in my grasp, in fear and fury. I plunged each of my limbs into that ball of lightning, tearing it into decoherence. I flung the remnants of the Eye's consciousness into the void, bolts of psychic energy that traced a long arc as Izulz pulled them into a wide orbit. Its scream echoed in my mind as it fell away from me. With nothing to interfere with it, someday the fragments of the Eye could recombine. Perhaps enough to maintain coherence, even consciousness. Izulz's terrible radiation would prevent that. The anti-particles would tear at the incoherent matrix over thousands of years, gradually wearing it away into nothingness.

Perhaps I would return someday to rescue it.

Eventually.

21

Gloria tumbled through nothingness. Far above her, assuming "above" had any meaning here, a riot of colors burst in stellar explosions. Reds clashed with blues, yellows interwove with greens. Squeals and shrieks of static followed the explosions. Somehow it didn't doppler away as she fell. The noise wasn't being carried through the air. There was no air here. There was barely even a "here".

A massive shower of blue sparks surrounded her, the conceptual debris of her mindscape. That *thing* had shattered it when it erupted into the world. No, not "thing". That was *me*. She tried to remember that, although she wasn't sure how she was supposed to feel about it. She had seen my apocalyptic form once before, but then it had appeared as a savior. Not a destroyer.

She plunged deeper into the void, if that was possible. The lights of my battle with the Eye diminished. Stranger lights took their place. Distant waves of color swam at the far reaches of her vision. It was as if she was falling through a cloud lit by weird lightning. Far away, discordant chimes jingled. There was something familiar about them. Familiar and disconcerting.

What had I done? She realized I must have torn free of my own nightmare.

Likely I had destroyed the entire mind-prison in the process. How much control did I have? Obviously not enough. Gloria had constructed an entire conceptual space to help her navigate between the nightmares. I must have destroyed it as collateral damage. Almost instantly. Luci and Dorothy had been inside Gloria's mind when the space collapsed. I had thrown them all out. Into where?

Into some psychic void. Gloria had read about some of this. The books she'd acquired with her mentor's help generally referred to it as the astral plane. One could reach numerous other realms from here, albeit not physically. Such as wherever the not-so-good doctor and his agents had acquired the dream eater. *Zedu heth baagu.*

You could move through it. That was the important thing. Her mentor, the one she'd been hiding from me, had briefly described the astral plane, then dismissed it as an irrelevant distraction from the real work. It was something like lucid dreaming and also something like the technique she'd use to build her mental control room. She didn't need a seal to do it, which was the important part. She had no idea how she'd fuel a seal if she had to scribe one right now.

Gloria spread her arms wide, trying to catch the debris of her conceptual space. If she could rebuild her control room, then surely she could find Luci and Dorothy. The storm of sparks swirled around her. It gathered up speed, pulling together in a glimmering cloud. She pictured the space, the curve of the walls, the solidity of the floor. She drew a blueprint in her mind, willing the motes of psychic energy to cohere along the glowing lines. The arches began to coalesce around her, all coming together to form a dome above her head. The framework of a floor took shape at her feet. It was *working*. She was going to rebuild her mind-ship. Give herself something to stand on, a reference point against which she could measure the void. She just had to make the light *solid*. Solid enough to hold its shape, solid enough to support her. She almost had it. So close…

But the energy slipped through her fingers, becoming like sand, like water. She could bring the power together, she could even give it shape, but she couldn't give it form. The hazy framework dissolved, trailing motes of light as it fell through the void with her.

Gloria let her head fall back against nothing and screamed in frustration. This was too much. Her studies hadn't prepared her for this. She'd pulled herself this far on guesswork and inspiration, but now this was as far as that would take her. Her mind adrift in a featureless void while her body wasted away in the basement of a haunted hospital. What an absurd thing to say.

"I just need a little help," she whispered. "Something to point me in the right direction."

The soft words floated away into the astral. Then she slammed back-first into a wide, flat surface. It was hard and cold but didn't hurt. She didn't have the parts to hurt with, here. Nonetheless, a strange, uncomfortable sensation rippled through her psychic form. Like the memory of pain, as her mind sought something familiar to process this sensation.

Gloria rolled over, pushing herself up on her hands and knees, trying to see what she'd found. It was just a floor. Black and blue tiles formed a herringbone pattern. It stretched out for miles behind her. In front, she was near one corner of the… space? Platform? There were no walls, nor a roof, only two tall arches of blue stone, striated with paler blues. They were hung with heavy blue drapes, which fluttered irregularly despite the lack of breeze. A man stood between the arches. Or at least, what Gloria thought was a man. Certainly he was man shaped. He wore a thick robe, hood down to show his bald, grey-skinned head. The cloak's hem decohered into smoke and shadow, waving indecorously in the still not-air. It almost seemed to Gloria that it was beckoning her closer.

Then the man turned to face her, and Gloria stifled a scream.

He had no face. It wasn't that his skull was entirely covered in blank skin, or that his head was under shadow. There wasn't a gaping hole where a face should be. Instead, the man had a shifting nothingness, like the physical equivalent of radio static. It hurt to look at. Almost as much as it hurt to hear him speak. It wasn't a voice in her ears. More like words being dropped into her mind, leaving uncomfortable ripples echoing in their wake.

As the creature greeted her and asked what took her so long, Gloria recognized him. Them. It. The nameless guest from her nightmare. Whose voice was sickness, whose laughter was venom. The one the books called the Ageless Stranger.

"I thought you were just something I dreamed," Gloria whispered. "Something that monster had made up."

It should not have been possible for the Stranger's broken kaleidoscope of a visage to smile, but nonetheless it managed. It explained that it had been watching this place for quite some time now, waiting for an entity clever enough to upset the board. Was she such a person, it wondered?

Gloria set her shoulders and lifted her chin, trying to project a confidence she didn't truly feel. "I don't have anything to prove to you."

But she had people to save. Unless she was comfortable freeing only herself? It was all the same to the Stranger. Events were already moving forward to its satisfaction. Perhaps it should simply move on.

"Maybe you should," Gloria said. "I'm not in the mood for games or tricks. You gonna try and eat my soul? Let's go. Otherwise, state your business or shove off."

The Stranger stared at her for a moment. Then she felt a sensation like a thin sheet of rusty metal bending back and forth in the pit of her mind. It took her a second to realize the Stranger was laughing.

Gloria didn't blink. There was no point, here in this conceptual space without eyes to dry out. Nonetheless, in one moment the Stranger was standing several yards away, at the corner of the platform. In the next, it was standing in front of her.

The Stranger's robe rippled. It lifted something that was probably a hand of some sort. A line of blue lightning flickered between its phalanges. The Stranger tugged on it, and Gloria felt a wave of vertigo. She looked down and saw the line of lightning was coming out of her chest. The other end stretched off into the void. The Stranger lifted its other appendage to reveal a second line. This one was pale, less energetic. Gloria worried it might snap at any time. Like the first, it stretched from her mind-form and out into the nothingness.

"This is what remains of the seal, isn't it? The one connecting me to Luci and Dorothy."

The Stranger radiated condescending approval. She couldn't help but think it was behaving like a trainer watching a clever pet perform a complicated trick. She swallowed the words that came to mind, as she had done for as long as she could remember and said, "So if we're still connected…"

She took hold of the stronger thread. Her perspective shifted immediately. She was far away, plummeting through the void again, this time without any control. Fear filled her mind. Fear and longing for me. What was happening? Where was I? Why wouldn't I save her?

Gloria gasped and forced herself to drop the thread. She returned to herself with a shivery shock. The Stranger regarded her, curious.

"Luci. That was Luci!" Gloria said. "Then this other thread must be my link to Dorothy. That makes sense. Luci's my best friend. I barely know Dorothy."

She looked at the Stranger with a grim expression. "What are you offering?"

Knowledge. The equations she would need to master this space… or at least, well enough to traverse it.

"And you're just going to give that to me?"

Of course not.

"I already have a mentor."

This would be a one-time transaction.

"What's the cost?"

Whatever it was, she would find it acceptable.

"How do I know that?"

Because if she didn't pay it, she would lose her friends.

Gloria was silent for a moment. Time ticked by, one inexorable second after the other. Did time pass the same here? No way of knowing yet. But she couldn't afford to waste it, or to argue with the Stranger's logic. She didn't have to like it. But for her friends, their minds falling further and further away into nothingness, her degree of comfort with the situation meant nothing.

"Okay. Do it."

The Stranger extended one digit. There was one other condition.

"What's that?"

The Stranger's head inclined. For a moment, Gloria thought she saw alien sparks that could have been blazing eyes floating around its hairless cranium.

///TELLNOONE///

It touched her forehead. Her mind filled with data. She saw the equations fall into place, shaping not merely a conceptual space but an entire personal world. Or a ship. She had all the power she needed for this operation waiting in the wreckage of her previous attempt. She reached out again, feeling the motes of power draw in, spinning around her as she rebuilt her control room, making it the heart of a disc-shaped vessel. She leaned back in a chair of flowing silver metal, looking out through an oval glass dome, eye-shaped. Each hand rested on a control disc, connected by levers to the complex array of churning equations that were the ship's engine. Gloria gestured with the discs, and the ship rotated in the psychic void. She maneuvered it along the thread connecting her to Luci's presence. She was more confident in her ability to follow that thread than Dorothy's. If she was right, Luci could help her find the other woman.

The Stranger had disappeared, but Gloria felt a lingering echo of its presence wafting through the astral space as the ship flew away. No need to render payment now. She had already sacrificed enough for one day. The Stranger would return at a more opportune time.

She pushed that out of her mind for now. She concentrated on flying her ship. An age passed. No time passed at all. She saw Luci in the distance, floating at the end of a line of blue fire, her presence shining. Gloria gestured as her ship approached, and it unfolded like a metal flower to catch Luci.

"I am running out of the potential to be surprised," Luci said as she hugged Gloria.

"How are you feeling?"

"Discombobulated. Kind of stretched out."

"That makes a lot of sense."

"I hate that. Do I even want to know where we are?"

"You remember telling me how you were reading up on the Theosophists?"

"Sure. Oh, hell."

Luci stared at Gloria, half aghast and half annoyed.

"The astral plane? What are we doing here?" she asked.

"I pulled you and Dorothy both into my head," Gloria said. "I think we've all been pushed out of it, and this is where we ended up. I can get us all back, though. Trust me."

"Well, obviously," Luci said, becoming agitated. "But Dorothy must be terrified. She has no idea what's going on!"

Gloria doubted that very much. Dorothy had been involved with the hospital for far too long to be as ignorant, or innocent, as she played. Her nightmare had proven that. Gloria kept that to herself for now, though. No sense causing discord while the rescue was still ongoing.

"We're going after her next," she said, with forced casualness. "I need your help to do that. I don't have a strong connection to her. We've only just met tonight. You two, on the other hand... you have, ah..."

"An *intimate* connection, let us say," Luci said delicately. "What do you need me to do?"

"Sit up there." Gloria pointed to a seat ahead and to the right of her captain's chair. She resumed her position. "Pick up the controls and focus on Dorothy."

A small gleaming object rested on the flat console in front of Luci's chair, a palm-sized ceramic disc inside a larger metal ring. It was a miniature version of the ones Gloria used to control the ship. Luci fitted her hand around the inner disc and held it out in front of her, letting her fingers float in the narrow gap. The invisible force made her fingers tingle.

"What do I do, exactly?" she asked.

"The controls are all conceptual," Gloria said.

"Should that mean something to me?"

Gloria rolled her eyes. "Just focus on Dorothy. I'm going to use your thoughts as a lens to strengthen my connection to her."

Luci's brow furrowed. She waved the disc vaguely in front of her and concentrated, picturing Dorothy in her mind. She saw the other woman sitting on a park bench, smiling coquettishly. Then she saw Dorothy wearing her candy-striped uniform, pushing a gurney and looking frightened. Then the gurney fell out from beneath her and she was falling through nothingness, screaming for help. Luci leapt from her chair, turning to aim the disc in Dorothy's direction.

The thread connecting Gloria to Dorothy flared to life, blazing with power. Gloria gestured, twisting the ship until it was oriented along Dorothy's thread. Then she sent the ship hurtling through the astral void.

They heard Dorothy before they saw her. Her screams shivered through the astral plane, rippling across the skin of the ship. It rumbled as it approached her, and the shaking grew stronger as they closed in. It wasn't like whatever had destroyed Gloria's previous conceptual space. That had been a single great force, overwhelming her with its presence. This was *directed*. And it had to be coming from Dorothy. It felt like a warning, or a shield, manifesting in the astral space as waves of force pushing them away.

I think there's a reason that nursing program picked her, Gloria thought.

"Something's blocking us," she said aloud. "I think it's Dorothy. We can't get any closer."

"Blocking us? How in the world could she do that?" Luci asked, incredulous.

"More things in Heaven and Earth, Horatio," Gloria said. "We'll figure out the 'how' later."

She slowed the ship to a stop, letting it bob in the astral turbulence. It hung several—yards? miles?—from Dorothy, holding a steady position. Or, perhaps, falling into nothingness at the same speed as her. For now.

"Okay," Gloria said. "I have a theory."

"A *theory*." Luci raised a skeptical eyebrow.

"Fine, I have a guess. I'm *guessing* she's doing this somehow. Maybe she picked up something from the not-so-good doctor. Or maybe you have a type."

"A *type*."

"Gals with weird abilities."

"Oh, will you cut the gas?"

"Look, all I know is that I can't get this imaginary ship any closer without Dorothy shaking it apart and leaving us all floating in nothing again. She won't let me in. But I bet she'll let you."

Luci opened her mouth to speak, but words wouldn't come. Tears welled in her eyes. She turned away from Gloria and looked out the windows at her former lover. When she finally spoke, it was in a whisper. "If she was willing to do that, we'd still be together."

"Luci…"

"She was the one who ended it, Gloria. It was *her* choice. She didn't want to be with me anymore." She gestured at the waves emanating from Dorothy's terror. "This is actually what it was like in the end. Dorothy pushing me away because she was too scared to be with me. To be herself. I couldn't get through that before. You think I can now?"

"Look, I don't know what it's like, being in that sort of relationship. But people don't put themselves in these situations for just anybody. She got mixed up in this because she still cares about you. She reached out to *you* when we saved her from her nightmare. I think she will again."

Luci stared up at Dorothy and let out a deep sigh. "It's worth a try."

Gloria took up the controls again. At her gesture, the ship unfolded like a flower. This time a slender platform rose from the center, with Luci atop it. The thread connecting Gloria to Dorothy ran up the platform and through her. It would be a lifeline if she needed it. They hoped.

There was no gravity here. Or if there was, it was in whatever direction she needed it to be. When the platform was high enough, Luci's feet gently lifted off its surface. Then she was falling, falling toward Dorothy. The force of her screams hit Luci like a strong wave. It felt as if it should have sent her bowling over. Luci felt a wave of vertigo, then found herself in Dr. Sutherland's office. The not-so-good doctor stared at her down his round nose as if she was an insect pinned to a board, a curiosity. Or perhaps a simple tool he might have a use for. He spoke to her now, his words lost to imperfect memory but his tone unmistakably condescending. He held an asymmetrical crystal in one hand, rubbing its facets with his thumb as he spoke. She could have sworn it briefly glowed with a weird inner light.

The wave passed. The void dissolved into place around her. Luci sucked in a gulp of air that wasn't there. Dorothy was still ahead of her, closer now but still distant. Luci plunged forward.

Another wave hit. Luci was sitting on a university dorm bed, staring at herself, holding her own hand. A surge of vertigo threatened to overwhelm her until she heard Dorothy's voice come out of her own mouth. She was in Dorothy's memory of their breakup. She watched a thundercloud pass across her own face as Dorothy tried to explain that it was foolishness, that they could never be together, that all girls felt like this at some point but it was time to grow up…

A brief respite in the void. Then another wave. Dorothy, younger now, looking down at her hands as her mother tried to explain the sorts of things nice girls didn't do, *especially* not with other girls…

Another wave. Dorothy standing over a hospital bed, staring at a woman covered in bandages, her wrists strapped to the rails. Something was writhing in her stomach. Dorothy could see the way it pushed against her skin from inside. It had to be painful, but her jaws were wired shut. All she could do was moan pitifully…

Another wave. She stood in the corner, hands against the wall, shivering in a plain cotton shift. A bucketful of ice water dashed against her head and shoulders, forcing out a scream. A thick voice above her promised to wash away her sins…

Another wave. She was lying in the back seat of a car, feeling Luci's warm weight between her legs, Luci's soft lips against hers, Luci's hands running over her body, inside her blouse, up her skirt…

Luci dove through the brief gap between waves. She reached out to Dorothy, catching her in her arms, pulling her close, holding her tight. Dorothy stiffened, then slowly melted as she realized who it was, sobbing against Luci's neck and clinging to her as if she was a life preserver on the surface of a bottomless, alien ocean. The screaming stopped. The turbulence subsided. The astral space stilled.

Gloria felt a pressure behind her, at once alien and far too familiar. It placed a flesh-crawling phalange on her shoulder. Impressive, wasn't she? Perhaps the payment could be rendered now.

"Perhaps I'll figure out what sort of ward works against things like you," Gloria said.

There were no things like it. No matter. Payment would not be required now. It simply wanted to see. And for Gloria to see.

Space shivered, and the Stranger disappeared again. Gloria set her mouth in a grim line and brought the ship in close. It came up beneath Luci and Dorothy, petals spread wide to make a gently rotating platform. Conceptual gravity reversed, and the pair slowly floated down until they landed safely. Luci gave Dorothy one last comforting hug, then disentangled herself and rose to her feet. Dorothy let her go with some reluctance. As she stood, she reached out for Luci's hand and looked hurt when Luci evaded her.

"I don't know what's going on," Dorothy said, her voice dull and sullen.

We'll see about that, Gloria thought. *Later.*

"We're not out of the woods yet, but we're at least out of this particular problem," Gloria said. "I'm going to get us back to where we're supposed to be. Then we're all going to leave this awful place."

She gestured again with the control discs. The petals of the platform folded, twining together to form three glowing portals surrounding the central platform. Gloria felt an unmistakable pull toward the arch behind her—the portal designated as the entry to her own brain. Luci and Dorothy turned to face their own portals, following the same instinctive pulls.

"Let's not waste any time," Gloria said. "I have a feeling that things in the real world are getting serious."

Luci nodded, her expression firm. "We wake up, we grab Amelia, and we run for the elevator. *All of us.*"

I don't think Amelia's going to be so easy to budge, Gloria thought.

The three women ran through their portals. Behind them, the astral ship dissolved into motes of energy from the inside out. The motes gradually decohered into swiftly fading sparks. A writhing shadow hung in their place, a cruel smile across its lack of a face.

22

Reality snapped back around me as I returned to the local cross-section. The Amelia facet was making increasingly strident demands for priority access to the sensorium and decision making. Sensing no immediate threat remaining, I determined it was safe to shift Amelia forward. Yet I retained primary control as a precaution and did not *turn* from my apocalyptic form.

The hospital room was a mess. A half-dozen gurneys had been thrown against the walls. Three of them, the ones that had been closest to me when my apocalyptic form manifested, were twisted and bent nearly in half. Thankfully, my friends hadn't been in them. Gloria must have pulled them to the floor when she did whatever it was that she did. It had most likely been to facilitate the seal she drew, but fortunately it had also spared them from harm. From my wrath.

My flesh rippled as a sick chill spread through me. The alternative paths were still there, readily in view. I could see an afterimage of Gloria cradling Luci's broken body, cursing me. Gloria and Luci lying against the shattered walls, their spines and limbs bent at sickening angles. The three women on their gurneys, their minds hollowed out, waiting for instrumentality. I screamed, denying these realities. *This* was the timeline that mattered. The one in which my friends lived.

The afterimages vanished as I asserted reality. Gloria rose to her knees, grabbing her messenger bag. Most of her supplies had been scattered across the room. She looked about for the Eye, or rather, for the poor dead vagrant who had been forced to be its host and prison. The body lay in pieces on the floor, scattered amidst the tangled wreckage of the wheelchair. I evidently hadn't been gentle when I had exorcised it.

The Eye is no longer here, I sent. *I dealt with it.*

Gloria winced as my words entered her mind. She'd never been fond of telepathic communion, and even less so coming from my apocalyptic form. Luci, however, immediately sat upright when she felt the caress of my presence. She looked for me, relief flooding her face when she recognized me.

"The Eye?" Luci said. "You mean that monster who trapped us?"

The Gaze That Chains. The Eye sees, the Cage imprisons. That is the designation the Archivists gave it. I do not know how it refers to itself. I doubt that it does. That would imply that a distinction between itself and others matters.

"But you dealt with it," Gloria said. "How exactly?"

I removed it.

"From the body?"

From this planet.

Gloria hid it from her face, but I could see the quiet terror washing over her forebrain. She made a quiet reappraisal of my abilities. Although she was far from ungrateful, the thought that I could do that and speak of it so casually unsettled her. It unsettled the Amelia facet as well. She was demanding full control now. I did not relent. The danger had not passed after all. I now perceived that the true danger had arrived. My expanded senses threw warnings at my consciousness. Three new vehicles had arrived in the parking lot. Three white vans with identical markings to the one that had taken Ralph Connor away. Twenty-two identical men sat inside the vans, with white jumpsuits, close-cropped blond hair, dark sunglasses, and a chemical sameness. Dr. Sutherland sat in the passenger seat of one van, mopping his sweaty brow with a handkerchief. An older man with graying hair and a short salt-and-pepper beard sat in a second van. I couldn't detect his name; his mind was shrouded in that familiar frustrating slick blankness. His body language was far more relaxed than that of the doctor, however. He calmly filled in a small notebook in shorthand while the identical men filed out of the vans. The identical men in the left and right vans formed lines of eight. The six men in the center withdrew a complicated mechanical apparatus from the back of their van, setting it up in the parking lot. A dish-shaped antenna array unfolded from its top.

Over Amelia's objections, I pushed her aside. I didn't think she had the stomach for what would come next. It was a mercy to assert full control over my apocalyptic form, as well as a practical necessity.

No more talk, I sent. Shomo-Elnak *was holding us here for others to claim. They have arrived.*

"Others?" Gloria said, glaring at Dorothy. "What others?"

"The ones who took Ralph," Luci said. "That's it, isn't it? This whole place is a testing facility. And we were going to be—"

"Test subjects," Gloria said. She stepped closer to Dorothy, who backed away in shock. "What did you know about this?"

More than she let on but less than you fear, I sent. Whatever fog had blocked my perception earlier gave way to my apocalyptic form's presence. I could see the truth dancing in Dorothy's mind. *Irrelevant at this juncture. You are not prepared for this fight. You must depart.*

"F-fight?" Dorothy said, trying desperately to catch up. "We're not fighting anyone!"

That is correct.

I cast my consciousness across the basement. It was good to have full awareness of a space again. Numerous compartments connected to the gently curving single hallway. There were plenty of places to hide in the short term, but only two exits—the elevators and the stairwell, both at one end of the hall. They would be easily secured. Dr. Sutherland and the other man were upstairs in the mechanical room, ordering one of the custodians to shut the elevators down. Eight of their identical underlings were marching in step toward the stairwell. Eight more were taking up positions in the first-floor hallways. After thirty seconds of observation, I realized they were tracing out a wide circle around us. The final six had activated the machine in the parking lot. Weird energy coursed through it, sending an irritating vibration through local reality.

There are twenty-four men, I sent. *One is Dr. Sutherland. The others I don't recognize. They are all coming for us. I will stop them.*

"Stop them…" Gloria said. "You *can't kill them!*"

You will find that I can.

"No!"

Space rippled as I *turned*. My apocalyptic form remained in local space-time while Amelia pushed my way in. Gloria and Luci stared at me while Dorothy fainted. I ignored her, focusing my attention on my apocalyptic form.

"I'm not hurting anyone," I said firmly. "There has to be another way."

There will not be, I sent. *It was an unpleasant lesson, but a necessary one. These people mean my family harm. I acted to protect them.*

"I'm *better than this!* I can move through space and time! I *just* went to another star system! I can just take us somewhere else!"

It is too late.

Above us, the eight underlings had formed a complete circle. Moving synchronously despite a lack of detectable communication, they each withdrew an instrument from their jumpsuits. They were like mannikins made of metal. The underlings began humming, each slightly but significantly off-key from the others. In the parking lot, one of the underlings turned a dial on the apparatus, increasing its power output. Strange radiation poured out of the dish. Again moving in distant synchronization, the underlings on the first-floor twisted their instruments, moving their limbs through a sequence of significant shapes. They resonated with the weird radiation. Space solidified above and around me.

They are sealing us in. Prepare yourself.
"For what?" Luci asked.
"No!" Amelia cried. "I have to stop this!"
You did.
The other eight underlings were tromping down the stairs. They would be upon us in less than a minute. We were utterly unprepared for anything but violence.

Or a feint.

I took hold of my Amelia facet. This was my anchor to this cross-section. I couldn't risk being harmed. I had to return Amelia to safety before the underlings finished their seal and locked down space-time completely. I struggled against my apocalyptic form, desperate to remain present. Space-time splintered around us as I fought to remain in this juncture, fought to *turn* myself to safety. The Amelia facet was tenacious, but my apocalyptic form had raw power. Amelia screamed in frustration as I forced myself back outside of the local dimensions.

All of this occurred in the time it took my human friends to draw a single breath.

The seal locking us in was nearly complete. Fortunately, my internal struggle had provided the opening I needed. Space-time is flexible, to a point. It was already starting to snap back, similar to but entirely unlike a sheet of rubber. For the next few minutes/weeks/eras, the immediate vicinity would be unstable, though not nearly as much as in the next five seconds.

I rode the instability up to the first floor, my apocalyptic form screaming in furious electromagnetic radiation as it burst through seemingly empty space in front of a surprised underling. The white-suited man fumbled for another instrument—a weapon, perhaps, something he hoped could disable me—but far too slowly. I lashed out, striking him across the midsection with a tooth-rattling *thud*. He flew down the hallway, smashing through a wall into an empty patient's room. The impact didn't kill him immediately, assuming he was something that even counted as "alive". All his limbs were broken, as well as half his ribs and his spine in three places. His blood was thick and milk-white instead of red.

I did not waste time examining him. With one component gone, the ward collapsed. The rest of the security detail turned their heads in my direction. They began moving, re-spacing themselves out, expanding the ward's dimensions even as they compensated for one component's loss. That would take time, and I had plenty of that now. I reached through space and grabbed Luci, Gloria, and Dorothy. One moment they were in the basement. The next they were tumbling across the floor of their borrowed van. The collection detail filed into an abandoned room, littered with junk but with no sign of life besides a sudden inrush of air.

Get them to safety, I sent to Gloria. *I will rejoin you when I can.*

I'm sorry. I love you, I sent to Luci. *I'll see you soon. Promise.*

Don't even think about it, I sent to the unconscious Dorothy, although I knew she would.

I gave the van a *flick* ten seconds before the ward slammed into place. I couldn't risk trying to place them more accurately, so I simply sent them skipping across space. No more than two or three miles, I was sure. Far enough to facilitate their escape without being detected. Not so far that inertia would cause serious injuries. I couldn't control how they landed, after all.

With my friends safe, I turned my attention to the swarm of white-suited invaders. The collections detail was already running upstairs, while the security detail had completed their adjustments. The collections detail had weapons at the ready. Confrontation was inevitable.

And then it was simply violence.

I could have escaped if I had truly wanted to. I do not say that out of braggadocio. The Eye was a far greater threat than these experiments by the Apollonian Society's latest castoffs. These were glorified insects, fragile bags of contaminated water wrapped around something entirely unlike bone. Had I been willing to unleash more of my powers, I could have freed myself easily. Not even the fullest extent of my strength. Just more than I displayed at this juncture.

But if I did that, considerable collateral damage would have followed.

The Amelia facet stayed at the edges of my perception. Holding me back. Reminding me that this was more than just an Apollonian Society facility. It was a real hospital, full of normal, fragile humans who had come here to be made well. It was a curious form of armor, though in my-as-Amelia's judgement it was simply despicable.

I restrained myself. It was the correct thing to do. From a human perspective. The cosmos as a whole has no sense of ethics.

But the human perspective mattered to Luci and to Gloria. And so, it mattered to me.

Thirty-three minutes later, I found myself trapped in a corner of the hospital cafeteria. Four of the identical underlings surrounded me, holding out their instruments to focus the weird radiation. A fifth stood one floor above me, a sixth one floor beneath me. A seventh stood off to one side, holding up a metal placard covered in familiar symbols. It glowed red hot, searing the flesh of his hand, although he did not seem to notice. My rugose skin burned where he had torn space around me. In my confinement, I couldn't rotate my damaged matter away. I crouched within the confines of hostile geometry and seethed.

But these seven were all that remained of twenty-two. I took a fierce satisfaction in that.

Once they were sure the violence was finally over, Dr. Sutherland and the other man entered the cafeteria. Sutherland wore his white lab coat over rumpled pajamas. The other man, half Sutherland's height, sported a jumpsuit that was a photo-negative of those worn by his underlings—black with white shoulders connecting to a V-shape across the torso. Though both men's thoughts were hidden from me, their body language was familiar. I'd seen it enough times within the Bureau to understand it. Sutherland was incensed, his movements stiff and jerky. No doubt he was tabulating the cost of everything we'd accomplished tonight. The bearded man was far more relaxed, as he'd been when he arrived. His mannerisms reminded me of Agent Thomas, the infrequent times he wasn't angry, or of Agent Pickman when he was about to begin an experiment. His gait was casual, the set of his shoulders light. His thin mouth turned up in something like a smile, but more like a sneer.

In another place, the scars on my right arm burned.

"This is a mess," Dr. Sutherland was saying. "An absolute mess. We'll be recovering from tonight for months. Maybe years."

"I have every confidence in your abilities, Graydon," the bearded man said.

"Oh, that's nice. That's very nice, Octavian. So this is all *my* problem."

"I don't ever recall giving you permission to address me by my first name," the bearded man said, his voice mild.

Sutherland stopped abruptly. His sweat came more heavily.

"I *do* recall you saying that this facility was *your* domain," the bearded man continued, not deigning to look at the not-so-good doctor. "I recall that very distinctly. And repeatedly."

So sorry about the mess, I sent. *I hope it's difficult to clean up.*

"It communicates!" the bearded man said, sounding pleased as punch. "And much more clearly than the lost asset. That's an unexpected dividend."

"That 'asset' represented a significant investment of our resources, *Mister Director*," Dr. Sutherland groused.

"And this one represents a much smaller investment, Graydon," the bearded man said, "and with a potentially much greater return."

The bearded man dismissed Sutherland with a twitch of his head. He walked a partial circuit around the ward, head cocked to one side, regarding me as if I was a fish in a bowl. He tapped his finger against his chin thoughtfully.

"If I'm right, you can communicate even more clearly than this, mm? Yes."

He snapped his fingers, speaking now to the underlings. "Pattern Theta 5, if you please."

The underlings did not speak. Instead, they manipulated their instruments, flipping their limbs through another sequence of positions. The ward rotated around me, compressing in some dimensions, slackening in others. It was forcing my apocalyptic form out of this junction of space-time, rotating in Amelia. How? Did he know about me? What did he know?

I had no time to speculate. Space-time dragged against my apocalyptic form, throwing up sparks as I pushed against it. Reality rippled around me. The air in the cafeteria whipped into a wind, sending dust and debris flying. Plaster and tile cracked, and timbers creaked as space shivered. Seconds skipped past, then dragged for minutes. I could break this ward, I was sure. It was such a small thing. No match for my strength.

"Neither is the hospital," I said as Amelia.

I stopped pressing but did not relent. I did not want to harm those who had not harmed me. At least, now I didn't. It wasn't that they mattered. But somehow they did. Still, neither could I let myself be taken by these low men and their toy soldiers. Not again. I couldn't bear it.

"It's all right," I said. "I can take it from here."

I'm a prisoner!

"I've been a prisoner for seventeen years, ten months and six days," I said. "This is just a different cell. I'll find a way between the bars soon enough."

With great reluctance, I acceded. Space returned to normal as I let my apocalyptic form be rotated away, *turning* the Amelia facet in its place. I sat on the fluid-spattered cafeteria floor, back straight, legs folded primly beneath me. I glared at the bearded man. He was speechless for a moment, mouth agape. I felt some satisfaction at that.

"Not what you were expecting?" I asked.

"Oh this… this is too good," he finally said. "If only you understood what we have here, Graydon. Mm. If I'm correct, this entity is more valuable than your little lost pet could ever hope to be."

He stepped closer to the ward, careful not to cross over the invisible line separating us. He smiled down at me, this time completely genuinely. That didn't make me feel any better.

"I know it might not seem like it now, young lady, but you and I are going to be very good friends. Yes."

23

Time passed, as it does within this segment of reality. Most entities can't skip back and forth across the local timestream. Their selves pass inexorably in a single direction. And yet, while time passes in an objective measure, human perception has its own method of time dilation. The hours Luci had spent with me in her dorm room had seemed far too short. The first five days she spent waiting to hear from me were interminable.

Worse, when she finally did receive a visitor, it wasn't me.

It was early in the evening on a Friday, and Luci's dormitory was largely empty. Most of the girls had left for various parties out in town. Hallowe'en might have been a week ago, but college students still found excuses to enjoy themselves. Luci, though, was in no mood for a party. She had buried her head in a pile of notes spread out across the pushed-together beds. She'd written down everything she could remember of the night at the hospital, adding it to the messy files she'd accumulated. Now she was poring through her notes for the third time that day, looking for connections. For a single clue as to where she should turn next. For where she might find me.

She didn't notice the first time her guest knocked on her door. Or the second. It took a loud rap on the door and a feminine voice calling her name to finally drag Luci out of her research. She let loose a string of foul words and dropped her notebook. Then she jumped up and stalked across the four steps from the beds to the door, yanking it open, not bothering to see who was on the other side before she started shouting.

"I told you already, I don't give a foul word about your fouling party, I'm *busy!*"

Dorothy flinched, holding a hand over her face. Luci's expression immediately softened. A wave of guilt washed over her. Guilt and something else. A tickle in the back of her mind, a sensation she barely noticed. She briefly felt as if a word was right on the tip of her tongue but wouldn't come. That feeling disappeared as soon as it came, leaving behind the guilt. She looked away, mumbling an apology in the direction of Dorothy's left shoulder.

"Sorry. Thought you were someone else."

Dorothy stared at her feet, hands clasped together at her waist. There was something Luci found so familiar about her body language. She didn't realize it at the time, but it reminded her of me when we first met.

"It's okay. I know you weren't expecting me," Dorothy said softly. She bit her lower lip, eyes sliding to the left. "Could we... would it be okay if I came in?"

Luci hesitated. She flashed back to the last real conversation they'd had, almost seven months ago now. To say it had been tense was an understatement. Her old resentment flared again, and when her eyes found Dorothy's, they were hard and hot.

"You sure about that, Dottie?" Luci said, her tone at once light and nasty. "Because I seem to recall you saying pretty clearly that you didn't want to come around my room anymore."

Dorothy's face crumbled. Tears welled in her eyes. Her lip trembled. "Please, Luci. I don't have anyone else I can talk to about... about..."

Now the guilt rose again. Guilt both at the way she had treated Dorothy over the past couple of weeks and at the feeling her tears were stirring. Luci let her shoulders drop in defeat. She pushed the door open and stepped aside.

"Come on in, Dorothy," she said, looking away again. "Mind where you sit.

I'm in the middle of something."

Dorothy's eyes widened as she took in Luci's current project. She stared at the cork board for ten long minutes, taking in the extent to which Luci had charted the conspiracy. She didn't understand most of it, but she recognized the name "ST. AUDAEUS". She approached the corkboard, putting two shaky fingers on that card and tracing the green string that led to Dr. Sutherland's photograph with a worried frown. Luci watched her, arms folded across her chest, waiting for Dorothy's reaction. Prepared to judge her based on it.

"I'm surprised I'm not on here," Dorothy finally said.

"Haven't gotten around to it," Luci said. "I'm not entirely certain where to fit you in yet."

She grabbed a notecard from the pile on her bed and showed it to Dorothy. It read "Dorothy's Nursing Program". She pinned it to the corkboard next to the hospital's card and connected the pins with a yellow string.

"There you go," she said.

"Oh, that's nice. That's real nice," Dorothy said, recovering a bit of spark. "It isn't *my* program. It's the only one I could get into. You act like I'm responsible for it."

She looked away, putting her hands on her hips. "And it's the New Hope Nursing Program, for the record."

Luci tightened her mouth into a thin pale line. That weird tingling sensation had returned, dancing at the back of her mind. Then it was gone, forgotten. She grabbed a felt-tipped pen from the jar on her nightstand. She crossed out "Dorothy's" with an angry slash and wrote "New Hope" beneath it.

"*There,*" she said. "Happy now?"

"*No,*" Dorothy said.

Her shoulders slumped. She hung her head low, staring at her feet, and wrung her hands together. A tear rolled down her cheek.

"I didn't come here to fight," she whispered.

Luci stared at her for a moment, her cheeks flushed. She shook her head, now angry at herself. This wasn't how she'd intended for things to go when she let Dorothy in, although it was how she expected it.

"Then why did you come, Dorothy?" she said softly.

"To talk to *someone*," Dorothy said. "I can't forget what happened the other night. But I can't tell anyone else. Who would believe me? Except for you."

"Except for me," Luci said nastily. "Good to know I'm just *someone* to you. But I guess that's what you wanted, isn't it?"

"What are you talking about?" Dorothy stared at her, broadcasting hurt and confusion.

Luci balled up her fists, gritting her teeth hard to hold back what she wanted to shout. Her mind burned now. Then it was gone, leaving only her anger. Whether Dorothy's confusion was genuine or feigned didn't matter to her. The mere fact that she wouldn't face the truth—Luci's truth—seven months later was more important. Long-held resentment leapt up inside of her, and for a moment she forgot that she was the one who had dragged Dorothy back into her life.

"You were more than *someone* to me, Dorothy Weathersby," Luci said. Her volume was level, but the head in her voice was enough to start a fire. "You were *special*. Someone I thought I could maybe spend my life with. But you? You wouldn't even give us a *chance*. And now you act like, what, I'm someone you can fall back on when you need me?"

"Isn't that what you did to me?" Dorothy shot back.

Luci flinched as if Dorothy had slapped her. She stammered some random syllables. She shook her head and turned away, trying to hide the guilty blush in her cheeks. Dorothy didn't relent. Now her dander was up too, and she was going to give as good as she'd gotten.

"We never *had* a chance," Dorothy said. "I'm a *woman*. We're *both* women. We can't... do you know what the school would have done if they'd found out about us? What my *family* would have done?"

In a flash, Luci was crouched in the bushes beside her neighbors' house, watching her first love's father hand his daughter over to the men in the white van. She felt his hard hand on her shoulder. Heard his voice asking what they thought they were doing.

She remembered eight months later, when Cora returned. The distance in her dark eyes. Her head hanging low, her hands constantly rubbing her arms. Wearing long sleeves even in the summer. She wouldn't acknowledge Luci was there. That hurt, but Luci couldn't blame her. She hadn't been able to save her, after all. She hadn't even tried.

The Riordans moved away not long after. Cora's mother told Luci's mother that her husband had gotten a new job in another city, but Luci's mother had told her that it was because he couldn't face his neighbors after what had happened. He was ashamed of what his daughter had done instead of what he had done. The coward, Luci's mother had said.

Cora hadn't even said goodbye.

"I know what they would have tried to do better than you think," Luci said. Her voice was thick with unshed tears.

"Then you know I'm right," Dorothy said, sad but resigned. "We could never be together, Luci. Not really, not the way you wanted. It was fun, but—"

"Fun? *Fun?*" Luci spun around, eyes flashing with indignation. "Is that really all I was to you? A little bit of *fun* until you landed the first doctor you batted your eyes at? Settled down in some Levittown? *Someone* you could keep in your back pocket until you needed me?"

"How *dare* you?" Dorothy shouted. "You didn't speak to me for *six months* until you *wanted* something!"

"Because it *hurt!* Because you said you *didn't* want me."

"That is *not* what I said! I said we *couldn't* be together, not that I didn't want to be! I *loved* you. I *still* love you!"

"I still love you too, you jerk!"

Dorothy grabbed Luci's face and pressed her lips against hers. Luci kissed her back, wrapping her arms around Dorothy's shoulders and clinging to her for dear life. Dorothy pulled Luci to the floor with her. Luci lay on top of her, between Dorothy's legs, while Dorothy ran her fingers through Luci's strawberry-blonde hair. It wasn't until Dorothy slid her hand beneath Luci's blouse that she broke the kiss. Luci pushed herself up on one elbow, catching Dorothy's wrist with her other hand.

"Stop. We have to stop," Luci said. "I'm not... I've moved on. I'm with someone else now."

Dorothy smiled seductively, her fingertips tracing circles against Luci's side. "That's not what you were saying."

"I—*stop that*—look, my feelings for you are a little more complicated than I thought—I mean it, that *tickles*. I'm with Amelia now. I *love* her."

"Who's Amelia?" Dorothy said, frowning. "We don't know an Amelia. Wait... oh God, is she that drab little thing who was with you and that colored waitress the other night?"

"And *thank you* for making this easier," Luci said. She pushed herself to her knees and stood. "Amelia is *not* drab. She's one of the most interesting people I've ever met. Next to Gloria, who is far more than just a waitress, thank you very much."

"All right, all right," Dorothy said, flustered and annoyed. "I'm sorry, okay?"

"What's wrong with being a waitress, anyway? My *mother* was a waitress. Her waitressing got me through most of my childhood, after she ditched my lousy fouling father."

"I *said* I was sorry," Dorothy said. "I didn't mean to set you off on one of these... whatever you call it when you get like this."

"*At least* Amelia's not afraid to be with me, Dorothy Weathersby, so you can just stick that in your shoe and beat it!"

What did I even see in her? Luci asked herself while Dorothy pouted.

I can answer that. It was Dorothy's behind. Luci liked to believe she was above shallow impulses, but in this instance? Even I had to admit that Dorothy Weathersby had a very shapely derriere, despite her many terrible opinions. That goes to prove something about human beauty standards, I'm sure.

Dorothy sat on the floor, frustrated, confused, and annoyed, watching as Luci paced across the room. Luci was trying to burn off the sudden restless energy Dorothy had inspired. She put her hands behind her head, digging her fingers in her hair, trying to focus on something that wasn't directionless anger (or, again, Dorothy's bottom). She turned sharply on her heel, staring at her conspiracy board. Luci dropped her hands to her hips, letting her hair fall down her back again, and locked her eyes on the photo of Dr. Sutherland. She traced the threads connecting him to the hospital, the Chambers Foundation, the rest of the conspiracy. The mental exercise worked. Her heartbeat slowed. Her jaw unclenched. That tickle in her mind was there again, but she dismissed it. She had no time for distractions.

Dorothy let out a frustrated sigh and climbed to her feet. She stood behind Luci, off to one side, and stared at the conspiracy board. She clasped her hands together in front of her, winding her fingers nervously.

"I don't really understand what happened the other night," Dorothy said. "You told me that you and your, um, friends had to see one of the patients. That he was in trouble. I still don't know why I let you in."

Luci looked over her shoulder. "Don't you?"

Dorothy flushed. "That's not fair. You just said you were with someone else."

"That's not what I meant," Luci said, rolling her eyes. "You say you don't know what happened. That you don't know what I meant that Ralph was in trouble. I don't believe you."

"Excuse me?"

"Do you know what this is?" Luci said, putting a hand on the corkboard. "This is a map of a conspiracy that goes back to before we were born. A conspiracy of men and monsters and *magic*, Dorothy, real-life magic. And you can stop looking at me like that, because that's what you saw the other night. *Magic*. And I'll bet you your hard-earned bottom dollar that it wasn't for the first time."

Dorothy's face went pale. "What do you mean?"

"I mean that St. Audaeus is in the thick of it. And so's this university. Your nursing program's connected to both, and it's not the only one. The Chambers Foundation, the same folks funding the hospital? They endowed the scholarship program my friend Ralph was using. *Is* using. I'll bet they're funding your nursing program too."

"But why?"

"Call it a jobs program. They need people doing their grunt work. People interested in magic, yeah, but everything else, too. If you have a hospital, you need nurses and administrators and janitors. People who are going to see things that maybe they shouldn't. So they have to make sure they have people they can trust—or at least control."

Dorothy's cheeks flushed, and she looked away. Luci nodded, as if Dorothy had just confirmed her suspicions. Mercilessly, she pressed on.

"The Chambers Foundation is using the hospital to perform experiments on people. Experiments involving—I don't know what you want to call them. Spirits or demons or aliens. Maybe it's all the same thing. I don't believe you were *involved*, exactly, but I think you've seen more than you're letting on."

Dorothy was close to tears now. Luci didn't look at her, but she could hear the sniffles. When they threatened to become sobs, she finally relented. Luci's face softened as she turned to put her hand on Dorothy's shoulder.

"Although maybe you don't remember all of it."

Dorothy burst into tears, falling against Luci's shoulder. Luci put one arm around her, resting her head against Dorothy's while the other woman cried.

"It's okay," she murmured. "Take your time."

"I *don't remember*," Dorothy sobbed. "I don't. I don't."

Eventually the crying stopped. Luci guided Dorothy to the beds, sitting her down on an empty corner. She grabbed a handkerchief out of her nightstand (which was, although she didn't notice it, monogrammed "D.W.") and passed it to Dorothy. While Dorothy blew her nose, she cleaned up her notes, organizing them into a neat pile. Once the space was clear, she sat next to Dorothy.

"I don't remember," Dorothy said. "But some of the other girls whispered about what went on in the basement. Secret experiments, like you said."

"Like we saw."

"Like we saw," Dorothy admitted. "And then there were the special patients. Mixed in with the others but only certain staff were allowed to see them. Like your friend Ralph. They said he was a burn victim, but that wasn't true. Was it?"

She furrowed her brow, racking her brain for memories that weren't there.

"There was something *wrong* with him. I can remember that, but I can't remember what it was. Why can't I? Oh, Luci, why can't I remember?"

Luci patted Dorothy on the back, trying to offer some comfort. Then she reached for the three-ring binder propped up against her pillow. She flipped through the pages until she found the one marked "Dream Eater".

"Because of this. 'Saydoo hayth Bahgoo'," she said, deliberately pronouncing it in a way sure to make the Watcher flinch. "They call it a dream eater, but it goes after memories. Or at least, that's how Sutherland uses it."

Dorothy stared at the page. It summarized what Luci had learned from the Watcher and I, as well as her own reconstructed experiences. She had included a sketch of the memory echo that had attacked us.

"A dream eater," Dorothy said softly. "You think this…?"

"Any time you saw something you shouldn't have," Luci said firmly. "It happened to me and to Ralph's mom. She got a glimpse of what had really happened to him, so the doctor took us both down to the basement and I don't know how, exactly, but he unleashed it on us. Took *hours* from us. Probably the easiest way to keep a secret. You can't tell what you can't remember."

"But I *do* remember," Dorothy whispered, staring off into the distance. "I remember *green*. Green and fear. And something…"

She grabbed a blank notecard and a felt-tipped pen. She drew a symbol, a stylized Y with a teardrop at the end.

"I remember *this*, all glowing green."

"Then that's another piece of the puzzle," Luci said, gently taking the notecard from her. She fished a paperclip out of her nightstand and clipped the card to the dream eater's page. "Don't have the box top, so we don't know what the picture's supposed to look like. But we're putting it together all the same."

Dorothy smiled prettily. "See? I'm helpful."

Luci smiled back, although not as genuinely. That tickle in the back of her mind had returned. "You are. Now, let's see just how helpful you can be. I want you to tell me *everything* you know about St. Audaeus Hospital and the New Hope Nursing Program."

24

"Apparently, she was recruited through her church, if you can believe it. 'A fitting occupation for a good Christian girl,' they told her."

"Huh." Gloria tapped her index finger thoughtfully against the telephone receiver. "That's an interesting wrinkle. What sort of church does she go to?"

"A generic Presbyterian one, as far as I know," Luci said. "'New Lights Harvest' or something like that."

"'Something like that' or exactly like that?" Gloria adored Luci, but sometimes she despaired of her journalistic instincts. "It's important."

"Okay, exactly like that. Sheesh," Luci said, annoyed. "Although, funny thing. It was renamed about four years back. Before that it was Oswald Street Presbyterian."

"*Huh*. Almost like it came under new management."

"That's what I was thinking," Luci said. "Hm! 'Good Christian girl'. Not when I was between her legs, she wasn't."

"Luci! This is a party line! Also, you're terrible."

"Sorry!" Luci sounded utterly unapologetic. "Anyway, I followed up on what Dorothy said. Almost all the program's staff go to her church. More than a few university faculty attend services there, too. I dunno if they're recruiting from the congregation or converting them after the fact."

"I suppose that's what you're looking into next."

"No."

"No?"

"I can't get distracted. This jigsaw puzzle is *huge*. There are pieces all over the place, and every one we pick up has a different picture. I can't jump back and forth across the table every time two pieces come together. Only one part of the picture matters right now."

"The one with Amelia."

"Right. There were three patrons who funded the hospital. I'm betting those goons were with one of them. That's what I'm looking into now."

"Be careful."

"When am I not careful?"

"I'm going to let that one slide. So, you have your plan. I'm going to go over my notes again, see if I can refine my processes. I don't want to waste our next chance, whenever that is."

"Can you do that?"

"I still have the first batch," Gloria said, meaning the Watcher matter we'd recovered from the alley behind Orr's Used Books. "I can get more if I need to."

"Now *you* be careful. I don't like the idea of messing around with that stuff."

Gloria absently put a hand on her abdomen. "I am. Trust me. But we're going to end up taking risks at some point. Isn't that what you're always saying?"

"Yeah, but I'm the irresponsible one," Luci said, cheerily. "You're the level-headed one. And Amelia…"

Luci's voice trailed off. The line was silent for a long minute. Gloria sighed as softly as she could, imagining Luci's face trying not to crumble into tears. She was probably using the phone at her dorm. It was far from private. Not that Gloria had any more privacy, talking from the first-floor hallway in her family home, but at least she wasn't surrounded by strangers. She forced herself to break the silence.

"She's coming back, Luci."

"What if she's not?" Luci said, her normally confident voice dropping to a shaky whisper. "We haven't heard from her in almost a week. What if they've hurt her? Or worse?"

"She's a tough girl. Probably tougher than either of us knows. We'll hear from her soon. And if not—"

"If not, we're going to find her," Luci said, suddenly vehement. "We're going to find her and bring her back."

"Right on the money." Gloria paused. "Have you heard anything from the administration at her orphanage?"

"No. Haven't seen hide nor hair of 'em."

"Same here."

"Now that you mention it, it's actually starting to worry me," Luci said. "Not that I want to hear from them. But if she's missing, you'd think they'd be snooping around."

"We'll keep an eye out for strangers. Even more so than before. If a man you don't know starts taking an interest—"

"I know. Take notes and pass it on as soon as I can."

Gloria was about to say something else when her mother called her name. "Shoot, that's dinner."

"Ooh, what are you having?"

"Nothing fancy. Pork chops and the usual. Potatoes and greens and such."

"Your mom's cornbread?"

"Of course."

"Lucky. I'm stuck with the cafeteria and my meal card again. Mystery meat, probably. Can't wait to see what horrors they've committed with Jell-O tonight."

"Yeah." Gloria laughed hollowly, ignoring the sudden pang in her stomach. "Have you considered moving off-campus? You could try lodging."

"I have, but how would I explain my corkboard?" Luci let out a long-suffering sigh. "Maybe I'll go down to the commons and bat my eyes until some nice thick jock takes me out for a burger."

"You are the worst, Lucille Sweeney."

Luci said something irreverent regarding her virtue, but Gloria didn't hear it over her mother calling her name, more sternly this time.

"I really have to go, Luci."

"Sorry, sorry! My love to your family. Meet you at the library at noon next Saturday?"

"Works for me," Gloria said, hanging up.

Her mother waited in the hall, arms folded across her chest. She looked at Gloria expectantly, clearly wanting an explanation as to why she was delaying the family dinner.

"Sorry, Mom," Gloria said. "That was my friend Luci. You know, the one with the sick neighbor? She's awfully worried and I'm trying to keep her mind off it. You know how she'll go on and on if you give her the chance."

Mrs. Lane's frown deepened. She didn't disapprove of Lucille Sweeney, exactly. She just didn't trust her. Luci was an unknown quantity, which meant she was likely to be bad news. In her eyes, Luci would get her only daughter into some sort of trouble that Luci would escape unharmed. I had to admit, that was a fair assessment, albeit not for the reasons Mrs. Lane suspected.

For the record, Verna Lane thought about the same of me, although not quite as strongly. She didn't know what to make of me. Luci was easy to type—a pretty white girl looking for excitement. I was harder to place. Still, at the end of the day, we were two white girls palling around with Gloria, and Mrs. Lane wasn't entirely sure why. I'd taken offense the first time I'd felt her suspicion, but Gloria had quickly set me straight. I didn't like it, but I'd seen the way passing police officers had reacted to Luci and me compared to Gloria. It wasn't fair, but it wasn't incorrect.

To her credit, Mrs. Lane's tone was much warmer than her expression when she said, "We'll keep her young man in our prayers. Hopefully he'll pull through. I don't suppose she's a churchgoer?"

It must be admitted that "warmer" is a matter of degrees.

"She never said what sort of church her people go to," Gloria said carefully, "but I know she's looking at a new one up in Regina."

That mollified Mrs. Lane slightly. "Good for her, then. It'll do her some good."

Gloria wasn't so sure about that but wisely held her tongue.

"In the meantime, that dinner your brother made will do *you* some good. You're looking skinny, Gloria. You haven't been dieting, have you?"

Gloria put a hand to her stomach, again feeling a slight twinge. "No, Momma."

"Good. These magazines put such ideas in a young woman's mind. Mrs. Barton down the street, she was telling me how her Clara fainted because she'd only been having water for breakfast and lunch the past three weeks. Water! And such a fine-looking young lady, too. I don't know. Nothing wrong with a little weight, your grandmother always said. Men like a *healthy* woman."

"I'm sure they do," said Gloria, who cared no more for what men liked in a woman than a cat cared for what was on television.

Nevertheless, she followed her mother to the dining room. Most of their family was already gathered around the table. Andre was bringing the last dish in from the kitchen—Verna Lane's famous cornbread. The two younger boys, Carlton and Daniel, were seated on one side of the table. Gloria took her usual place opposite them and next to Andre. Mrs. Lane sat at the foot of the table. The seat to Gloria's left and the one at the table's head were empty. Mr. Lane and Lucas were covering the evening shift at the diner today. Empty plates had still been set out for them, as was tradition. One way or another, the Lanes always ate as a family.

At her mother's request, Gloria said the blessing. The family folded their hands and bowed their heads while Gloria led them in a brief prayer, thanking their god for the family's health and safety. It was interesting. Gloria's connection to the presumed recipient of her prayer was shaky at best. She doubted anyone was listening except for the four people at the table, but that was enough for her. Her wish for their continued wellbeing was heartfelt, and through the prayer, her connection to them was strengthened. Their faith in their god was sincere. Hers was in her family, and it was no less so.

After they all said "Amen", a little needlessly loudly by the younger boys, they began passing around the serving bowls and plates. Everyone took a healthy helping of everything, although Gloria's face clouded when she looked at the mound of food on her plate.

As they ate, the family shared stories of their day. Andre told them about a truly absurd order he'd received that afternoon and complained about the new hire their father had taken on now that Gloria was "too busy" to work as many shifts as before. The younger boys told all about their adventures in the nearby park, while Mrs. Lane shared friendly gossip from around the neighborhood. Gloria herself said little, only offering comments here and there as she pushed her food around the plate. The smell of her brother's cooking made her mouth water, but each bite caused her stomach to twist uncomfortably. Her brothers didn't notice, focusing instead on demolishing their own plates. Mrs. Lane certainly did but held her peace. For now.

The moment it was polite to do so, Gloria pushed her plate away and asked to be excused, explaining that she needed to study. Mrs. Lane nodded, but Andre scoffed at her around a mouthful of mashed potatoes.

"What you got to study for?" he asked impatiently.

"You know full well Gloria wants to go to Hampton next year," Mrs. Lane said, shaking her fork at him. "And how many times do I have to tell you not to talk with your mouth full? A grown man?"

"Andre got in trouble! Andre got in trouble!" Carlton and Daniel chanted, waving their forks in the air.

"Now do you see what you've done?" Mrs. Lane said. "Never mind your brother, Gloria. Clean up your plate."

"Thank you, Momma," Gloria said.

She grabbed her plate and gave her mother a kiss on the forehead as she passed. Once she was safely behind her mother, she stuck her tongue out at Andre. He couldn't respond in kind under their mother's watchful eye, but he hid his hand under the table and nodded firmly. It was their old familiar signal that he was making a rude gesture at her. The two siblings laughed as Gloria left the room. Their mother shook her head patiently while trying to shush the younger boys, knowing that there were shenanigans about but not knowing precisely what.

Gloria quietly scraped her plate into the trash, then scrubbed and rinsed it in the sink. She knew she hadn't done as good of a job as she should have, but she was running out of time. Her stomach was churning now. She put the plate on the drying rack and hurried into the hallway. The laughter from the dining room floated past her as she ducked into the home's single shared bathroom. She locked the door behind her and turned the sink on full blast. Then she lunged at the toilet. She barely got the lid off in time before she started vomiting. A gout of bile and undigested chunks of food flew out of her mouth, burning all the way up. Her stomach heaved again and again, forcing its contents up and out. By the time she was finished, tears streamed down her cheeks. Her arms and shoulders shook with the effort of holding her up, and her stomach and lower back ached as if she'd spent hours doing crunches.

Gloria flushed her sickness away as soon as she was sure her stomach was done purging. She wiped up the mess as thoroughly as she could, leaving the toilet and the floor around it spotless. She pushed herself off the floor, limbs shaky, and propped herself against the sink. She splashed cold water on her face, washing away the last bits of vomit and leaving her feeling, if not refreshed, then somewhat recovered. She poured a cup of water and swished it around her mouth, trying to rinse out the stench and the taste. She spat it out and wiped her face again. Then she fixed the set of her shoulders, smiled mirthlessly at her reflection, and left the bathroom.

There had been consequences for her hasty, half-understood attempts to power the wards that night at the hospital. She had been right the first time—she wasn't made out of whatever I was. Her attempt to jump-start her metabolism with an untested seal had altered her body, most likely permanently. Her gastrointestinal system couldn't digest food anymore. She could taste food, she could swallow it. Her mind still craved her favorites. But her body rejected the food as soon as it reached her stomach.

When she was sure she'd hidden any sign of her distress, Gloria ducked out of the bathroom and hurried upstairs to her room. Her family was still carrying on in the dining room. They hadn't noticed anything wrong with her. She was grateful for that, yet still felt a pang of irritation that she chose not to interrogate.

It wasn't the only pang. Despite having just voided the very fine dinner her brother had prepared, her traitor stomach was complaining of hunger. A wave of dizziness struck as she mounted the stairs. Her body was about to start consuming itself again if she didn't find some way to feed it. Fortunately, she had something for that.

The makings of a seal were already set up in her room. She had a dedicated bag with a pre-scribed power seal and a collection of candles on her dresser. It also held a modified version of what she'd dubbed the "ambrosia seal", the one that had saved her life at the cost of her digestive system. She taped the seal to her abdomen, set up the candles on the power seal, and lit them. Then she sat down, running through the equation in her mind. Energy pooled within the power seal until it reached the desired level. Then it ran up the ink-stained twine, connecting the two seals. The ambrosia seal glowed with a dull amber light as it fed the energy into her metabolism, but the refined seal didn't burn. She was grateful for that, at least.

It took twenty-two minutes for the seal to finish "feeding" her. It didn't lessen the cravings. Her useless stomach still demanded food it couldn't digest. Still, she could feel her strength returning, and that would allow her to ignore her stomach's empty demands. It stopped churning, the fatigue left her limbs, and her thoughts came quick and bright. The ambrosia seal wouldn't truly replace food, as her gradually diminishing frame proved, but it was keeping her going. For now. Replenished, Gloria snuffed the candles, removed the ambrosia seal, and tucked the working away. Then she got back to work.

She had set up another seal on the short table that served as her writing desk. It was hidden beneath a legal pad—a camouflage that was also functional. A short string ran from that seal to a small candle at the end of the table. She lit the candle and waited. It wasn't long. A missive had been waiting for her. Long sentences in thin, cursive handwriting burned themselves into the topmost sheet as the seal pulled a letter from her mentor's desk, however many miles away that was. It wasn't comforting, but she hadn't expected comfort.

G.L.,

Sorry, still no fix for your condition. I've never even heard of something like what you've done to yourself. Which is impressive as hell, don't get me wrong. It takes a lot to leave me stumped these days. Unfortunately, it also means I can only be so much help. We're blazing this trail together, girl. I told you when you started that it was gonna be dangerous.

Chin up. You figured out a working on the fly and from memory, after your memory was attacked by an outsider. I'll say it again; I'm impressed. You're miles better than my last apprentice. Which is damned faint praise, I know, but I mean it. I knew I picked right when I reached out to you. You picked right when you answered.

I'll keep researching, see if I can figure something out for your messed up guts. It's slow going, since your friend saw fit to lose most of my library. In the meantime, keep working on the lessons I sent you. I don't care if they're boring. You need to practice your fundamentals if you don't want to foul up something worse than your guts.

Keep at it, kiddo. We're gonna do great things together.

M. O.

25

A nondescript car sat a block away from the Lane home. It was parked along the street, giving the men inside a good sightline to the house. With Gloria's curtains drawn, they couldn't see inside. Agent Walsh was satisfied with that. He wasn't comfortable staking out my friends' homes. Of course, he also hadn't raised any significant objections when the assignment was handed down.

"Anything?" Agent Poole asked.

"Nothing." Agent Walsh lowered his binoculars. "But I keep saying, if Amelia turns up anywhere, it's going to be at the Sweeney girl's dorm."

"So why aren't we there?"

"Because I'm happy to let some other numbskull get caught creeping around a co-ed dormitory. That's a hassle I don't need. The local police don't care what we do out here."

That was disgustingly true, but Walsh had other reasons for picking this assignment. My friends knew his face, and he expected Luci would be more likely to cause a scene if she recognized him. Agent Walsh knew the Del Sombra campus was enemy territory. He had no intention of being caught on what he considered a pointless detail. Let someone else take that risk. Ideally Agent Thomas, but sadly the Specials were too highly placed for mere stakeout duty. They were pursuing their own methods of facilitating my recovery.

The fact of it was, Agent Walsh knew that if I hadn't appeared with my friends yet, I simply wasn't going to. He understood me well enough to know that the only reason I wouldn't be with them now was that I couldn't be. That I was most likely a prisoner of someone other than the Bureau. Undoubtably of what he only thought of as "the opposition". The one he now wished he'd warned me about. Of course they would want me, just as much as the Bureau had. Albeit not for the same reasons, or so he still believed.

Yes. In the face of everything, Patrick Walsh still genuinely believed the Bureau's intentions for me were benign. That they, and he, were ultimately trying to do right by me. It made him difficult to resent and even more difficult to understand.

"Wish we knew what was going on in there," Agent Poole said. "Why haven't we bugged the phone yet?"

"Someone's always there, and Headquarters doesn't want to take any chances," Agent Walsh said. "And it's a party line. We'd end up sifting through hours of irrelevant conversation."

"So that's a no-go, then?"

Agent Walsh frowned. "They've got church tomorrow. We're sending a team in then."

Agent Poole didn't understand Agent Walsh's distaste for the operation.

"That's the best time," he said gamely. "Those people all go to the same church, yeah? Whole neighborhood should be empty."

Agent Walsh shook his head. "Yeah. Sure. Makes sense."

He tucked his notebook away and packed up his binoculars. "Come on. I'm calling it."

"What, now? We've barely been at this for two hours. The mission brief called for six, minimum."

"Who's the agent in charge of Amelia Temple, Nate?"

"You are, Pat."

For now. In light of my disappearance, Agent Walsh's tenure as my handler was under sharp review. Fortunately for his reputation, that information hadn't filtered out to the rank-and-file Bureau agents. Yet.

"That's right. Which means I direct any investigation into her whereabouts. And I'm saying this is a dead end. We're wrapping up the stakeout early. After they install the bugs, someone else can sift through hours of domestic crap instead of working."

"You're the boss." Agent Poole's voice was doubtful, but he followed the instruction. He turned on the lights and the engine. The two drove away, leaving the Lane home unattended. And Gloria's experiments hidden for another day. At least, hidden from the Bureau mainstream.

Dorothy Weathersby sat on a steel chair. Her hands were folded primly in her lap. Her head was bowed as if she was sleeping, but her green eyes were wide open, staring at nothing. Her mouth hung slightly open, and a small runner of spittle dripped down her chin. After a moment, one of the men staring at her helpfully wiped it away with a handkerchief.

"Waste of effort," Agent Thomas said, grinning cruelly. "She's just gonna do it again."

Agent Drummond shrugged and tucked the handkerchief back into his pocket.

"So," Thomas said, lighting a cigarette. "Temple's in the wind. After we learn about whatever debacle occurred at St. Audaeus, we start digging. We do not find Temple, which I am still not happy about. Instead, Marty, you bring me a candy-striper. And she didn't even jump out of a cake. Explain to me again why I should be impressed."

"You shouldn't," Agent Stark said with a shrug. "This was down to pure luck. We were following up on Temple's known associates and happened to strike something with this one."

"Temple's known associates." Thomas snorted dismissively. "A bunch of grown men peeping through curtains. What a waste of time. Temple's undergone manifestation. Based on the readings coming out of Dreamland, it's at least Level Six. That thing's not even pretending to be human anymore. The assumption it still cares about its human acquaintances is a mistake. A dangerous one."

"Agreed," Stark said, adjusting his glasses. "Nonetheless, Subject 19 was drawn to this group of people for a reason. Miss Weathersby here might have a partial explanation."

Dorothy's chest rose and fell with clockwork regularity. She gave no indication that she was aware of the half-dozen men standing in a semicircle around her. The room was dark, with only a single lamp bathing her in harsh light. From time to time, one of the men crept into the circle of light, checking her pulse or her pupils. One agent brushed back her bangs, revealing a small metal disc affixed to her pale forehead with red wax.

"She's close to the Sweeney girl, or at least she was," Stark said, reading from a cardboard file. "Apparently, they had a falling out a few months ago. Their classmates assume it was over a man. Nonetheless, Sweeney reconnected with her within the past month."

Thomas scowled. "Gossip. We have an ultraterrestrial threat on the loose and you're bringing me collegiate gossip."

"It's relevant, I assure you. This isn't reconciliation between friends, Randall. Weathersby works at St. Audaeus. In fact, she was on duty the night of the event."

Thomas' eyebrows shot up. He took a slow drag off his cigarette. "Okay. Now I'm interested."

"We never managed to get a man inside the hospital, but we have two in the university. We were able to acquire records from Miss Weathersby's nursing program. It's run by the opposition, just like the hospital."

"You're kidding me. This little chippie is one of them?"

"In a manner of speaking. Miss Weathersby isn't like Dowling or the one up in Oregon. We think they're looking for assets with particular qualities."

"We've got copies of her aptitude tests," Drummond said, handing a folder to Thomas. "They weren't testing these girls for their steno skills."

"Miss Weathersby scores moderately highly on three separate tests for psychic ability," Stark said. "A consistent sixty to sixty-six percent accuracy with Zener cards. A similar rating with the Grey-Frost envelope test. Nearly seventy-five percent accuracy with induced automatic writing. A flat zero on dice tests for telekinesis, thankfully."

"Jesus," Thomas said. "This frail's a low-grade psychic talent?"

"Hence why we're keeping her off-site," Stark said.

"She don't know it, though," Drummond said. "She don't remember any of the testing under hypnosis. And when we put her under, she went real easy."

"She's been hypnotized before," Thomas said.

"Probably pretty regular."

"So. The opposition is recruiting minor talents who don't know they're talents, then putting them to work in highly psychoactive environments." Thomas took another drag off his cigarette, looking deep in thought. "To what end?"

"That's an excellent question, Randall," Stark said. "Most likely one we won't be getting an answer to anytime soon."

"I think we can forget about getting a man inside the hospital for the foreseeable," Drumond said. "The opposition's in disarray, but not in a way we can turn to our advantage."

"Don't be so sure about that." Thomas stepped into the light, leaning over Dorothy. "We don't need to get a man inside. Not if we've got a woman."

"Her?"

"Why not her?" Thomas grinned cruelly. "You said it yourself. She went under easily enough. She doesn't remember the testing. Can she remember anything else?"

Agent Crux stepped forward. "We've interrogated her extensively. She doesn't know many of the details, but she confirmed the presence of ultraterrestrial experimentation at St. Audaeus. She also confirmed that Subject 19 and company were responsible for the incident four days ago."

"They were trying to break out the Connor boy," Stark said.

"Christ. Did they succeed?"

"Negative. The opposition had already moved him. She doesn't know where."

"Shame. Well, the Connor boy is a low priority compared to recovering Temple." Thomas rubbed his chin. "So. Temple and friends infiltrated the hospital, thanks to finagling an asset inside. Unlike us. They fail to recover Connor but find something else. Temple undergoes a Level Six manifestation, but these three frails *somehow* survive that and escape. That all sound about right to you?"

"That handily summarizes events as we understand them," Stark said.

"Which means Temple's associates are far more resourceful than we thought."

"And probably more informed," Drummond said. "We bringing them in?"

"Bringing them in? A colored girl and a lady pinko? Don't be thick," Thomas said. "No. I'm not risking the project to radical elements."

Thomas cocked his head to one side, a thoughtful expression on his face. "That doesn't mean they can't be useful. Temple won't go looking for them, but they're gonna go looking for Temple."

He stood straight and turned to face his agents. Five of the Specials clustered around the edge of the light, waiting for the word from on high. Agent Crux hung back, one arm folded across his chest, chin resting on the other hand, but his attention, too, was fixed on Thomas.

"Clean out Weathersby's mind. Write up the appropriate imperatives and impress them on her subconscious. Command words, sympathetic mannerisms, suggestions, the works. See if you can do something with that talent of hers. We wanted an asset in the hospital? Now we've got one. *And* inside Temple's gang of associates. That's what I call efficiency."

Agent Thomas grinned over his shoulder at the unconscious young woman in the chair.

"Welcome to the Bureau, Dorothy Weathersby. You're gonna make one fine Judas goat."

26

The room was all white, a space twenty feet by twenty feet by ten feet. I had a twin bed in one corner. A minimalist white nightstand sat next to it, holding a lamp and a radio alarm clock. The sheets were of a ridiculously high thread count, and the pillow was just the right balance of firmness and plush. A desk sat in the opposite corner, next to a short bookcase, both as minimalist as the nightstand. The bookcase was empty for now, but there was a very full library not a hundred meters from this wing of the compound.

I didn't have a kitchenette or a personal bathroom. Instead, I shared common space adjoining seven other bedrooms, as well as a wide bathroom and shower facility. All the other rooms were occupied, but I politely withdrew my perception from them. I could still see inside the rooms; I was simply deliberately not paying attention to what the occupants were doing. I just laid on my bed, hands folded behind my head, and cast my perception out wide. I let my perception drift down the halls of this, the second of three above-ground floors. The building had five other dorms identical to this one, each filled to capacity. A cafeteria, kitchen, and library sat between them. In contrast to the Bureau campus, this place was full of life. Students, or at least people whom I presumed were students from their age, milled about their common rooms and in the library. Three small groups were clustered around circular tables in the cafeteria, chatting amiably.

Every person I saw wore some sort of jumpsuit—mono-color in shades of blue, except for black shoulders and a black chevron running down the torso. Most wore baby-blue jumpsuits. Many of these appeared to be custodial and kitchen staff. Smaller groups, such as my dorm-mates, wore increasingly darker shades. Only seven wore a deep navy blue. These, presumably, were the ones in charge of whatever organization had taken me into custody.

My room's closet was empty, incidentally. It had a dozen wooden clothes hangers but nothing hanging on them. I wasn't sure what to make of that yet.

The first floor held little to interest me at the moment, filled as it was primarily with offices and other administrative spaces. Lecture rooms and laboratories filled the third floor. Five of the ten labs were blank spots in my perception. The five I could see resembled the too-familiar labs of the Bureau campus—small, square chambers adjacent to narrow observation rooms. Their walls and floors were slippery and stained with splatters of unusual matter.

I could tell that at least two more levels extended beneath the surface. I couldn't feel them properly. They were surrounded by a veil of familiar static. Luci would have been intrigued. I was simply irritated.

I cast out my perception wider, taking in the whole of the compound, a single large mansion in Edwardian style, sitting atop a low hill. It would have been green two months ago; now it was covered in dry brown grass. My perception stopped a hundred and fifty meters from the mansion. It was as if the whole space was sealed in an opaque bubble. I didn't find static at the edge of the barrier, just a slick nothingness. The compound obviously still had to be part of the Earth—probably—but I couldn't detect even the dimmest glimpse of the world outside. I was utterly sealed in.

I thought "probably" because I lacked any form of reference to locate this compound relative to Chatham Hills or Regina. To my friends. Somehow, the men who'd taken me into custody at the hospital had endeavored to temporarily *suspend my consciousness*. It wasn't as simple as putting me to sleep. I had slept before. Frequently. Even then, I retained a basic awareness of my surroundings. This time, I experienced the most alarming sensation of *discontinuity*. I had already had entirely my fill of that.

In one moment, I was in the hospital cafeteria, surrounded by identical men. In the next, I was in this room, on this bed. My return to awareness had been five days and six hours ago. How much additional time had passed in the interim? I could not yet say, and that gnawed at me.

Nonetheless, the compound's enclosure was not as perfect as it had initially seemed. I could feel the greater part of myself dimly, as if I were touching a numb limb through layers of thick cloth. For that I was grateful. I didn't know what would happen to me if this aspect of myself was cut off from the rest of me. I didn't even know if that was possible, but I was in no hurry to find out.

Whatever I was.

The rest of me drifted, for lack of a better term, in higher dimensions I could vaguely sense but not reach. It was possible some of the lost time was remembered there, if I could only fully reach it. If I could pierce the barrier. I couldn't move through or around it; I'd spent the first day testing its integrity and probing its substrates. I could break through it if I absolutely needed to, I was certain of that, but not without also doing horrific damage to local space-time.

With some effort, but less than I'd expend trying to escape, I thought I could rotate my apocalyptic form into local space. Possibly even other aspects of my anatomy even more inimical to local conditions. I hadn't tested any of that yet. I expected it would provoke a response from my captors I wasn't ready for.

I could still feel the spilled fluid against my skin, warm and thick and milk-white.

The *numbness* of my greater self bothered me. I *stretched* myself, trying to feel the rest of me. Distant nerves burned as awareness briefly flared. My form rolled, a vast bulk adrift in the aether, batted by cosmic winds and inverted stars. It dove *downward*, following the trail of thought emanating from my local cross-section. It did not breach but pressed gently against the soap-bubble shell of local space-time.

Above my head, a loudspeaker crackled with static.

"Miss Temple," a tiny, tinny voice said, "you have been advised against multidimensional movement in contradiction of facility regulations. This is your eighth warning."

"What happens on the ninth?" I asked aloud, eyes still closed.

There was no answer. My room was not equipped with a microphone. Besides, it was unlikely whatever technician was running the monitor room had an answer. Whoever these people were, I highly doubted they had any comprehensive rules covering me. Yet.

Twenty-five minutes later, someone knocked on my door. I opened one eye and rolled it at the door, annoyed. It was a man with thinning brown hair, wearing a dark blue jumpsuit. Two men in white jumpsuits flanked him. They were identical, both to one another and to the men I'd fought and destroyed in the hospital. All three wore the same stylized Vitruvian Man pins on their lapels. The dark-haired man's mind was wrapped in that familiar mirror sheen. The twins' minds were like an echo.

The three young people sitting in the common room pretended not to notice them. They focused their attention on their card game and the record player. It wasn't that they were afraid, exactly. It was that they understood very deeply that whatever these three were doing was none of their business.

I sighed and closed my eye, waiting for them to enter the room. They didn't. Two minutes passed. The mam knocked again.

"Miss Temple," he said. "You are awake, yes? We want to speak with you."

I sat up, staring at the door. The man in the common room stared at the door from the other side. Neither of us moved for a full minute until he raised his hand to knock a third time.

Just before his knuckles touched the wood, I said hesitantly, "Come in?"

The door opened slowly. I slid off the bed and stood, not wanting to be on it when a strange man was in the room. He did not enter, however. The man in the middle poked his head around the partially open door and smiled.

"Ah. Miss Temple," he said. "Good, you're decent. That will save time."

I folded my hands in front of me and quirked one eyebrow expectantly.

"The director would like to speak with you. If you have a moment."

I looked around the largely empty room. "Well, I do have a fairly full schedule at the moment, sir, but I suppose I can work him in."

The smile fell from his face. "Ah. A 'wit', I see. Well. I'm sure we can work with that."

He opened the door wider, gesturing at the door to the hall. "If you'll come this way?"

I cocked my head to the side. "Do I have a choice, Mister…?"

"*Doctor*, actually. Doctor Jeffrey West. And you always have a choice, Miss Temple. Even the thief has a choice when the policeman tells him to surrender, yes?"

So, it was going to be like that. Well, I couldn't say it was a surprise. I was accustomed to living like that.

"Then I'll choose to meet with your director, I suppose," I said.

The smile returned to Dr. West's face. He led me through the common room and into the hallway. The twins fell into place behind, flanking me. Their threat was, courteously, left as implied; the electric prods they carried were kept hidden in the thigh pockets of their white jumpsuits. My hands twitched at the thought. I could still feel their thick white internal fluids between my fingers. Even though I had washed my hands thirty-seven times since my first awakening here. Even though it hadn't been these hands that tore them apart.

Seeing my fingers twitch, one of the twins put a cautious hand on his thigh pocket. His fingers tested on the handle of his electric prod. I gave him a sidelong glance but kept walking.

"You might want to tell your heavies to relax," I said to the back of West's head. "I'm cooperating, aren't I?"

West chuckled without much humor. "My 'heavies', as you call them, are useful at what they do but have limited skill sets. And, of course, they've seen what you can do. You'll have to forgive them if they have you flagged as a potential threat. I'm sure that will change in due time."

"Have they?" I looked over the twins again, trying to determine anything that distinguished them from one another. "Were these two at the hospital?"

"That's immaterial," the doctor said, and declined to elaborate.

After that, we exchanged no more words until we reached our destination. It was a waiting room on the first floor, a simple rectangular space set up as a gate to the third largest room on this floor. Two statues carved of mottled gray stone flanked an ornate metal door. The statues were all flat angles suggesting androgynous humans, while the door was burnished bronze with a stylized sunburst stamped onto its face. A low gray desk sat off to one side. A young woman probably four years older than me sat at the desk, typing up a memorandum. Her jumpsuit was a blue just a shade lighter than West's. She didn't look up as we approached.

West gestured for the twins and me to stop at the door to the waiting room, then stood in front of the desk.

"Good afternoon, Delilah," he said. "I've brought our guest to see the director, as requested."

Delilah Thornton still did not take her eyes off the typewriter. Instead, she lifted one hand and pressed the intercom button to her left.

"Director?" she said. "She's here."

The intercom speaker crackled. "Excellent. Send her in."

Delilah looked past the doctor to me and smiled. It was possibly the least friendly smile I'd ever seen. "The director will see you now, Miss Temple. You can go through."

She finally turned to face West. Her smile widened, yet somehow became even less friendly. "I'm sure you can return to your lab now, Dr. West."

West's mouth twitched. He stared at Delilah, then at me as I walked past to open the heavy door. Delilah returned her attention to her memorandum. I ignored both of them. Whatever that was, it had nothing to do with me.

West continued to stare as the door closed behind me.

The room on the other side of the door seemed less like an office and more like a gentleman's smoking room. It was large enough for a dozen people to mill around comfortably. The wall to my right had a well-stocked wet bar. To my left, a dartboard hung between two tall bookcases, their shelves sagging beneath heavy leather-bound books. An octagonal table with a green felt top sat in one corner. An ornate wooden desk sat across the wall in front of me. I was unsurprised to see the bearded man from the hospital sitting behind it. On the wall behind him, a large portrait commanded the room's attention. It was an art deco interpretation of the Prometheus myth. A man with a burning torch held high fled the wrath of a terrible storm in the upper left corner. Stylized lightning bolts sparked above him, but none struck him.

The director stood. "Welcome, Miss Temple. It's a pleasure to meet you under more comfortable circumstances. I'm Doctor Octavian Pretorius, the director of this humble institute."

Two high-backed leather chairs stood in front of the desk. He gestured at them with the hand that wasn't holding a gin and tonic. I sat in the one to his left, crossing my leg primly over the other and resting my hands on my knee.

"No, you're not," I said.

The director blinked twice. He licked his lips. "I beg your pardon?"

"Doctor Pretorius. That's not your name," I said. "That's not anybody's name. Doctor Pretorius is a character from *Bride of Frankenstein*."

The Arcadia had shown the first two Frankenstein films as a double-feature two weeks ago. Luci had insisted we go see them. I felt they hit too close to home.

The director laughed. To my surprise, it sounded genuine. "Wonderful, wonderful." He sat back down and took a long sip of his drink. "In the course of events, it is sometimes necessary to adopt a sobriquet. Especially in this business. Is 'Amelia Temple' *your* real name, young lady?"

"Amelia is. I chose it," I said. "Temple is the name the Bureau gave me. I haven't had a reason to amend it, so I haven't."

I didn't see a need to explain what the Bureau was. The director nodded knowingly.

"As you said. How interesting."

"Quite. Where am I, exactly? And what is it that you want with me?"

The director's smile widened. "Getting right to it. I like that. Welcome to the Nova Anima Institute, Miss Temple. We're excited to finally have you with us."

Absolutely nothing about that eased my trepidation. Nor did it make my situation any clearer. I tapped my fingers against my knee.

"I meant more where I was in a geospatial sense, Doctor 'Pretorius'. Say, in relation to Regina, Maryland?"

"I know," the director said with irritating good humor. "I'm afraid that I don't intend to tell you that at this juncture."

"Do you really think that will stop me from leaving?"

"I would be willing to test that," the director said. "We take security very seriously here. We have to, after the way the Apollonian Society ended.

"But we're getting off on the wrong foot!" he continued, suddenly standing. He looked at his empty glass and waved it at me. "I'm sure you'd like some refreshment. I'm fully stocked in here. Soft or hard?"

"Just a Coca-Cola, if you have it," I said. "I'm only seventeen."

He winked at me. "Of course you are."

The director went to the wet bar and fussed around for a few minutes. He came back with another gin and tonic in one hand and a bottle of Coke in another. He set the Coke in front of me and returned to his seat.

"We don't want you to think of yourself as a prisoner here," he said, taking a sip. "We'd much rather you think of yourself as a collaborator. That's certainly how I hope to see you. We aren't the Bureau, Miss Temple. We recognize your potential, and we'd like to help you reach it. And in return, you can help us reach ours."

They were very pretty words. I had very little reason to trust them.

"What exactly do you think you can offer me?"

"Far more than you think. For example, do you know where you came from?"

"From a woman, doctor. I remember that quite vividly."

"Would you like to know her name?"

I recognize that I have something of a temper, particularly at that age. Recent events to the contrary, I try very hard to regulate it. I do not like having uncontrolled emotional outbursts. It feels bad, and terrible things tend to result.

Nonetheless, for a few seconds cold fury flared within me. My heartbeat quickened without my direction. The blood ran away from my face.

"That's a dirty trick," I said between gritted teeth.

"It isn't a trick, Miss Temple," the director said. The humor was gone from his voice. He was serious, but not unfriendly. "The Apollonian Society for Illumination is gone, but it has many successors. You and your friends have figured that out, mm? My institute is one of them. The, shall we say, program that produced you is another. After the disagreements that resulted in the society's collapse, we've abided by an unspoken pact of non-interference, but we've all kept tabs on one another.

"I know who your mother is, Amelia Temple. And I know where she's been kept. And if you help me with my research, I will help you find her.

"Who could ask for fairer than that, hmm?"

As a "show of good faith", the director allowed me to return to my dorm without an escort. He promised me the run of the facility if I accepted his offer of collaboration, excepting a small number of sensitive, highly controlled spaces. Off-campus travel rights were to be determined later, provided by continued cooperation. All in all, I couldn't shake the feeling that this was at best a lateral move.

I had requested time to think it over, to which he agreed. We would meet again tomorrow at 10 a.m. He didn't say what would happen if I refused, although by the tingling in my right arm I could hazard a guess.

I passed more Institute personnel as I made my way through the mansion's complicated maze of corridors. Most of their minds were open to me. They stared at me as I passed, although they tried to hide it. I was the only person here not wearing a color-coordinated jumpsuit; the only person who did not clearly fall somewhere within the Institute's hierarchy. They didn't know how to process that, but as I walked as if I had every right to be there, they let me pass unobstructed. Would that change if I accepted the director's offer? The thought did not appeal.

A slight tingle started in the back of my mind, like someone psychically tapping me on the shoulder.

"Well?" I said. "What do you think?"

"We don't trust him," the Watcher-As-Lucas said. They appeared to be walking beside me, hands folded at the small of their back.

"Neither do I," I said. "This is all entirely too convenient. And I can't tell how much the director is lying about. Which is annoying."

"They do seem to know more about you than the Bureau," the Watcher said. "Possibly more than we do, under the circumstances."

"That does seem to be the case."

"Which means they're more prepared for you."

"So they probably think."

"As much as we appreciate this newfound confidence in your abilities, Amelia, we do have to advise caution," the Watcher said. "So far, the Institute has imprisoned you more successfully than the Bureau ever had."

"No. The Bureau imprisoned me very successfully when I was young and ignorant. The Institute has imprisoned me successfully by taking me by surprise."

We turned down an empty corridor. I stopped at the second door to the right. It was a broom closet. After a quick glance to ensure the coast was clear, I opened the door and stepped through, but not into a broom closet.

"I'm wide awake now," I said.

We were standing in a metal-walled chamber in the second sub-basement. The floor was split-level; a short metal staircase led down to what looked like a hospital room. Hanging plastic sheeting surrounded a single bed. Ralph Connor's body lay atop it. He was no longer hidden under stained bandages. There was no longer any need to hide his affliction, after all. Nor respect for his modesty. Ralph lay exposed, his tortured flesh bare except where covered by restraints or medical cuffs. He was still on a ventilator and an IV drip, but both were silent for now. His biological functions were paused, his metabolism frozen in the space between a heartbeat. A seal covered the metal grate beneath his bed, presumably the cause for his stasis.

I had found where the Institute was keeping him three hours after waking up in the mansion. No one had thought to conceal his location, and with a few adjustments to the space around him, they wouldn't be able to. I could come see him whenever I wanted. Most likely, I could break him out whenever I wanted, too.

But first, I had to know what the Institute was really up to. And learn whatever I could from there. I turned to the Watcher. "I'm not trading one prison for another. But I can't pass up this opportunity. We'll work with them for a while. Find out their plans. Find out what they know about me. And then, when we're ready, we'll get Ralph out of here."

The Watcher-As-Lucas looked at me thoughtfully.

"Speaking of prisons…" they said.

"Yes. I promised we'd find a more long-term solution for you," I said. "I'm not unleashing you on this world. I still don't trust you, either. But you deserve to exist freely, if you can do it without hurting others."

"A new compact, then?"

"We'll see."

The Watcher smiled. "You know, these animals won't be happy about you using them. And the Bureau isn't simply going to let you go, either."

"I know that."

"So then?"

"So then I'll deal with them as I need to," I said.

We left Ralph's lab. This time the door took us to the hallway outside my new dorm. I walked through the common room to my own bedroom, ignoring my new neighbors. They all looked up from their amusements as I passed with a mixture of curiosity and fear.

I lay back down on my bed, hands folded beneath my head. I reached out with my awareness, once again testing the limits of this place's barriers. They were smooth and solid, with no weaknesses I could find. Yet. I felt a twinge of sorrow. I missed Luci and Gloria already. I hated that I couldn't reach out and feel their presence. That I didn't know when I'd be able to see them again.

But it would be soon. I promised myself that. I had allowed the Bureau to keep me from finding love and companionship for nearly eighteen years. I wouldn't allow this Institute to do the same. I would get what I needed from them. And then I was leaving.

"And if they try to stop me," I said, "I'll burn this place to the ground."

ABOUT THE AUTHOR

Vivian Moira Valentine is a rad trans lady who loves monsters. When she was a child, she found the Crestwood House Monster Series at her local library and it's all been downhill from there. Now everything she likes is horrible. When not writing, Vivi enjoys card and board games and plotting out more tabletop RPG campaigns than she will ever have time to run. Vivi lives in Virginia Beach with her amazing wife Frankie and their son, as well as an ever-growing collection of action figures. *Against Fearful Lies* is her second novel in the Amelia Temple series, and she has also written short stories in the horror genre.

Milton Keynes UK
Ingram Content Group UK Ltd.
UKHW042324040424
440618UK00001B/16